PREDATOR
PREY
THE PHOENIX AND THE FIRE

KATE STEWART

For Malene Dich.
You will never know how many times you've saved me.

PART ONE

The Phoenix

PROLOGUE

THERE WERE A FEW THINGS I KNEW ABOUT WHO I WAS AND TWO words that described me: order and excellence. It was not vanity that led me to confess this but fear. For as long as I'd been in charge of my own life, those two things have kept me motivated, kept me breathing.

I could blame the way I was on the way I had been received into the world. I wasn't born in a hospital. No, my mother assured me I was born in the crosshairs of gunfire—in "a spray of bullets." She would remind me every year we didn't celebrate my birthday. And every day of my life, she encouraged me to believe I would go out the way I came in.

For some reason, I had always believed her.

She was my mother after all. I lived in a constant state of fear the first ten years of my life. Every gunshot I heard I assumed was a warning specifically for me that my time was coming. The fear consumed me, was ingrained in me, and made my already desperate situation a hell that I had to dwell in until my escape.

As soon as the realization hit me that I didn't have to become a product of my mother's greasy fucking environment, I turned the tables on my pre-destined fate she cursed me with.

That's when I discovered order, cause, and effect. You see, I watched them. I'm good at that. I observed and interpreted. I'd always prided myself on knowing the good from the bad, and how to read people.

I'd been wrong only once, and I intended on keeping it that way. I had a past that kept me in shackles until I freed myself with excellence. It was my camouflage, my way of escape.

I became bulletproof.

CHAPTER 1

THOSE EYES…THOSE FUCKING DARK EYES WERE THE REASON FOR MY trip, but if it didn't pan out this time and I didn't get his attention, I was giving up.

Look at you, Taylor Ellison, obsessing over a man.

And I should have been ashamed. I'd done everything in my power to get his attention without being too obvious. When my friend Violet had introduced me to The Rabbit Hole—a sex club just outside of Savannah—I'd been excited about the prospect of having my own Rhys, my own version of her beloved husband. He was a strong Dom with a good heart that treated her well. I didn't want to have *exactly* what she had. But I did want something of my own.

I'd been working my ass off for so long that I'd almost lost sight of having a life completely. I needed more than an impressive bank account and a set of fast cars. Though I'd reached my goal, I knew I needed something more to be satisfied. Months of worthless visits to The Rabbit Hole had turned my excitement into dread. I had frequented it in hopes of finding a man to suit my sexual taste. Nothing too crazy, but just to be sated would be enough for now. I'd fucked a few too many that led to dead ends.

I'd all but given up, until I saw *him*.

He was there each time I went, often alone at a table, sipping his drink, sometimes with friends. I'd seen him come and go, but he had never taken on a member of the club. While there, he'd never visited the private rooms. The first time we made eye contact, I saw the recognition in his. There was a spark, an amount of heat. *Something* was there.

Maybe I was obsessing out of boredom. I closed my eyes tight in frustration as I sat in my car facing the double doors of the club.

This was it. If it didn't happen tonight, I might have to find a date the old fashioned way.

But that was part of the problem. I didn't date. I wasn't good at the getting to know you aspect of the evening. I liked the fucking portion and had always preferred to get to that. I very much had the dating mentality of a twenty-one-year-old man—casual sex and nothing serious, no attachments, that sort of thing. I wasn't against those in love and actually saw myself going down that road a time or two. I'd been hurt by a man I had affection for, and I was sure I would eventually try that again with the right person. But now, I was just restless. I needed a partner who understood my needs, my body. I'd been settling for far too long.

In my most figure revealing dress, I walked into The Hole and was greeted by Tara, a nice enough bartender who had often tried to strike up a conversation with me. It was obvious she swung both ways, which was fine, but not for me. I had serious issues when it came to women. I couldn't stand ninety-nine percent of them. I guess you could say I was a tad bit of a misogynist. I preferred, and had always preferred, the company of men, whether as friends or fuck buddies.

It had a lot to do with my mentality. I didn't find the conversations interesting, or the unnecessary drama appealing. I didn't talk about feelings, or revel in a good pair of shoes. I'd tried—really, I had—but women weren't especially receptive to my brand of honesty. The kind that wasn't sugarcoated and saved time.

The only woman I had let even remotely close to knowing me, aside from Violet, was my work partner, Nina. She was the exact type of woman I most loathed when I met her: pretentious, all about appearance and image, and had an unnatural fascination with shoes. I never saw us becoming close, but ever since all that went down in her personal life, and because she had been so genuinely good to me, I had let her in a little. She had changed so drastically in the two years I'd known her.

Sitting at the bar now with a crisp chardonnay, I couldn't help but be happy for her, if not a little envious. In the last few months, my friend Nina had come through a personal hell that would break most women. She had finally found her peace and was now benefiting from the release of her struggle. While she was off on what could only be described as a new beginning, I was pining for a man I hadn't uttered a single word to.

He's not here, Taylor.

He'd always taken the table in the corner behind the frosted glass. The first time I'd seen him, I'd rapidly drank him in. He was tall, that much I knew from his stature in the oversized seating of the club. His inky hair was slightly long and styled back to cradle his ridiculously beautiful face. He had naturally dark skin. I guessed him to be of Hispanic descent. His attire was impeccable and mainly consisted of double-breasted suits. His pleasure at the club seemed to be to sit back and observe. I liked that. It was a habit I had formed myself.

I pushed out a disappointed breath as I sipped my wine. It was time to let Mr. Mysterious go. The last time I'd seen him, we'd locked eyes for several minutes, neither of us turning away until he was approached by a beautiful brunette that left his table shortly after she had stopped. I refused to believe he was gay. I couldn't see it, couldn't fathom it. Not *this* man.

This is boredom. Go home and watch a CSI marathon.

As soon as I'd convinced myself to leave, he appeared at a barstool next to me, and I smirked into my wine as he spoke.

"I think it's time we introduce ourselves."

"Taylor," I offered as I turned in my seat to drink him in. He was close—so fucking close—and the feel of his eyes as they met mine made all my nerve endings light on fire. I sucked in a quick breath as he pushed the loose hair away from his face. He looked all business aside from his contradictory hair. It was short enough to tame, but its unruly presence seemed to be a big *fuck you* to the conservativeness of his dress.

"Daniello," he rasped out with a thick accent. Maybe not Hispanic, but he didn't look Italian, either. I couldn't place it. But at that moment, that was the last thing on my mind. He was too perfect, too immaculate looking. This man wasn't southern grown. I'd fucked enough southern beauties to know *this man* was in a league of his own. His thick, silky hair was beautiful and almost feminine, but he could never be misconstrued as that due to the sheer size of him. I guessed his height at least a foot and half taller than mine. His build was just a hair shy of monstrous. My eyes wandered to the sprinkling of dark hair that covered his wrist as his hand descended to the tumbler of amber liquid delivered to him by Tara.

I'd never been so intimidated…until that moment.

Fuck that, Taylor. Stick to order.

My eyes shot back up to him and I watched.

"Tell me what you were thinking," he mused with a whisper of a smile that tilted his full lips. His eyes weren't dark up close; they'd changed to a lighter, more iridescent brown. I was mesmerized.

"That's privilege you are asking for," I stated plainly, my eyebrows raised in challenge.

"It is conversation," he whispered low, so low I had to strain to hear it. "Would you prefer I asked you where you are from and what you do for a living?"

"Are you really interested in those things?" I replied as I took more of him in. If I could change anything, I wouldn't. Not a single fucking thing. His broad features were chiseled to perfection. His skin was a beautiful hue of deep bronze that made his eyes shine brighter in contrast. Penetrating eyes looked back at me as I decided to give him an answer to his original question.

"I was thinking we've been playing cat and mouse," I said bluntly. He smirked and heat spread through my midsection. I loved his size, the intimidation factor. My imagination was on fire with the possibilities. If he could see how clearly attracted I was to him, I was fine with it.

The look in his playful eyes told me my gamble to finally stop our charade might pay off.

"And which are you, Taylor? The cat or the mouse?" The R of my name rolled off of his tongue and made my toes curl. Two things were clear to me in that moment.

I wanted to fuck this man.

And he would be very, *very* bad for me.

"You assume I'm one or the other. What If I'm both?"

He nodded as if he already knew my answer then turned to me before looking at the door where a few men were making their exit.

"Taylor, it was a pleasure meeting you." He gestured at Tara who winked at me as he stood. Deflated, I looked up at him with a curt, "You, too."

"I look forward to more of our game." Before I had a chance to respond, he was walking out the door.

"I have to say, I have never seen a better looking man come through those doors. I have no idea how you remained glued to your seat. You aren't even sweating!" Tara exclaimed as I drummed my fingers on the bar.

"He's just a man," I muttered as I finished my wine and

pulled my wallet out of my purse.

"He bought your wine and the next if you'd like another one." Tara had the bottle in hand, cork ready as I nodded a yes.

"Why not?"

"Green or red?" A man took the stool next to me. He was referring to the level of kink I was into, which no longer seemed appealing. Neither did the club I'd frequented for months in vain. It would be my last trip.

"Neither," I said coolly, trying my best not to show my disappointment as all my nerve endings settled back into the dull thrum they'd become accustomed to.

"I can give you what you are looking for," he whispered, too close for comfort.

"I'm not interested," I reiterated as I picked up my wine.

"I could—"

"Hey, asshole, you know the rules. Move on," Tara defended as I kept my eyes on my wine. Tara was as brazen as her clown-colored, red hair. Her right arm was covered in tattoos and she had a rough look about her, but her face was soft and feminine.

"Thank you," I whispered to Tara as the space next to me emptied.

"Don't give up, girl. You will find your man," she encouraged. I was suddenly irritated at the weakness I was showing and was more uncomfortable than I could remember being in years.

Knowing I would never see Tara again, I admitted the truth.

"There is no such thing for me."

CHAPTER 2

Three Weeks Later

I SAT AT MY DESK WITH MY MONITORS CUED UP READING MY DAILY reports. I had nothing but good news to share with my partner, Nina, when she returned from Key West. Nina had started the company with her cultivated fortune using my lone idea and we'd built it from the ground up. Scott solutions had revolutionized the protocol of the modern day inventor. We saw an idea we thought the consuming masses couldn't live without, we invested, and it had paid off in spades.

I'd started off as her assistant and was now half owner of the company, a goal I hadn't intended to meet until much later, but was rewarded to me by the amount of work I'd invested. The day Nina had pushed those papers across my desk, I thanked excellence.

Our building was located in downtown Charleston, South Carolina. I'd only moved here from New York when the position was offered to me. I'd always thought I would remain a New Yorker but was surprised for my love of both Charleston and the historic south it represented. It was very different from the desolate and depraved, shithole town in Tennessee where I once lived.

Six months in the city had me convinced that I no longer wanted any part of New York, and after my first mild winter, I was convinced I'd moved to paradise. I had a successful career and more money than I hoped at the age of twenty-nine, which afforded me a life more comfortable than I'd thought possible.

I had achieved my goal.

And I was bored out of my mind.

"Taylor, line four." I picked up without giving my new assistant, Ross, the scolding she deserved. I didn't like being surprised by who was on the other end of the line.

"Taylor Ellison," I barked.

"And good morning to you," Nina joked as I sat back in my chair with a smile.

"How's it going in the Keys? Is Devin still alive?" I joked back.

"Barely. I've pulled my gun on him twice." I chuckled knowing that might be the truth of it. I'd recently taught her how to use a pistol and she was a natural and never left home without it. Nina was now a far cry from the more timid woman I'd met. Recent events had ensured she would never be the same.

"Remember clean shots only and leave the important parts. I have a meeting in five but is there something you need?"

My office door opened and Nina walked in with a smile. She had a deep-set tan and her eyes were glowing with mischief. I was instantly envious, though I made sure my face gave nothing away.

"I thought I would take this one," she remarked, ending our call and sitting across from me to look around my new office. "This looks great. Are you happy with the turnout?"

"I am, thank you," I offered as I took in her appearance. She was glowing from weeks of sex aboard her boyfriend Devin's boat. They had sailed away together in an attempt to reconnect. "You look good," I admitted with only a slight grudge. The truth was, she deserved the smile she was sporting more than anyone I'd ever known. She'd gone through hell to get it.

"Thanks, I feel good. Look, I've been away for long enough. It's time the favor was returned. Seriously, Taylor, you haven't taken a day off...ever. It's time."

"I—"

"It's an order," she said, half-joking.

I ignored her as I began to type up my final notes for the meeting I had in two minutes. I was never late and I wouldn't be to this one, either. "Thanks, really, but I'm good. Maybe I'll take you up on that in a few months."

"Don't you have family to see? Someone to do?" She knew I'd been frequenting The Rabbit Hole. That club had turned out to be part of her horror story, and another good reason for me to stay away.

"No." I stood up then walked toward the door. "Want to sit in? The clients are in the conference room."

"I'm aware. I got your 6:00 a.m. email." There was concern in her voice. She'd been trying to get anything she could out of me for months. I'd told her I'd try to loosen up a little more with private details about me for the sake of our growing friendship, but one minute before a meeting was not the time.

With a sigh, she looked at me as I stood next to her at the door. "Taylor Ellison is all business all the time."

"Yes, ma'am," I confirmed as she followed me out.

Thirty seconds.

I counted them down as we reached the conference room door.

Three, two, one...excellence.

CHAPTER 3

"You stupid fucking slut! Who the fuck do you think you are! You are no better than me! If you leave me like this, I will find you. I will kill you."

"You won't find me, Lazarus, and do you know why? Because you won't have any idea where to look."

"You think your sumtin' with that scholarship, don't cha? Well, I have news for you. They can smell trash. They'll be able to smell you a mile away. I'm all you've got."

"No, Laz, you are all you've got. Insult me again, and I will blow a hole through you."

"Fucking whore, you—"

I aimed and pulled the trigger, shooting a clean hole through his thigh. His agonizing cries only fueled me as I squeezed again, this time clipping his ear.

I opened the door of the hotel room then looked him in the eye. "Don't come looking for me or I'll finish the job."

"Red, don't…please." The voice belonged to the boy I used to know. As I looked into his eyes, I saw equal parts affection and hatred for me. He didn't want me to belong elsewhere and that was where the hatred stemmed from. The affection was something we'd started years ago and would never go away, regardless of how completely screwed up our relationship was now.

Even through all of it, I still cared for him. As I stood in the doorway, prepared to leave and never lay eyes on him again, I let my feelings show, but only briefly.

"I can't stay. I told you that. I'm sorry." He shed a single tear as he glared up at me.

"I'll come for you," he warned.

"No, you won't." His shoulders stiffened as his greasy hair spilled over his face. He looked down at his worn shoes in defeat. I lowered my gun and walked out the door.

I shot up in bed, completely ruined from my dream because that was just it. It wasn't a dream. It was a reality in a different world I had escaped and hadn't thought about in years. Glancing at my clock, I saw it was barely 10:00. Uneasy and still reeling from the clear vision of the look in Laz's eyes, I took a hot shower. Ten minutes later, I was seated on my couch, preparing for a sleepless night, and a marathon of some mind numbing TV.

Looking around my lavish condo, I realized I'd picked out absolutely nothing in it, including the blanket covering me.

Awareness came over me in waves.

I was trapped again, but in a different kind of reality. Did I have order and excellence to thank for that?

I shook off the throw blanket, walked into my closet, and threw on my first hanger. I didn't design or throw together my outfits like most women. I took complete looks from the mannequins in the stores. From top to toe, I used the outfit and the jewelry they used to accessorize the plastic. It had worked for years and it continued to work now. Except that now the mannequins sported a much higher price tag. Of that fact, I was proud.

Going into Harvard my first year, I had no idea what fashion sense was. I'd come from nothing and been thrust into a world of wealth I couldn't have been prepared for. I had no TV as a child, no internet aside from the two computers in our high school of eighty students, no anything. I'd only gotten my first pre-paid cellphone when I was sixteen. Even then, it was outdated due to the limited supply of my shit town. I'd almost felt like I had come from an alternate planet when I'd entered Boston. If it weren't for the time I'd spent fucking Memphis's wealthiest man, I would have been even more lost.

The dress that covered me tonight was nude and left little to the imagination. I put on matching pumps in the exact same color. The dress made my long, dark red hair stand out in comparison. Slipping on my stockings and garter, I admired the body I'd worked hard for in the last few years. I had a solid muscled core and rounded hips and was thankful for a smaller but ample bustline than one that would match my top-heavy mother. In minutes, I had carefully layered my makeup the way I was taught then grabbed my keys.

I might have nothing to do on a Saturday night, but I had toys to play with if I so desired. I owned an array of muscle cars, which I paid the association extra to keep covered. These were my babies, and I needed no chauffeur to take advantage of them. This was my one indulgence, and I had no shame when it came to them.

I slid my finger along my Charger I'd nicknamed Bomber. It had the exact sleek look of the fatal plane. Completely blacked out from roof to turf, she was my pride and joy. I'd rarely taken her out in the last few months and decided tonight was the night. Slipping in, I turned the ignition as she roared to life, the idle alone heightening my senses. I was instantly turned on by the heavy repeat of the engine.

I'd fantasized about having the right cock in this car, but in my original daydreams, he had owned the car himself. I was sure there were plenty of men out there who owned a muscle car, but the new woman I'd become was slightly choosier for a different breed of man than those who owned a car like this.

Was I a hypocrite? Yes, maybe. The type of man I was now

suited for wouldn't own this type of car. His would be a lot more expensive and way more foreign.

This car and all my others were my way of keeping a small part of that Tennessee girl inside of me, and I would not fucking apologize for it.

Pulling into downtown, I bypassed the bustle of King Street to drift a little further, driving toward a piano bar I knew encased the company I was looking for. I would have a few drinks to take the edge off, and maybe a willing cock to exhaust me.

The young valet took one look at my car and then the small flash of my bare pussy as I exited and was hard as a rock by the time I handed him my keys.

"Fuck...is this heaven?" I heard him murmur as I smirked, leaned over, handed him a twenty as I whispered, "Which part? Take care of it and you may get a taste."

Before he had a chance to answer, I was through the door. Though the music was far from what I enjoyed, the atmosphere was more desirable. Intimate tables were lined throughout the small bar and on the back patio were a set of couches surrounded by lavish plants, small trees, and highlighted by soft electric blue lighting. I walked up to the bar, getting a good share of attention as I passed by without looking in any direction. I was more than aware that the good ol' boys, the ones who felt they ruled the city, congregated here. Tonight, I'd decided to play with one of them in my bed. These men valued nothing but money and power. But I knew they had a weakness for quality women and tonight that's what I'd offer. It only took minutes for the first to approach. Unfortunately for him, I would have to pass.

Davis Jeffries, CEO of Blue Corp, was the first to make a move, approaching me just as my drink was set in front of me.

"I've seen you before. I think we've met," he said as I turned to him with a smile. I heard his inhale as he studied my face, letting his eyes drift down to my chest before moving back up. He made no apology as he appraised me. He was bold, and maybe he could back it up. It was a shame I was on the prowl and I wouldn't take the first bid.

"You have. Taylor Ellison, Scott Solutions. How are you, Mr. Jeffries?" He gave me a small smile as he motioned to the bartender.

"Davis, please…ah, yes, Taylor. I hear congrats are in order," he remarked of my new partnership in my company.

"Thank you," I murmured before taking a sip of my drink, feigning interest in conversation and in him as I looked at the couch full of millionaires behind him. They all owned a small portion of Charleston, textiles, travel, and one of them actually the last name of several landmarks of the city. None of them were interested in their conversation as they stared at Davis's back to see his progress. It was clear I had my pick. In fact, I recalled two of them had propositioned me at one point. Two men I didn't recognize had their backs to me and were in a heated discussion.

"…and I swear I had. Would you care to join us?" Davis finished as my eyes roamed back to his. He was attractive with dark blond hair that had been tamed neatly with the proper cut and product. His suit was tailored, outlining a fit body, and I was sure he would make for an interesting evening. Still, before I made a decision, I wanted to weigh my options. I allowed him to lead me to my buffet. Every man stood aside from the two who were clearly having a deep conversation. The patio was dark, and I nearly stumbled as Davis led me to sit on the white couch next to him. The rest of the men greeted me with lust filled eyes and soft hellos.

"Gentlemen," I said sweetly, my intent anything but. I set my drink down and took a corner seat, distancing myself from Davis enough to let them know I was fair game. The inner me cheered as they all began to speak at once.

"Taylor Ellison, right—"

"Scott Industries, I heard the stock was soaring—"

"I've been meaning to introduce myself—"

I gave a soft laugh as the men fumbled over each other, and I saw Davis tense. It was game on. I replied to a man I knew owned two textile plants and a nationwide retail chain.

"John, yes, hi. We actually have a meeting in a few weeks," I admitted as he leaned in from across the table.

"Yes, we do." He grinned as if he'd won the upper hand, and he might have until the man that had just been in an aggressive conversation with the man beside him set down his empty glass with a loud clink at the table opposite me.

"Daniello," I said on a whisper in surprise as his angry eyes met mine. I was sure the anger was misplaced due to his recent argument with a man that stood to leave. He looked gorgeous in his ever present, double-breasted suit and wingtips. He was perfectly put together, aside from his slightly mused, slicked back hair. His eyes were intense and his jaw firm as he addressed me.

"Taylor," he rasped out as he took in my dress and the men who surrounded me.

"What a coincidence," I said, making polite conversation. "You have business in Charleston?"

"I have business everywhere." His words covered me in curiosity, but before I had a chance to respond, Davis moved slightly my way to engage me.

"I have an idea I'd like to run past you," he whispered as I kept my eyes on Daniello, who looked ready to jump over the table and hurt Davis, or me, or both of us.

"Oh yeah," I flirted, finally turning my eyes away from the man who had haunted my thoughts for months to focus on Davis. "What's that?"

"I was wondering—"

"I had hoped to finish our game," Daniello interrupted

without apology as I crossed my legs to dull the ache that began to grow the minute I saw him. "You have not been back to the club."

"I grew bored of it," I said simply and without looking at him as I averted my conversation back to Davis. The men next to us shifted uncomfortably, sensing the undeniable tension in the air. The only one seemingly oblivious was Davis as he continued. "I was wanting to ask if you are free—"

"You look bored now," Daniello said smugly as he lifted his empty glass. "You should put your mouse down, Taylor."

Davis turned to glare at Daniello who sat confidently as a fresh drink was delivered. He stopped the waitress by putting his hand on her bare leg as she stood next to him. Her eyes were hot on him, and I knew immediately anywhere that hand wandered she would welcome it. Her lips were parted as he rubbed the back of her thigh with his fingertips. "Thank you," he whispered to the waitress, stroking her as his eyes challenged mine.

"Why don't you put *your* mouse away?" I snickered as his hand drifted up further, brushing just beneath her skirt. She opened her legs slightly as the men at the table looked on in awe and frustration. A few of them averted their eyes, clearly uncomfortable at the display. I was both shocked at the abandon of the waitress and at the same time not at all surprised. Daniello had that effect. I knew it the minute I saw him at the club months ago.

After an uncomfortable lull in conversation, uninterrupted by whimpers from our fearless waitress, one of the men next to me cleared his throat loudly and began speaking. They all joined in, leaving Daniello, Davis, and I to our own discussion.

I turned to Davis. "Looks like the help is busy, and I could use another drink."

"Say no more," Davis said with uncertainty, looking between Daniello and me as he stood, but not before staking his claim with a kiss on my cheek.

"I am rather enjoying my mouse," Daniello whispered as his hand slid up even further, brushing her where I knew she was as hot as the burning between my legs.

"You do that." I winked. I kept my game face on, but inside I was dying and refused to let it show.

"I love satin," he complimented her on what I was sure was a soaked pair of panties as he stroked her. She made a small whimpering sound but stood, taking his attention as he fucked me with his eyes.

I became slightly paralyzed as I heard her exhale when he slipped fingers inside her. I cursed my pale skin knowing it was probably red with the mix of my desire and the alcohol. At the same time, the dark cover of the club revealed little. I had to strain to see Daniello's movement. I looked up to his mouse's hooded eyes as she began to pant.

"Eager little mouse, isn't she?" I challenged.

"She is," Daniello complimented again as she slid her hand down to cover his beneath her skirt. She was on the verge, and more than anything, I wanted to see her come. I'd watched couples at The Rabbit Hole fuck openly, but it had never been as hot as this man pleasuring this woman with his fingers in front of my peers and Charleston's elite. The men shifted next to me, some of them no longer hiding the fact that they were now watching.

Her legs began to shake as Daniello increased his pace. "You Americans are way too guarded with your sexuality," he declared as he pulled her down into his lap and spread her slightly, reaching his hand back up to resume his work. "You hide your needs and keep them hidden," he declared as the waitress laid her head back to rest on his shoulder, abandoning any lingering notions of timidity. I was sure management would be coming by at any moment, but I doubted she cared in the least about anything but Daniello's hand and what it was doing to her. She moaned and gripped his thighs as she rode his hand, unashamed. "Money here buys you that discretion, but your filthy fuck clubs are deceitful. They only add to your betrayal of what you truly want." And with that and a flick of his wrist, the waitress came hard, her limbs shaking as Daniello reached up lightning fast to present her face to me by gripping it in his hand. Ecstasy is what I saw written all over her features. The men next to me stilled and took it in, as did I. Once her orgasm subsided, she collapsed against Daniello as he stroked her hair.

"Good little mouse," he murmured, his eyes still connected with mine.

"I'm afraid I took a guess on your drink." Davis returned, completely clueless as the rest of his group stared at Daniello, who seemed to have put our cocktail waitress in a coma. A small part of me wanted to laugh. The rest of me was filled to the brim with sexual tension.

"Excuse me, gentlemen," I said as I stood, my voice full of desire. "Davis, you have my number. It's getting late, and I need to get going."

After months of waiting for Daniello to speak to me only to watch another woman come by his hand left me furious. Not only could I not engage in anything I desired due to our environment, I was more turned on than I had ever been in my life.

"Don't leave so soon," Davis said, glaring at Daniello, who was still murmuring to his mouse and testing me with his attention.

"Call me. We'll set it up," I said hastily, ready to explode, before taking my leave. I pulled the valet ticket from my purse and waited eagerly as the heat between my legs coated my thighs. The same valet greeted me with a smile as he pulled up. Gripping his shoulder, I leaned in and made a desperate offer.

"Want a taste?"

He pulled away in shock as I grabbed my keys. He had to

be about twenty-five. He was attractive enough but looked like a deer in the headlights. I rolled my eyes and got into my car as he spoke to the other valet.

"Marcus, I'm taking ten," he said hastily as he rounded the car and got in. I pulled forward and into the dark parking lot next to an idling SUV. I didn't give a damn whose driver it was. They were about to get a show. As soon as the car was situated, I turned in my seat and spread my legs over the console, letting one land on the dash and the other rest next to him in the passenger seat, damn near hostile for relief. The guy wasted no time diving in fully as his tongue began to lap at me, completely unskilled. It didn't matter. I was on the verge of exploding as my back rested against the driver's side door. I sank further into the seat, wrapping my legs around his neck as he greedily sucked my clit. Digging my nails into his scalp, I pushed him further down. "Lick it," I commanded as he sloppily lapped my pussy, missing every single pleasure point and further frustrating me. I felt the stare before I saw Daniello peering through the window behind the valet. I gripped his hair and bucked my hips, spurring him on. It was too dark to see Daniello's expression, but I assumed it was smug.

"Fuck, I can't believe this is happening," my hungry companion said through a mouthful of my soaked pussy.

My eyes still glued to the man who I was sure could only see a small amount through the window, I pushed the valet's head away so I could reach my ache with my fingers while he fumbled with his tongue. With a few flicks of my wrist and the right amount of pressure, I came undone, hard and loud, still engaged in the man who stood outside my car. My eyes closed as I let the desire spread over me and when I opened them, Daniello was gone, as was the black SUV that sat next to us. The valet was unzipping his pants, but I stopped him.

"Look, um…" Jesus, I didn't even know his name.

"Derek," he answered, revealing nothing I desired for as he exposed himself.

"Derek, sweetheart, if you can't give proper head, it can only get worse from here. I appreciate the effort, but put that thing away before you embarrass yourself further."

He looked at me in confusion before I finished him off. "No."

He sighed, putting his cock back into place as I pulled my legs into my seat and nudged him toward the door. "I offered you a taste. I delivered. You did not. Get. Out."

He looked at me as if I would offer a punch line, but I kept quiet. I felt bad for his future wife. Maybe he would try to improve for his own sake.

"Can I call you?"

"Hell no. Goodbye," I said, starting my car.

"Bitch," he whispered under his breath as he exited. With a sigh, I placed my forehead on the steering wheel, completely baffled by what I had just let happen. I'd gone into that upscale bar to bed an equal and ended up letting a valet tongue fuck me because of Daniello.

I smiled slightly at how good he had gotten me. "Son of a bitch."

I couldn't damage my career or reputation for a sexual need, that was a given. I'd left hoping I looked like I was offended to the rest of the group, but a complete stranger knew better. Daniello knew better. He knew I was into kink and he'd used it and had gotten the best of me. He'd beat me at a game he'd roped me into for the second time. His plays were taunting, and I'd fallen for it twice. Though I should hate him already, my hunger only grew. This was lust, and this is what he was capable of, and I hated that I'd become desperate and at his mercy.

And still, I wanted him. And I wanted the feeling to last. The uncertainty, the need, it made me feel alive, excited.

I laughed once more as I thought about the fact I may never see him again, and I'd run away with my clit on fire and my tail between my legs.

Tonight I had walked out of my home a tiger on the prowl and ran back home as a mouse…but that was far from boring.

CHAPTER 4

A WEEK LATER, I WAS IN MY OFFICE, PACING. "YOU HAVE TWENTY minutes to deliver what you promised, or I'll find you in breach of contract," I snapped, irritated with my situation. Murphy's Law had found a way to make my workweek hell. I had absolutely no patience for bullshit and was getting a solid stream of it spewed at me over the phone line. I looked out of my office window at downtown Charleston as tourists lined the city streets. Couples holding hands or families roamed the sidewalks of the historic city as young kids on their bikes pulled others around by cart. Some were crowded in horse-drawn carriages as they were given a guided tour telling of Charleston's history. It was summer, and that meant more were on their way to drown in the humidity and crowd the beaches. I looked out the window with longing, thinking it may be time for me to finally take a few days to myself to do the same.

I heard my office door open and close and kept my gaze on the city, assuming it was my assistant, Ross, waiting on me.

"I don't like to repeat myself, Warren. We've given months of leeway here and hundreds of thousands of dollars. If you've pissed it away on shitty mechanics, that's your issue. I want the new prototype in four days." I cut the line and threw my headset on the chair next to me. "What is it, Ross?"

"Ross has gone for coffee." I froze for a brief moment before turning around to find Daniello sitting in my desk chair.

Of course, he took my chair.

"My time is valuable, Mr.?"

"Di Giovanni."

"Italian?" I asked, finally given the opportunity.

"Some of me," he answered vaguely. As I surveyed him, I was sure God had granted my wish and poured the perfect man into an expensive suit. His looks were unmatched by any other man I'd ever met. I gave myself a brief moment to appreciate him before taking a step toward him to bite.

"As I said, Mr. Di Giovanni, my time is money, and I'm pretty sure you aren't here on business."

"I wanted to see where you reign, Ms. Ellison." He looked slightly amused, as always, but somehow I knew the bitch in me would be far more hesitant to let him win in my playground. I dug in.

"Great, months of watching each other and now we both have a last name. You're here and you've seen my office, anything else?"

"I want to share a little time with you," he said, steepling his fingers under his chin and leaning back in my chair.

"Do you? And what would be the purpose?"

"Pleasure, companionship, things we both crave," he replied, sure of himself. Confidence and arrogance ran through him in abundance.

"Pleasure is better left outside of my office, and companionship…well, let's just cut to the chase. You aren't that type of man." I flicked my hand and gestured for him to move out of my seat.

"Let us not assume anything about the other," he said in a surprise move to give me back my throne. "You are angry with me for not pursuing you sooner," he taunted. "You want to be the one coming on my hand, no?"

My sex pulsed as his truth came out. "My time is valuable as well. I want to share time with you while I have it and I want you to agree. What do I have to do to make that happen?" As he spoke, he walked slowly around, picking up various items off my shelf to study them. "No pictures. You have no family?"

"We aren't assuming, remember?" I pointed out, taking a seat in my chair and watching as his expansive frame moved throughout my office. The man was incredible and looked completely out of place handling my knickknacks. "Are these your things?" he asked, knowing the answer.

"Decorator. So I suppose I should just agree to this since you seem to think you know what I want?"

He placed the last knickknack down and stared at me. The connection was just as electric as it had been the first time we locked eyes. Dispelling a breath, I tried to force myself to remain unclouded. He was intoxicating.

"I know exactly what you want," he taunted, slipping off his coat. I stared at his build, stunned by his ability to shift gears to intimate so smoothly.

"And what's that?" I smarted at him, way too confident. He smirked as my heart began to pound and blood pooled below.

He rounded the corner of my desk and without warning unzipped his pants. I glanced over at the door and noted it was locked before turning my full attention back to him. He stroked over his pants, his length thickening in front of me, and I envied his hand. I felt my desire kick into overdrive as I watched his hand move back and forth, shortening my breath. He was taunting me again, and I was letting him.

Because I wanted it.

"Don't flatter yourself." I straightened just as his full, thick shaft came into view. I stared, riveted.

"You hurt yourself with your lies," he hissed as he began to stroke himself right in front of me. "I am not afraid to admit I have been thinking of you. I have hunger for you." In an attempt to even my breathing, I rested my hands on my thighs and slowly rubbed them back and forth.

He was long and thick. The head looked silky and my mouth dried at the moisture gleaming from the tip. My tongue fought hard to remain inside my mouth as I watched his skilled hand stroke the perfect, hard, full cock.

"Who are you?" I asked aloud, though I didn't mean to. He paused his hand and leaned in with a whisper.

"I am the man who will disappear from your bed without any explanation."

He resumed his strokes and pulled harder, gripping himself tight. I leaned forward, entranced, waiting for his invitation. He pulled away to make sure I didn't touch as he circled his perfect, throbbing dick and pumped.

I couldn't believe the sight in front of me. In all of my wildest sexual imagination, I'd never pictured anything like it. I was stunned by his boldness and at the same time not surprised at all after his display at the club. He towered over me as I sat there appraising him, an inferno of need growing hot inside me.

He pulled at himself as he watched me watch him. "You see, there are bad men out there who will not hesitate to pull the trigger...rape, steal, and climb with hungry claws to get to where they want to be."

I was so turned on I could barely get the words out as he cupped, stroked, and claimed his cock without any help. Unable to hold back, I put my hands on his thighs and licked my lips as I looked up at him.

"And you are one of them?"

Suddenly, he jerked my head forward, and I parted my lips. He yanked a handful of my hair and tilted my head back, commanding my eyes on his as he slid his full length into my mouth. I took it eagerly, licking and sucking as my pussy pulsed out of control. The salty taste of him spurred me on as I felt him harden further. He watched my mouth with molten eyes as I finished him without hesitation. I couldn't control it, and I didn't want to.

"No." He smirked down at me as I bobbed and sucked eagerly. "I am the man who stomps on those men with my heel." He fisted my hair tighter and shot his hot release into my eager mouth as I consumed every drop, cursing my desire for him. Daniello leaned in as I savored the rest of him and placed a gentle, lasting kiss on my lips. Liquid brown eyes burned into mine as I rubbed my thighs together.

"I will be good to you. I will be as honest as I can, and when the time comes, I will end it," he declared. "I am giving you the choice to start something only I will finish, and when I finish it, it *will be* over, Taylor." I was still entranced and equally disheartened as he zipped his pants and brushed his thumb over my lip. Cornering my desk, he grabbed his suit jacket and slipped it on. "Think about it. Think about me." As soon as those words were out, he was gone.

CHAPTER 5

T<small>HAT NIGHT</small>, I <small>LAY IN BED, DOING NOTHING BUT FANTASIZING ABOUT</small> Daniello. He wanted to share time? I already knew I would agree to what he offered. What I was pondering were his conditions. Though he disguised it in a gentlemen's way, and only after he'd spit his cum down my throat, he'd given me a clear indication that he would be in charge. Sexual control was a different story.

I could very easily let him objectify my body, but giving him the ability to control our situation and the nature of our relationship down to the point of where it would end, that was an entirely different kind of power.

Still, I loved having his silky, huge cock in my mouth. Even then, I wasn't in control. I'd spent hours cursing my stupidity and inability to handle myself.

But wasn't that what I was looking for? A man who could easily take the reins as I lost myself in him? I'd given him so much power over me in showing my arousal, my need for him, and my eagerness to please him.

Daniello was a force to be reckoned with. Could this finally be the man who topped me in every way?

Had I let him make a fool out of me or had I simply given into what I wanted?

Indecisiveness was not my forte.

I could keep things strictly sexual. That wasn't an issue for me, never really had been since I started college. Lazarus was really my only reciprocal experience with matters of the heart. And my other experience…well, it was far from the norm.

I'd never, not once in my life, uttered the word love in declaration to any man.

So Daniello wanted to share time with me. He'd clearly told me he was dangerous. And from what he'd gathered from me so far, I was all bark and no bite. I actually liked that fact.

It could make things extremely interesting.

Okay, Mr. Di Giovanni, let's share some time.

"You son of a bitch," I heard Nina yell from her office as I passed by it the next morning. I laughed along with Devin as I heard a small crash and the breaking of glass. I paused by the door to make sure my girl was holding her own.

"Do not throw that, Nina. I simply asked you a question." I could hear the amusement in Devin's voice.

"And the answer is no. Get out of my office!"

"Jesus, woman, you are insane," he scoffed as the knob twisted and the door opened. Devin gave me a raised brow as he caught me eavesdropping.

"Good morning, Devin." I smiled as Nina fumed behind him. "I see you are leaving her in a good mood for me today."

Devin was a beautiful man. I'd always thought so, even when I was tempted to kill him for the hell he'd put Nina through. I noted his impeccable dress as he shook his head slowly back and forth while Nina muttered obscenities behind him.

He gave me a smug grin as he spoke. "You know, you think

the woman would be grateful to be asked to be the next Mrs. McIntyre."

"Well…" I paused trying to hide my chuckle. "The last one did end up in the nut house."

"True." He grinned wickedly as he looked back at Nina. "So I take it that's a no?" He winced as she lifted her stapler. "Okay, baby, see you at home." He turned to me with a nod. "Taylor."

"Give her time." I winked as he retreated down the hall toward the elevator.

I turned to Nina and couldn't hide my smile as her chest rose and fell in hurried breaths.

She gave me wide eyes. "Is he crazy!?"

I took a step into her office. "No, Nina, he's in love and wants to make an honest woman out of you. Congratulations."

"It's barely been a month," she huffed as she paced her floor.

"What do you want?" I asked as I took a seat.

"I want to marry him, of course," she snapped. "But he's still the man who lied to me for almost a year and then kept some pretty serious shit from me for the remaining time I'd known him. No way. Not now." She crossed her hands and pulled them away quickly in gesture.

"I forgot to leave this," Devin said softly, unaffected by her rant as he crossed the room with an open Tiffany's box and placed it on her desk.

"You're broke. You can't afford that," she snapped without looking at the ring.

"I plan on marrying a millionaire," he said as he stood in front of her now, lifting a single finger to stroke her cheek. "Stop being such an ungrateful bitch about this." I saw her face soften as he leaned in and brushed her lips with his. I stood to leave. "Taylor, you stay, he leaves." Devin pressed his lips into a thin line and again made his way out the door. "Later, Mrs. McIntyre."

"That name is a curse," she called after him. "You can keep it."

"Hyphenate," he called back over his shoulder. "I love you." I heard the elevator and turned to her with a smile. They were absolutely perfect for each other, and I knew no matter how much she resisted there would be a wedding sometime in Nina's future.

"What are you so afraid of?" I asked as she looked at the box.

She gave me an *Are you kidding me?* look.

"Okay, aside from the obvious nightmare you two endured to finally be together. Would it be so bad to live with the man you love?"

"I already live with him. He hasn't gone home since we got back from the Keys. I actually asked him to stay with me." She sighed as she paced, fighting herself on an answer she knew she wanted to give.

"And how's it been?" She picked up the ring with tears in her eyes and slipped it on.

"Perfect. But, Taylor, I swore I'd never get married again. I don't need that. I don't have to be his wife."

"Maybe *he* has to be your husband," I suggested. "His track record is just as tainted."

"I know, trust me. I didn't think he would ever even talk about marriage." She looked up to me with a smile. "He wants to marry me."

"Well, my job here is done." She laughed at my retreating back. She knew I was uncomfortable with these talks and let me off the hook. "We have the Bledsoe meeting in an hour," I reminded before I shut her door, her eyes glued to her finger.

"Un huh," she answered absently.

Walking back to my desk, I willed away the sick feeling in my stomach. I remembered the day my college friend Greg declared his love for me and told me he wanted to marry me. In reality, he hardly knew me, but Greg was the closest I'd come to an adult relationship. His affection for me validated all the hard work I'd put into my efforts of becoming someone else, someone better than the helpless redhead that had committed her first felony at age fifteen.

Cedric, my only friend from my past, and Nina's bodyguard, was the only one who knew me both as the penniless piece of white trash and the business mogul. He'd never judged me, making moves himself to get out of the timeless hell we'd lived in. But he was never anyone I could love or ever have sexual interest in. He had been like a brother to me until I disappeared from Tennessee, and he had done the same himself a year later to join the Army to better his situation. From what Cedric told me, all of our friends from those days were either dead, in jail, or still up to the same shit they had been when we'd escaped. Now, I had only one thing keeping me tied to Tennessee.

And one day soon, I would have to face my demons to rid myself of that life once and for all.

I wanted the way Devin looked at Nina for myself one day, but deep down I knew the man who would wholly capture my heart would have to know all the parts of me, and the truth was I knew I would never share that part of myself with *anyone*. Love had and always would be an illusion to me. I wasn't incapable, my circumstances were. And I honestly didn't know if I would ever let myself become a victim to it…again.

So it was time to put away the ridiculous notion that it could happen for me. Suddenly, I was excited about the no-strings arrangement with Daniello. Little did he know he was already giving me exactly what I needed.

Walking out of work that evening, I felt confident in my decisions about my future. As lonely as it might be to keep my past out of my present, I couldn't commit. I refused to live another lie, so I was walking tall before I reached my Stinger. I smiled as I noticed the black SUV idling next to it, waiting for me. The chauffeur opened the back door as I approached and I slipped in without hesitation and sat opposite of Daniello. We greeted each other with appreciative eye appraisals. He was dressed in jeans and a designer black shirt that accentuated his perfectly cut chest and showcased his thick, muscular arms. I kicked off my stilettos and tucked my feet beneath me, making myself comfortable, which seemed to please him.

"Have you thought about what I proposed?"

"Oh, you mean the scenario where you are in charge of absolutely everything and I am supposed to just accept it and enjoy the ride?"

He let out a heavy breath with a quick, "Exactly."

"You are extremely arrogant," I said with a smirk.

"I do not deny this," he replied with a devilish grin.

"How often are you taken up on this offer?" I asked out of curiosity, and to simply irritate him. I could tell he got his way often, if not always. So did I. The thought already had me hot.

"Every time."

"Then I'll be the exception," I said, noting the irritation on his face. His eyes trailed down my body in hot survey as my panties coated in welcome to him.

"Then we have no more to discuss?" he asked, slightly confused.

"Sure we do. Take me to dinner. I'm starving."

He smirked, and I could tell he thought he would sway me, but I had only one point to negotiate. "*Either* of us can end it at any time. I'm no one's possession, and I'll *choose* to submit, but I have the right to opt out whenever I want. If you can live with that, then I'll share time with you."

He ran his fingers through his hair and looked at me dead on. "And if I do not agree?"

"Then we have no more to discuss," I said evenly. "What would be the alternative anyway? I tell you I'm finished with you so you take me against my will?"

"Yes," he countered wickedly. "That could be fun. Rocco," he instructed his driver, "let us take the lady to dine."

His voice was baritone silk and laced with old world charm. His English, though unbroken and smooth in delivery, lacked modern colloquialisms. He was a complete contradiction to the men I'd usually be attracted to, and yet it was undeniable.

We said little as we stared one another down. I was all for conversation. I was curious about him, but it wasn't in the cards for our drive to dinner. I saw his erection grow in his jeans as we wordlessly expressed to each other our intentions. The cabin grew thick with tension as we fucked each other without touching. My hunger for him had reached unbearable.

"Did you enjoy watching me?" I asked, referring to the valet buried between my legs.

"No," he snapped. "I intended to finish what I started."

"You're going to have to move faster than that," I said coyly.

"You did not enjoy it, either," he remarked coolly.

"It was your game," I said heatedly. "Still is."

"Tonight, my game is simple. I am going to fuck you...hard. And I am going to hurt you." His eyes were deadly.

Instead of his tone setting in fear, it set me on fire.

"Your game, Daniello, though I must warn you since you were kind enough to do the same. I'm not so easily broken."

"I have no intention of trying to tame your will. It is one of the things I like about you."

I smiled. "It's the *only thing* you know about me."

"Well, you can tell me more at dinner." He gestured as the

driver opened the door.

"Thank you," I said, taking Rocco's hand and stepping down from the truck. Without acknowledging me in any way, Rocco closed the door behind us and resumed his seat behind the wheel.

"What polite help you have there, Mr. Di Giovanni."

"He is not a fan of Americans," Daniello remarked, amused. "Do not bother trying to befriend him."

"Fine by me."

Daniello grabbed my hand, ushering me into the small seaside restaurant. Though I may have demanded dinner, Daniello seemed to have arranged it already as we were led to a very small and intimate private dining room. As I sipped my white wine, I asked my first question.

"So, you clearly aren't a fan of American's, either, seeing as how you criticize our ways of keeping sexual acts behind closed doors. Exactly which country should I frequent where finger fucking is allowed at a local bar?"

He smirked as he sipped his brandy. "You people lack passion, romance."

"And that was your idea of romance?" Though my voice was steady, I was having a hard time hiding my reaction to the sight in front of me. Every inch of Daniello was perfection, from his brown toned skin to his dark hair and perfectly etched but full features. His size was an absolute turn on. He filled his clothes out effortlessly and I knew what lay beneath was a solid, if not muscle covered body. I also knew his cock was massive and just as beautiful.

He crossed his arms. "No, that was easy gratification. Her eyes told me she wanted me and so I gratified her with my fingers. I appreciated her lust for me, and I returned it to her. She was in need and did not require romance."

"Is that what you call what you did?"

"Yes, that is what I call what I did as I spread her out on her back that night and filled her pussy with my cock."

I sat shocked as he leaned in. "I see the jealousy in your eyes, Taylor."

"You see what you want to see," I quipped. "And for the record, it's not my concern what you do with other women." Frustration rolled off of me. "I could end this before it starts. You come off as a pompous ass right now, which I do *not* find attractive. You talk a big game and have a beautiful face, but you should know those traits are not isolated to wherever you came from. In fact, that's *very* American. I could throw a stone and hit another man just as full of himself. You came after me, try not to forget that."

"I have offended you. I apologize," he said, picking up his water glass.

"Are you sure you know the definition of passion? Because from where I'm sitting, all I see is boasting. For all I know you may have no clue how to use that beautiful cock."

"Now you are the one being rude," he snapped, pulling out his napkin and smacking the air with it before placing it in his lap.

"This was a mistake," I said, pushing my chair from the table.

"One night," he said, stopping me before I stood. "One night, Taylor." I loved the way he said my name. The way his voice accented it so ornately it seemed important. And by the way he was looking at me, I felt that way. He didn't want me to leave. There was no plea, no question. Just a simple command.

"I've got nothing to lose," I rasped out, straightening in my chair as the food was set before us.

"That is where you are wrong."

"Are we back here again already?" I rolled my eyes and nearly jumped back as Daniello stood quickly, took the two steps to my chair, and pulled me from my seat. "Taylor," he breathed as his fingers brushed my face before he cradled my head and stopped his lips a hairsbreadth from mine. He held me snugly to him as if I was precious, and I fought the urge to disintegrate the last of the space between us.

"I look at you, and I truly want you, Taylor. You are not angry with me. You are angry with your need." His breath tickled my skin as he leaned in further, brushing his lips against mine before he spoke. "What you need, what your body is screaming for, I want to give it." I felt a strange tug inside of me as his hands held me delicately. He stood perfectly still as his eyes wandered to my lips. "If this night is the extent of our time together, I will try to show more restraint...until I get you alone."

All I could do was nod as his lips gently descended on mine. Once connected, the inferno took over. My moan reverberated throughout his mouth as I opened for him and his skilled tongue stroked me tenderly and thoroughly. All my anger vanished and anything left unsaid fell away as he tasted me completely with his tongue. Unable to control my reaction, I melted into him, gripping his shoulders to keep myself standing as we moved in unison, unable to get enough. Just as I expected him to pull away, he dug in deeper, completely ruining my chances of escape.

His tongue was velvet as it stroked mine and our mouths molded together. The only thought swirling inside of my head was that I didn't want it to end. When he'd had his fill, he slowed our kiss, still tasting me gently with his tongue and swiping my lower lip and sucking it into his mouth. I kept my eyes closed as he finally pulled away, afraid he would see what was in them.

"Taylor," he urged gently.

"One night," I said, certain it would be all I could handle. I could compartmentalize lust, but this attraction was far too strong. He was like the opposite end of a magnet, and I had no choice. I opened my eyes to see him watching my face carefully.

"I cannot wait to taste all of you," he whispered, pulling my lip inside his mouth again as I kept my whimper inside. "Watch you come all over my cock."

"Okay," I said as my knees turned to Jell-O. He laughed loudly as I tried desperately to keep my cool. He let go of me and pulled out my chair. I took it, thankful. When we resumed dinner, the air had changed around us. It was no longer filled with contempt, just lust and longing. I finished my scallops with a low appreciative moan.

"That was delicious, thank you," I murmured.

Daniello set down a large amount of cash on the table, stood, then held out his hand for me. I took it without hesitation as he led me through the front door and guided me into the waiting SUV. Once seated, he pulled me into his lap, and our lips crashed together, as if not a minute had passed since our kiss in the restaurant. Daniello pulled his mouth away and leaned over, removing my heels before smoothing his hand up my leg, and not stopping until his fingers lightly brushed my sex. I jumped in surprise as he pulled my chin with his other hand so I was staring right at him as his fingers pushed my panties to the side and invaded me hard and fast.

"Oh," I said, trying to get my face out of his grasp as he plunged in and out of my center with his skilled digits. In an attempt to control my reaction, I closed my eyes. His fingers squeezed tightly around my jaw, and I opened them immediately, giving him what he wanted.

"Your pussy is so fucking wet, Taylor. You need me?"

Without hesitation, I moaned out a yes.

"Show me your desire for me. It pleases me," he commanded. "I will be good to you, beautiful woman. I will covet you."

"Please," I pleaded, begging for relief. "Free me like you did her."

"Were you jealous?" he asked as his finger flicked my clit with expert speed.

"I wanted to see her come," I said truthfully. "But I wanted it to be me."

"Ahhh, and I wanted your attention. That is passion, Taylor, no?" He still had me gripped in both of his hands as I braced for freedom. His hand stilled, and I damn near burst into tears. "I asked you a question, Taylor."

"Yes, yes," I said in agreement, pushing against his hand for more friction.

He lifted me from his lap, so I straddled him and pulled my skirt up so it sat at my sides. I moved to unzip his pants, but he stopped me by placing my hands on his shoulders. I leaned in for a kiss, which he granted with a greedy tongue. He pulled my legs further apart so my sex was hovering over the bulge in his pants and then snapped my underwear away at my hip so it lay on my opposite leg against my thigh. Pulling away from our kiss, I looked down at the exposed dripping mess between my legs.

"Beautiful," he murmured. "Keep your hands on my shoulders," he ordered roughly. I nodded as he slipped his middle and pointer finger in my shuddering mouth and I sucked quickly, wetting them. The wet digits moved between my thighs, and I damn near jumped at the spark that ignited with the regain of his touch. His fingers worked quickly as I studied the beautiful heat residing in his ever-changing brown eyes.

"Obedience pleases me, Taylor."

I looked upward, briefly unable to hold our gaze, and felt the sharp slap of his hand on my thigh. It was painful, and I bucked into his teasing fingers as my angry eyes met his. His smirk told me he liked my reaction.

I felt the wave of pleasure begin to pulse and bloom as he plunged in and out and then covered my needy clit with my desire before diving back in. He repeated this until I began to come apart at the seams, my body begging for relief though I remained wordless.

"Patience," he whispered as I played into his hands. The SUV slowed and stopped, and I moved to pull my skirt down.

Removing what was left of my panties, I tucked them into my purse as I questioned him. "I don't play Russian roulette with my body. Are you covered?" He seemed surprised by my question. I had an implant in my arm that ensured no surprises but needed reassurance from him regardless.

"I do not, either. This is not an issue." I nodded as the door opened. All members of The Rabbit Hole had to be tested monthly, so I didn't bother arguing with him. When I recognized where we were, I looked up at him in question.

"Shouldn't you be extended an invitation?"

"Your home is the only place we will have," he said, taking my hand and leading me toward my condo.

"Do you know everything about me?" I asked, slightly irritated.

"Only the geographical, the rest I will learn from you," he answered as I slid my key into the lock.

"I'm afraid there isn't much to—" My breath was knocked out of me as he slammed my back against the door, knocking it closed. Before I had a chance to react, his mouth was on me, and his hands caressed every surface of my body.

"Enough talk," he barked as he pulled away, ripping the bottom half of my blouse open. He pushed my skirt up again so it cradled my hips and lifted me off of my feet. Carrying me down the hall, he spotted my bedroom and sat me down gently on my king bed. We matched breath for breath as I explored him while he undressed. His shoes and jeans went first. His build was more than I could have hoped for. Thick bulging ridges covered his stomach and chest, leaving a wonderland of exploration just inches away from my fingertips. His legs were thick, muscular, and perfectly proportioned to his upper body. I stayed motionless as he revealed the rest of himself to me. My mouth watered as his boxers remained, the only thing between me and the view I'd been wanting for months. Daniello walked up to me near the bed, his ripped stomach in full view and a light dusting of hair leading down into his briefs.

"Take," he bit out on edge. "Take what you want just this once," he insisted.

I wasted no time freeing him from his shorts and attaching my lips to the sparse hair on his abdomen. Flattening my tongue, I explored every divot, every hard ridge, and down past his waiting cock to suck his large sack, and then descended even further to lick the sweet spot behind it. His moan was welcome as he ran his large hands up and down my back to encourage me. He was perfectly groomed, which I appreciated as I gripped him hard in my hand, looking up to his stone face. Teeth gritted, jaw firm, he was holding back, and I was further convinced as his length twitched in my hand when my mouth finally enveloped him.

"You like my taste," he bit out as I sucked hard, leaving a trail of hot steel in my wake. I pulled and gripped my jaw around him as I got another groan out of him. Somehow, I knew it wasn't an easy feat.

When I looked up at him, he broke the connection from my mouth. I reached for the buttons he hadn't torn on my blouse, and he slapped my hands away, pulling at the shredded tails of my shirt and lifting them up so my arms were encased. He left me that way, arms trapped above my head as he laid me down, pushing up my bra over my peaking tits.

"Is there any part of you that is not perfect, Taylor?"

I was just thinking the same as he hovered over me, his strong cheekbones and sculpted lips capturing my attention as well as his dark lashes that fluttered as his mouth captured my waiting nipple.

It was then I knew that the minute his cock entered me I wouldn't be able to handle our connection. It was too much. My alabaster skin looked beautiful in comparison to his dark tan. His silky black hair fell over his face as he drifted from one breast to the other. Then he sank his teeth in. I screamed out in an attempt to protest but was useless with my arms bound above me. My whole body bucked as he bit harder and I felt the skin break. Tears sprang to my eyes as he pulled away, soothing his bite with his tongue. He grinned, knowing if my hands were free, I would've slapped him. He lifted my leg and rammed into me without hesitation. The tears threatening broke free as I looked up at him in shock, my whole body tensed with the pain of being impaled. I choked on the breath I attempted to regain as he stared down at me.

"The answer is no. There is not a single part of you that is not perfect. Feel me, Taylor," he gritted out as I tried to relax around him. His strokes were unforgiving, and he was hurting me as promised. I waited patiently for him to free my arms as his thrusts blinded me with pain and ecstasy in equal measure. Seeming to read my mind, he pulled my arms free from my blouse, and I immediately dug my nails into his flesh, drawing blood. His knowing grin told me I'd just rewarded him. He swiveled his hips and closed his eyes as he slowed to a stop.

The sheer size of him was intimidating as he looked down at me. I gripped his torso with my thighs, wrapping my legs around him as he towered over me, motionless.

"Now that I know the feel of you, Taylor, I will want more."

I didn't have time to respond before he pulled out and slammed back into me. My body rose to meet his thrusts as he twisted his hips perfectly, and I felt my whole body tense in expectation. I opened my eyes as he crashed into me one more time and I detonated.

It was the first time I'd ever screamed a man's name when I came.

Shockwave after shockwave ripped through me as I opened

my eyes to see Daniello still thrusting but watching me intently. It lasted far longer than I was used to, and with another quick movement of his hips, I dissolved again.

Daniello rose to his knees, keeping us connected and me wrapped around him as he pounded into me without mercy. With one hand wrapped around me to keep me centered, he used his spare hand to clutch my throat. I lay limp in his arms, fighting the constriction of my airway as my spent body took every hard inch of him.

It was ecstasy.

With a grunt of exertion, I was released and fell back into the bed as Daniello threw his head back and let go. I watched his muscles tighten and his jaw clench as he thrust one last time and came.

It was the best fuck of my life.

I heard heavy breathing and froze. I couldn't remember the last time I had allowed another man to sleep in my bed. I also couldn't remember falling asleep for that matter. I moved to get up but was trapped by a captive arm and silky, dark skin. He curled his fingers around my hip and stroked lightly before he released me. I looked at him sleeping and inwardly groaned. His hair fell over his face, covering my appreciative view aside from the sheet that revealed a ripped muscled back and the top of his perfect, firm ass. He took immaculate care of his body, and it was evident as I stared at the side of his rippled torso that led down to his perfect, solid cock. His only imperfection was a large scar that wrapped around his trim waist. He was massive and completely capable.

One night, that's what we both agreed to.

It was over. And the truth was, I didn't want it to be. Sure he was arrogant to the point of infuriating, but in bed, he was an enigma. He could read my body and gave it exactly what it longed for. I was ravaged and sore from last night but felt the evidence of my lust renewed as my pulse thrummed between my legs.

We didn't have to be best friends to have amazing sex. Hell, we didn't even have to talk. But it was more than that. He intrigued me. Reaching over, I brushed his dark hair away from his face to reveal two golden eyes gazing up at me.

"You like me," he whispered with amusement.

"I like the way you fuck," I answered honestly.

"So am I to assume you want another night with me?"

"Nope," I said with a small smile.

"That is the first time I have seen that," he said, brushing my exposed nipple with his fingers as I sat before him, bare and uninhibited.

"Seen what?" I asked as he moved to stroke my naked thigh, his fingers leading sensation from the place he was coveting to the center of my soaked core.

"That is the first time you have smiled for me." Seeming to read my needy body, he pushed me down beneath him. "I will maybe think about it."

"Think about what?" I asked as he centered himself at my entrance and began to stroke my pulsing clit. I licked my lips as I looked up at him. He stared down at me, a solid wall of beautiful, raw man.

"Fuck," he hissed as his pulsing, hard cock entered me slowly. He looked down at me with lust in his eyes but a smug grin. "Sharing more time with you."

"Oh, go to—" And my words were sucked away with one hard, hungry thrust. Appraising him with lips parted, I saw raw and primal hunger. The man was surreal, and I decided then I did want more from him. I knew it last night. I also knew I didn't have to think twice about getting my emotions involved. Our sexual connection was off the charts, but I was positive I could keep my emotions out of it. It wasn't something I even had to worry about. And just as I thought that, his eyes softened slightly above me.

The truth was, I wanted him to think about it. I wanted him to think about me, crave me, and end my wait of finding the perfect sexual partner, no matter how temporary it may be.

Suddenly, he withdrew and slunk down between my thighs, lifting my lower half up with his palm and cupping my ass in front of him as if I weighed nothing.

Flattening his tongue, he devoured my pussy eagerly as I gripped his shoulders. It took no time for my orgasm to build. "You like being in the palm of my hand, Taylor?" The curl of his tongue around my name had my orgasm surfacing.

"Mmm," I answered as he darted his tongue expertly on my clit. He stopped his torture and looked up at me just as I was about to breach.

"You are a good little mouse in bed, no?" I glared at him as his head descended, and just as I was about to feel his tongue again, I pushed him away.

"No," I said as I positioned my fingers on my clit and he watched me rub out my orgasm. I could tell he delighted in my rebellion as he witnessed me come with an amused grin.

He flipped me suddenly, and his weight settled between my thighs as he curled his arms around my shins pulling them up with him as he impaled me. I screamed out in ecstasy, feeling his hot breath on my neck.

"Do you want a lover or do you want a master?" he gritted out as he pulled back and sharply thrust again.

"Oh fuck," I cried as I reached out for anything to hold onto, finding leverage as I gripped the edge of the mattress.

"Answer me, Taylor." He pushed in again and took all of my good sense as I gave him my one-word answer.

"Both," I begged as he hit me again and again, fucking me hard, leaving my throat dry with wordless cries.

"You want to be dominated, that is why you go to a club and beg for it, no?" his question dripped with sarcasm as he swiveled his hips, making sure I felt every single movement. "You like to play with little boys who demand your obedience and tickle your little cunt with feathers. This is the kind of man you need?"

"Oh, God." I braced myself against the sheer force of him as he drove in hard, deep, and punishing.

"Fucking amateurs," he hissed as he gripped my hips and pulled me off the bed, holding all my weight as he jackhammered his hips until I screamed. "Do you not agree?"

"Daniello," I pleaded as he stroked hard and I buckled and crashed under him. He didn't let up as he continued his taunt. "Ah, are you begging, Taylor?"

More rough pounding with precision had my whole body wound tight, and I felt myself tremble as he hit me again where I needed him. I succumbed and felt my release coat him and wash my thighs. I'd never come so hard and chanted my praise.

"I feel that you agree with me," he whispered as he slowed to a stop, setting my legs down and lifting my upper body so I was on all fours. Pushing his fingers into me, he captured my orgasm between them and rubbed it over me as he continued. "I need no feathers."

"Daniello," I whispered, exhausted but wanting more, needing more.

"I like the way my name falls from your lips." I felt the heat of his hands as he massaged my back in slow circles. "A good lover does not need to ask permission." Daniello's touch ignited me further, and even after two powerful orgasms, I pushed my ass out, seeking more from him.

"We will do this my way, and my way only. Where I choose, when I say, understood?" I moaned as his fingers curled inside of me, drawing out more. I buckled slightly, and he slapped my pussy hard in warning.

"Understood, Taylor Ellison?"

"Yes," I conceded, still on fire.

"You have pleased me this morning." I felt his cock brush my thigh as he continued to rub the muscles of my back, leaving me sinking into him.

I didn't need time to realize he was exactly right. A good lover didn't need permission. At that moment, I was willing to do whatever the hell he wanted, and do it with enthusiasm.

Lover was suddenly a powerful word. And the clear definition was behind me now, making me feel even more powerful with each stroke of his hand.

He moved to lie down, and I instantly hovered, aligning my tingling center to his greedy stiff cock.

"Make me crave you, Taylor," he whispered as our eyes locked.

I sunk slowly down, reveling in the feeling. The friction was unbelievable as I dug my nails into his chest. Daniello's eyes closed briefly at our connection before opening. I basked in the intensity for only a moment before I began to move my hips.

This wasn't just sex. It was an experience.

I rode him hard, showing my appreciation as he controlled me only slightly with his hands on my sides.

"Let go," he ordered as he looked up at me and my controlled movements. I let my head fall back and did as I was told as our bodies crashed together.

"Taylor," he hissed as his cock jerked inside of me with his release. His resignation pushed me over, and I braced myself as the wave hit me. Daniello sat up quickly as I began to come, taking my mouth and my moans. In his kiss, I felt something powerful: need, passion, and tenderness. My moaning continued as his kiss softened and his hands soothed me, covering me from my shaking shoulders to my quivering hips. Our tongues did our bidding in place of words as we took and took until both of us were forced to take a breath. I gasped as our lips parted, seeing recognition in his eyes as he pulled away.

Exhaustion quickly set in as I tried to gather my senses. I felt his breath on my shoulder before his lips came down and caressed it. He made his way slowly from one to the other in reverent kisses before he sank his teeth into my neck, covering it with his warm mouth. I was instantly renewed as he caressed my back with his hands and laved me with his tongue. His touch was gentle as I recovered and we both separated slightly away to study each other.

Instantly uncomfortable with the intimacy, I freed myself from our tangled limbs and made my way to the bathroom without looking at him for a reaction. When I exited the hot shower, I checked my emails, seeing I had an hour to spare before I had to head to the office. I opened the door to find my bedroom empty.

I didn't know if I expected to find him there and now I had my answer.

The man was a ghost.

And now I knew they existed.

The purple bruise on my breast and the soreness between my thighs told me so.

CHAPTER 6

Days later, I was in my office scrolling through my emails. I'd been debating whether or not to take the time off Nina had urged me to, but I had no idea what I'd do with it. I'd tried to keep my mind off Daniello but found my hand beneath the sheets every night to the memory of him.

It was that good.

I went through my day as I always did: with precision and without distraction. I had a company to run and being in a dick daze was not an option.

A delivery of solid white roses arrived toward the end of my day, and I immediately threw them out. Before anyone—including my assistant, Ross—had a chance to ask, I made an excuse that they were a thank you from a client.

Irritated, I left work that night looking for an SUV but found nothing.

It was clear to me then I didn't like the situation. I needed order and some control. I had none, and I was longing for him. I went to bed that night with my hands firmly planted beneath my pillow.

The sun was unforgiving as I sat on the curb in front of the five and dime, waiting on my father to gather his weekly list at the tractor supply store across the street. I was filthy from head to toe from a day's worth of cleaning and could feel my throat closing from thirst. I spotted the shiny metal underneath a small patch of grass growing in the crack of the sidewalk and lunged for it. I was met by what felt like a brick wall as my fingers grazed the quarter.

"I saw it first," the wall replied. "Too slow."

I shielded my eyes from the sun and audibly whimpered at the loss as I tried to get a good look at the boy who had just barreled over me.

"Give it back," I shrieked as my thirst outweighed my fear. He was taller than me, and I assumed a couple years older. His dark brown hair stuck to the sides of his head in a sweaty heap. I noticed his clothing was tattered, torn, and way too small for him. It was nothing out of the ordinary here. Very few of us sported new clothes, even at the beginning of the school year. I didn't recognize this boy, though.

"Please," I pleaded. "I'm thirsty. I'll buy you a soda, too. They are only fifteen cents. I have five more in my pocket." The only soda the Lil' General sold were old, flat cans of Shasta. Even as cheap as they were, it was a rip-off.

He shook his head as he stood above me. "Sorry, kid, I have plans for this."

"It's just a quarter," I said, standing in front of him.

"But it's my quarter now," he said, taunting me.

"Fine, take it," I said, dusting off my shorts. He leaned in, and I could see the large amount of freckles covering his nose.

"What are you willing to do for it?" he asked playfully, his blue eyes twinkling with amusement. "Maybe if you wash my bike I'll consider it."

I looked around with a small amount of excitement but saw no bike. None of my friends had one, and I'd never learned how to ride. I don't know why I thought this boy would be willing to teach me.

"You don't have a bike," I said, clearly irritated. "And I wouldn't wash a thing for you."

"Sure you would. And if I give you this quarter, it won't be helping my *chances of owning one."* He put the quarter in his pocket and tilted his head sideways. *"I've never seen hair as red as yours. You look like a circus clown."*

I huffed as I looked up at him. *"And you are the ugliest boy I've ever laid eyes on."*

He laughed as if my statement was ridiculous. *"How old are you?"*

"None of your business," I said testily as I scanned the street for my father. His old, beat up Chevy was still parked at the supply store. I suddenly wished he'd hurry up so I could get away.

"Look, Red, I'll make you a deal."

I looked up at him with anger. *"Don't call me Red ever again."*

"Anyway, Red, I'll buy you a soda if you agree to wash my bike."

"You don't have a bike. And do you really think fifteen cents is worth it?" I rolled my eyes as he smiled at me.

"I will own a bike, and you sure look thirsty."

I was covered in sweat at that point and knew my time was running out. *"Fine, but only once, and I doubt you'll ever get one anyway."*

He didn't say another word as he walked into the store and came back minutes later with a grape soda. I looked at him curiously. *"I could give you my money and you could get yourself one."*

"Good idea," he said, holding out his hand as I popped the top on the ice cold can and swallowed half of it while digging in my pocket and handing him my money. He took it and slipped it into his pocket as he remained standing in front of me.

"Well, aren't you going to buy one?" I asked, giving him an odd look.

"Taylor," I heard my father call from across the street. I looked to see him hoisting up two bags of fertilizer and throwing it in the back of the truck.

"Coming, Daddy," I shouted, taking my eyes back to the strange boy on the street.

"Taylor," he said, grinning. *"I'm Lazarus, but you can call me Laz."*

"Okay," I said quickly. *"I have to go, bye."* I handed him my remaining soda, which had only a sip left, and he smiled at me.

"See ya," he said a few beats after I started to walk away. I looked

back over my shoulder and saw he was still smiling, so I gave him a small smile back. Deep down, I hoped he really didn't think I look like a circus clown because I lied when I said he was the ugliest boy I'd ever seen.

I got back into the truck with my father and slammed the door hard like he taught me so it didn't open suddenly like it had the last few times I'd ridden in it.

"See you met our new neighbor's kid." I looked up at him curiously. My father and I rarely spoke. My new neighbors were news in this town. No one ever chose to live in Dyer. The nearest house to ours was nearly half a mile away and was a little more run down than our farmhouse.

"Yeah, his name is Laz. He bought me a soda."

"Laz, huh? Odd name." I nodded, not knowing if he saw me. That was the last we spoke as we made the fifteen minute drive home.

The following week, I saw Laz with a brand new Huffy riding down the dirt road toward my house. The moment I saw him, I couldn't explain the amount of pride I felt for him. He was the first person I'd ever met that actually did what he said he was going to. I ran to meet him just as he cornered my driveway.

"You got one!" I said in sheer delight as he smiled at me proudly.

"Told you I would," he said, catching his breath.

"You want me to wash it now?" I asked as he put down the kickstand.

"Nah, some other time." He studied me for a long minute before he looked back at the bike.

"No one in our school has one," I said, "except for Lucy Hardin. She has everything." I snorted in disgust. "Her parents own half the town. I can't stand her."

It was on the tip of my tongue to beg him to let me try to ride it, but I knew better.

Laz studied me for a moment before piping up. "You going to let me come in and see your room?"

I took a step back and shook my head. I hadn't even thought of the fact that he shouldn't be here. I was reminded when my mother's shriek interrupted my thoughts.

"Taylor, get your ass back into this house!" I jumped when the screen slammed shut and winced when I saw the shock on Laz's face. My mother weighed less than a hundred pounds and was a horrific sight with deeply etched pockmarks covering her face and her signature out of control dark red hair. She had once been a beautiful and voluptuous woman from what I gathered from my father, who to this day still bowed down to her every whim.

"Who the hell is this?" she seethed as she took a step down from the porch. "You the new neighbor?"

Laz nodded, still assessing my mother's looks, and remaining silent. "Don't you know it's dangerous to be here, boy? Didn't anyone warn you away? Go on…get."

Laz nodded again and turned to me, a deep sadness in his features. Somehow, he knew then that my mother was the bane of my existence, and I nodded in reply. He simply said, "I'm going," then got on his bike and left.

I turned to my mother just as she lifted the glass pipe to her mouth and sat down on the top step. She'd never made any effort to hide her addiction, and I prayed Laz wouldn't look back to witness her taking a hit.

"That boy is trouble for you, and I better not see him again, got me?" She exhaled a steady stream of chemicals as Amber screamed from the kitchen.

"Yes, ma'am," I said grudgingly.

"Get inside. You know we have things to do."

I nodded, picked a rag out of the bucket then I stepped into the house. The house we lived in was spotless, but on a daily basis, she made it her mission to soil every single rag we had with cleaning. Her addiction drove her to madness as my father kept to the fields, ignoring her and us as we were made to work day and night, sometimes to the early hours of morning cleaning a spotless house.

"You'd think you'd know better than to bring a friend here," she hissed as she followed me inside. I pulled a piece of ice out of the freezer and handed it to my sister who was still howling from thirst. After she'd wet the bed last night, my mother swore she wouldn't have another thing to drink. Amber, who was only three years old, took the ice greedily and sucked it

while choking on her subsiding sobs.

"What the fuck are you doing?" my mother hissed, taking the ice from her and fueling her cries.

"Momma, it's hot. She hasn't drank anything today," I said in her defense as Amber threw herself on the cheap, chipped laminate floor.

I felt the slap on Amber's thighs as she screamed louder and looked up to me for help. My mother hit her again and again as I began to scream with my sister.

"Stop, please, Momma, stop!" I begged as Amber's voice went hoarse before she let out another loud cry.

When she refused to let up, I dropped the rag I was using to clean the staircase and walked up to my mother as she continued to redden my sister's thighs with vicious slaps. I reared back, struck her across the jaw with my open hand, and heard her surprised "oh" as she stumbled back. I was only eleven years old, but I knew then that I might be taking my last breaths. Still, I'd resigned myself to punishment of the worst kind. Anything was better than hearing my sister cry. My mother stood to her full height as I braced myself for her wrath. Thinking fast, I grabbed Amber and ran out of the house into the field, flagging my father down. Looking annoyed, he stopped his sad excuse for a tractor as he saw me rushing to him.

"Daddy, she's doing it again. She's hitting Amber over and over. You've got to stop her!"

"Taylor Jean," he barked with an eye roll, "what have I told you about getting in your mother's way!"

"She was hurting her, Daddy!"

He wiped the sweat from his brow as my mother screamed for me from the house, hell and fury in her voice.

"Get back inside and take your punishment," he said, irritated.

Feeling the frustration roll inside of me, I couldn't stop myself. "You ain't no real daddy! You are chicken shit. A real daddy wouldn't let her hurt us!"

My father's shocked face didn't stop me. "She's a crack whore just like Aunt Stephanie said," I unleashed as Amber cried in my arms. My father dismounted the tractor and stood above me as my sister trembled in my arms.

"You don't like the way things are around here, missy, you can get." I
shook my head as he gripped my upper arm and pulled me toward the house.

"Daddy, please for once just tell her not to hit Amber. Please, Daddy."
I begged and begged to no avail as he dragged me into the house with Amber
still in tow and deposited us on the living room floor. He looked up at my
mother as a sinister smile covered her face.

"Handle your daughters," he barked as he gave me one last look.

When the screen slammed shut, I looked on as my father crossed the
drive back into the field. I swore from that day on I would never trust a man
to protect me.

That Saturday, I was at home running on my treadmill and burning off a binge of tacos I'd partaken in the night before. I was on
my third mile when I spotted a dark figure at the door.

"What the fuck," I screamed as I tumbled off my treadmill
and landed on the floor. I was on my feet in seconds as I looked
up to a howling Daniello. He looked gorgeous in black slacks
and a T-shirt.

Fire raced through my veins as I took the two steps to confront him.

"How the hell did you get into my condo!"

He raised a brow. "Not happy to see me?"

"Not at all and answer my question," I snapped as his chuckle slowed, but his smile deepened.

"If I want in, I get in," he smarted back as I brushed past
him, my breathing heavy. I didn't want him to see I was turned
on. He stopped me and brought me back to him. I was covered
in sweat, and he smelled like a man, and soap and heaven, re-
minding me of our last encounter. I wiggled to get away as he

held me tightly to him and whispered in my ear.

"You thought of me," he chided, feathering my hard nipple with his fingertips, his breath whispering over my goose bump covered skin.

"Let's get something straight," I said, still wrapped in his embrace, eyeing the alarm on my front door. It was lit green, and I couldn't understand how he'd bypassed my system completely. "You are not welcome here anytime you choose. You want to pl—" My sentence was cut short as his hand slipped beneath the thin fabric of my sweats. "Play," I finished. "You make arrangements to play."

"I want to lick your pussy," he whispered as I involuntarily shivered in his arms. "A taste of you before I leave." He scooped me up and carried me to my couch, taking off my sneakers. "I have been craving you, Taylor. Does this please you?"

I didn't answer as he eyed me, pulling down my sweats and then my panties to spread my legs.

"Don't send me flowers. I think you knew better," I said as he kissed the inside of my thigh.

He paused his movements, his hands braced on my thighs, and his stare turning deadly.

"I do not fucking take orders," he said with menace, his fingers digging roughly into my skin. My lips parted at his change in demeanor. He'd gone from playfully sexy to downright deadly in mere seconds.

And with the introduction of his wrath, the spark of need I was feeling turned into an addiction.

Noticing my change, Daniello quickly removed his hands from my thighs. "What a fucking shame," he sighed.

"What is?" I asked, lifting myself up to sit on the couch and pulling a blanket over my naked bottom half.

He stood with a sigh, his erection bulging, and just inches from my watering mouth.

"Your fucking mouth," he snapped as he walked toward my front door. Turned on and completely confused, I rambled after him.

"Look, I'm sorry. It was a nice gesture, but I like to keep my professional life—"

"You will receive no such kindness from me again, I assure you," he said, his hand on my door. "Goodbye, Taylor."

"Wait…what?" I stood and wrapped the blanket around me. "Look, you caught me off guard, breaking into my house and I'm…"

No, Taylor, fuck that. This is a power struggle…He's playing with you.

"See you around, Daniello," I spouted, lifting my chin defiantly.

A slow, satisfied smile covered his features before he opened the door and closed it behind him.

I walked quickly to the door, armed the system then threw the blanket to the floor. The ache between my legs refusing to ease, I decided on a hot shower and my hand. I stalked toward my bathroom but only made it a few feet before I heard my alarm disarm. I turned to look back and saw the green light and wiped my hand down my face in frustration.

I picked my phone up from the counter and typed a quick text to Cedric.

Me: Damned alarm has gone haywire. I need it checked out and fast.

Cedric: I can be there tomorrow morning.

Me: See you then.

Cedric would know within minutes what was wrong with it. I trusted him implicitly. He'd installed it only a year ago. If there were an issue, he'd fix it. I'd have the locks changed as well.

Throwing my soaked sports bra and T-shirt on the floor, I turned on the shower and stepped in, already massaging my soaked center. Fury rolled through me as I fought hard to relieve myself and failed. If I'd only shut my mouth and let him do his bidding, I was sure I'd be gasping in release.

I moved my hand furiously, coming up empty as the hot water dripped over my aching slit, even more convinced I hated our arrangement. He'd said goodbye, and if that meant it was already over, I cursed him further for the state he'd left me in.

It was a shame…my fucking mouth.

"It's fine, Taylor," Cedric said as he pulled the instrument away from my alarm, unplugging the wires and giving me a concerned look. "A solid hour and nothing. Are you sure it disarmed?"

I looked at him exasperated. "I was standing right there." Realization dawned on me. "That son of a bitch."

"Who?" Cedric asked, intrigued.

"So…" I looked down at my bare feet. "I may have fucked a bad guy."

Cedric smiled. "And this is news?"

"A bad guy could probably trip my system, right? Like if he wanted to get in?"

"No," Cedric said with certainty. "Hell no, you can't just trip this alarm or disarm it easily, Taylor. I told you that."

"What if he's a really, really bad guy?" I asked pensively.

Cedric threw his tool into his kit and stood with his arms crossed in front of him. A million times, I'd wished I were attracted to him, and a million times more my body refused to react. I took in Cedric's shaved head, subtle but attractive features, accusing eyes, and wished just one more time.

"What are you doing?" he snapped, knowing my definition of a bad guy was exactly that.

"Isn't the question who?" I piped, turning my head with a smile full of teeth.

"Don't. You aren't cute, especially in a Vols T-shirt," he said, pushing past me to make himself at home in the kitchen.

Cedric hated anything that had to do with Tennessee, while I kept subtle reminders of where we came from close to fuel and motivate me. Not that I needed them with my recent dreams.

"So I met a guy at The Rabbit Hole," I started as his glass paused at the ice dispenser. "And he claims to be a bad guy. And, well, we kind of had a rendezvous here, and I think he's the reason—"

"Are you listening to yourself?" he asked as he sipped his water and gave me a wary look. "Seriously, Taylor."

Digging my nails into my palms, I cursed my bad decisions. "I'm not this stupid."

Eyebrows raised, Cedric looked out my window at my view of the marsh. "You're lonely."

Standing motionless, I waited on his backlash, but to my surprise, he gave none.

"I'll replace it with something new, change the locks. I'll take care of this." He turned, giving me a stern look. "Do I need to go further?"

I knew exactly what he was asking. Though to my friend and business partner, Nina, Cedric was legitimate security—and he was—he would go a lot further to protect me if I needed it. I shook my head in a no. I was sure Daniello wasn't a threat to my life, but then again, I knew absolutely nothing about him, except he was beautiful, infuriating, and apparently liked to have uninterrupted access to the women he 'shared' time with.

Cedric emptied his glass and put it in the sink, surveying me from head to toe. I didn't fidget under his scrutiny. "You can take care of yourself, Taylor. I know this, but if you ever—"

"I know," I said back with a small smile. I wished one more

time for the sake of wishing that I could have affection be-yond friendship for Cedric. He truly was a decent looking man. Covered heavily in tats and a well-muscled body, I was sure he had his fair share of companions. Still, I had to ask.

"Are you…lonely?" Eyes crinkling, he took a step toward me.

"You finally going to quench that curiosity?"

I pushed at his chest in jest. He smirked and took a step back. "No, Taylor, I'm all good in that department. But do your-self a favor and try and remember you just got your last wish granted by taking a hold in that company. Don't fuck it up falling into old habits."

I nodded, knowing damn well who he was referring to: my *original* bad guy, the one who used to be his best friend. A name we didn't speak between us, and a name I would love to forget.

"You smell like bleach. Blech," Laz said as he helped me out of my bed-room window. We'd been meeting up at night after my mother had finally let me go to my bedroom to 'do homework or whatever and go to bed.' I'd flip my light on and off a few times as Laz watched from the field for my signal. We'd decided at school today to meet up so he could teach me how to ride a bike. It was late and I was exhausted but got my second wind thinking of taking the driver's seat for the first time.

"My momma," I huffed as if he would understand. I attempted to explain better, "She makes us clean every day."

"Us?" Laz said, looking past me with concern.

"Amber," I whispered, "my little sister. She's not old enough…Forget it."

We stood in close proximity as Laz's half-shadowed face studied me. I pushed the frizzy red mess out of my face and lifted my chin. I shouldn't care what he thought, and I knew it, but I couldn't help the embarrassment I felt at what he had already seen.

"Let's go," he offered, grabbing my hand. I felt my chest tug at his small gesture and looked up at him in confusion.

"Don't get the wrong idea, Red, I'm not into you," he snapped, pulling his hand away. "It's dark, follow me."

We had no street lamps and were screwed for light as far as the time of day, but I didn't care, and it seemed neither did he. He brought me to the halfway point between our houses, onto the smoothest possible dirt road. I knew the road by heart as it led to a small fishing pond that my dad used to take me to when I was much younger. Saddled on the bike, I looked to my right and could barely see Laz with the small amount of light shed from the crescent moon.

"Balance yourself and just peddle," he instructed gruffly. "Don't think too hard or you'll fall. Push off hard, steer straight, and don't stop peddling."

"Got it," I said enthusiastically.

"I'll hold onto you for a bit, but then I'll let go," he warned.

"Don't. I don't want your help," I snapped.

"Look, Red," he said, indignant.

"Stop calling me that!" I argued. "I've got it."

I pushed off without warning and pedaled hard. I held on tightly to the handlebars and felt a sharp high as the breeze sifted through my hair. Overconfident, I failed to balance and I fell on my side the first ten seconds then cradled my arm that was full of embedded rocks.

"Shit," I heard behind me. "I told you I would hold on." I turned to admit defeat, but Laz simply wiped the dust off of me and picked up the bike. "Get back on."

"No," I said quickly. My arm was burning, and I was sure I was bleeding.

"Hmph," he said defiantly. "Didn't picture you as a chicken shit. It's a scratch, Red. You want to ride a bike, here's your chance." I didn't need to look at him to see he was disappointed. I was crushed. Taking a deep breath, I made my decision and reseated on the bike.

I didn't wait for Laz to react and took off again on my own, but before I could get my first push out, Laz stopped me by gripping the bars and the back of my seat.

"Hardheaded or stupid, you can't be both," he snapped. "Hardheaded will get you your way sometimes, but stupid will get you hurt. Which one are you?"

Without hesitation, I answered. "Hardheaded." Smiling into the darkness, I pushed hard on the pedal, ripping myself from his grip. That time I made it almost thirty seconds before falling, but when I got back up, I made it to the end of the road. I didn't need to see Laz's face or even hear his congratulations to know somewhere at the opposite of the dark road he was smiling.

Jumping in my seat at the horn incessantly sounding behind me, I turned onto the highway as the car blew past me, still blaring their horn with a friendly one-finger salute. I shook thoughts away of anything Lazarus, but not before I noted that I was no longer just dreaming about him. He was in my thoughts again, invading my days. I turned the radio up and stopped at the next light, adjusting the rearview toward me, expecting to see the bleach covered eleven year old with bright, frizzy red hair. The woman in front of me was perfectly put together, her now dark auburn hair sleekly knotted at the top of her head, perfectly applied lipstick, and aviator shades covered any telltale sign of her age.

I'm not there and he's not here.

Irony struck then as a biker crossed the walk in front of me. Deciding I needed a drink as the sun faded, I turned into my condo, prepared to dine seaside and quench my thirst. Walking into my home, I set my alarm and, out of new habit, watched as it remained armed. Two steps into my living room, I froze as the hair on the back of my neck stood at attention. It was too late for me to get out of the condo. I lunged for my curio cabinet, taking out my .38mm. It wasn't my gun of choice, but it would do in a pinch. I crept toward my bedroom, my cellphone in hand as I surveyed the house. If someone was waiting for me, they were aware I was here. Creeping closer toward my bedroom, I stopped at the sound of water falling.

The shower.

It was probably a distraction. Turning quickly into my bedroom, prepared to shoot and ask questions later, I saw it was clear and nearly jumped out of my skin when I heard the voice.

"If you are going to use the .38 on me, you might want to make sure your aim isn't off. Bullet wounds just anger me. It would be wise to believe you like me angry."

I noted the suitcase next to my nightstand and sighed in relief as I let the gun trail to my hip then turned to see the source of the noise, gloriously naked through the shower glass. Putting the gun on the counter, I crossed my arms.

"You will not figure it out, so do not try," he mused, his beautiful ass on full display as he soaped his hands and I fumed over his security breach. "Though I must tell you, it took me some time to get through this new one," he murmured, crossing his hands over his chest to his thick arms to rinse the soap away. The man was huge and on full display. I could see every indention, every perfect, God-given carving on the surface of him. I was entranced at the hard muscles of his back, his full rounded tight ass, thick thighs and the deep crease of his muscled calves. "Have you been well?" He turned to me with a dazzling white smile, the water running through his dark hair and outlining his exotic features so beautifully I had to fight to keep my wits about me.

"Last time I spoke, I scared you away. You sure you won't take offense to anything I say?" I smarted, giving him attitude. An attitude I swore I would try to keep in check the next time one or both of us was naked and in close proximity.

Fear was something I held onto dearly to protect and remind

myself that I was still alive, and yet even with a second security breach, it struck me I wasn't afraid of him.

"You should be afraid," he said smoothly as I let my eyes wander to where his hands roamed.

"Get out of my head, Jesus," I pleaded, throwing my shades on the counter. I waited patiently for him to speak as he turned off the water and stepped out of the shower, the scent of his soap and steam wafting through the air. Sex clenching, he moved past me to grab a towel, and I moved aside.

My mouth refused to keep its words. "Clearly you enjoy seeing me irritated."

"Women always play—" he furrowed his brows, thinking of the right word "—dumb to what they agree to with a cock buried deep inside of them," he mused, wiping his chest then starting on his legs.

"I know nothing about you." Digging in, I stood my ground. "I'm fine with your damn rules, but this is an invasion of privacy."

"You have three more guns in the house," he said without hesitation. "I am a man who has to be aware of his surroundings. That is not something I am willing to stay curious about."

"Ask," I hissed as he pushed past me, wrapping the towel around his waist.

"It is not that simple, Taylor." He lifted his suitcase from the floor and opened it, pulling on jeans and a T-shirt. He looked up at me. "Your dress will do."

Raising my brow, I turned my head in a *come again* gesture. Daniello nodded toward me. "Your clothes…they will do."

"Oh, thank you," I said, using my southern accent heavily as I placed my hand on my chest.

He put his hands on his hips to mock me. It looked ridiculous, and I couldn't help the small laugh that escaped me. He smiled and took my breath. "I'm guessing bitchy doesn't look good on me, either." I narrowed my eyes as his smile deepened.

"I could still grab that gun and piss you off," I mused, unable to stop the grin that crept across my face.

"You could, but would you not rather find out what I have planned for you tonight?" His accent was so thick, his voice deep. This strange, beautiful, foreign man was tickling my senses, dizzying me and making my heart beat a little faster. So, without hesitation, I answered, "Yes."

I asked Daniello for a moment and decided I needed my own shower. I picked up his soap and took a huge whiff as my eyes darted through the glass doors to make sure he didn't see. It smelled divine, and I couldn't place it. It was masculine but fresh with a hint of mint. I dropped it when I heard his voice.

"I brought you a gift, you bitchy," he joked from the kitchen, battering the words.

"Sucker," I joked back as if we had been doing this routine for years. Maybe he had. Maybe it was his norm. I admitted to myself then I had no idea what territory we were in. This was completely out of the norm for me.

"You should know this is my last attempt at a gift," he said, much too far away. I made quick work of changing into a casual sundress and wedge heels, applied light makeup, and twisted my wet hair into a tight bun.

I joined Daniello in the kitchen as I saw he had a bottle of wine poured and handed me a glass.

I took it with a polite thank you and sipped it eagerly to calm my nerves. Fucking him would be easier than casual conversation. As usual, he caught on quickly.

"Relax." He nodded at my glass. "What do you think of the wine?"

"It's delicious, thank you," I said, taking another sip.

"Taylor, you are lying," he whispered.

"No, I'm not." Softening my tone, I tried to raise my enthusiasm. "It's really good. Is this my gift?"

Daniello sighed and began to laugh softly. He shook his head in exasperation and took my glass from me. "Thirteen-year-old award winning bottle from the vineyard," he scorned still amused. "Taylor, what do you like to drink?"

"Wine, this is—"

"Baggianate. Bullshit, you lie," he snapped, setting his glass down. I couldn't help my smile with the way his accent slaughtered the words. What came out sounded like bowel shit. I chuckled as he narrowed his eyes.

"There is only one way to solve this mystery," Daniello said, nodding in agreement with himself.

The man was strange. Maybe he cheered for himself daily. Maybe he was a full-fledged team: the player, the referee, and the scorekeeper. I laughed harder as he drug me out of the living room and I escaped his grip to run back to the counter and sip the wine again. "Yep," I confirmed, wrinkling my nose as he looked back at me, hopeful. "Tastes like shit."

It may have been a growl that erupted from him as he pushed me through the front door and waited for me to lock up.

"By all means," I prompted, gesturing toward the door in hopes that he unearthed a key.

"Taylor," he sighed.

"What?" I said innocently. "Be a dear and lock up for me." Turning without looking back, I made my way toward the SUV. I heard Daniello mumbling in the background. I hopped in the back of the SUV, greeting Rocco, who refused to give me anything other than a nod in return. I felt loose and alive and was positive the wine had everything to do with it.

"It is final," Daniello said sternly, "no more gifts."

"Fine by me." I gave him a wink and nodded to my front door. He rolled his eyes. "Rocco."

Rocco pulled away from the curb sharply, and I clung to my seat. Daniello was opposite of me as he took in my dress.

"You are beautiful tonight," he said appreciatively. I felt the heat of his compliment. My whole adult life, I'd gotten attention from men. Some had openly gawked at me, and I knew the power of sex, but when Daniello complimented me, it mattered. I realized then it was because he was so beautiful, his words were made more powerful. I thought it ironic.

Beauty is power. Money is power. And even though in his eyes I had both, with him I felt a little weak.

Shifting in my seat, I changed the subject. "So what are your plans?"

"They have changed," he said with a shrug.

"Not my fucking mouth again?" I said, testing him.

"Of course," he replied, his tongue dragging out the words.

"So you said some of you was Italian. What is the rest of you?" *A harmless question and not too personal.*

"My father was Egyptian. My mother was Spanish and Italian."

"Which makes you a mutt," I joked. He didn't like my joke. *Shit.*

"Sorry," I offered.

"What is a mutt?" I froze, unable to form words. It sounded much worse in explanation than it did in jest. I stalled.

"I grew in both countries—Egypt and Italy—so I do not understand all of your American slang. What is a mutt?" Fiery eyes confronted me as I dug my fingers into the seat and crossed my legs.

"It's a dog of mixed breed," I muttered, trying to hide the fear in my voice. "It's perfectly acceptable to say in jest, um, when you are joking…It wasn't meant—"

Before I could get the words out, I was snatched by my arms and pulled forward. I landed on Daniello, who was ready for me as he pushed me beneath him on the seat he was just sitting in and cupped my face roughly.

"Shut the fuck up, Taylor," he growled before his lips slammed into mine. I moaned loudly as his kiss disintegrated thought, disintegrated space and time, and lured me into a desperate state for more. I was lost as I clutched him to me as tightly as I could and pressed my angry, hard nipples against his chest as he stroked me with his tongue, tasting, sucking, and fucking my entire world up. I was completely wrapped in him, my body begging for more as his hand slid up my dress and stroked over my lavender lace panties. Lightly, I pushed my hips up, needing more.

"Yes," he whispered, licking his lips and eyeing me as he pulled me up to sit next to him.

The car stopped, and I gave Daniello a curious stare. How long had we been kissing?

Daniello adjusted his ready cock, and no amount of it could cover his arousal. Rocco opened the door, and I took his hand and stepped out. We were at The Boathouse, a restaurant I wasn't familiar with but had heard of for good dining. I looked to Rocco who was whispering Arabic at Daniello, drawing the conclusion Rocco was Egyptian or part mutt as well.

I walked away, into the restaurant, leaving the two to argue, realizing that Rocco was the same man that Daniello had been arguing with at the club a few weeks back.

Why didn't he just fire him? Maybe they were family. Still, the relationship seemed strained. I shook off those questions, deeming them intrusive, and held up my finger to the bartender. I was looking over the marsh as the sun began to set. Orange and pink hues wafted throughout the restaurant as diners ignored the obscene beauty that surrounded them in lieu of conversation. I had no issue with my own company as I watched the show unveil in front of me. Snow white heron birds with majestic wings patterned around the water, dipping their feather tips on the cool surface before flying into the mix of grassy marsh and then further to clear water. I hadn't traveled much in my life, never straying further west than Tennessee before making a beeline for New York after Boston. And there was something to be said for the beauty of the Smoky Mountains, but unfortunately for me, I never got to enjoy those.

But Charleston couldn't be summed into words. Charleston was a feeling. The city had more breathtaking sunsets and more settings to paint those sunsets than any place I'd ever been.

"It is beautiful," Daniello whispered as he joined me. I made a small hmph sound as he pulled me from the bar where I had yet to be served and guided me behind the hostess to our table where we got a front row view of the last of the show.

"I'm sure it's nothing compared to Italy," I noted, saying a small thank you to our hostess.

"You have not been?" He seemed surprised.

"I skipped the backpacking through Europe trip in college," I said absently.

The server greeted us, asking for our drink order.

"I'll have a white wine, your choice." Smiling, I addressed the waiter.

"She will have a vodka," Daniello corrected.

"Very good, sir," the waiter walked away, and I looked at Daniello, confused.

"You twist your nose every fucking time you take a sip of any wine. You do not like it."

"What?" I asked, wildly confused.

"Just be truthful, you do not like wine," he said crossly.

"I order it everywhere," I said confidently, knowing with him I was transparent.

"And yet there is not a bottle in your house. Not one." He sat back in his chair defiantly.

"I'm not much of a drinker." I shrugged.

"Because you hate wine," he insisted.

"Daniello, I'm really trying here, but how the hell would you know what I like and dislike?"

"I know you love my tongue in your mouth, my cock in your pussy, and I know you do *not* enjoy wine."

"Fine, vodka it is," I hissed, taking a sip of our newly delivered drinks and hating it. Daniello saw it and motioned to the waiter.

"No," he said, ushering the waiter back. "Scusami...what is your name?"

"Chris..." the waiter answered, smiling between the two of us as if he were in on the game.

"I will pay for every drink you deliver to this table until we find something she enjoys," Daniello said. "Gin, something with gin."

"Way off," I snubbed.

Daniello raised his brows as if I'd already lost. He tapped his fingers on his lips pensively then took another guess. "Scotch?"

I shook my head and blew out an exasperated breath, looking at our eager waiter. "Whiskey on ice."

Daniello chuckled as Chris looked at him. "Per favore." Daniello steepled his hands in mock prayer. "Please give her some whiskey, Chris."

Chris nodded in reply and walked away with the fresh order.

"Why would you suffer with wine all this time?" He wasn't asking, gloating was more like it. I shrugged and eyed my menu, not giving either recognition.

Whiskey is not the drink of a lady, Taylor.

It had been a while since I'd thought of that voice, a different ghost, a different life. I straightened in my chair, refusing to explain myself. The voice taunted me.

"You will order white wine at every event. You will sip it slowly, and you will never have more than two."

Minutes of silence followed as Daniello scrutinized me, and

I ignored him entirely, instead watching the sunset.

"I would like you to be comfortable," he offered in small apology.

I smirked as I looked up. "And that was handled perfectly."

"I find myself answering to you, and it does not please me." I almost laughed, even more exasperated as fresh drinks were delivered. I took a long sip as Chris waited and watched me.

"Yummy." Managing a wink at Daniello, I turned to our waiter and beat Daniello at his game by ordering for the both of us. "We'll both have the filet, medium rare, rosemary potatoes, and the lobster tail. House dressing with our salads."

Chris nodded, his gaze turning to Daniello, who was laughing loudly as he waved Chris away.

"Woman, you have no idea how much you amuse me," he said, sipping his stiff drink.

Three drinks later, my body buzzed from the amber liquid as Daniello remained light in our conversation. Whiskey had always been my drink of choice, but had the effect of a syringe full of truth serum, so I tried to avoid it at all costs. I reminded myself to remain tight-lipped as I sucked on a piece of ice.

"Why were you at the club?" I asked boldly. "You never entertained any of those women."

He wiped his mouth, finished a bite of salad, and watched me suck my ice before answering.

"I was there with a business partner who frequents the club. I had no desire to…*entertain*."

"Kind of judgmental, isn't it? You could have tried it at least once."

Serious eyes looked at me, watching my chest rise and fall, drifting up to my neck, and then landing on my lips where they remained with his next words.

"I got all I wanted out of that club."

"So did I," I replied quickly.

"Ah," he said, pushing his salad plate to the side. "My first compliment."

"Thank you for the wine and the flowers," I said in a daze, buzzing from the electricity between us and the whiskey running through my veins. "I still hate that you break into my house."

"And I will continue to," he said flatly.

"Well, I may shoot you."

"I look forward to that fight." Smirking, he moved his hands from the table as his plate was delivered. We ate in comfortable silence and lingering glances that told me what I was in store for.

"How old are you?" I asked, knowing he couldn't be much older than me.

"Thirty-three."

"Do you—" I squeaked and he chuckled.

Fucking whiskey.

"Do you have a large family?"

"Large, define large in American terms," he ordered as he cut his steak.

"I don't know," I said carefully. "Five brothers and five sisters, big?"

"There were thirty-one people at our last family dinner."

"That's a family reunion," I said, stunned as he looked at me in question. "It's a gathering of family you haven't seen in some time," I said in explanation.

"We do not do this. We do *not see* each other for a long time," he said, amused.

Our worlds were completely different. It had never been more apparent to me.

"That's…that's good." I'd been jealous all my life of families who were close. It was nothing new, but suddenly I found myself glad Daniello had that for himself.

"And you?"

His tone was uninterested, so I waved him off in reply.

"I do not accept that, this gesture with your hand," he snapped.

"One sister."

"And your family union, how many of you are there?"

I didn't bother to correct him on his verbiage. "Two."

One day. One day, a reunion of two.

"I see." It wasn't pity that covered his features. It was indifference, and it confused me. Up until that point, he had seemed interested. Maybe I was asking too much.

"It doesn't reveal anything about you if you have a big family, Daniello." My damn mouth.

"Let us go," he barked, lifting his hand to get Chris's attention.

"You know if I can't speak without pissin' you off, I don't see the point."

I'd heard it. He'd heard it. Not just my words, but also the accent. I sat back in my chair and folded my arms at his slightly shocked expression.

"It's a southern accent. You know…we talk *this* way. You aren't new to this." I stood as he threw enough money on the table to pay for the meals of everyone dining. Chris would be over the moon. I was under the bus where I'd thrown myself and was now being guided by the elbow out of the restaurant.

"You seem to have more people living inside you than I can care for, Taylor Ellison," he chided as he guided me down the stairs.

"I can walk," I barked as he pushed me up against the side of the wood building the minute we reached the landing.

"Fuck, woman, just give up. I want to fuck you, and you want to fuck me. Your pussy is on fire right now and this"—he pressed his hard dick into me as I moved my hands to his shoulders—"is in need of that mouth."

"Go to hell." I pushed away from him and turned to head

for the waiting SUV.

I was furious with myself for revealing so much. This man wasn't interested in me in the least. He wanted a fuck and I wanted…What did I want?

I didn't want to be involved but I damn sure didn't want to be ignored, or feel it when I made polite conversation. I heard another sigh behind me.

"You want me to care, or you do not? Make your choice, Taylor Ellison. I grow tired of your fits. I have fucked you only once and from what I can see you may no longer be worth the trouble."

I saw red as I turned and lunged at him, the whiskey a perfect excuse for me to lose my ever-loving mind. "You son of a bitch," I shrieked as I pounded at his chest with my fist. "Who in the hell do you think you are! Forget this whole situation, and to hell with you." I turned on my wedged heel and fell flat on my indignant ass. Daniello howled behind me as I whimpered at the pain in my ankle. I pulled myself up with no help from him and limped to the SUV where Rocco opened the door without any emotion on his face. Daniello followed behind me with a snide comment.

"Rocco, you must find a red hair south woman and give her whiskey. That is an order!" He laughed loudly and clapped his back before he climbed in behind me. I felt the pain in my chest as I tried hard to stifle my laugh and glared out the window.

Fuck, it *was* me and completely me.

I'd shied away from every single thing Daniello had done to show affection and responded only to the sexual advances. I had to own that. I didn't need him to care, but in a small way, I wanted him to. The truth serum had shown that to him and to me.

His laughing slowed as I remained trained on the world passing by us. "I don't need love, Daniello. I don't."

"I know," he said, agreeing with me. "You are not that kind

of woman. But every woman deserves appreciation."

"And respect," I added, pulling my leg up slightly to inspect my ankle. "What I'm trying to say is…"

"When you talk you want me to hear you," he said simply. I nodded.

"I have not missed a word," he assured me.

I felt a small amount of emotion break in my throat at his words and hid it by clearing it and giving him an embarrassed smile.

"I guess you know why I stick to wine," I offered quickly.

"You will drink whiskey with me." The car stopped before I had a chance to ask if he was serious. For such a bad man, his sense of perverse humor seemed to be intact.

I asked as much as we entered my condo. "What kind of bad things do you do?"

He paused mid-stride in my living room, his back to me as I realized instantly I'd gone too far.

I felt the shift in the air as Daniello sharply turned on me, his features simmering.

Taking a few tentative steps forward, I took a leap. "I own part of a legitimate business and have no interest in seeing all the hard work I've done disappear due to guilt by association. Can you guarantee your work won't interfere with my life in any way and won't jeopardize my company?"

His answer was quick. "No."

"Personally or professionally?"

"Professionally seems…unlikely. Personally depends on you."

I tilted my head with more questions.

"Taylor, I will not give you more. We have already discussed this." He turned away from me then walked to the kitchen, searching the cabinets. He pulled out a bottle and placed two pills on the counter, pushing them toward me and filling a glass full of water from the dispenser.

The mood was suddenly…awkward.

I did the only thing I knew to do at that moment. I let him lead. Taking the pills from the counter, I popped them in my mouth and downed the water. He knew I'd drank too much. It felt strange to be cared for in this way and yet I welcomed it. I stood watching him as he studied me. It looked like he was trying to figure out what to do with me.

"Maybe I'm just not going to be good at this," I said, giving him an out. As much as he intrigued me, as much as I wanted another round with him, and as much as my time with him had been anything but boring, I had to admit I was acting a total fool. I was out of my element because, in a sense, we were dating.

"You are horrible at this."

I grinned. "Thank you."

"I like your south accent," he said, taking a step forward.

"It's southern," I said, correcting him and then cursing myself for it. I held my hand up. "I'm going to bed before I say another word." He smiled deep in reply. I paused, completely unsure of how this was supposed to go. I forced myself to think back to college when I was in my first adult relationship. He was nothing like Daniello. It took my ex the better part of a year to get sleeping over privileges. The dynamic between us then was completely different, and I was not cut out for it then or this… whatever the hell this was. I simply turned and headed toward my room to leave him to go as he pleased. Disheartened by the fact I would not be having spectacular sex and would most likely wake up alone and with a headache, I stripped to my panties and slipped into bed. I tossed for what seemed like an eternity, curious if Daniello was still in my condo. His suitcase was still beside my bed so I knew at some point he would return. Unless he'd decided I really wasn't worth the trouble and made a beeline for the door. And honestly, I wouldn't blame him.

I was so fucked up.

He hadn't advanced on me sexually the way he had our last meeting. He hadn't really tried. I pictured his naked body as he'd showered earlier and found myself writhing in bed. I tried to relax as the whiskey continued to course through me. Restlessness won as I wandered to my living room, slightly dazed to find him watching a muted CNN in my large lounger. I looked at the clock on my mantle and saw only an hour had passed since I'd attempted to fall asleep.

"You cannot sleep?" he asked, sensing my presence before I'd made it known. I kept my mouth shut as I circled his chair and saw his eyes light when he saw my dress or lack thereof. I stood there motionless, waiting for any sign from him that this, me, was something he still wanted. Nearly naked and vulnerable for a man for the first time in years, I stood waiting on something, anything.

He gave me nothing as his dark eyes met my green.

Complete opposites, nothing in common, nothing to bond with but our shared bodies, I gave in to the one thing we both wanted.

My intention was clear as I watched him watch me. Nipples peaking and sex clenching, I slowly knelt in front of him as he lifted his hand to cup my chin, rubbing a smooth thumb over my parted lips. I pulled on his jeans after unfastening them, and he lifted his hips to help me as his fat cock sprang free and stood proudly. I moaned and licked the tip of his thumb before diving to clench him between my lips. He let out a long puff of air as I sucked greedily, stroking every inch of him with my tongue. I looked up to watch his face tense and his dark eyes absorb my licks. I inhaled as his scent hit me, sucking harder, needing more of him, wanting more, craving his hands and his hunger. He gripped my hair hard and pushed me on him slightly in encouragement as he thrust his hips up and began to fuck my mouth.

I felt the wetness slide out of me between my thighs and soak my panties as I swallowed him whole, willing him to come in my mouth. It wasn't an apology, but it was as close as he was getting to one.

"Fucking mouth," he hissed as he thrust his hips up hard before pulling me off of him and wrapping both hands around my neck, bringing me up to his waiting lips. We collided, tongues thrashing as I moaned into him, my bare breasts rubbing against his ready and soaked cock. Still locked in a kiss, I felt him move to the edge of the recliner, his legs encasing me as I remained kneeling before him. Limbs burning with need, I gripped his length between us and stroked. He pulled out of our kiss and grabbed my hips, lifting me from my knees and turning me away from him. Bending me over slightly with his hands, he rid me of my panties. I stood, legs parted in breathless anticipation.

"Perfect," he growled as his finger tested then entered me slowly. I was lost in sensation as he once again gripped my hips, easing me into his lap and onto his rock hard cock. I gasped at the feeling of fullness as he impaled me inch by inch. Once completely seated, I felt his breath on my neck before I felt his tongue as it traveled from my neck to below my ear. He reached between my thighs and adjusted us so I was leaning back slightly and began to stroke my clit in slow circles. I was gasping repeatedly at every new sensation as he then reached around with his free hand and stroked my nipple. Trapped in a world of complete bliss, I moaned loudly as he began to move his hips, prompting me to do the same. Placing my arms on the side of the recliner, I lifted myself up and ground my hips as I lowered, meeting Daniello's solid thrusts.

Whimpering and so completely full, I rested my head against his shoulder as his solid cock stretched me.

"You fit me now." His voice was low and filled with threatening lust.

Unable to take all the sensation, I burst around him, gripping the hand on my clit and the one kneading my breast, encouraging them to move faster.

"You are good at this," he complimented of my earlier comment as he started moving again, ignoring the limpness in my spent body and fucking me ruthlessly. I gripped the back of his head as he moved us forward so my feet were planted firmly on the floor.

"Ride my cock, Taylor."

I pushed off with my feet as his arms slid around my waist and gripped me tightly. Moving furiously on his lap, I wasted myself on his thick dick, appreciating the sound of the rumble in his chest that led to the growl in his throat. I dug my nails into the flesh of his thighs as I rocked against him, the buildup burning through me. Arms still wrapped around me, his hand slid down my now slick body, his fingers teasing my pulsing clit.

"Again," he murmured to my back before biting down hard just as I gave into his demand.

"Oh…fuck." I detonated, washing us both in my orgasm. His grunt ripped through my body as I felt his dick harden and pulse out his release in hot spurts inside me.

In his tight embrace, I gained my wits and stiffened slightly. Sensing my retreat, he moved back on the recliner, taking me with him.

"Look at me," he coaxed as I kept my head on his chest. "Taylor," he warned, his thick accent covering my drying flesh in goose bumps. I braved a look at him and was completely captured when he gave me a small smile before claiming my lips in a kiss just as powerful as the one we'd shared before. Surprised and thoroughly confused, I kissed him back with as much fervor.

Our bodies still connected, his arms around me, I dove into him, my hands in his thick hair, my body warming as he kept our mouths connected. When we separated, foreheads touching and breaths heavy and rapid, I sighed. He laughed.

"Did that please you?" I asked with sarcasm and a small smile, my breath still escaping me in quick spurts.

He bit his bottom lip and studied me. My sex pulsed as I watched his face lit only by the TV, but couldn't read his expression.

He turned me in his lap so I faced him fully and stood. I wrapped my legs around his waist as he walked us to the bedroom.

He never answered me, but by the time the sun crept into my bedroom, I was pretty sure I got my reply.

I woke on my stomach, wrapped around an oversized pillow. Pushing the dried, sweaty red mess of hair off of my forehead, I turned to see I was again alone. It did little to stop the smile on my face.

In the shower, I went over my loss of control and the way I'd handled myself with Daniello. He might have found my lack of etiquette amusing, but I found it disgusting. Last night I'd lost order and to a complete stranger.

"Act like a lady, you'll get treated like one."

It had been years since I'd even thought of the voice that belonged to the man who had groomed me to become one of Tennessee's finest debutants. Squeezing my eyes tightly shut, I cleared my head until the image of him dispersed, forcing thoughts of Daniello and our night together to take their place.

Washing between my thighs, I felt the delicious ache, burning, and Daniello's absence. He'd been gentle last night. I assumed he'd sensed my vulnerability. He was good at reading me and yet he'd commented more than once that I was acting like a crazy person. Pressing my forehead to the shower wall, I groaned in embarrassed agreement.

If having Daniello near me aided in helping me abandon my good sense, maybe the whole situation needed to end. At the same time, I was having way too much fun to stop our charade. In the end, it was up to me to get my shit together. This wasn't about emotions or the possibility of falling in love. This was about him seeing behind more than a decade old façade and wanting to uncover what lay beneath.

And once again, it was up to me to make sure that the poor piece of Tennessee white trash laid dormant to the woman I'd evolved to. A force to be reckoned with, business owner, and woman of means.

"Keep it tight between the ears and between the legs, and you become every man's fantasy."

"Ray," I whispered as if anyone could hear me. It seemed all the ghosts of my pasts were making an appearance these days. While turning the shower off, I had expected ghost number three to show up in the reaper's cloak and tell me to change my wicked ways before it was too late.

But this wasn't *A Christmas Carol*, there was no Tiny Tim, and the only family needing more compassion were whispers, images, faces of my past that took residence with the rest of the ghosts in the audience while my life played out on the screen. I'd left them all behind, but it seemed these days I wasn't trying hard enough.

It had been months or longer since I'd thought of Ray Tyco. Turning off the shower, I wiped away the moisture from my skin and cleared a visible path across the mirror to take a good look at the woman across from me.

"If you intend to play with the big boys, kitten, you have to keep your emotions in check at all times. The only time a man shows any sort of emotion in the business world is when he's screwing or being screwed, and even then he may be hard pressed to reveal it. The world you are about to enter has no place for quivering lips and a weak mindset."

I owed everything to that man, and yet he'd collected. He'd collected a piece of me I would never get back.

An involuntary shiver drifted down my spine as I gave myself a stern internal lashing.

Maybe it was thoughts of Laz and Ray or the fact that I knew it was time to try to reach out to Amber again. Either way, my past had nothing to do with my present or my situation with Daniello.

I sat down on my couch and texted Cedric.

Me: It's time.

Cedric: I'll make the call.

The last time I'd seen Amber, I'd just graduated from Harvard. I barely had enough money to get us by, but I was determined to try to get her away from my parents. My mother intercepted our reunion as Amber remained locked in our house, peeking out the window behind the same tattered curtain that I'd been forced to hit with a broom daily. Her face haunted me as it looked so much like my own, a younger and far more burdened version of myself.

The confrontation on the front porch that day had been a long time coming, and I recognized the fear in Amber's eyes as she stared at me through the window. I hadn't seen her in several years, but I could see the itch in her posture, the constant movement of her eyes from me to the front door. She was thinking of fleeing as my mother screamed at me in her meth-induced state. Though I tried to barrel past her, she pushed me hard on my back and began tearing at my clothes. I managed to get her off me as I watched Amber fall apart before my eyes, her indecision to leave showing in the agonizing look that painted her features. I'd gone back later that night to find her window nailed shut. My mother kept watch through the living room, pacing continually like a rabid guard dog to keep me at bay. She had her drugs to thank for her watchdog abilities.

Amber was fifteen then, and as I looked at her through the

window, I saw myself so clearly. The resemblance was uncanny. And also, I knew her life, and I knew her need to escape. I wanted nothing more than to give it to her, and though I wasn't exactly in the position to be a parent, I couldn't help but linger.

I waited for her after school, as we'd agreed through hushed whispers through the window glass the night before, in vain. Maybe it was out of fear that she hadn't shown, or maybe she resented me for leaving her all those years ago at my mother's heavy hands. Either way, this time she'd left me. I'd waited for hours knowing she'd had a chance to break free at least once in the day and fought hard to respect her decision, though the urge to rip her away was debilitating.

Forced to leave town due to the danger of Laz finding out I had returned, I fled back to Boston, no closer to getting my sister out than I had been when I left. With me, she'd had a chance.

She'd never left Dyer, this much I'd found out through Cedric, who still kept up with a few people in town. She was nearly the same age that I was when I went to see her. I'd spent so many years buried in my career and working hard to get myself into a better situation, I'd abandoned her altogether.

I'd hoped she'd do the same for herself. I'd hope to have to track her down one day and find her married, happy, and success-ful. What burdened me was the fact that she hadn't left, which almost guaranteed all my hopes for her were for nil. Dyer wasn't a place to build a life. It lacked life, lacked oxygen, period. The town was a dead end cloud of dust that could only suffocate.

And I was sure my future would bring me back to it sooner rather than later. I jumped on my couch, deep in thought as my phone vibrated.

Cedric: She has your number.

I'd reached out. That was all I could do. It was up to her at this point. Deep down, I'd hoped for a reunion of two.

CHAPTER 7

IGNORING THE FACT THAT DANIELLO WAS A DANGEROUS MAN HAD been an oversight…until today.

I'd spent the morning working through my day at neck breaking speed, ignoring the now roaring curiosity regarding my new sexual interest. I hadn't given a man I hardly knew permission to invade my home on his sexual whim, but in a way, I'd allowed it.

I didn't have enough information to have Cedric run a background check, but I had a feeling I wouldn't find anything I was truly interested in knowing with that information anyway. It was up to me to get it out of him, and even as I thought of getting inquisitive, I wasn't sure I was brave enough.

"Taylor, line four, Mr. Di Giovanni." I straightened in my seat as if he'd caught me red handed in my thoughts and then rolled my eyes. I ignored the slight flutter in my abdomen.

"Taylor Ellison."

"I find myself answering to you again, Taylor Ellison. This does not please me."

I couldn't help but smile at his irritation. "I'm confused."

"I am calling to ask your permission to enter your home. It seems your security has been watching for intruders."

I muffled my laugh, knowing the flashlight cop that rode around my complex on a golf cart had probably cornered him.

"Rocco does not think this funny." I heard it then, the dangerous situation I'd put the security guard in. I asked Daniello to hand him the phone.

"This is Taylor Ellison. The two men that are at my front door have complete access to my property. I apologize and will email the association."

"Thank you, Ms. Ellison." I could hear the smugness in the man's voice and let out a breath of relief for his safety. Somehow, I knew without a shadow of a doubt that situation could have turned deadly.

Before I had a chance to speak, the line went dead. I sat back in my chair, completely baffled.

Mob, he was in the mob. He had to be. They had no patience or regard for authority. And his name Di Giovanni had mob written all over it. He paid for everything in cash, and that left him untraceable. He knew his guns and had surveyed my condo to make sure his ass was covered. He commanded respect and took without asking.

He'd practically admitted it in my office.

Great, I'm involved with a mobster.

No, you're fucking a mobster temporarily.

Either way, this wasn't good for me, or for business. Daniello had commented he thought it interfering with my business might seem impossible. Being involved with a member of the mob could easily tarnish my business reputation. How could he not see that?

Then again, we both knew our arrangement was temporary. He apparently isn't high profile and kept his business to himself, and told me it wouldn't affect me personally. Actually, he'd said it was up to me.

No closer to drawing a better conclusion, I made my way

home where an angry part Hispanic, part Italian, part Egyptian mutt mobster waited on me.

When I arrived home, my condo was empty aside from his suitcase. I looked in vain for a note, knowing that wasn't his style. Confused and yet satisfied that the slow burn I'd held for him this week would be satisfied, I showered quickly and plucked out my favorite mannequin look. Underneath, I sheathed my skin in purple lace and scented oil. I'd just finished putting on my stilettos when I heard the door chime with his entrance.

Unsure of how to greet him and determined to not screw up this round, I kept quiet as I entered the living room. Daniello's fiery eyes greeted me as he washed my body in his stare. He was dressed in a dark suit and silver tie and looked absolutely fucking edible. His towering presence seemed surreal in my tasteful but understated living room. Anger seeped from his every pore. Small drops of blood splatter adorned his white shirt just below his tie line. He pulled off his jacket to reveal his gun strap fully loaded on each side with twin Glocks. Dispensing the guns on top of his jacket, I remained silent as he further assessed me and noticed his hands were slightly stained pink.

Blood.

He hadn't bothered to wash them fully before returning to me.

Fear should have taken over my senses at that moment. I should have demanded an explanation. I should have been terrified...instead, I was turned on.

I ignored every warning that went off in my head. A man so dangerous shouldn't have thrilled me. I should have demanded he leave and take his crime littered laundry with him. Instead, I waited on him.

Unclasping his cufflinks, he barked his order.

"Go take off that dress," he whispered, moving to unbutton his shirt. "Leave the shoes on and lay face down on your bed."

My breath hitched as he watched me for only a second before pulling off his shirt. I hesitated, but only briefly, before I walked into my bedroom and stripped down to my lace panties and heels. I waited face down, breathing heavily as I heard him in the kitchen. Anticipation for his thickness alone made me wet as I lay patient and panting. I wasn't the best submissive in the few times I'd been to the club. I'd never met a Dom strong enough to top me. Daniello had a way of bringing me to my knees by just anticipation alone. I loved that about our arrangement. I loved his dominance and his ability to put me in my place when the mood struck him, even if I was less than cooperative. He'd waited for me to come to him the last time we were together. This time, I was the one who had to demonstrate patience.

In my world I ruled, commanded attention, and ran an empire. I controlled all things. In his world, I was his to rule, to control, to command, and I happily handed over the burden. That's what attracted me to the submissive lifestyle, but I was quickly realizing I'd been barking up the wrong tree with that club.

I couldn't hand the power over to just *any* man. I'd been waiting on *this* man.

Fingertips brushed over the base of my spine, trailing down to the skin my panties didn't cover. I let out a long breath of appreciation.

"You are selfish and almost cost a man his life today playing games." His voice was so rough, his accent thick, his anger obvious.

"I didn't know Rocco would go all Rambo," I said, slightly breathless as my breathing escalated and his fingertips drifted over my entrance, my panties soaked.

"He has no patience, and now you have angered him."

On edge and needy for his fingers to keep their pace, I replied with caution. "The guard was doing his job, keeping the bad guys out."

"You are a smart woman, Taylor." It was a scolding I wasn't in the mood for.

So I'd asked security to look over my condo. It wasn't my fault he couldn't keep his dog on a leash. I moved to turn over and face him when I felt the sting of his first slap. I inhaled deeply with the pain and before I could recover, a burn coursed through my scalp as he twisted my hair in his fist. His hair tickled my shoulder as his weight covered me and his breath hit my ear.

"Do *not* fucking move."

I shivered in response, no longer able to keep my breathing inaudible. I felt his full cock harden as it teased the valley of my lace-covered ass.

I lay perfectly still as his fingers stroked and probed and his fist slowly let go of its hold on my thick hair. I was aware of everything in those moments I waited for him. The ticking of my wall clock, the sound of the fridge clicking on, the scent of him, the thickness in the air between us all filled my senses before the second slap shattered my attention to detail.

Burning coursed through me as I gripped the sheets tight and arousal leaked from me.

In that moment, I surrendered all.

Another soft stroke over the top of my panties strummed my clit, and then I received another hard slap just below my ass. I buckled slightly at the bite and was rewarded with a harder slap.

I'd moved.

My clit throbbed, need going unanswered. I fought the urge to writhe and beg. I lay motionless as he went on with this for a small eternity, never touching my clit, only feathering my skin with the slightest touch before each punishing strike.

After another agonizing amount of time had passed, I was lifted onto my knees as his tongue found the most heated parts of my flesh and soothed them with long tongue strokes. I moaned in thank you as he soothed each burn thoroughly before landing another hard series of slaps and tearing the lace off of me in the process. I screamed in both desperation and relief as he shoved his huge cock inside me in one quick thrust. Unable to maintain my position, I fell flat on my stomach and was rewarded with strong hands gripping my hips and leading me back to my knees. His thrusts punished me as my raw ass screamed while he grunted above me and pulled at my hips mercilessly. I felt the tremble in my abdomen as Daniello remained eerily silent, voicing his anger only by the fury of his hips and the punishing of his strokes.

Still on all fours, he lifted my leg, anchoring over his forearm and dove deeper as I shrieked in surprise.

Full.

There was no other way to describe it as his cock filled me repeatedly, rubbing every surface inside of me. Unprepared for my orgasm, I shifted under its weight and sudden arrival. I was rewarded with a powerful slap and bucked my ass up, grinding into the bed as Daniello continued to fuck me.

I let out a yelp once again as he tilted me to go deeper and I choked slightly on the pain. Lace panties interrupted my next moan as they entered my mouth.

Rocked to the core by his cruelty, I stilled slightly.

As if sensing my hesitation, Daniello pulled his punishing cock out of me and turned me over to face him. His eyes were soulless, empty, void of any emotion, and I quickly understood.

This was the touch I was used to. The use of my body as a vessel for a greedy offender. This I understood. This I knew.

There was an instant recognition in his eyes, an unspoken agreement of submission on my part. I kept the damp panties in my mouth, tasting my arousal and moaning again as my hands drifted from the bed to clutch at his broad chest. He lifted my legs, anchoring me to him. This time, he entered me harder than the first. Every muscle in his form rippled in effect with his effort. The sparse hair on his chest led down to a perfectly toned stomach and defined abs. My eyes drifted to where we met, and I watched his hardness furiously fuck me while coated with my arousal.

Powerful thrusts encompassed my every limb as I held onto him tightly and crumbled a second time. He ripped the lace from my mouth as the orgasm hit and replaced it with his smooth tongue. I clung to him, desperate for relief in my burning muscles. I got none as he continued my punishment without words, only action.

Exhausted and spent, I watched him tax his anger, my drenched and pulsing pussy gripping him. A low growl erupted as he stiffened and gripped my head, pulled out, and coated my chest with his hot release. I gripped him hard as he spent the rest of himself, covering my bare breasts and neck. I collapsed back as the last of him pulsed onto me.

Thick air clouded the room as he left it, and the sound of the shower echoed through my bedroom.

I stood in front of my mirror and noted the long line of smeared mascara that marred my face. My body was covered in marks from angry fingertips, my backside a deep red. I ran my hand through the glistening on my chest and neck, opting to shower in my guest room.

Freshly showered and eager for sleep, I walked into the kitchen and noted a freshly corked whiskey bottle with a drained glass of ice next to it. I picked up the glass, slipping a piece of flavored ice into my mouth, knowing it was pointless to check my bedroom.

He was gone.

CHAPTER 8

"*You ever been kissed, Red?*"

"No," *I snapped quickly at Laz, who was skipping stones across our pond.*

I looked at him closely. In the last few years, he'd become my very best friend. We took turns mastering our own self-made bike trails and sneaking turnips off of the Jameson farm. We spent our nights fishing and swimming in the pond between our two houses. There hadn't been one day that we weren't side-by-side, aside from the time he had to head to Memphis for his aunt's funeral.

We often went to Laz's best friend Cedric's house to practice shooting. Cedric liked to hunt and would fire off round after round with his rifle, while I used my father's gun and was careful with my only box of bullets. Both boys seemed impressed with my ability to shoot, but Cedric was always quiet when I was around and looked at me as if I were interfering. It took a while for him to grow warm to me, but once he did, he would spend some of his summer with us.

"You can't miss," Cedric would note as he studied the target closely then study me. "You're a marksmen."

I felt a tremendous sense of pride when both boys agreed and smiled at me.

Cedric and I would lie on the grass, listening to crickets when Laz had to go home early. He would tell me about how he would be a soldier one day. How his father had been one and his grandfather too. I would simply listen to him talk, dreading the inevitable trip home. Cedric would always give me an odd look when we parted with a quick "night." I would run home and shake from head to tail at the horror of being caught and sigh in relief when I made it to bed, my latest adventure unnoticed.

Amber would start to ask questions when I got home, saying "Where have you been?" and "Promise not to tell." I felt guilty for leaving her a prisoner in that house but was thankful she now had school as an escape.

I had Laz as mine. Today was the last day of summer before we started at separate schools and Laz had been quiet all day. It was if he knew everything was about to change. He was going to be a freshman, and I was still stuck in middle school. I'd watched his body change and wasn't immune to the heavy looks he got when we went into town together. Laz had somehow charmed my mother into letting me out of the house. I didn't ask questions and took my freedom without hesitation. As I stared at Laz now in long cutoff jean shorts and nothing else, I felt a slight twinge of something I'd never felt. When he'd asked me the question, I'd immediately crossed my arms over my budding chest and stood awkwardly in my too small bathing suit.

Laz laughed at my posture and shook his head slowly. "Uncross your arms, Red. It's just a kiss."

"Maybe I don't want a kiss."

"Sure you do. I see the way you look at me." I huffed and rolled my eyes. I'd never wanted to kiss him. I'd never even thought about it until he'd asked me. Well, maybe once. I picked up a few rocks, tossing them beside him. Laz kept his eyes on me for only a second before he dropped the rest of his rocks and wiped his hands on his jeans.

"See you later," he said, pulling his T-shirt over his head. I stood with my handful of rocks, stunned. The sun was still high in the sky. I was sure I had a whole day of freedom left. I panicked as he began to walk off in the direction of his house.

"Wait!" I shrieked as I followed him.

He turned and gave me a bored look.

"Why are you leaving when we have the whole day?"

"To do what, Red, skip rocks? My friends are down at the river getting high while I'm playing patty cake out here with you."

I wrinkled my nose at the thought, and he rolled his eyes. I spoke without thinking. "I could go with you. I could get…high." The only thing that occurred to me was smoking meth, and I knew in that moment there was no way I was doing that. I shrugged as I took the last step to face him. He'd grown a good foot since I'd met him.

"Not that kind of high, Red." He must have seen the relief in my features as breath rushed out of me.

"Look, I'll see you later, okay? I'll come to your window tomorrow." My heart was sinking as I watched him start to walk away and the words stumbled out. "I want you to kiss me."

Laz stopped and looked back at me. "No you don't."

"Don't tell me what I want, Lazarus Walker. I said I want you to kiss me."

I stopped my moving mouth as he approached, pushing my shoulders out, and looked up without flinching when he again stood before me.

"And I never said I wanted to kiss you," he taunted as he studied my face.

"Well, you brought it up, you ass, so sumthin's got to be done about it." I put my hands on my hips and raised a brow in challenge.

"You look like a circus clown. Why would I want to kiss you?" He smiled, his blue eyes shining the way they always did when he knew he was aggravating me.

"You are all talk," I huffed. "You've probably never kissed a girl a day in your life."

"Sure I have. Kissed Lucy last week." I felt the burn in my face as I confronted him.

"Well, now I hate you, Laz, so good going," I mouthed, kicking the dirt up in front of him. He'd beat the snot out of Johnny Reid for announcing the arrival of my period because of Lucy Harden's big mouth. Lucy had been responsible for the most embarrassing moment of my life, aside from

Laz seeing my mother for the first time.

"Don't go all half-cocked, Red. 'Sides, you ain't my girlfriend," he snapped after gripping my wrist.

"Nope, I ain't and I won't ever be." I felt my heart break in that moment and lashed out further. "But one day you'll wish I was, and you won't get your way. To hell with you, Lazarus!"

I made my way through my window, bypassing my mother, and sat on the ledge, wiping the wet streaks trailing down my face with annoyance. That night, hearing my mother pace up and down the halls, I imagined for once her feet would make their way down the hall and out the door, but she wouldn't stop there. I prayed for the day she would just keep going. I hoped that my daddy would be glad about it and that Amber and I could finally have some peace. I must have drifted off because I woke to a light tap on my window. I thought about ignoring him out of spite, but the truth was that Laz was the only thing I had to look forward to.

He was all I had.

I opened the window part way and poked my head out.

"What do you want?"

He smiled and shrugged. "You still mad at me?"

"Did you really kiss Lucy?"

He nodded in reply.

"Then I'm still mad at you. Get."

Laz gripped my head as I began to retreat, leaning in to place a hard kiss on my lips. I pulled away slightly, but when he wouldn't let go, I let his lips linger on mine a beat longer. He pulled away with a grin.

"I'm your first kiss, Red. Nothing will ever change that, and you can't do a thing about it."

I wiped my pulsing lips as I lashed out. "Wasn't nuthun'."

He ignored me and kept walking as I got into my bed, wide-eyed, my heart beating out of my chest.

I jumped when I felt little hands touch my arm.

"Aylor, I did it."

I pushed out an impatient breath as my little sister interrupted my moment of reflection.

"Amber, we're going to get caught one day," I scolded as I grabbed a clean sheet I hid underneath my mattress.

"Onwe wittle bit," she promised as I stood to see she had already pulled the urine-stained sheet from the mattress. I studied it, noting it was just a small amount. I grabbed her wet panties and the sheet then crept down the hall to rid them of the smell. I sprayed a little starch on it for good measure and hung it out the bedroom window along with her panties to dry.

"I sorry," she said as she climbed back into bed and looked at me. She was almost six years old and was afraid of her own shadow. Her speech hadn't improved since she'd started school, so I did my best to help her. "It's I'm sorry."

"I'm sorry."

She was so small, and on a daily basis, I was forced to watch her endure horrible cruelty. Where I had air and sunshine, she was kept a prisoner, covered in bleach that burned and irritated her skin. What my mother did to me never mattered. I could bear it with thoughts of soaking in the pond with my best friend.

My mother seemed to spare me most days in lieu of hurting her, but in the end, I knew she did it because it hurt me more. There were days I would practically beg her to take it out on me, but I gave up when she only punished my little sister harder. Watching Amber sleep that night, I made a promise to myself that I would get us out of there.

And for years, I did nothing but think of a way to do it. Laz and Cedric got caught with drugs their first week of high school and were sent away to juvie in Memphis.

And when they came back, everything had changed, including Laz. Cedric had seemed just as determined as me to get out of Dyer and swore on everything the day he was of age he was signing up for the Army. I secretly and selfishly hoped Laz wouldn't follow, though he considered it.

It wasn't until a much later that I realized I should have used my wish more wisely.

CHAPTER 9

DAYS TURNED INTO WEEKS, AND I TOLD MYSELF I WAS BETTER OFF without Daniello. And in truth, I was. He'd kept his word and left me without explanation. I'd spent a few days reflecting on our time together and decided it was for the best. A small part of me mourned his absence, the banter, the sex.

God, the sex.

I kept my days full with work and making money. That was what I did. It was oddly comforting. I still hadn't heard a word from Amber since Cedric had made the call giving her the option of contacting me. I wondered how I would respond if I found out she wanted anything to do with me. How she could possibly fit into my life? I could have called myself. I should've called myself, but I couldn't bring myself to do it. I was a coward in that sense.

And when it came to her, I felt unimaginable guilt.

Sipping on a tumbler filled with the whiskey Daniello had left me, I sat on my patio overlooking the marsh. I'd been so immersed in my past lately that I'd been remembering more and more.

I thought about the first time I'd met Ray and the night that changed my future. My prince didn't come along and save me.

He was no white knight, but a benefactor with the right amount of money to buy me at the right price. I'd sold my soul to him for privilege. I'd lied to every soul I knew about my departure from Dyer, including Laz. It was my biggest skeleton and my most well-hidden secret.

I'd been someone's whore in exchange for my education.

In my world, there were no saviors aching to find an under-privileged girl and make her dreams come true. There were no miracle scholarships to Ivy League colleges, regardless of my high school GPA. I'd made strides from the age of eight to keep perfect grades at school. I'd never been encouraged by my parents or even acknowledged for my collection of A's. I did it for me in hopes of leaving town for college one day, no matter where it may be.

I read each book on the summer reading list *twice*. I read materials beyond my comprehension level and studied them over and over again until I understood them. I spent the time in Laz's absence at the public library, which was actually a broken down corner of a vacant shopping center. It seemed no one in Dyer had cared about the future of their youth and the library had a ridiculously limited selection. I'd jumped at every chance to accompany my father on his rare trips to Memphis to get a glimpse of life outside of Dyer. More than once I'd kept my hand on the door handle with the itch to escape, to step out of his truck, put one foot in front of the other and never look back. Thoughts of Amber and her future always kept me planted to the seat and obedient when I returned. I began to resent Amber for my predicament. I knew as soon as I was on my own I would find a way. I'd never doubted my ability to take care of myself. It was always the guilt of my mother's cruelty that weighed me down. Amber would suffer if I left, more than she ever had.

On my seventeenth birthday, someone had heard my prayers because Lucy Hardin had talked her father into taking us to Memphis for dinner. She'd approached me when Laz was sent away and told me she had meant for us to be friends. I had no one at the time, so I went along with every detail of our "friendship." In a twist of sick fate, I had no idea while she was applying a heavy coat of makeup on me that I would be meeting opportunity that very night that would make me both villain and victor.

It turned out Lucy's father had only agreed to take us with him in order to meet a business partner. Lucy's family was the wealthiest in Dyer. All too often, I found myself resentful of it. I spoke with Lucy as I devoured my salad and steak and then chose the biggest dessert available. All the while I caught the man eyeing me with a smile as he spoke to Lucy's father.

"Who is that man?" I questioned Lucy as I tore through my food, moaning in appreciation.

"Just one of Daddy's business partners."

"He's staring at me."

Lucy threw a linen napkin in my lap. "Because you have chocolate all over your face."

In the middle of dessert, I found myself alone at the table with Ray.

"Happy birthday," he said in a dry tone as I licked the chocolate off my spoon.

"Thanks," I said, completely immersed in chocolate that was no longer on my cutlery.

Ray leaned forward. "Look at me when I talk to you." I stiffened at his tone. It was the same tone my mother used when I expected the worst. Setting down my spoon, I turned to face him.

Ray wasn't as old as Lucy's father. In fact, he was much younger. He had big blue eyes that reminded me of Laz. He was well dressed and reeked of money, which was easy to spot when you had none.

"You live in Dyer?"

"Yep," I said, quickly averting my eyes to see if Lucy and her father were on their way back.

"Yes, sir," he corrected.

"Yes, sir," I agreed. "And I'm getting out as soon as I can." I didn't know where the words came from, but I decided to widen my lie. "I'm going to Harvard."

His laugh was both cruel and amused.

My cheeks flushed as he reminded me who I was.

"Do you have any idea how much it costs to attend a school like Harvard?" He crossed his arms over his suit jacket and tie as he stared at me expectantly.

"Hundreds of thousands," I answered with dread, waiting for the inevitable.

"And you'll need prep school. Good grades aren't enough, and even with the right breeding there is no guarantee you will get in." He cleared his throat, demanding my eyes again as I looked at him. He wasn't a bad looking man. In fact, he had a nicely cut face and full lips. For a flash, I saw him recognize that I was assessing his looks and he smirked. "You are aware of all this?"

"Yes, sir," I smarted with pure contempt.

"Good, quick learner. You seem sharp. You could manage a state school." It was a crack. No matter how subtle, it was a gavel decision he'd made about my future that I had no say in. I dug my heels in.

"You graduated from Tennessee and probably had money before you made any. Sorry you couldn't do better." I threw my shoulders back and glared at him as his laughter bellowed around the restaurant.

He shook his head as he looked down at his cuff links. "Little girl, you are something else. Tell me, how did you know I went to Tenn—"

"Probably a Vols fan, too. That's unfortunate," I added smartly as Lucy and her father began to make their way back to the table.

"You want Harvard?" he asked in challenge, pulling out his wallet. I sat stunned, praying Lucy would walk faster. I was relieved when Ray slid a card in front of me, a small smile on his lips.

"Call me when you're serious about it."

"I won't need to," I said, pushing the card back his way.

"Taylor…this card will get you out of Dyer." I could feel the tension leave me slightly with his words as if the truth of them didn't exist until he uttered them. I looked at him for long moments when Lucy and her father returned, trying to piece together why a man like him would possibly help me. I put the card in the purse Lucy let me borrow to match my dress and taped it to the top of my dresser drawer when I got home, where it remained for a year.

That card had turned out to be exactly what Ray had promised, but with a cost to the both of us.

"You look lost."

I jumped in my seat as Daniello's shadow covered my sun-exposed skin. Shielding my eyes from the bright sun, I lifted my hand and studied what I could of him. He was dressed casually and was looking down at me with an expression I couldn't read.

"I'm…What are you doing here?" I realized I was dressed in nothing but a ratty T-shirt and illegally cut jean shorts. I crossed my legs in my chair and poured another long drink over my lingering ice.

He turned his head as if he smelled something bad as he answered. I tried not to laugh. "I am here for you, of course."

He sat next to me in the vacant chair. Elation in my chest, I looked over and smiled at him, completely taken with the fact that he'd returned. It had been weeks without a word. I'd been sure it was over.

"You thought I would not return." His tone was far from the one I'd experienced the last time we were together. It reeked of sincerity and amusement.

"Yes."

His smile matched mine as his eyes trailed to my bare feet then scanned across the marsh. He picked my glass up from the table and threw it back in one long gulp.

"Rough day?"

"Rough," he murmured as his hand shot out and he gripped

my foot, bringing it to his lap. He was dressed so casually in a V-neck T-shirt and dark jeans. His black hair hung loosely around his ears, accenting a face that could grace the cover of *GQ*. His biceps bulged slightly as his strong, warm hands massaged me. I felt lucky in that moment to have captured the attention of such a beautiful man. His touch was gentle as he worked the bottom of my foot. My lips parted as he dug in deep, the tension in my shoulders rolling away.

"What do you do in your pastime…for fun?" I almost hadn't heard him as his touch became intoxicating. "Taylor?"

I smiled as he picked up my other foot, giving it the same undivided attention. His eyes moved from my bare legs in a hot trail up to my lips before they met mine. I felt the tension grow thick as he continued his massage.

"I work."

"Surely, there is something you do that is just for you?"

I paused and bit my lip. "If I show you, then your hands will stop."

He lifted a brow as his hands continued. We sat in silence for a few minutes as we looked at each other. Oddly, I wasn't shying away from the intimacy, and it seemed he didn't intend to let me.

Already wet from the mere sight of him, I was thoroughly seduced, slightly buzzed from the whiskey he'd gifted me, and acutely aware that I'd missed him.

I remembered Cedric's words to me that I was lonely.

"Do you get lonely living this way?" It was an intensely personal question, another that according to our arrangement I had no right to ask, but really wanted an answer to.

"I get exactly what I ask for in this life."

"Wow."

"What?" he asked, tilting his head and stopping his hands.

"You are really good at bullshitting." I stood before he had a chance to scold me for my mouth. "Come on, you wanted to see my hobby." He stood, towering above me, leaned in, and then took my lips in a slow kiss.

"Hello again, Taylor Ellison."

"Come on," I said as he followed. I needed a shower, I didn't have a single stitch of makeup on, and I was pretty sure he'd noted the spaghetti sauce stain on my T-shirt. I walked to my garage entrance and turned the knob, gesturing him in before me. I was quick to catch up, curious about his reaction. He turned to me after standing perfectly still for several moments.

"Interesting," he said, circling my Bomber and bracing his hands on the frame to peer in. He took his time studying each car and paid special attention to my GT-500. He looked up at me finally with amusement. "You have the habits of a man."

I nodded in agreement. "I guess in a way I was raised by men."

"No mother?"

I shrugged in reply.

"You do these things in place of words with your hands and your shoulders. I do not accept this." He shrugged, mirroring my movement.

I fought my smile. "Everyone has a mother." My answer was just as evasive as his, and he gave me a dead stare. I moved past him and opened the driver's door to the GT, my arms braced over the top of the window. "Shall we?"

"You want to challenge me?" He laughed loudly as he opened the door to my Bomber.

"Not exactly, Well, not *you*."

A deep grin spread over his features as he caught on. He reluctantly closed the door to the Bomber and took the passenger side of the GT. The engine roared to life, we gave each other a knowing grin as the garage door opened, and I gunned the vehicle into the street, slowly pulling past Rocco so he could clearly see us. I could feel his fury as we raced out of his sight.

"Let's teach him some manners," I said, cruising slowly through the downtown streets as Rocco followed closely. As soon as we hit open highway, I dropped gear and floored it, smoking Rocco in the SUV. Daniello barked a loud laugh as Rocco struggled for mere minutes before he became close to invisible in my rearview.

I sucked in a harsh breath as Daniello's hand gripped my knee, his fingertips pressing into my flesh possessively. I caught a glimpse of the fire in his eyes before I shifted and let the GT reach its potential. Muse's "Mercy" drifted through the air as I sped past the world around us, weaving through the inconvenience of sharing the road.

"You thought I was no more and yet you have not had another man," Daniello stated heatedly as his hand drifted up to the small strip of fabric between my thighs.

"No," I confirmed quickly and was rewarded with the stroke of his fingers. "And I'm not going to ask how you *know* of no other man."

"You want no one else." It was another statement. And it was a true statement.

"No." I exhaled loudly as his fingers stroked my bare pussy beneath my shorts. I was slick with need and felt the air of the cabin thicken as he slid his thick digits up and down my slit. Grazing my clit, he continued his slow torture as we torpedoed down the highway, thoughts of Rocco and anything else abandoned.

"Tell me what you feel with my fingers inside you."

Words, he wanted words as I fought to maintain control of myself, of the car. It had been too long without him. How could I tell him that? I couldn't.

"I…oh," I moaned as he gripped the back of my head with his other hand and slid two fingers inside me. I was helpless as I took my foot off the gas and was instantly left empty.

"No!" I protested loudly. I gripped his retreating hand and again resumed my speed.

His fingers also resumed, and my insides trembled in appreciation.

"Tell me," he coaxed, bringing me close to the edge, his fingers curved perfectly to hit me *there*.

"I don't want you to stop."

"That is too obvious of an answer, Taylor. Tell me more."

I let out a deep breath. "I've never felt so go—God, ah, Daniello, I'm going to come."

"Take the next exit," he said quickly. "Tell me more."

"I love the way you touch me, fuck me. I love the way you taste."

"How do you feel when I fuck you?" His fingers moved from my insides and stroked up to my clit. I reached for his hand, and he pulled it away. Two miles to exit, I panted out my plea. "I need this so much, please."

"What do you feel when my cock is inside you?" he hissed as his fingers plunged deep, taunting me before bringing my wetness to my aching clit.

"Everything," I answered as frustrated tears slid down my face. "I feel everything." I took the exit and raced through the stop sign as his fingers remained constant. His breath hit my neck as he inched closer and I spread my legs wider.

"I want to come with you inside me," I pleaded, my eyes fighting hard to remain open as I skidded onto an abandoned country road.

"You will come the way I want you to," he reminded me as I began bucking my hips to meet the thrust of his fingers.

"I want you so much," I confessed, cursing my mouth and honesty, and his effect on me. He pulled his hand away and sucked his fingers as I finally came to a stop near a tree line. We lunged for each other, the console keeping us separated where we wanted to be joined the most.

"I have thought of you so often, Taylor, my cock stays hard," he offered into my mouth as he pulled me into his lap. His thick accent, his smell, his dark eyes all created the perfect storm inside of me as I began to come undone. I rubbed my hot, wet mess over his lap repeatedly. "I have thought of your mouth, your taste, being deep inside you, and hearing your noises." He pulled my T-shirt up, tearing at my bra to free my breasts as they peaked for his dark, hungry eyes. "Fuck." It was the first time I saw his arousal weaken him. He closed his eyes, humming in appreciation as he sipped my nipple before enveloping it deep into his mouth. I arched my back, offering him more as I rode his lap.

Another long kiss had us both moaning and desperate as he pulled the button on my shorts and pushed them down my thighs. I lifted my hips, pushing them off the rest of the way, my need bringing a whole new level of desperation. Daniello plunged his fingers back inside of me without hesitation as I gripped his belt.

Before I could release him, he reached beneath him, reclining his seat back, and pushing me so my back was against the dash. I stared down as he spread me wide, lifted my hips, and dove tongue first into my aching pussy. I screamed his name as he devoured me like a hungry madman. I held myself up, my hands on his thighs and his lust filled eyes keeping mine as he fucking ruined me.

In that moment, I wanted nothing more than to belong to him and to be as claimed as he made me feel.

He pressed in, flicking his tongue over my clit with expert skill, and the visual along with the sensation sent me falling into a blissful heat before I exploded on his tongue. He lapped up my orgasm and slowly set me back on his lap. His hand traveled across my collarbone softly before he cradled my neck, leading me back to his lips. He kissed me deeply, and I threaded my fingers through his hair, pulling him as close as I could, unable to get close enough.

I'd never been kissed that way, touched that way, cared for that way, fucked that way, and I was truly addicted.

And I'd never in my life wanted a man more than I did at that moment. I pulled away briefly to look at him. The same heat accompanied his as he held me just as closely to him.

Everything *was* what I felt, and that was no exaggeration.

Fear, excitement, hope, want, need, completion.

"I feel you, Taylor." My whole body was trembling as he pushed me back on his thighs, his eyes never leaving mine as he started with his zipper. "I will fuck you so thoroughly tonight, I will be in your every thought."

Before I could object to the weight of his statement, a black SUV with a furious Rocco skidded to a stop next to us. Rocco jumped out of the SUV, and Daniello pulled off his T-shirt, quickly covering me as angry Arabic was sprayed on the outside of my window.

I knew instantly something was off. Daniello listened as Rocco unleashed and looked at me with regret.

"I guess our plans have changed," I said, knowing Rocco's anger had less to do with the stunt I'd pulled and more to do with business. Rocco disappeared behind the SUV as Daniello helped me gather my shorts. When I pulled them up and resumed my seat at the wheel, Daniello grabbed my hand, bringing it to his lips.

"Tell me," I implored as he paused briefly before pulling his T-shirt back over his head. "You can trust me." I waited in vain as he exited the car and disappeared behind the SUV. Suddenly frustrated, I slammed my car door and rounded the SUV to see Daniello loading two Glock magazines. He eyed me warily as I pressed in.

"You know enough about me," I said to his back as he smacked a clip in with his palm.

"Bitch, you leave here now," Rocco snapped with so much venom I took a step back in surprise. Rage covered his features as he took a menacing step toward me.

Daniello intercepted just as Rocco was closing the gap between us. More angry Arabic was exchanged as Daniello held up his hand and pointed in my direction.

"Go, Taylor, *now*," Daniello barked angrily between his back and forth with his driver, who was apparently anything but.

I didn't argue and made my way toward my car. By the time I had my door shut, the SUV had taken off, leaving me stunned. Stunned about Daniello's departure, stunned by Rocco's blatant hatred for me, and stunned I was dismissed so easily after what Daniello and I had just shared.

Furious with the situation, I quickly fired up my GT and caught sight of the SUV just before it disappeared. I knew I was playing with fire and my curiosity could very well get me in the path of Rocco's vicious assault.

Still, I followed.

I stayed as far behind as possible, exiting at the last minute, and keeping as much space between us as I could. It was impossible to disguise the red sports car, and I'd clearly be made if they so much as looked in their rearview. My hope was that they were distracted by whatever had called Daniello away.

I saw the sign for Port Authority and followed the narrow road. With no sign of the SUV, I gunned the car in an attempt to catch up. Coming around a sharp curve, my whole body tensed in fear as I spotted Daniello in the middle of the road in front of the SUV, blocking both lanes, his arms crossed in front of him. I slammed on the breaks, missing nailing him by inches. Without hesitation, he came toward my car in a blur, pulling me out of it and slamming me against it.

For the first time since I'd met Daniello, I was afraid of him.

"Do you want to fucking die today, Taylor!" Rage and cold eyes greeted me as I managed to get some breath back into my lungs.

I looked around us for Rocco and saw he was nowhere to be seen. Daniello gripped my shoulders painfully as he tore into me again. "*Never* would I trust *you.*" He gripped my T-shirt, handling me like a ragdoll, opened my car door, and then threw me into the backseat. I sat up, indignant, in an attempt to defend myself.

"All right, you've made your point," I snapped with slight fear as he pulled the seatbelt free behind me along with all the excess belt, wrapping one of my wrists tightly and snapping the belt into place so that it hung above me. He tied the other the same way, leaving me tied to the back of my car, completely helpless.

"What the fuck are you doing?" I screamed. "I said I got it, all right. I'll leave!"

Daniello cursed and hit the roof of the car repeatedly before his breath hit my face and he snarled his reply.

"I am save your fucking life, and I will not do it again, Taylor."

"It's saving, Jesus, and you can't fucking leave me here like this!" I was grasping at straws. I knew damn well he had every intention of doing so. He got into the driver's seat, pulling my car over to the side of the road where I'd be less likely to be hit. He pulled out the key and slammed the door without another word. I fumed as I watched the SUV speed away.

That was fucking stupid.

I pulled at the seatbelts to no avail. I felt his anger in the bite at my wrists as I pulled at the belts. Giving up after about a half an hour, I tried to ignore the pain spreading through my chest at his harsh words.

He was just supposed to be a fuck, a distraction. Why the

hell did I care what he did when he wasn't in my bed? The longer I waited, the angrier I became, and the more I distanced myself from my situation with Daniello.

As of that moment, I needed to be done with him. I'd made the decision for myself, even if he'd already decided the same. Hours passed as the heaviness in my bladder kept me on angry edge. Eventually, night fell as I sat tied to the backseat of my car. Panic crept its way in the more time passed. I hadn't seen a car the entire time I'd been tied up. Civilization seemed a million miles away.

That was really fucking stupid.

I didn't need this shit. I'd had enough of complicated to last me a lifetime. I didn't need to add some crazed mobster and angry sidekick to the mix. As sweat gathered at my back and I fought the urge to relieve myself, I thought about the fact that Daniello had been intrigued with my car collection.

I'd told him that men had raised me, and it was the absolute truth.

Lazarus might have taught me to ride a bike and eventually shoot a gun, but the valuable truths I learned didn't start until the day he returned from juvie.

"Wow, you're almost full grown now, Red." I stiffened as I pulled my nightgown over my head and turned to see him smoking a cigarette outside of my window. No one had ever seen me bare the way he'd just witnessed and I felt a small thrill at the thought that he liked what he saw. He had grown at least another half a foot taller as he watched me through sharp blue eyes. His brown hair had grown slightly longer, and a smile graced his lips around the pull of his cigarette.

"I was sure you had forgotten about me," I huffed, unimpressed with his failure to write me a single letter in reply to the dozens I'd sent him.

"I had to go hard in there, but I kept them all. I couldn't let them see me writing to a girl in there. I had no privacy. I had nothing."

"Doesn't matter," I said, bracing my hands on the window to help

myself out. He gripped me by the hips, pulling me out and closer to him. He smelled like sweat, cigarettes, and a hint of soap. I gripped him tightly to me for a brief moment, letting myself feel the false safety I always did when I was with him. He hadn't stopped the last few years from happening, and my hero worship for him was short lived when he failed to save me from it.

"Why doesn't it matter, Red?" he asked curiously. "You can't lie and say you didn't miss me. I have it in writing."

"Yeah, I missed ya," I agreed. "But I think you should know I'm the one leaving next." I brushed past him as the breeze played with the hem of my long T-shirt.

"Oh yeah? Where are you going?"

"Anywhere. I can't take it here with her, not anymore. I want to go to college."

Laz stayed silent, and when I turned to look at him, I saw he was staring at me openly with something new in his eyes.

"You're beautiful, Red. I knew you would be, but I didn't think it would hurt so fucking much." He made two quick strides toward me.

Surprised and confused, I asked, "Why would it hurt?"

Flicking his cigarette, he placed his hand on his chest, rubbing back and forth as he gripped my hip and pulled me closer. "Because when you want something this much, it hurts." I looked up at him as he smiled down at me. "And it's time to make you mine."

I didn't have time to answer as his mouth descended. I inhaled as he kissed me with hunger and separated my lips to explore with his tongue. I felt my nipples tighten in response to him as I kissed him back. Eager fingertips gripped me tightly to him as I wrapped myself in his need for me. The sensation of his closeness, his tongue, his taste, his touch had me leaning into him, wanting to feel more. He pulled away, placing his forehead on mine. "I missed you. I thought about you every day."

"You could have written one letter," I scorned, though his kiss melted every single bit of anger I'd harbored. It was the first time anyone had touched me tenderly in years.

"I couldn't do it. I knew…" He gripped me even tighter. "I knew I'd

fucked up. I knew it would be hard on you with me in there." He kissed my lips again softly then pulled away and ran a frustrated hand down his face. "Fuck, Red, I was so fucking worried about you, but with every letter you sent, I knew you could handle this without me. You had to."

"I didn't want to," I said tearfully. "Laz, I almost ran away so many times. She's so much worse now."

"We will leave," he said and pulled me back to him. "You believe me, right? I will get you out of here, I promise."

I nodded into his chest as he tilted my head up at him.

"You have an objection to being my girl?"

I shook my head no.

I didn't know why he'd decided I was his in his time away, but I was beside myself with the knowledge he wanted me. Still, a large part of me was wary of his words. It seemed liked so much more time had passed since he'd left. The hell I'd had to endure at home and the hundreds of hours I'd spent daydreaming about my escape and starting a better life. None of those dreams had ever included him, and now I felt guilty as to why. He took me by the hand and made his way to our pond.

We sat for hours as he told me of the friends he'd met in juvie. He'd decided not to go back to school and start working with Cedric's father. Cedric was hell bent on staying out of trouble, and Laz explained he would be keeping his nose clean until he left for the Army.

"He blames me for the bust, Red. He barely spoke to me in juvie. It was my fault." Somewhere between his guilt for Cedric came his promises to me. "I'll make some money, and we'll get the hell out of here, first chance." He pulled me to him, engulfing me in his arms. "You are the only reason I came back."

"I am?"

He simply shook his head as if I should've known better and promised me again. "As soon as we have enough money, we are gone."

With all my heart I wanted to believe him. To trust him to help me escape the hell of my mother and the gun toting traffic that had become more frequent in the last year. I clung to Laz until the sun came up and we were forced to separate. He kissed me again—the kind of kiss full of promise and seemed more important than anything else you could do.

That was the night I learned that a promise in a kiss was a lie.

I came to with the blaring of the interior light and the door chime. How I managed to drift off with a full bladder and burning wrists would remain a mystery. I saw the softness in Daniello's stare as he assessed me and took the driver's seat. I remained silent on the drive to my house as he kept me tied up like a dog, full of rage and humiliated. As much as I wanted to assault him with an arsenal of choice words, I remained silent as he glanced at me in the rearview. Once inside my garage, he pulled the seat up quickly and started my release. He sat on the edge of the back seat, blocking my exit as I pumped my hands in an attempt to get the blood flowing.

He was expecting an explosion but instead got a stare full of blatant hatred.

"You want me to be sorry. I will not be. You will get no apology from me." His tone was arrogant, as if he was speaking to a child after time out.

He really had no idea who he had fucked with.

"As soon as I get a gun in my hands, I'll be using it on you, so I suggest you make your exit, Daniello, and don't fucking come back."

He gripped my arm, and I pulled it away with ease. "I explained to you—"

"I'm done," I seethed. "This isn't worth the trouble. *You* are not worth it! Take your fucking watchdog and leave!"

I saw nothing change in his expression as he watched me. "Get out! Get the fuck out!"

He again reached for my hand, and I slapped it away.

"Fucking lies. Jesus, I'm so used to it," I mumbled, more to myself than to him.

"What are you saying now, woman? More words you do not mean." He looked bored, which only fueled my anger. I flew at him, fists balled. "Fucking bastard!"

He laughed as he easily dodged my angry fists.

I worked up the best mock accent I could muster. "I will treat you well." I curled the L in horrid exaggeration as I snarled at him.

He burst out laughing, and I opened my hand and struck him hard in his smug face.

Before I could register movement, my back was flat against the garage wall, and Daniello's hand was wrapped around my neck.

"You get in the way of my work again, Taylor Ellison, I will not hesitate to end your life, understood?"

"Hey, asshole, I know my 'south' accent is funny to you, but I said it pretty clearly, we"—I gestured between us—"you and I are over." He let go of my neck as I blew past him and ran to my bathroom, slamming the door behind me. My relief was audible as I drained my bladder, my face in my hands. I was sticky from sweating in the car, and my arms were weak. I felt the anger bubble from inside and couldn't help the small sob that escaped me. I picked up the clock off the shelf beside me and threw it at the wall. I ripped the clothes from me, taking deep breaths to calm myself. Fighting the urge to make good on my threat, I stepped into the shower. More angry tears bubbled and spilled over as I placed my hand on the shower door in an attempt to calm down.

This kind of anger had always been dangerous for me. It reminded me of a time when I'd lose control and lash out without consequence. The result had never been pretty.

I was utterly confused at the arrival of my tears, but it took very little time to remember why.

I'd tried to trust another man with just a small part of my-self, and the same thing happened that always happened. I got fucked, lied to, and made to feel unimportant. But I couldn't entirely blame Daniello. No, this was a sickness I'd started a long time ago with Laz.

I'd always wanted to believe and trust in the wrong type of man.

I heard the bathroom door open and saw Daniello sweep up the glass from my shattered clock before stripping bare and joining me uninvited in the shower. I hid my tear-streaked face under the showerhead, avoiding his eyes.

"Just leave," I said, defeated. "I don't trust you, either, and I don't want to."

I ignored the large build looming over me, perfectly cut, and completely viral. Nothing about Daniello was subtle. "Those tears are for me, Taylor," he said, holding my face with one hand while he pushed me gently against the tile.

"My tears are for my stupidity, you *unbelievable* asshole." He leaned in, his grip tightening as I tried to resist his kiss.

"I will be taking my pussy tonight, Taylor. You fight me, and I will take it anyway. It has been a…rough day," he admitted, using my words, "and I just need my woman's legs around me."

"I'm not yours." I resisted as he cupped my face, pulling me close. "I'm not your woman."

"You know that is a lie," he countered, forcing my eyes to his. "That changed today."

"We fucked. You got no such confession from me. If you think a good fuck negates my intelligence, think again," I said tearfully as they continued to fall. Daniello sighed as he released me and dropped to his knees, burying his forehead in my stom-ach. I froze as his hands began to mold my body with his touch. I gripped his hair hard in an attempt to yank him away from me as he held onto me tight as his touch roamed, tested, teased. Angry at my body, my mind, and the sudden erratic beating of my heart, I protested.

"Stop!" I screamed in anger as weakness seared through me.

"No," he said simply, lifting me to straddle him as he pulled me out of the shower. I clawed his shoulders, and he completely ignored me.

"CAVE MAN!" Soaking wet and fighting, I screamed as he pushed me on the bed beneath him and held me, wrapping my legs around his waist. He leaned in, taking my lips. I bit his hard, tasting metal.

Pulling back with a roar, he commanded my eyes and made his declaration. "Everything I tell you is for you! Everything I do and do not do is for you! Goddamn it, woman, you have moved me, and I cannot fucking stay away from you! Stop fighting me! I am giving you everything I can give you!"

I stopped my struggle to stare up at him, all fight in me vanishing with the heavy hit of each of his words. Without hesitation, he placed himself at my entrance and pushed inside. Crying out his name as both a curse and prayer, my back arched at the feeling of fullness around his solid cock. My thighs trembled along with the rumble of emotion in my chest as his eyes tore through me and his body slid along mine, powerful, consuming, intoxicating, each stroke a hard hit to my resolve. Gripping his hair, our mouths collided, insatiable with need. With his next thrust, I came so hard I buckled completely beneath him.

Deeper and deeper he consumed me as my freed hands pulled him close and my body tilted, meeting each movement of his hips.

With one last powerful push, he lifted my hips as if to prove his point and poured his hot release inside of me, holding us tightly together. Powerless and so full, I stared up at him as he slowly lowered himself to hover above me.

"When you leave..." I couldn't bring myself to say the rest. As bad for me as he was, as infuriating and as wrong as the situation had gone, I wanted him. And if our arrangement led me to being just another women whose bedside he left without explanation, then I was asking for warning. My legs still holding him to me, he hovered, his eyes seeing right through me.

"You want to know."

I nodded.

He pulled away, lying on his back next to me, and lifting my leg by the knee, bringing it over his torso to stroke it.

"Then I will tell you, but you have to tell me something in return."

Turning my head, I met his eyes as we faced each other on our pillows.

"Why do you feel the need for so much protection?"

A shallow laugh escaped me. "Kind of a ridiculous question coming from a man with blood stains on his shoes and who just threatened my life."

He didn't respond as he waited for a worthy answer.

With a sigh, I turned to face him. "I shot my first gun at age nine. I stole it from my father's bedside and spent an entire summer practicing. And I don't miss. A gun for me is like lipstick in the purse for any other woman. I can't explain it any better."

He remained quiet and turned to stare up at the ceiling fan, still stroking the bend in my leg.

"What about you? What made you decide to be a bad guy?"

He chuckled dryly, his eyes mischievous as he turned back to look at me. "I decided to make myself incredibly wealthy. It came with the job."

I found it ironic then that I'd fought so hard to leave the life behind to become something other than the gun-slinging misfit I was while my lover bought into the life purposefully.

"We are two completely different people, Daniello," I

mumbled with a long breath. "I fight hard every day to be legitimate, while you effortlessly remain corrupt."

"And yet we are still a match."

"Made in hell." I half-laughed, half-moaned as he rolled himself on top of me. His grin was infectious as his newly hard cock nudged me.

"Tell me, Taylor Ellison, do you think I am the devil?"

"No." Staring into his etched features, I had no choice but to draw my conclusion. "I think you are his greatest creation."

Alone again, I dressed and was at the office early. Nina had been taking on more and more clients, and business was thriving. In my early years at Harvard, I'd pictured a career, any career that meant money, security, things I'd never had before. Never in my wildest dreams had I imagined being a part of something so lucrative and satisfying. If I had nothing else in my life, I had a career to be proud of. I stared down at the tourists, a cup of coffee in hand, as I wondered what it was like to again be one of them. It was simple, really. Just a few hours touring around Charleston with a couple hundred dollars in my pocket, buying useless but necessary items from the market, hearing the history from one of the many tour guides. It seemed so simple, and yet the thought of going alone saddened me. Nina had grown up here and probably had no interest in doing such a silly thing, but at the same time, I was too embarrassed to ask. For a second, I thought of Daniello and me in a horse-drawn carriage. That happy thought was immediately interrupted by an angry Rocco on the opposite side of the carriage, glaring at me. This brought a fast laughter that rang out through my office.

"There's something you don't hear often," Nina remarked as

she joined me at the window. She followed my gaze. "Thinking of finally taking some time off?"

"Soon," I replied, turning away from our view.

"Taylor, God knows you work your ass off, but let me clue you in. You own half of this company. You employ close to two thousand people. We will survive. I'm sure there is something you can do for a few days."

If she only knew my only thought was to tour the city I'd lived in for the better part of three years she would probably laugh, or worse, pity me.

"So have you said yes to Devin yet?"

Her eyes narrowed as she sat behind my desk with a sigh.

"No, and I won't. I said I was never marrying again and I meant it."

I nodded, knowing it was bullshit. Devin was a magician when it came to Nina, and his brand of magic was suited just for her.

"Knock, knock." I looked up to see Nina's younger brother, Aaron, greet us. Nina jumped from her seat in obvious surprise and met him at the door in a long hug. For a split second, my envy got the better of me before I composed myself and smiled.

"Good to see you again, Aaron." He gave me a warm smile and replied, "You too, Taylor."

"How long will you be staying?" I asked for Nina's sake. I knew her little brother meant the world to her.

"A month or so. I want to try some courses here, and Florida is getting pointless." Aaron was a semi-pro golfer and was recovering from a terrible accident as a result of being too close to Nina's boyfriend's psychotic ex-wife. He'd been an innocent bystander to all the events that led up to Nina's newfound happiness and had almost been a casualty.

"Healed up nicely?" I asked as Aaron's eyes appraised me as they had the first time we'd met. He was attractive and had an appealing warmth about him. If I were into nice guys, I'd be tempted to learn more.

"Doc says I can ease into it," he replied as Nina eyed him warily.

"I call bullshit. I'll call him myself," she huffed and grabbed Aarons arm, pulling him out of the office while she addressed me. "See you at our three o'clock. This one should be interesting." She gave me a wink before pulling a protesting Aaron through my office door. I smiled after the two and silently wished for Amber to call. It had been weeks and still no word. I texted Cedric.

Me: Are you sure it was her who got the message?
Cedric: Still no call?

I didn't reply. He knew as well as I did it was a long shot and Amber was apparently holding some sort of grudge. Or even worse, she may not wish to know me at all. Still, I hoped for the chance to at least see her. To know my mother hadn't tainted her to the point she was unrecognizable.

Finishing up my day, I let my mind wander to the last words Daniello said before I drifted to sleep the night before and he again disappeared from my bed. Words I knew he hadn't meant for me to hear.

"Si che paralizzato?" *Who crippled you?*

I woke to more angry Arabic and groaned as I looked at the clock and it read 4:00 a.m. Daniello had made another appearance tonight, which did nothing but confuse me further. During dinner, I was sure an apology was on the tip of his tongue but had never made it past his lips. He seemed distracted, and I hadn't bothered to ask why. All I did know was that his threat to hurt me if I interfered with his business hadn't been dismissed from my thoughts.

Pushing off the covers, I winced at the soreness between my legs and walked to my dresser. Pulling on a T-shirt and panties, I made my way to the living room to find Daniello at my front door, facing off with Rocco.

The two were whispering heatedly, and as soon as Rocco saw me over Daniello's shoulder, he narrowed his eyes and pointed in my direction. Daniello all but pushed him out the door before turning to me with reassuring eyes.

"He will not return to your home."

"Great. And he was never invited in the first place, and neither were you," I added, starting a pot of coffee in the kitchen.

Daniello cornered the counter and gripped my T-shirt, pulling me to him. "You are such a mood woman."

"Yes, yes I am." I grinned. "And it's moody."

"Bitch woman." He grinned back.

"It's bitchy," I smarted, resisting his pull and slapping at his greedy hands.

"Stop correcting my English. I am aware I have not mastered it," he scorned as he gathered more of the material of my shirt in his fist and I slid hesitantly toward him. If he filled my senses with his scent, I wasn't sure I would be able to resist him, and my body needed a break. He'd fucked me to the brink of unconsciousness after our quiet dinner.

"Why do you not just say what is on your mind, Taylor?"

I turned my back to him and braced my hands on the counter, watching the coffee brew.

"I will not beg you to tell me your mind."

I rolled my eyes at his statement. His English tutor should be shot. The man couldn't even scold me without needing correction. It made it comical, but at four in the morning, it made me brave.

"You threatened my life. I don't think I'll be able to get over that. I don't think I want to. And I still don't like you."

He gripped the back of my shirt, turning me to face him. His tight hold outlined my body, and my nipples peaked under his watchful eye. "Then it is a good thing I play so well with your body." Heat invaded me as he leaned in, sucking my nipple through my T-shirt until it was painfully hard. Pulling out of his grip, I crossed my arms.

Bowing his head, he let out a long breath.

"You want apologies for words I mean when I say them. Do not let your curiosity about me get you killed, Taylor."

I took a step forward, my eyes as cold and steady as his. "And *you* would be the one to kill me?"

"Would it ease your mind if I told you I would have no choice?"

"I don't know." And I didn't. The man stood in my living room weeks ago with enough DNA on him to convict him for life. Was I really that surprised he would do the same to me?

"And if I end this now?"

He scrubbed his face with his hand, agitated as he answered. "That is your choice. I will honor our agreement."

We stood facing each other in a silent standoff, the ever-present current passing between us.

"What made you think I was the type of woman to deal with your life, your choices?"

He smirked as he sandwiched me between him and the counter, his ready cock pressed against my leg.

"Are you not?"

He had no clue about my past. He couldn't possibly. There was nothing about it to be found on any piece of paper or hidden in any database. I had no criminal record. The only people who knew about my past were me, Laz, and Cedric. If Daniello thought me a woman worthy of handling him, he'd drawn that conclusion on instinct alone. Maybe that's why I was reluctant to let him go. He was more than capable of handling me sexually, and from what I'd gathered would probably think my corrupt past laughable.

Still, I had no order. I couldn't seem to make up my fucking mind when it came to him. There was nothing structured about indecision.

And I knew without a shadow of a doubt that this decision could cost me my life. He'd admitted as much. It should have been a simple one, but half an hour later as he bent me over the bathroom sink and licked the inside of my thighs, I decided order could wait a little longer.

After Daniello had licked my center raw and soothed it in the shower, I couldn't help the distant voice that ran through my mind.

"Stupid or hardheaded, Red, you can't be both."

CHAPTER 10

WEEKS PASSED WITH NO WORD FROM DANIELLO. I WANTED TO believe that he would keep his word and tell me when his departure would be his last, but the more time that passed, the more certain I was that I'd imagined his sincerity. Were women disposable to him? It seemed the case when it came to matters of business. And yet each time I was in his arms, surrounded by his warmth, and felt the passion behind his kiss, I felt completely worshiped.

Suddenly, I was clouded by foreign feelings, the need to be close, to be wanted by him. Was I feeling for him or simply craving what his touch evoked?

Falling in love with him would make me an absolute fool. I didn't know if I was even capable anymore. Being addicted to his touch was just as dangerous due to the nature of our relationship. Obsessing over him had been a constant since the moment our eyes met.

And I longed for those eyes, the light color of them that twinkled when he was amused, and the dark brown irises that greeted me with desire when he was hungry.

My heart pounded each time I turned my key in the door and fell flat with a quick sweep of my empty condo.

I hated everything about what I felt and yet I silently willed the new vicious cycle to end with an appearance, a whisper, one more moment, one touch, a kiss.

I'd become possessed by a ghost, both in body and in mind.

Another week passed as I remained a prisoner in my house, hoping for any sign of him and coming up empty.

Hell had officially frozen over. I was living for a man.

Disgusted with weakness, I'd made it a point to leave my condo every night the following week. I'd spent hours shopping for shit I didn't need, tripling my workload, and exhausting my body with workouts to the point of passing out without a shower. I was doing the opposite of what I set out to do and simply went through the motions.

Nina had noticed my change in behavior, taking me to lunch twice to ask what my hang up was. At the second Spanish Inquisition, I'd finally admitted I'd gotten involved with an overbearing, infuriating ass of a man with an oversized ego and a persuasive cock. It was the most I'd ever shared, which sickened me even more.

"You sound like a woman in love to me," she'd said with a shit-eating grin.

"Not love, lust. Definitely just lust," I said confidently as we both finished our plates. "I know hardly anything about him except that I lose myself in him so easily…" I drifted off as I tried to explain his effect, but was at a loss for words when it came to explaining how he made me feel. "The situation is all wrong. We…us together…we are all wrong, but I just want to know why he feels the need to be so damned—"

"You are over-thinking this, Taylor, and dare I say, you

sound kind of…needy." She laughed loudly at my discomfort.

"You're right. I don't want to hear it."

She straightened in her seat and ran a manicured nail down the side of her water glass. "Taylor, who taught you there was anything wrong with developing feelings for a man?"

I gave her a straight face as I confessed the truth. "Every man I've ever developed feelings for."

She simply nodded as she averted her eyes, not pressing me further because she knew I wouldn't go there.

"Taylor, this relation—this thing sounds like a low maintenance relationship with no strings, no expectations, and incredible sex. Tell me again what the issue is, because from what I can tell, it's perfectly suited to you."

And that was the bitch slap I needed to put the whole thing in perspective.

No longer obsessed with Daniello's motive for control over me in and out of bed, I kept my routine of perfect order. Once again comfortably alone at home washing dishes, I heard my phone vibrate as I worked suds into a coffee cup.

"Taylor Ellison."

Silence on the other end had me about to hang up when I looked at the screen and felt the shock wave drift through my limbs. It was a Tennessee area code. I waited for words on the other end of the line with heavy breath.

"Taylor…it's…it's me, Amber."

"Amber," I repeated as I dropped the cup into the sink, hearing it break and staring at the broken pieces. Her voice was nowhere near what I was used to. It wasn't the voice of the little girl I'd left or the soft-spoken teen that I'd had a conversation with through a bedroom window. It was the voice of a woman.

"I…" A harsh sob escaped her. "I need your help."

Picking up the broken pieces of the cup, I nervously rushed through, "I'm here, Amber."

"It…I…it's…"

"What is it, Amber?" I pressed, "Talk to me."

"Hello, Red." Gripping a broken piece of coffee cup, I felt it cut through my flesh. Cold sweat seeped out of my forehead as I addressed the voice I never thought I'd hear again.

"Laz, don't you fucking touch her!"

"Me? Nah, wouldn't hurt her for the world. She's my girl, Red. I take really good care of her."

Blood pooled in my hand as I discarded the broken glass into the trash and braced myself on the counter, dread racing from the center of me throughout every limb, every nerve, and every fiber of my being.

"Don't hurt her, Laz. I'll give you anything you want, just don't hurt her."

"From what I gather, you have about a thirteen hour drive. I'll be sure to have a welcome home party well underway. You remember the place, right?" I heard Amber shriek in the background.

"Laz, please—"

The line went dead as I stood dazed in my kitchen, my past barreling over me like a tidal wave. Grabbing a kitchen towel, I wrapped my bleeding hand and took a deep breath. The Laz I'd left was a criminal and unpredictable, but a large part of me knew then he didn't want to harm me. *Then.* The last time I saw him, I'd left him crying and bleeding in a hotel room, begging me not to leave.

What I was sure of was the man I'd just spoken to on the phone wanted nothing more than to hurt me. *Now.*

And I predicted he would be more caustic than the ghost I

fought in my head.

Pushing down the terror that raced through me, I raced through my condo and pulled a bag from my closet, mindlessly shoved some clothes inside, grabbed some cash from my safe, then texted Nina.

Me: I need a few days.

Nina: It's about damn time.

Functionally numb, I pulled out onto the street, leaving the life I'd built to face the one I'd left behind.

CHAPTER 11

Adrenaline took the place of fear as I raced down the highway at neck breaking speed. Heavily armed and prepared to do whatever it took to resolve the situation, I pushed myself back to a mental state of ruthlessness that I hadn't visited in years. The agony of not knowing what my sister faced fueled me as I thought of a thousand scenarios that Laz could come up with to punish me. My sister had finally given me the chance I'd been so desperate for, and I would not let her down. I hadn't realized until I crossed the North Carolina border that I'd been seeking redemption. Connection and redemption were what I craved. My love and loyalty for my sister went beyond the simple reason of blood, but it was a selfish confirmation I needed from her. I wanted to prove to her and to myself, I'd done the right thing by leaving. Now that I had the means to help her in any situation, to get and keep her free of the life I had so purposefully abandoned, I could convince her to leave Dyer.

She was all I'd ever really had.

Laz, and later, Ray, had taken away both my innocence and faith in men. I refused to let anyone, especially Laz, take any more from me. If he wanted a fight, he had one coming his way.

"Nora, the fucking anhydrous tank is short again! When I catch the fucking thief, I'll put a goddamn bullet in his head!"

I heard the shouting back and forth as my mother and father speculated on any one of their list of enemies stealing the precious liquid from their tank.

For any common man, anhydrous was a fertilizer for farming. For meth dealers, it was an essential ingredient in the mix of the drug. All hell had broken loose in the last few months in the Ellison household due to a new supplier in town and the constant threat of my parents slowing traffic threatening to ruin their monopoly as the town's best source for meth. They had gone from using meth to selling my father's biggest cash crop one propane tank at a time. They'd started to make a substantial amount of money showboating around town in new cars and spending it on anything but the disrepair of the house and new clothes and proper nutrition for their children. I'd always blamed the majority of our despair on the fact that we had never had money. After a year of watching my parents live well while my sister and I still suffered, I had no choice but to accept they were simply monsters who had no place as parents.

I stayed on constant high alert and remained silent and obedient in an attempt to keep my mother's wrath at bay. My grades were soaring, and academically I was being recognized while going home felt brutal.

Often times from our beds, Amber and I would hear gunfire in the distance, followed by the hasty retreat of our father's car in the driveway. He was after the thief stealing the one cash crop that had ever brought him prosperity, and it had nothing to do with his dying fields.

What my parents did not know was I was the one aiding in the thievery.

It was my boyfriend who was doing the taking. And it was my boyfriend who my father now had to compete with for the sale of the drug. Laz had spent a few months out of juvie working with Cedric to tar roofs. Cedric had offered him a job with his father's company, which he gladly accepted until he realized how "Shit pay would take forever to get us out of Dyer." Cedric continually looked out for me, especially when Laz decided to start cooking and testing his product himself. He saw it as quick money, and I saw it as the death of us. Cedric had come to my window, warning me away from Laz, telling me that he'd changed since before juvie, telling me a few convincing secrets I knew Laz would kill him for.

"You deserve better, Taylor. You deserve more," he'd said as I shivered in the newly fallen snow. It was just after Christmas, but you couldn't tell in my household. There had been no "fucking tree messing up our house," no music, no laughter, no gifts. It had come and gone unnoticed, as it had every year.

"He will come around, Cedric. He's just trying to do right by me," I defended.

"You could come with me. As soon as I sign up, we could get housing."

"Wouldn't I have to marry you for that?" I asked as he looked at me with that same wistful look I had before now mistaken. He stepped forward. "We could fake it." It was then I knew he wouldn't have been faking.

"Cedric," I offered as he took a step away. Rejection eating his features, he spoke up quickly. "It's a way out, and I thought that is what you wanted. Mark my words, that guy doesn't love you more than himself."

I could see the puff of my exhale as he walked away, the crunch of snow under his boots. I remember thinking he looked a little angelic in his white jacket and sweats among a blanket of snow.

But his cruel words scarred me, as he didn't come back after that night. And Laz remained my constant.

We argued all the time, and though I knew I loved him, a part of that died the first time I saw his pale skin go clammy, his eyes dilate, and the warmth leave him in lieu of drug-induced paranoia.

After the first month he used, I put down my ultimatum. "It's meth or me." Laz looked panicked as he glanced around the hotel room he'd taken up residence in just outside city limits. He still worked with Cedric during the day and stayed awake most nights cooking in different fields to make the "real" money. He was thinning quickly and looked sick. We'd spent nearly no time together since he'd declared me his girl. He claimed he was doing everything he could for us. I was still a prisoner at home and forced to be in by nightfall every day. Laz would pick me up around midnight each night and take me on his drug runs or to go gather supplies. Twice I'd shot my gun in defense while he drove recklessly through town. I'd missed purposefully, and Laz knew it, but we were quickly becoming known in the meth community as the Bonnie and Clyde of Dyer. Laz was shunned by his mother, and my parents seemed entirely oblivious as I lay low shortly after our brush with rival dealers. Ironically, the biggest rival of all were my meth addicted parents. I'd been cluing him in on when it was safe to go steal from my father, and my reward was to be drug around at all hours of the night, watching the boy I loved ruin his body, his mind, and our future. Like most nights, I watched in horror as he produced the drug that had ruined my life. At first, I had justified it as a means to an end, an escape route.

It was all temporary.

"I can't watch this," I cried as Laz weighed and bagged his new obsession with soulless eyes. "It's me or meth, Laz. I can't do this with you anymore. You know what this shit did to my family, to me!"

"You. I pick you, Red. I'm sorry. I know better. I'm just trying to get us out of here."

"Look at me," I pleaded. His blue eyes glanced up at me, and all I saw was his shame. "Please, we can find another way."

"Like what!" He stood, overwhelming anger caused by the drug rolling off of him in waves. "What's your fucking plan, Red? I'd love to hear it. I have about four hundred saved after the car. We won't last longer than a week or two. I want to give you a good life. We need a decent start. I want to get as far the fuck away from this place as possible, and we don't have enough!"

"Laz, don't…" I stopped myself. There was no reasoning with meth. "Can you take me home? I have a test tomorrow."

Laz looked around the hotel and scratched the back of his neck anxiously. "Just let me bag the rest of this shit and we'll go."

I nodded and sat at the table across from him and watched for three hours as he obsessed with his drug, weighing and reweighing while Sevendust's "Black" stayed on repeat in the background. Laz made frequent trips to the bathroom to smoke, thinking I was naïve enough to believe he wasn't. I'd grown up in it. I'd lived it long enough. When I'd finally had enough and Laz had hit the bathroom for the third time, I left the room without a word to him and started the fifteen mile walk back to my house. An hour later, Laz pulled up next to me just as I crossed the city limits.

"Red, I'm sorry."

"I don't care, Laz. Go back. I can walk."

"Get in the car. You have school in a few hours," he barked.

"Not that you give a shit. Get. I've got this." He pulled forward, blocking me and waiting while the car idled. I walked past it without a second glance.

"Hardheaded, get in the car!"

"Not with you hyped up on that shit!" He opened the door and rushed me, pulling at my hand and placing the keys in it.

"Then you drive," he offered, his head hung. "I just want you home safe."

"I don't know how," I said weakly.

"No time like the present." Without another word, he walked to the passenger side of the car, opened the door, and took the seat. He'd recently bought the car from Cedric's grandfather. It was an old Thunderbird that looked like a scrapyard project but ran like a dream. I walked slowly to the driver's side, sure he would change his mind at any moment. When he didn't object, I adjusted my seat and took the wheel. Hiding my smile, I pulled onto the ever-deserted road that led into town and floored it, elated. Laz's smile widened with every turn I took. It took me only minutes to learn how to maneuver the car, and with Laz's occasional instruction, I was driving with ease. I drove for hours as he spoke of our life after we left Dyer. Of the places he would take me before we settled down somewhere like California or Florida. It seemed he'd been dreaming of our escape as much as I had, and I couldn't stifle my excitement as I parked at our pond. I had only a few hours before sunrise, and I knew it would be another tired day at school, but the talk and the drive were enough to keep me awake just a little longer as I listened to what my new life would be like.

"We can go anywhere, really."

"I want to go to college, Laz."

I turned to face him as the call of a thousand amphibians echoed through the dark night and all around us Led Zeppelin preached softly in the background.

"Come 'ere," Laz ordered as he pulled me into his lap to straddle him. I hesitated, knowing the moment was already tainted. He was high, and I hated it.

"You're high."

"High on you. Do you trust me?" He threaded his fingers through my hair as I nodded my reply.

"Let me touch you," he said heatedly as he pressed his lips to mine. I kissed him reluctantly at first and then thought of the moments that had led us to the one we were in. I thought of how he'd always cared for me, protected me. Loyalty led me to return the kiss as his hands drifted low. I let him unbutton my pants and sneak a finger beneath my panties as my body became warmer to his touch.

Breaking our kiss, he whispered, "I want to give you something." I gasped in surprise as he dipped a finger inside me and brought it up, massaging me. Sensation blossomed deep in my belly as he rubbed me continually while his lips explored my neck.

"Touch me, beautiful," he pleaded as I gasped and bucked, meeting his finger. I reached for the bulge beneath me and hiccupped in surprise when I unbuttoned his pants and he bared himself. Lost in sensation, I gripped him with my fist and pulled hard.

"Fuck, I can't wait to put it here," he whispered as his finger dipped in and out while his thumb kept rhythm. I felt the surface of something and paused on his lap.

"It's okay, baby. Go with it," he murmured as I gripped him hard, sweat building on my forehead and running down my back.

"Oh…Laz. Oh, I…oh," I gasped as the feeling reached the top and boiled over. Every limb shook as he laid me down on the seat and moved his fingers faster while I quaked beneath him.

"You are so fucking pretty." Kissing my lips gently, he pushed himself *into my hand, encouraging me to move again. I looked up at him with wide eyes as I stroked him, watching his face contort.*

"I'm so fucking hard," he hissed as I worked my arm faster and harder *until he stilled, spilling thick and hot down my hand.*

"Baby, fuck. Baby, I love you."

I felt the knot form in my throat as he ruined it for us both. He was high, and I didn't know if it was him or the meth talking. I refused to give him the reply I'd always wanted to because of it. Suddenly, I was furious. I left him with a short goodbye before making my way home. I didn't want to hear those words from him. Not that way. He'd taken that from me. I cried as I crawled into bed, knowing deep down that he hadn't really chosen me.

"She's a beauty," the grease-ball pumping my gas remarked while surveying my '78 Chevelle. I'd spared no expense on the candy apple red paint, the refinished leather seats, and what lay beneath the hood. Of all my cars, it was my favorite. It was sleek; it reeked of recklessness and spoke for itself on the open road.

"Thanks," I said dryly, completely uninterested in the envy covering his features. When he turned to me with a mustard toothed smile, I cringed. "The car isn't so bad, either."

"How much do I owe you?" I asked, pulling cash from my pocket.

"Depends. You want full service?" His suggestive tone disgusted me. I was sure he hadn't seen a toothbrush…ever.

"Nope, just the gas." I was somewhere between Knoxville and Nashville and had absently chosen to get gas in bum fucked Egypt. More afraid for my sister than the creepy eyes the man made at me, I handed him fifty dollars and headed to the driver's seat with the belated realization that stretching my legs had been a mistake.

"Jack, come out here. You have got to get your eyes on this one." I sighed deeply knowing that the state I was in was far from hospitable. I willed the man coming toward the vehicle to do the right thing, but the second I saw his greasy hair and toothy, knowing grin widen, I knew he'd made his decision. He wanted either me or the car, or both, and I wouldn't put it past either of them to try and take what didn't belong to them.

"Come on, honey, show us what's under the hood," Greasy Jack prompted as I strapped on my belt.

"I'm in a hurry, fellas. Maybe on my way back through." I jumped as Greasy reached in the driver's side, popping the hood. He smelled of liquor and piss, and I had to turn my head away to keep from gagging. As soon as the hood was lifted, I leaned in my glove box and grabbed Leroy—short for Leroy Brown, the most lethal of my guns—unlocked the safety then stuffed him into the back of my pants. I exited my car and rounded the hood to see them peering inside.

"Like I said, I'm in a hurry. Close the hood please and I'll be on my way."

"She's in a hurry, Cody. You hear that?"

Fuck.

I maintained my patience as the two men began to fidget with the motor. I watched them like a hawk to make sure they weren't trying to keep me immobile as I glanced around the deserted area. There were no cars coming in either direction, and it seemed to just be the two of them.

I wasn't afraid; I was annoyed and finally made it known.

"I paid. I'm done here. Close the hood." Cody looked up at me with a sneer.

"Calm your attitude, girl. We haven't seen one of these '78s before, I'm guessin'."

"Good guess. Take a picture if you want," I snapped, "And

please, shut my fucking hood."

No longer able to control my rising temper when the two didn't move, I lifted my hand to close the hood when Greasy Jack gripped it tight.

"You don't want this fight," I warned as they gave each other a look and then burst out laughing.

"No, baby, we don't want to fight you. We just want a taste. Why not take us for a ride?"

I lifted a brow. "You have a business to run, and I have business to attend to. What is it going to take to leave here?"

He pulled my hand he was gripping toward his stiffening cock. "How about a little—"

Before he had a chance to finish, I ripped my hand away and lifted Leroy inches from his smug face. The look of surprise was quickly replaced by panic as Cody took a step back and declared loudly, "I think I'm in love."

"I'm tired. I've had a long day. Cody, what do you say we close the hood and let me on my way?"

"Sounds good to me, darlin'." He shut the hood and gave Greasy Jack a nod. "Best do what she says, Jack."

I saw the scenarios race through Jack's three-celled brain as he eyed my finger on the trigger. "Don't be stupid. I promise you, I'm not worth the trouble." Jack's Hyde surfaced as he lunged for me, and I whipped the side of his face with my pistol-clad hand. He howled with fury as he hit his knees and covered his newly broken nose.

"I'll be on my way, then," I hissed, kicking Jack hard in the back so he went down on all fours.

"Don't be a stranger." Cody looked on in amusement as I started the Chevelle, taking off like a bat out of hell.

I'd told Nina months ago that I'd come from a place of dirt and metal grass and even compared Tennessee to the Wild West. But I was certain as I left the situation behind me I was a magnet for trouble, and even more so a beacon for evil men. I knew after years of being away that men like the two I'd just left behind didn't exist to most women of the world. I'd stopped at a shady gas station in the middle of nowhere because it wasn't intimidating to me. It felt like home. It felt like Dyer.

It was just the kick in the ass I needed to remind me of what I was about to face.

Men like Greasy Jack and Cody were exactly the type of people I hated most. Their sense of entitlement to take what didn't belong to them fueled me past anger. They'd probably never worked for anything a day in their life, and yet they felt they had to right to corner me into giving them whatever they decided to take. It took all my willpower not to turn around and put a life-altering hole into each of them.

More dangerous anger brewed as I thought of how Laz had demanded my appearance with a phone call. As if I owed him something.

He'd made his bed, and I had nothing to do with it. He'd want my money, some sort of control over me, this I was sure of, and he would use my sister as a bargaining chip. This I was prepared for.

I'd never taken anything that didn't belong to me but my freedom, and even when I took that I'd felt like I was doing something wrong. My life had never been my own until the day I'd left Dyer and fled into the waiting arms of Ray Tyco.

But he too was a different kind of evil. A selfish sinner disguised as a saint. Cold and calculating. An angry king.

And now with Daniello, I was dealing with the same selfish demon.

Burning road, I raced through the night with more resentment fueling me and keeping me alert. I looked at the dash clock.

Soon.

CHAPTER 12

"I'T'S BEEN MONTHS! WHERE IS THE MONEY, LAZ?" I STOOD IN THE same disgusting motel room staring at stained maroon carpet as he finished his shower. We hadn't had sex yet, an issue he hadn't pushed, and I wasn't comfortable enough with him sexually to confront him while he was naked. He'd been preoccupied anyway, with his new obsession.

"You have to spend money to make money. Just give me a little more time." His words were empty and carried little weight with his tone.

"I think you like it. No, you love it. People crowding around you like you are somebody. You can't keep doing this, Laz. You'll get caught, and I'll lose my mind."

"I won't," he snapped, exiting the bathroom naked. I averted my eyes as he stood in front of me, water dripping down his every limb. I felt a stir in that moment. Laz was beautiful and sought after by most of the girls in town. He had grown into a muscular body and a perfectly masculine face. His blue eyes shone brightly in contrast to his dark brown hair. I felt him slipping away from me daily as older girls with more voluptuous bodies eyed me with distaste as we made our rounds around town. I knew I needed to stake my claim. I knew eventually he'd want all of me, but I knew I wasn't ready. He was lying to me constantly, and I didn't want to reward him with the last piece of me.

"Look at me, Red."

"No, put some clothes on!"

"How about you take yours off?" he whispered, plucking the strap of my sundress.

"Laz," I said with a shaky voice.

"I love you, and I know you love me. You are just too hardheaded to admit it. I've been patient with you, baby, haven't I?"

"Yes." He took my hand and led me to the bed. "I'm going to teach you how to touch me, how to suck me."

Face to cock, I looked up at him with wide eyes.

"Wet your lips," he said gently, rubbing his fingertips over them. I stared at his hard dick, completely intimidated.

He cupped my face and rubbed his fingers back and forth lovingly across my skin. It felt beautiful, and his touch made me feel even more so. It was like a drug the way he looked at me. I found my resolve crumbling as his eyes pleaded with mine.

"I want you so much," he whispered as I opened my mouth timidly and took him inside it.

"That's it, Taylor. You are so fucking beautiful." He smiled down at me as he gripped my hair, pushing and pulling me as I took more of him inside. "That's good…ah…that's perfect."

Something inside me snapped, and I moaned as I worked him harder, clenching his hardness tightly between my lips. Nothing about it felt wrong, and I felt his body tense as I sucked harder, moved my tongue faster.

"Jesus," he whispered as he gripped me tighter, pulling me to him. "Let go," he ordered as I jerked my mouth away and he fisted his release on the bed. He lay down and pulled me to him in that disgusting room, and I felt the world fall away as we spent a few minutes in quiet.

"I love that no one else has kissed you, touched you the way I have. I'll wait as long as it takes for the rest."

I nodded in thank you as he put me at ease. "I'm fucking up, Taylor. I know I am. It stops now. I only want you." I nodded as happy tears fell and wrapped myself around him as we listened to the rain fall outside.

"We'll leave on your birthday."

I sobbed into his chest in relief as he held me to him. I wanted to tell him in that moment that I loved him. I'd decided to wait until the minute we pulled out of Dyer for good, but I never got the chance.

Two weeks before my birthday, I found Laz pacing the motel with fury on his face.

"We've been robbed. We can't leave!"

Every bit of hope I'd had fell into a large pool of despair as I watched him carefully. He was using again and heavily. I blanketed the loss of Laz, unable to deal with my shattered heart, and played into his game, though I knew he was lying.

I hadn't taken enough to stifle our trip out of town.

"By who?"

"If I fucking knew that," he seethed, "I wouldn't be standing here!"

I played devil's advocate. "Okay, so who knew where you kept the money?"

"Me," he snapped as he grabbed his keys off of the table.

"I'm coming with you."

"The hell you are." He turned to me with contempt. "Go home, little girl, and do your homework."

Tears built up quickly but I pushed them down in lieu of lashing out.

"This 'little girl' has been by your side for months, selling meth, helping you steal, and watching you wreck yourself. As far as I'm concerned, it was my money, too." The truth was I was terrified of his retaliation and who it might be directed at. I'd known for the last two weeks that Laz had no plans of leaving Dyer anytime soon. Cedric had told me as much when I had met him to pick up Laz's last paycheck. They'd had a falling out on the job due to Laz's lack of appearance and Cedric was done covering for him. I was, too.

It was time to admit the truth to myself. I'd told Cedric I was leaving, *and he had tried to talk me into waiting for him, but I had already learned not to trust anyone but me.*

Meth had brought misery and claimed every single person in my life, and now it was destroying Laz. I couldn't afford to be selfish and wallow in my despair. I had to do something and fast. I'd called Child Protective Services on my parents twice in the last three months, and we had yet to get an initial visit. I wanted Amber out of that house before I left, but I was failing miserably. When I realized Laz wasn't leaving, I'd watched his every move to find his stash spot. I'd only helped myself to enough to get me far out of Dyer. I'd left the majority of the money.

I was leaving without him.

I'd betrayed him, but he'd lied to me long enough. He was caught in the world I was desperate to escape, and I couldn't save him.

"I'm not going to get in your way. I just want to—"

He began shaking his head before I'd even finished. "It's too dangerous. Just go home, okay?"

"No, to hell with that, Laz. I'm coming, deal with it."

"RED! GODDAMNIT!" He rushed me then lifted his hand as if he was going to strike.

I saw it then, the side Laz had purposefully kept hidden from me. It was a brutal realization and struck harder than his hand ever could have. I took a step back, fearful, but kept his eyes.

"I'm coming, deal with it."

Furious, he gave me a deathly look I ignored until he pulled out of the motel parking lot.

"You have your piece?" I nodded, unable to miss the agitation in his voice. I'd been carrying my father's gun with me everywhere for months. I pulled the small gun out of my hoodie and flashed a part of the metal to him.

"When we get there, you don't say a word. Just let me handle it, okay?"

"Where are we going?"

"To make a deal."

I sat quietly as he pulled up to an old, abandoned school that desperately needed to be condemned. We made our way through the loosely boarded back door, and I looked around us, terrified. There were kids my age, some younger, and adults alike hitting the glass hard and oblivious to those around them. Laz had taken me to a smoke house.

I glanced up at him in question, and he warned me with a clenched jaw to remain silent.

"Laz," I heard a voice call and turned to see a blonde a little bit older than me with vacant eyes walk over to him with a smile. "I've been saving myself for you," she purred, completely ignoring me and running her hand up and down his chest. Her clothes were filthy, and she would have been beautiful if it weren't for the fact that she was grossly thin and had a veil of meth covering her features.

As if I was an afterthought, she looked over at me. "You don't mind sharing him, do you? We had one hell of a good time last weekend."

Cringing with the weight of the blow, I looked to Laz, who pushed her away as if she was full of venom.

"Fuck off, Trina. This is not the time."

"You know where to find me," she piped happily as she saw the devastation on my face. She'd made her point and accomplished her mission. All the loyalty I had for him died in that moment as I gagged on the realization that everything he'd ever told me was a lie.

I ignored the stabbing pain as I followed him down a long hallway filled with dilapidated and unhinged lockers. It was eerily dark, and I could barely see a few feet in front of me. It irked me that Laz cruised around the halls with ease. Obviously, this place was something else he'd been keeping from me. Laz knocked on a door that read Asst. Principal and I waited with bated breath to see who would answer.

We didn't wait long as the door was ripped open and a menacing guy with a crew cut and a map of tattoos covering every inch of his skin greeted us with contempt.

"Laz," he said, looking past him to stare at me. "Who is this?"

"This is my girl, Red."

The guy raised his brows in question. "Long time knowing you, never mentioned a girl."

"Didn't need to. Rudy seeing people? I need a word."

"He's in a mood today, make it quick." Laz nodded and walked into the office, shutting the door behind him and leaving me with Crew Cut. I ignored his open stare as I looked around.

"I'm Jay. You want a hit?" He extended the foil and glass my way, and I shook my head. "No, thanks. I'm good."

Leaning against the office door, I strained to hear anything I could and got nothing. Jay looked me over as I waited patiently for Laz to make his deal.

"You don't look like the type of girl Laz would get with," he mused as I crossed my arms over the tits he'd decided to concentrate on.

"I'm not, and I'm not his girl." The floor was covered in a mix of trash, gravel, and broken glass, which I assumed were used pipes. I couldn't imagine choosing to spend my time in a place like this. And suddenly I wanted no part of whatever plans Laz had. I wanted out, and I wanted out now. Whomever he decided to blame the missing eight hundred dollars on was entirely on him. He'd have no proof. His actions would be his own. I was leaving, and I was doing it soon.

And then, when I was feeling the most helpless, the most desperate, I remembered the card taped to my dresser. Suddenly, the door opened behind me, and I stumbled as Laz's arms caught me. He gripped me tightly, leading me out of the school and to the car.

"Red, about what you heard," he started to explain as he turned the key. "It's not true."

"No, it is true. You fucked her and forgot that you loved me. I wasn't giving you what you needed, so you got it someplace else. And that isn't why this is over."

He hit his steering wheel repeatedly in fury before turning to me. I didn't give two shits about the reason why he had so much anger. Maybe it was guilt. Maybe it was because he got caught. He took a deep breath and turned to me. "It's not over. I love you."

"It is over, and it has been. We can't be who we were anymore. I can't

save you and you sure as hell are in no shape to save me. We both failed."

"No," he whispered as he read my expression. He knew it then that I was the one telling the truth.

"If you think I'm just going to let this go, think again," he said coldly as he made his way back to the hotel. "It's always going to be you and me against the world, Red. Always. You need to remember that."

I stayed quiet, knowing he didn't even believe his own words anymore.

"Ray Tyco."

I fumbled with the cord and went completely blank as I contemplated hanging up.

After a bout of silence, he tried again. "Hello?"

"Ray, it's me, Taylor Ellison. You...gave me your card." I looked around the motel lobby nervously, knowing Laz was in a sleep coma after being up for several days.

"I remember you, Harvard."

"You said—"

"I know what I said."

"I'm ready to leave. I-I need to leave."

I heard glasses clink and assumed he was in a fancy restaurant surrounded by other wealthy diners as he spoke in a hushed tone.

"I'll come for you."

"No," I pushed out loudly. "Don't do that. I'll come to you. I just need to know where I'm going."

"Tell me something, Taylor. Do you still want Harvard?"

"Yes," I said without hesitation.

"Then that's where you are going." Tears slid down my face as I did my best to keep it together. Last night, I had watched my mother tear Amber apart for spilling bleach on our twenty year old carpet. I'd prayed for the first time in my life for her death.

"Taylor?" He was now surrounded by silence as I tried to keep the shakiness out of my voice.

"Please, just tell me where to go."

Salvation from my situation came at a price I never thought I could afford. Days seemed endless without Laz, who had only attempted to mend fences with me once. It only reaffirmed what I already knew. His new life as the kingpin had taken the place of our life, the one we were supposed to have.

I'd decided the night of my eighteenth birthday to see him one last time. I was going to wait until the last minute to break it to Amber, who I was sure would never forgive me, but decided against that confrontation altogether. She would cry and beg me to stay, and I couldn't afford to back out at the last minute for my sanity alone. On the day I left Dyer, I replaced the books in my backpack with clothes and attended one last day of school. I walked the shorter distance from the school to the motel without bothering to look around at the outdated buildings and the bone-dry landscape. I waited until nightfall in front of the motel door and was just about to give up and head for Memphis when he pulled up. He shut his car door, stuffing his hands in his pockets as I stood slowly, trying to assess his mood. His face gave nothing away.

"I'm leaving."

"No you aren't," he snapped as he approached the door.

"Laz, I just came to say goodbye. I got a really prestigious scholarship to this prep school, and I've taken it."

It was another lie. Something I was getting entirely too good at. The truth was, I was leaving to run to a man I'd had one conversation with, who promised the same thing Laz had failed to deliver: freedom from Dyer, from my mother, from the hell on earth I'd been living in for the past seventeen years.

Laz dug his nails into my arm and pulled me inside the room.

"You think you can just fucking leave me? You think I'll let you?"

"You made your decision, so I made mine," I snapped. "You lied to me. We were never in this together. For all I know, you used my feelings for you to get me to help you rob my dad!"

It was if I had slapped him. Hurt in his deep blue eyes, he shook his head in disbelief.

"The only fucking thing I have ever done is protect you, and you didn't need to know everything. It was better that you didn't."

"Like the fact that you were selling meth before juvie? That you were slipping my mom a bag so you could take me with you at night?" It was one of the secrets Cedric told me. I worried about that confrontation.

Shock was all I saw as he gawked at me.

"I'm not an idiot, Laz, and you have done far more bad than good when it comes to me, so spare me the righteous 'It was all for you' act. The truth is, things changed, you got selfish. And while I've been helping you, I've been living in the same hell. Maybe you'd forgotten that, maybe you don't fucking care. Either way, I realized it was up to me."

"I got robbed. I told you it would take more time," he said weakly.

"I took your fucking money," I snapped. "It was the last thing you taught me. Look out for number one."

In two steps, he was in front of me. I heard the slap before I felt it. Face burning, I cried out in pain, palming my cheek as I stood again from being knocked off my feet.

"Fucking bitch, you stole from me?" Time slowed unbearably as I looked for the boy I loved, once lived for, only to realize he was gone.

"You lied to me! Cheated on me and used me to peddle your filthy fucking drugs!" Rage burned through me from the years of hell I'd endured, believing in him, in us, in what we had.

"Where is it?" he said, unaffected by my words as he began to pat me down.

"Go to hell!" I screamed as he threw me on the bed and pinned me.

"Maybe I'm there, Red," he spat over me, his large, terrifying pupils a sign of every monster I'd ever faced. "Maybe this is hell, and maybe I'll

get a better seat or earn my keep by taking what I should have from you a long time ago."

On his knees, he ripped at my jeans as I kicked him hard in the stomach.

"Fucking bitch," he roared as he reared back and braced his hands above my face.

"Do it. Make it easier on me," I challenged. Boiling over, I couldn't stop the anger, and I let it take me over.

He looked at the red he'd already stained on my face and broke. "Fuck, I'm sorry, I'm so sorry. But I can't let you leave, Red. I can't."

I pulled my piece out of my hoodie and pointed it at him. Never in all our years together had I ever thought it would come to this. What we'd just done could never be undone. We'd just hit a whole new level of fucked up. Everything inside me screamed for me to stop, that the person I had the gun trained on was Laz, that he loved me and would never hurt me. Still, I let the anger win and kept it on him as I backed away from the bed and he sprang to his feet.

"You stupid fucking slut! Who the fuck do you think you are! You are no better than me! If you leave me like this, I will find you. I will kill you."

"You won't find me, Lazarus, and do you know why? Because you won't have any idea where to look."

"You think your sumtin' with that scholarship, don't cha? Well, I have news for you. They can smell trash. They'll be able to smell you a mile away. I'm all you've got."

"No, Laz, you are all you've got. Insult me again and I will blow a hole through you."

"Fucking whore, you—"

I aimed and pulled the trigger, shooting a clean hole through his thigh. His agonizing cries only fueled me as I squeezed again, this time clipping his ear.

I opened the door of the hotel room then looked him in the eye. "Don't come looking for me or I'll finish the job."

"Red, don't…please." The voice belonged to the boy I used to know.

As I looked into his eyes, I saw equal parts affection and hatred for me. He didn't want me to belong elsewhere, and that was where the hatred stemmed from. The affection was something we'd started years ago and would never go away, regardless of how completely screwed up our relationship was now. Even through all of it, I still cared for him. As I stood in the doorway, prepared to leave and never lay eyes on him again, I let my feelings show, but only briefly.

"I can't stay. I told you that. I'm sorry." He shed a single tear as he glared up at me.

"I'll come for you," he warned.

"No, you won't." His shoulders stiffened as his greasy hair spilled over his face. He looked down at his worn shoes in defeat. I lowered my gun and walked out the door.

CHAPTER 13

ELEVEN YEARS AGO, I WALKED OUT THE DOOR THAT I WAS CURRENTLY mesmerized by. I had no idea what to expect when I walked through it now. I stared at the dented metal door and realized time had stood completely still in Dyer—always had. Nothing had improved or changed in any way. It was the land that life had forgotten. The eerie feeling I had now was the same damned dread that stayed with me from day to day while I dwelled here. Even the night air seemed stale.

Taking a deep breath, I tucked Leroy deep into the back of my pants and the pocket-sized pistol in my bra. Laz now knew where I lived. He probably knew of my success and wealth. What I was unsure of was whatever charade he intended to play out here. I could not bring this personal war back to Charleston if I intended to move on with my life.

I tested the door, and it opened easily. Instantly cringing at the sight before me, I pressed through, shutting the door behind me.

"Fuck, now it's going to get good. Jesus, Red, you are fucking perfect." I met his eyes dead on as he fisted the red hair of who I assumed was my sister as she sucked his cock. With one hand, he led her, and with the other, he held a Glock to her temple. Body tense and ready to strike, I was about to reach for my gun when I heard a whimper in the corner of the room. I turned to see Amber cowering in a chair, eyes wide as she looked between Laz and me.

"Remember the first time you did this, Red?" He snickered as he pulled his cock out of his victim's mouth and spilled over her chin. "Damn, I needed that. Thank you, baby."

"Never pictured you as one to hold a woman at gunpoint to get off," I said, taking him in. Laz was still beautiful despite apparent years of abusing his body. He had grown taller, more muscular, and had a wall of tattoos on his etched chest. Most of them looked to be angels and demons. His hair was a little longer than I remembered, but his eyes were the same true blue.

"Long time, baby," he said with a wicked grin as he zipped his fly. "How you been?"

"Amber, my car is parked out front. Why don't you go get in it. Me and Laz will have a chat."

"I don't think so. I mean, who would want to miss the re-union?" he said, pulling the girl who still had yet to clean him off of her chin to her feet. "And don't worry, Red, Lucy here is the one who gets off on sucking cock at gunpoint."

Lucy!

She turned to me, an empty shell, a meth addict, and a far cry from the proud, rich girl I'd known since I was a kid. Meth had apparently claimed her, too. Jesus, didn't anyone ever leave this place?

"Tell me what you want straight out. I'll give it to you and be on my way."

"I want you to suffer," he said heatedly as he wiped Lucy's mouth with a towel. She looked zombified as she strolled over to where her discarded dress lay on the floor and slipped it on. Without a word, she left the room.

"So, Harvard, huh? Here I was trying to rub dimes together

to make millions when I could have married my winning lottery ticket."

"So it's money you want," I said quickly. "I have plenty. How much to buy you out of my life?"

If I didn't know better, I would say he looked hurt.

"After all the time we spent together as kids, I don't mean anything to you, do I?"

"No," I said, glancing at Amber. She was shaking and gray and looked eerily like me. If we weren't years apart, we could have passed for twins, except her eyes were brown, mine were green.

"Laz, I've been in the car thirteen hours. Trust me, I've suffered. Tell me how to end this," I pleaded as he gave me a wary look, wiped his chest, and then pulled on a T-shirt.

I walked over to my sister and grabbed her hand. She looked at me with soulless eyes. "You made her smoke!"

"Fuck no. She put the pipe to her mouth herself. I simply lit it for her like a gentlemen."

I pulled my gun without a second thought as Laz grinned at me.

"Ah, so here we are full circle. How is that temper of yours helping you in the workforce? Are your employees dodging bullets?"

"I got the fuck out of here to make something of myself. *You* could have done the same." I gripped Amber's arm, pulling her from the chair and moved toward the door.

"The party is just getting started. Don't leave yet," he said, arms out and palms up. For the first time since I entered the room, I felt a pang of fear. This was too easy.

"What's waiting for me outside the door, Laz?"

He winked and plucked a cigarette from the dresser next to him.

"You were high and you hit me. You deserved that bullet.

This can't be about a bruise I gave you eleven fucking years ago!"

He flicked his Zippo, and I saw the deep pockmarks on his face for the first time illuminated by the light of the fire. He blew out smoke and tapped his temple. "Smart woman. Okay, I'll give you a fighting chance. I've set up a type of obstacle course for you. If you can make it out of Dyer tonight with your sister in tow, I'll list my demands, and we'll conduct our business then I'll be on my way."

"And if I fail?"

"This isn't the type of course you want to fail, Red."

"Why the fuck are you doing this?"

"I jumped through hoops for you. You can play hopscotch for me." His words were cold as he took a long look at Amber. "See you later."

The words escaped my mouth before I could weigh them. "I could just shoot you."

"You could." He nodded, taking another drag of his cigarette, and stretching his arms over his head. "Well, what are you waiting for?"

"Damn you to hell, Laz."

"Like I told you the day you left me bleeding in this hotel room, this is hell, but now I rule it." His grin was evil, and his eyes were filled with hate...for me.

I rolled my eyes as Amber began to shake and scratch. She was withdrawing. "Can you walk?"

She nodded as I opened the door, gun pointed in every direction as I shut it quickly behind me, walking Amber to the car and shoving her inside. I hauled ass to the driver's seat and pulled out like a bat out of hell only to be tailed.

Welcome back to the Wild West.

I gunned the Chevelle as I drilled my sister. "Is it true? Is he running the town?"

She looked at me with wide eyes and laughed dryly. "He's

running all of Gibson County."

Hearing gunfire, I dropped the car into gear and skidded to a halt on a bridge in front of a razored tire strip.

"Jesus," I whispered as the car blazing bullets gained on us. Having no choice, I put the car in reverse and told Amber to get down. I grabbed Leroy from the console and put the barrel against my forehead in prayer. I yelled at Amber on the floor, "Stay down!"

This made no goddamn sense. If Laz wanted me dead, why wouldn't he do it himself? I had no clue why he would drag me thirteen hours to release the hounds of hell when he could've done the honors himself. It dawned on me then. He had no intention of letting me die tonight.

He was playing with me.

And even as certain as I was, the men on the other end of the guns had no idea I was onto them. I stopped the car just as they approached and got out, placing myself between the Chevelle and the vehicle racing toward me. I took aim and began to open fire as bullets buzzed several feet away from me. These idiots were either trying to miss or really horrible shots, and I'd bet my life on my first conclusion.

Laz really should have warned them who they were up against.

I stood perfectly still and took aim with my exhale, opting for a Hail Mary shot to the front tire, and my bullet ripped through it just as an SUV came out of nowhere and T-boned right into them. My enemies repeatedly flipped until they landed on their side. A dark figure exited the SUV and jumped onto the crushed car, pulling open the door and firing inside. I hauled ass back into the Chevelle and pulled away, certain that Laz would not be happy with the outcome and that he'd picked the wrong night to play cat and mouse with me. His enemies clearly had no issue interrupting our game. I ran to clear the path of the tire shredder and then took off like a shot, thankful for my lust for fast cars. I drove aimlessly through roads my GPS couldn't lead me out of, cursing and keeping my eyes fixed on the rearview.

"Amber, if you happen to know where the hell we might be, now is the time to speak up." As much as I'd like to think I knew these roads like the back of my hand, it had been too many years. I was completely lost. She stared straight ahead as I tried to snap her out of her dazed state. "Amber!" She leaned forward just as I yelled and emptied her stomach on my dash and floorboard as I went into panic mode.

Two days ago, I was leading the corporate world, with endless resources at my fingertips. Today, I had pulled my gun three times and was toting my sick, meth-addicted sister around the country, lost and completely alone. I pulled the car to a slow stop keeping the car idle as Amber recovered.

"Well, this isn't exactly how I pictured this would go." I laughed softly while glancing over at Amber, who was still retching, the putrid smell filling the cabin of my car. I rolled down my window and pulled the fresh air through my nose. "I thought we could start with something simple like 'Hello, how have you been?' and then move on to the questions like 'Are you married? Any children?'" I looked over at Amber, who was staring at me like I'd grown another head. "I can see now those aren't exactly the right questions." I was rambling nervously, and it only made the situation worse when I wouldn't shut up.

"Or how about 'How's Momma? She dead yet?'"

Finally, my sister spoke up. "Yes."

I shot back a little in my seat, taken aback by her words and not sure I wanted the details, so I asked another question.

"How did Laz find out about me contacting you?"

"He looked through my phone."

I crossed my arms and let out a breath. "Jesus, Amber, you actually socialize with him!"

"He's been watching over me since you left."

I turned on the cabin light, grabbed a water bottle out of the back seat, and handed it to her. She drank it slowly and said a quiet "thank you."

Before I had a chance to ask any more questions, she opened her door and threw up again.

"How long have you been using? Be honest."

"Years."

"Jesus, Amber, after—"

She pulled the hair away from her face as she glared at me. "I appreciate the maternal concern and all, but do I really need to point out now is not the time."

"No, I guess—"

Before I had a chance to register what was happening, I was pulled out of my car by a dark shadow. I struggled and reached for my gun as the words he spoke knocked the wind out of me.

"Taylor Ellison, do you mind telling me what in the FUCK IS GOING ON?!" I paused in my struggle to look into the eyes of my lover and sagged in relief against him.

CHAPTER 14

WE WALKED A SMALL DISTANCE AWAY FROM THE CHEVELLE AS Daniello eyed Amber in the front seat.

"Your sister," he concluded as I turned to face him and nodded.

I breathed in his scent that felt unnatural in the environment we were in and looked him over in the contrast of my headlights. He was dressed casually in jeans, a black T-shirt, and boots, and looked absolutely beautiful. I realized again that I had missed him and knew that was dangerous. The how and why he was here as he stood in front of me were far too much for me to wrap my head around. I hadn't noticed the Glock in his hand until now, but the curiosity written all over his face was the most intriguing.

As much as the time didn't call for it, all I wanted to do was melt into his arms, kiss him endlessly, and fuck him until I was covered in the smell of his soap.

Then I realized the SUV that had just saved my ass belonged to him.

"I thought you weren't going to save me anymore."

He grinned, suddenly amused as he answered me. "A woman brave enough to step out in front of a moving car full of bad guys while she fires a magnum deserves some help."

I smiled back as we both chuckled together inappropriately.

"Who the fuck are you, Taylor Ellison?" He didn't want an answer as he stepped toward me with kind and ever amused eyes.

"Who the fuck are you?" I countered, just as intrigued.

"Amon Daniello Stamatio Di Giovanni." I cupped my mouth to stifle my laughter.

"I know it ridiculous," he smiled.

"It's ridiculous. Or it is ridiculous."

"I save your life, and you still correct my English." He gripped the back of my head, pulling me an inch from his lips. "I fucking need to feel this mouth." I moaned in agreement as his lips crushed mine in a need-filled kiss. I opened for him and gripped his huge biceps as he pulled my taut body to his. Just as I was about to start begging to shed clothes, he pulled away.

"Come, I will take you back to Charleston."

"I can't leave," I confessed, staring at the sharp grass between our feet. "I have to finish this. I can't have it following me home."

"And what is this?"

I looked up at him with the truth. "A fight I started a long time ago."

"Tell me," he urged, taking in our surroundings. We were in the middle of nowhere, the Chevelle lights seeming to beam on forever in the distance. I wasn't sure what else Laz had planned, but I knew staying idle like a sitting duck was asking for trouble. Sweat began to cover us both in the humid summer air.

"We have to get out of here. I don't know how many more there are coming." I paused, knowing my next words would anger him. "Thank you for the help, but you can go. I'll see you back in Charleston."

He stiffened, indignant. "I just shot three men trying to kill my woman."

I couldn't help but smile again. "And you were upset they

were going to beat you to it?"

He looked down at me with intense eyes as he brushed the wind-blown hair from my face. "I saw the blood on your kitchen floor. I did not like the way I felt."

Before I had a chance to start what was sure would be another argument between us, I saw sets of headlights flip on one by one. A row of trucks stood a quarter mile behind the Chevelle, lighting up the empty field.

"Fuck," I whispered as Daniello turned to face the intrusion.

I heard the boom of Laz's voice through a bullhorn on top of one of the trucks as he addressed Daniello.

"You must be lost, partner. Allow me to show you the door."

Daniello pushed me out of the way as bullets meant to hit us flew by our heads. I made a beeline for the Chevelle, knowing that Laz was no longer playing games. Daniello had killed his men and worsened the situation. I looked behind me to see Daniello pull his Glock and take out several of the headlights on the truck that lit up the field. He dove into the Chevelle as I killed my lights and sped away from the trucks heading toward us.

Amber screamed as a bullet ripped through her passenger side mirror. I was confused by Laz's attempt to take us out with Amber in the car. He'd apparently spent so many years caring for her, and I wondered if his hatred for me was enough to make him forget all about it. They gave chase as Daniello grabbed Leroy from my console and fired out of Amber's side, the gun going off like the small cannon it was and ripping through the metal of the trucks behind us. With only three shots left, he took his time aiming carefully and taking out two of them. I yelled at Amber, who was still shrieking with each shot.

"Give him more bullets out of the glove box. Now, Amber, do it now!"

Just as the trucks closed in, I turned on my headlights and saw the SUV shoot past us, launching a small arsenal at the trucks.

Two of them veered off the road, engines on fire as the others pressed on toward us. Daniello reloaded and managed to shoot out the tires of another truck so that we were only left with one, that I knew Laz occupied. The truck sped in front of us, and I slowed, following it until it came to a stop, knowing that I had to face him again. That if I didn't end this now, it would never end. Our headlights beamed into the cab where Laz stared back at me through his rearview.

We all stayed still for mere seconds as we tried to contemplate the other's next move. The silence was broken as the SUV skidded to a stop next to us and Rocco addressed Daniello, who was staring at me from the back seat.

"Wait," he ordered Rocco, who was once again spraying angry Arabic at Daniello.

I met Laz's eyes in the rearview, unsure if he saw me watching him. He tilted back in his seat and hung something on it.

"It's your necklace," Amber whispered.

"He never gave me a necklace."

"It was for your eighteenth birthday. He keeps it on him all the time."

A solid lump formed in my throat as I watched the back of his head. "Laz," I whispered. It was then that I thought maybe he *had* loved me all those years ago. That he was just a fucked up kid, as I was, but that he'd wanted to keep his promises.

Just as I thought it Laz pulled away and Rocco waited next to us for the word. Daniello watched me carefully and ordered him to back down.

Confused by Laz's attempt to keep us engaged, Daniello instructed me to follow Rocco, who seemed to know the way back to civilization. Half an hour later Rocco stopped a few towns away from Dyer, and we checked into a decent motel next to the interstate in amicable silence.

Exhausted and overwhelmed, I sank into the bedside chair

as I watched my sister sleep. Was she in on this whole scheme with Laz? She'd told me she needed help, but if he were her protector, why would she ask for my help? I would get my answers as soon as she woke. Muscles aching from too many hours on the road, I opted for a shower as Daniello and Rocco argued in the room next to us.

I stripped to nothing and let the water wash away one of the most fucked up days of my life.

My mother was dead.

I allowed myself to think about her and couldn't muster one single emotion from the news of her death. I slipped into a T-shirt and shorts and walked out of the room to knock on Daniello's door. Rocco opened it and pushed past me with his shoulder, his eyes telling me what I already knew. The man despised me.

"Come in," Daniello said as I watched Rocco get into the SUV and drive away.

"Where is he going?"

"Back to Charleston, and then home." I shut the door behind me and watched as Daniello pulled an array of guns out of a long, sleek black bag.

"And where is home?" He didn't answer me as I sat at the table opposite him. He remained evasive as he loaded each gun and placed it back into the bag. I watched him without a word as the lust grew inside me. He bit his full bottom lip as he concentrated, occasionally looking through the scope of a few guns and checking the chambers. He was all too alluring as I remembered our time together, and what his lips and hands could do to me in seconds.

Unable to resist, I lifted from my seat and walked over to his, straddling him and bracing my hands on the back of his chair. He ignored me, working around me, and kept at his task as I began to nip at his neck, breathing him in. He loaded another gun as I licked the divot in his throat, tasting the salty sweat that'd dried on him and went back for more. I began to grind my hips onto his hardening dick and pulled back after a few minutes of working myself up to see the fire in his eyes. Heat worked its way between my legs, and I leaned in to take his lips just as he moved his head to dodge my kiss. With a sigh, I began to pull away when he put the gun he was holding back on the table and grabbed my hips, bringing me back to his lap hard.

"Who is he?"

"Just a man I know who is holding a grudge against me."

"Why?"

"Because I didn't want to stay here. Because I left him here." Admitting the truth was easy. It was the look that Daniello gave me that was hard to swallow. "You being involved in this is only going to make it worse. I can handle him. I can handle this on my own."

He gripped my arms as his breath hit my face. "I am not going to leave you here so he can play his games."

"I'm going to talk to him tomorrow, and then I will leave with you." I pointed to the table. "We don't need all of this. No one was supposed to die tonight. He's sick, and he's hell bent on making me suffer."

"Then I will handle him."

"It's not your place."

"I am not asking your permission!" He lifted from his seat, forcing me off his lap and leaving me stunned at his anger.

"Please," I begged, knowing the outcome if the two men ever faced each other. "Please, just give me a day. I'll come back to Charleston with you."

"You continue to gamble with your life, Taylor, as if it means nothing. Why are you so intent on dying?" He pulled his shirt over his head and slipped off his shoes as he waited for my answer.

"My mother used to convince me I wouldn't live long, and after she'd said it enough, I began to believe her, to accept it."

He remained silent as he watched me, trying to figure me out.

"I need to go check on Amber."

"No, you do not. She will not wake."

"What do you want from me?" My voice was gravelly with exhaustion. He crossed the room wearing nothing but his jeans, his ripped chest begging for the stroke of my tongue. He hovered over me, masculine, dangerous, and beautiful.

"Fuck me," I pleaded. "Please, just fuck me."

Without hesitation, he pushed me against the door, his arms braced above me. "Why?"

"Because I want you."

"And your affection for this man...Laz?"

"You're jealous?" I saw his anger and couldn't help the full feeling expanding in my chest. He gave me little time to bask in my victory as he leaned in and bit my neck. A cry of surprise erupted from me as I clawed at his bare chest. He stilled my arms, soothing his bite with soft lips.

"God, please don't make me wait." He pulled me toward him, his lips still attached to my neck, and pulled my clothes off in a rush. I breathed out his name as he pushed two fingers through my waiting, dripping pussy. I leaned into his touch, thankful for the reprieve of my busy brain.

"Do not go numb on me, Taylor," he hissed as his digits explored me and a third finger slid into my back entrance. He caught my gasp with his mouth, his tongue stroking velvet licks against mine. Intoxicated and completely full of him, I moaned into his mouth as I kissed him. We melted together, our movements unrehearsed but perfectly synced. I pulled his cock from his pants, rubbing the silky tip with my thumb before stroking its thickness.

He pulled his fingers from me, and I sank to my knees, kissing down his manicured chest, keeping a firm hand on his cock. Once there, I worshiped him as I heard his steady exhale. He began to fuck my mouth hard, moving his hips and gripping my head possessively. Without warning, he pulled me up by my hair and gripped my hips, impaling me. I screamed out in a mix of pain and pleasure as he nailed me to the wall in rough, thorough strokes. My back slid up and down the rough surface as he punished me, his eyes as penetrating as the muscle he was fucking me with.

He gripped my bare breast with his teeth and bit down hard before sucking it deep into his mouth. I clawed the crown of his head, pushing him away as he pounded into me without mercy, my body tightening to the point of pain before I exploded my release. I heard the sound of our sex as Daniello flexed and moved inside me, never slowing, never stopping. Our bodies covered in sweat, we exchanged needy tongues, fueling our hunger.

On the floor minutes later, my back screamed at the feel of the rough carpet. Daniello moved inside me, fucking me, owning me.

I heard his grunt as he pulled away from me sharply, fisting his cock and spewing his hot cum all over my chest. He brought his soiled hand to my lips, and I licked it clean as he rubbed his orgasm all over me.

"Beautiful," he rasped out as he circled my nipple with his drenched finger. "You are the only woman I see."

A large part of me melted in that moment as he looked at my body in awe. His fingers drifted down to my sex as he again pushed them inside of me. I moaned in protest, sore from his brutal cock, as he began to kiss me. Minutes later, I shuddered with release as he fingered me to the point of orgasm, *twice*.

We showered together, and for the first time, bathed one another with gentle hands and shared long tongue-filled kisses.

We toweled each other off with soft smiles and spent the night in the dark motel, confessing from our separate pillows, my leg wrapped around his torso.

"My home is in Italy," he murmured as his fingers strummed my thigh. "Barga."

"It must be beautiful," I whispered, close to sleep with the steady movement of his fingers. He pulled my thigh up to get a better reach as he whispered.

"It is home, and yes it is beautiful. It is the only place I do not feel pressure, expectations."

"From who?"

He stiffened at my question, but for the first time gave me an answer. "My work, Rocco."

"Why do you deal with him? Just get rid of him. All you seem to do is argue." I felt his chest move with his chuckle and pulled my head back from him slightly to study what I could of his face in the dark room. The cold air whirred through the vent, and I pulled the cover over us and burrowed into his warm body.

"If I got rid of all the people I argued with, we would not be sleeping in this bed."

"Threatening to kill me again?" I rolled my eyes as he pulled me to him tightly.

"I will make you the promise that I will never say those words to you again."

"Oh, well, thank you for that," I said sarcastically.

"That does not mean I will not kill you," he chuckled as I pinched his nipple and twisted hard.

"Fuck, woman," he bit out in pain, pinning me to the bed, his hips spreading my legs as he made his way between them.

I felt his hard stare on my face as he spoke next. "If I trust you with this tomorrow, you will not get a second chance."

"I know," I whispered.

We spent the rest of the night whispering back and forth as

he told me of his home in Italy, of his one sister, Tula, and her nine children. He'd even confessed his love for airplanes and told me he owned a small one he flew at home. I only put a word in here and there as he told me stories of himself and a younger, less angry, Rocco, who was his cousin. The last thing I remembered was a caress of lips on my collarbone before I drifted away.

CHAPTER 15

I woke up just as the sun was peeking through the motel blinds and went back to Amber's room, lying down next to her, watching her sleep. She shook and twitched, clammy, and covered in a thin veil of sweat, but remained asleep. I used to watch her for hours when she was young, worried that one more abusive hit or word from my mother would break her. But every day she'd wake up, ready to face her. It was if she mentally prepared herself in the few minutes from the time she woke up before she went downstairs.

I wondered how she'd conquered her stammer and lisp. She'd spoken perfectly last night, without pause. I assumed my mother's death had a lot to do with it. I turned to stare at the ceiling, contemplating how to get out of my predicament with Laz without more bloodshed. What I did know was that money talked in these parts and it spoke volumes. I could give him enough to start a new life somewhere. It wasn't too late for him. I realized last night, no matter how much he hated me, how much he wanted to hurt me, I wanted different for him.

Seeing him last night had physically hurt, though I didn't let it show.

But his choices were his own. I wasn't responsible for the

way his life turned out. Life after Dyer was anything but easy for me. I had struggled long after I left, at the cruelty of Ray, at school, at life. And why the hell was my sister so tied up with Laz? She could've left like I had. She could've done whatever it took to get out of here like I had.

"I have a son," my sister whispered, startling me. "They took him a week ago."

I turned to her. "His grandmother, she found out I was using again. I can't deal without him. I've tried to get clean so many times, but it may be too late."

"How can I help you?"

"I have to show I'm capable. I have to get clean, have a stable home for him. It's legal now."

"What's his name?" I asked, curious.

"Joseph. He's two." I imagined a ginger baby with brown eyes just like hers and a sweet smile. "I cannot live without him, Taylor. I fucked up. I'll do whatever it takes. I can't be this person anymore."

I nodded, knowing this I would help her with for however long it took. "Why didn't Laz help you?" Even as I said the words, I was glad she'd contacted me.

"He's a well-known drug dealer, and even if he gave me the money, Dyer isn't where I want to raise my son. Laz never wanted me smoking, and he never gave it to me. I started on my own. He lied last night to get under your skin. He's not the monster you think he is."

I shook my head. "Then why all the theatrics last night, Amber? What the hell is wrong with him?"

"I think he loves you and hates you in equal measure. I never thought he would pull shit like that when he called you. But I'm guessing he didn't plan on extra company." She nodded her head in the direction of the motel room next to us as her lips began to shiver involuntarily.

"Yeah, about him," I said as I eyed her. "Let's not air our business in front of him. He already knows too much, and he wants Laz dead."

"Who is he?" she asked, pushing her auburn hair away from her forehead.

"Good question. Go shower, clean up. I have to talk to Laz, and we'll get you back to Charleston."

"Charleston?"

"Yeah, I live there. It's...so fucking far from here." At my remark about the distance, Amber began to crumble.

"Joseph," she whispered, closing her eyes as tears streamed down her cheeks. "I can't leave him."

"You aren't. You *are* just getting your shit together." She nodded slowly, got up, and made her way to the bathroom.

"Laz is a good man," she assured me. "He has always been good to me."

"No, he's not. He's a could've been." She pulled the door shut, and I pulled some spare clothes from my bag and stuck them in the bathroom for her. It amazed me she could think of Laz that way when the situation I'd entered last night was anything but wholesome. He was getting his cock sucked by a zombie, and she was being forced to watch.

My sister sure had a contorted image of good. Then again, this was all she knew.

I changed into a T-shirt and jeans and made my way next door, expecting to find Daniello gone. I was surprised when I found him dressed and waiting.

I smiled and he didn't. I wanted to go to him, run my fingers through his hair. My sex pulsed at the thought of us repeating last night. I wanted him every minute I was with him. I wondered if he felt the same. He'd been so open last night. It was obviously a fluke because he was slightly closed off this morning.

"I think—"

"Don't you dare. You cannot change your mind. This is not your decision!"

"Do you know who he is?!"

"Yes! I've known him my whole life. And now, apparently, someone got an update while I was next door. How the hell did you even find me anyway?"

"Why even question how?"

"Because you invade my life! You demand my body and demand answers and give nothing in return!"

He moved to stand in front of me, his eyebrow quirked. "Nothing?"

I blew out all the air in my lungs as he smirked. "You like seeing me this way, agitated and pissed off," I concluded as I put my hands on my hips.

"I like you other ways as well," he murmured as he slid his hands underneath my T-shirt and caressed my skin with his fingertips.

His thick lashes shadowed perfect, golden eyes as he studied me. "Just let me try this my way. If it doesn't work, we can do it yours."

He nodded and took a step back just as Amber knocked on the door. I opened it and noted that Daniello made himself busy loading his bags and bringing them to the trunk. Apparently, he didn't want an introduction. So I didn't give him one.

I handed Amber my phone, asking her to text Laz and have him meet me at our place. She had a question in her eyes but did as she was told. Driving into Dyer, there was an eerie quiet in the car. Daniello didn't miss anything as he surveyed the ghost town and caught my eyes in the rearview. We passed what would have been the town square, which were just a few buildings opposite of the other, all abandoned and crumbling brick. The further we went, the more the dread in my chest built. It was everything I'd remembered it to be: desolate, deserted, and forgotten.

Desperate to escape the town I'd fled, I gripped the wheel tight as Amber stared out the window emotionless. This was all she knew.

Daniello remained quiet as I slowed past our old farmhouse to study its state, curious about my father.

"He died a few years ago, heart attack." I nodded, knowing that it had everything to do with meth and wondering why fate had taken so long to take him. Daniello's stare burned a hole through me in the rearview as he caught my eye, no emotion in my face. I concentrated on Laz as I pulled to a stop on the dirt road that separated our old houses. I looked at Daniello then back at Amber.

"There is forty grand and a cellphone in my bag in the trunk. Use it to start over, Amber, get Joseph back and leave. I have a friend named Cedric programmed in the phone who knows about you. He will get you two set up and back to Charleston."

"I will get her to Charleston," Daniello spoke up. "You do not need to go alone."

"Please, we agreed," I pleaded. Daniello glanced out the window and nodded.

I gave him a long look, memorizing his features, and he refused to look at me. I could see the tenseness in his body. He was fighting with everything in him not to end this on his terms.

I made my way down the dirt road toward our pond, a thousand memories hitting me like painful bricks. I took a deep breath as I saw the truck that Laz had driven last night.

"He with you?" I heard as he rounded the truck bed and looked past me.

"He's in the car," I answered. "So is Amber. I'm taking her home with me, to get clean, for her son."

Laz stood a few feet away, his features showing exhaustion.

"Thank you for taking care of her, for being there. Laz, I'm sorry about what happened. I've—"

"Bullshit," he snapped. "You didn't give a shit about me then and you don't now. You just want a clean getaway."

I took a step toward him. "I want that, yes. That's all I'd ever wanted, Laz. I'm sorry."

He pushed a rock around with his boot then without hesitation met my green eyes with his blue. I couldn't help the familiar pain that spread through me as I remembered better days at this pond. I could see the recollection in his eyes, too.

"Pretty smart asking me here." He grinned menacingly. "Take your sister and leave."

"That's it? No more games?"

"If I decide it that way."

"Laz—"

He reached for my throat with both hands and squeezed hard as he bit out his words. Clawing at his hands, I felt the burn from lack of oxygen as my head pounded and realized what a fool I'd been.

"You fucking owe me, Red, more than you will ever know. And *when* and *if* I feel it's time to collect, I fucking will. You and that man you decided to bring to my fucking house won't be able to do shit about it. Now get the fuck out of here before I change my mind."

I gasped as I fell to the ground, seconds from unconsciousness, tears welling in my eyes. He kicked me solidly in the chest, and I felt a rib crack under the weight of it. I reached for the gun behind me and pulled it around as Laz kicked it from my hand then backhanded me. Blood immediately started pouring from my nose as I stood slowly and glared at him, ready to fight tooth and nail.

"If you think you would've ever won with me, Red, you are sadly mistaken."

"No," I hissed through my pain. "I lost with you a long time ago."

No matter how much time had passed, here at our place, memories of soaking up the sun with the blue eyed boy I loved ran through me like waves, forcing the point of loss home. My Laz was completely and utterly gone and replaced by a monster I didn't recognize, and that I refused to surrender to.

He smirked as he watched me wince in pain and I took a step full of contempt toward him, chin lifted, ready for war. I knew I would lose but not without inflicting lasting pain. I heard Daniello's shout from a distance and saw Laz grip the gun in his pants before leaving it where it sat on his hip and walking toward his truck.

"I'm not doing this for you," he hissed as he ripped his cab door open.

"I know," I said, looking back to see Daniello coming toward us full force, eyes blazing in anger, his gun pointed at Laz.

"Get him the fuck out of here, Red," Laz bit out as Daniello's first bullet ripped through the metal on the side of his truck. I saw their eyes connect and the hate that ran between them and stepped in front of Daniello's next shot. He roared in anger as Laz sprayed gravel with his departure.

"Goddamn you, woman!" Daniello yelled as he caught up with me, fury all over his face. He ran after the truck, cursing in every language he knew while unloading his gun.

"I know, I know, no one can abuse me but you." He moved toward me and gripped my head, his eyes roaming what I was sure was a purpling neck. I pulled my head away as he inspected my nose. "I'll let you strangle me next time, okay? Can we please just leave? It's over."

"He will be dead by morning," he promised, glancing over my shoulder for the long gone truck.

"NO!" I didn't know how to make him understand. "Please, it's over," I lied. "Promise me. Promise me right now you will not hurt him."

"You ask too much of me." He closed his eyes as I wiped the blood away from my nose and onto my T-shirt.

"It's over. Take me home." He nodded.

"This I will do."

"Promise me."

"No."

He gave me a deadly glare as he checked over my appearance and seemed satisfied I was in one piece. We walked silently back to the car, Daniello glanced in my direction every few seconds with what I thought was concern. Amber was waiting next to the car door, fidgeting nervously.

"Let's go," was all I said as I rounded the driver's side. "I drive," Daniello muttered, pointing to the passenger seat. I got in without argument as we made the bone aching drive back through Dyer. Daniello routed us back through without needing any direction and slowly drove through town, taking it in for the second time.

"Can you please stop on Maple Street? I want to see Joseph before I leave."

Daniello looked at me with question. "Take a right up here."

Daniello eased onto the street, my Chevelle sticking out like a sore thumb. But the street, like every other road, look deserted, and I was sure we went unnoticed.

"Stop here, please." Amber quickly exited the car and walked up to what looked like the most well-kept house on the block. I watched her knock before she was greeted by an older woman, who I swore I recognized. She quickly made her way into the house, and I sighed a little in relief.

Daniello got out of the car, taking long strides away from it. Puzzled, I followed him until he was at the end of the street, looking each direction.

"What are you doing?"

He turned to me with more emotion in his face than I ever

thought possible. "This place…Jesus Christ, this is where you come from?"

I felt the lump gather in my throat as he looked around, desperate for some sign of life, some sort of way to believe places like this didn't exist. He got no relief. My lover was full of untold emotion and words as he turned to me.

"Don't pity me, Daniello. I—"

He gripped my arms and looked down at me, completely exasperated. "I do not pity you, Taylor Ellison. I could never pity a woman I admire. You…what you have done, leaving here, the woman you have become." He leaned in, claiming my lips and covering me in warmth as he held me tightly to him, giving me the most passionate kiss I'd ever received in my life. I ignored the pain burning through my side as I let him have his way with me. Just when I thought I couldn't get any closer, he pulled me tighter to him, roaming my mouth with his tongue, his strong arms not giving any leeway. He pulled away after several minutes, my body molded to his and whispered to me, "Phoenix."

As his realization dawned, so did mine. This man understood me.

Amber's shriek interrupted our moment as she begged the woman at the door for her son.

"Please, he belongs with me. Please, just let me have him!"

Daniello and I headed her way as she sat on the steps in front of a closed front door.

"Leave me here. I can't leave him. I can't," she said with a shaky voice.

"If you want him back, come with me. I will help you. We can get you on your feet. It's the only way."

Daniello remained silent. I was sure all of this drama was far from what he was used to dealing with. Then again, he had a sister with nine children. He stared at Amber absently, and I nodded my head toward the car.

"Amber, there is no future here, you know that. It won't be long. I'll hire the best lawyer in the city. You just have to do your part."

She nodded as she looked back at the door.

The ride back to Charleston was odd, to say the least. Maybe it was the reprieve from the severity of the situation that had us all in better spirits. The minute we were miles from Dyer, Amber's eyes lit up as she looked around her wistfully.

"Have you ever been out?" I asked as she shook her head.

"Never, not even to Memphis."

"Get ready for a little culture shock," I said, looking at her in the backseat. "I live near the ocean. That's the first place we will go."

She smiled then, a deep, genuine smile, though I knew her skin was crawling with need. It would take weeks to break her habit, and she was handling it better than I thought possible. I would get my doctor to write her a prescription to help her sleep most of it off. I was curious about Joseph but didn't want to bring up such a painful subject while she smiled. Daniello tapped his fingers to Breaking Benjamin's "Sooner or Later" as I played DJ most of the way. He seemed to like my taste in music as he test drove my Chevelle through Tennessee.

"I think I will get one of these for home," he mused and then added, "Maybe one that smells better."

"Uh, yeah, sorry about that," Amber muttered as she kept her eyes closed, the pain of withdrawal hitting her hard.

I had tried last night to get the smell out as I cleaned up my sister's vomit out of my sixty-thousand dollar classic car, but the scent still lingered.

When we finally arrived in Charleston, I saw Rocco sitting idle, waiting. Daniello parked the car with ease next to my collection in the garage.

Amber wandered into the condo as Daniello turned to me.

"I will return."

I chuckled at his attempt at a more stable relationship. We were so screwed.

"Will you call, too?"

"No," he barked as he took my lips and then walked out the door. I shook my head and raced after him, my rib screaming at me for it.

"Hey, you." I caught up to him and placed a slow kiss on his lips. "I like you now."

His slow smile made my entire body flutter with need. "Ah, Taylor, you have always liked me."

"No, no I haven't," I said, truthfully. He laughed loudly as he took my lips again before whispering in my ear. "Enjoy your family union."

It was on the tip of my tongue to correct him, but he gave me a knowing smirk.

Rocco's stare out of the damaged SUV was deadly. I gave him a wink and a wave as Daniello climbed into the driver's seat.

I wondered if he was going home to Barga. I wondered how our relationship would change with my sister living with me, even if it was temporary. I smiled as I remembered his description of me.

"Phoenix," I whispered as I watched my fire drive away.

CHAPTER 16

Laz

I stared at the box before I barked my order. "You fucking done yet?"

"In a minute!"

"Rub it in good." The itch raced through me as my blood boiled with thoughts of her still running through my head. All of that fucking beauty and I had smashed it with the back of my hand. I'd squeezed the life out of it, almost to the point of no return. I plucked a cigarette from my pack and lit it with a slow inhale.

She fucking broke me.

And after all this time, I'd wanted to return the favor more than I'd ever wanted anything. Killing her with my bare hands would've been the most righteous way. She deserved to die at the hands of the man who had made her. I'd shaped her into the woman she was, and she was fucking some foreigner who had no rights to her.

She was supposed to be mine as she had promised.

"Now, right fucking now," I ordered as I crushed my cigarette into Lucy's expensive carpet and pulled out my cock. I'd been hard all day thinking of crushing the bones in her perfect face and watching her lying lips go blue. I'd sacrificed more for her, done more for her than I'd ever thought I would do for anyone.

She didn't appreciate shit. She'd never loved me. Her eyes lied, her lips did the same.

Lucy came out of the bathroom wearing nothing but the same shade of hair that'd I'd ordered her to keep up. My skin itched, and I needed release as I jerked her by the arm and slammed her head down on her kitchen table.

"Please, don't hurt me."

"Please shut the fuck up and take your medicine." I spat into my hand and rubbed it over my cock before positioning my head. "Fuck you," I hissed, slamming into her and hearing her scream. I gripped the red locks, pulling hard and feeling a few give in my hand. I fucked her hard as I cursed her for every fucking thing she'd ever done.

"Liar, whore, thief." I shook with rage as I pounded into her over and over, hearing her cries. Each prayer from her lips fueled me as I shoved into her, all of my frustration centered on my cock.

It was only when I saw the blood that I slowed and released her. She crumpled to the floor, broken as I unloaded in the hair shielding her face. "FUCK YOU!"

Minutes passed as I sat in my jeans at the table and smoked a foil as she gathered herself from the floor.

"NO MORE!" she screamed. "I can't do this anymore! Laz, please, I'm sorry I didn't mean to—"

"You cost me my son, you fucking cunt!" I stood and slapped her back to the floor where I watched her fall apart. "You and that fucking running mouth of yours. Couldn't leave it alone, could you? Had to spray the habits of everyone in town with that fucking mouth!"

I pulled my cell from my pocket and saw the text.

Amber: Here.

Me: Good girl. I know you can do this. Get our son back.

I would've killed Taylor today for bringing her new boyfriend to meet me, but I figured with the sacrifices I'd made she owed me this before I took her life. I couldn't do sentimental, not anymore. I needed her connections and money to get back the only thing that mattered to me.

Joseph.

And when Taylor served her purpose, I would show her just how much mercy I had displayed today.

She really should have stayed gone.

PART TWO

The Fire

CHAPTER 1

Taylor

SOFT LIPS CARESSED MY SKIN AS I GRIPPED HIS SILKY HAIR IN WELCOME. Ecstasy coursed through my veins as the tip of his hungry cock brushed up and down my body while his mouth covered every inch of my naked flesh. His warm hands covered what his lips left behind.

"Daniello," I moaned, now fully awake as my lover slipped his skilled fingers inside me, stretching me for his ready cock.

"Phoenix," he murmured as his lips drifted over my nipple in a whisper before claiming it hungrily, sucking it stiff before taking a sound bite.

"Ah," I protested at the pain his teeth caused while his fingers twisted inside me, beckoning my orgasm.

He paused when he reached my lips as I leaned in to offer my mouth.

"Did you think of me?"

"No," I lied.

"No?" I could feel the twist of his lips against mine. "You are such a chicken head woman."

I stilled his touch, unable to keep the laughter from bursting out of me.

"I'm sorry, but I believe the expression you are looking for is pig-headed."

"English is my fourth language," he scolded, taking my lobe in his mouth and licking it before sliding up the shell of my ear. "And watch your fucking mouth, or I will have you suck my cock with no reward."

I moaned again, unable to mask my need for him.

"Yes," I whispered as he positioned himself at my entrance and he lifted my leg. "I thought of you."

His intrusive thrust ended our conversation, and I clung to him while he reclaimed my body, fucking me so hard I had to muffle my screams by biting his shoulder. I took his heavy dick, greedy with all the thoughts of him that had consumed me in the week he'd been absent.

"I want to see you," I requested as my hands roamed his chest, locking my legs around his middle. I heard a pained grunt as he continued to fuck me without acknowledging me. I got lost in his unforgiving strokes and whimpered when he pulled out of me as I was just about to break.

Before I had a chance to react, I was being taken to the edge of the bed, my legs spread wide to accommodate his size as he pressed his hand flat against my stomach and pushed down before filling me so full I ripped my sheets in an attempt to grip them.

"Oh . . . God, fuck yes," I begged as he tore into me like a man possessed.

There were no words from him as he pushed me down further so I couldn't move; I could only feel. Opening wider for him, he swiveled his hips as the fire spread throughout my lower half. Pain and pleasure burst through my every pore.

I could only see a small amount of his face through shadows

created by the window and searched desperately for his eyes. I wanted to see the beautiful man taking me in the way I craved. In truth, I had very few days where I hadn't thought of him. He was literally, at that point, the man of my dreams.

His absence had somehow enhanced my ability to work overtime and effectively. It was, in fact, the perfect set up. As soon as my sexual cravings reached their peak, he would appear and sate me, but at the same time leave me hungry for more. I was, for the first time in my life, satisfied, and instead of worrying about how long it would last, I embraced it.

The air between us thick with electricity, I took his punishing cock and moaned in approval when he finished us both together.

Daniello lifted me without a word and took me to the bathroom. When he searched for and found the light switch, and I was finally able to see him fully, I gasped in shock.

"What the hell happened to you?"

"Ah, questions of a concerned girlfriend." He grinned as he started the shower, holding his hand in front of the running water to test the temperature.

"Don't go there," I said in warning, assessing his damage.

He furrowed his brows. "Go where? Where would I go?"

I sighed in an attempt to hide my smile. But one look at his body, and there wasn't another humor-filled tell to give. He had small cuts all over his muscled back and a deep gash just below his Adam's apple. He pulled me into the shower with him and began bathing us. I examined the gash and determined he needed stitches, though it wasn't bleeding.

"I can stitch this," I said carefully as I looked up at him. "What happened?"

"I got into a fight with an alligator," he joked. "Never go to golf at midnight in Charleston."

I was not amused. He poured shampoo into his hands and

began to massage his scalp. I studied his chiseled face as he ran his fingers through his midnight hair. He had the build of a gladiator, the face of a statue, and eyes that could melt metal. He was intimidating even when he was at his most vulnerable.

"Daniello, please," I begged once more.

"Why, Taylor?" he replied with one eye open as soap slid down his cheek. "It will change your opinion of me; everything will change. Are you unhappy with this? With our arrangement?"

"No," I answered quickly. "Not at all. I'm . . . happy with the way things are."

He nodded in my direction as if that was the end of it.

"Are you *that* bad of a man?" I asked, my voice barely audible.

"Is your sister doing well?" he countered. I breathed out heavily in defeat and nodded.

He pulled me to his chest, and I wrapped myself around him, trying to stifle my frustration with his refusal to give me more. Our bodies were so intimately connected, but Daniello was still a stranger to me. I gave in, knowing our time was limited. We had only a few stolen hours left. "She's been asleep for the entire week. I've barely seen her."

"She cannot sleep forever. You will get your reunion." I smiled at his proper use of the word.

Though our relationship was odd and unconventional, we both got something from the other. He gave me every imaginable orgasm, and I schooled him on proper English usage. It was a win-win.

I'd been working late the past week, and I wasn't sure if it was to avoid Amber or the situation altogether. Aside from constantly thinking of Daniello, I had thought of nothing but Laz's reason for letting me go.

"I'm not doing this for you."

I had my suspicions, and I wasn't sure if I wanted Amber

to confirm them. Because if they were true, I would never be free of Laz or Dyer, and I would have one hell of a fight on my hands.

The whole situation was odd, and I cringed at the thought just as Daniello turned the shower off.

"What are you thinking of?"

"It's late. I have a meeting in a few hours," I answered absently as I watched Daniello towel off. I stopped him before he could make his way out of the door.

"Before you disappear, Houdini, let me take care of that alligator bite." Daniello smiled and lifted his hands in surrender. I spent a few minutes on his superficial cuts as he stood before me naked.

Upon closer inspection, I saw the gash was already closing and smeared disinfectant cream on it before covering it with a bandage.

"I see you were prepared for alligator fights as well," Daniello noted of my large first-aid kit.

"Decorator, she staged . . . um, set up this whole place. I don't shop."

"No?" Daniello looked down at me, amused. "A wealthy woman who does not shop?"

"It's totally boring," I said, finishing off his bandage.

"Boring," he mused as he held my hands to his chest. "What amuses you, pig head?"

"Can we just stop that right now, please? Before you start with English expressions, let's start with mastering the basics. *Who* in the *hell* taught you those?"

"A tutor," he said absently as he placed my wrists around his neck and began to move us around my bathroom.

"What are you doing?" I asked when I realized he was swaying . . . dancing . . . with no music.

"You are helping me with my English, and I am sweep you

off your feet."

I put my head to his chest and laughed loudly, knowing my sister was sleeping mere feet away.

"You want to know what amuses me? You, you amuse me," I said with a huge grin, looking up at him. "You." I kept my smile as he danced me awkwardly around the bathroom until I let go and went with it.

The man was insane and beautiful and dancing with me in my bathroom at four o'clock in the morning, oblivious to his nudity and what looked like a painful gash at his throat.

Feeling privileged with that information, a strange new emotion burst through my veins, threatening to spill out of my pores. I was fucking . . . giddy.

"In some moments, you look at me with the wide eyes of a child," Daniello said as he slowly spun us around the space.

"I've never danced before," I said with a nervous glance his way.

"This does not surprise me," he replied with a knowing smirk.

"I'm not *that* bad," I defended as his smirk deepened.

"There is nothing wrong with keeping a part of yourself like a child."

"I have never really *been* a child," I whispered to him. "I don't know how to be one."

He stopped our movement, his eyes serious. "Have you ever been suspended on the surface of water? Your arms behind your head, your feet up, nothing to hold you but the water?"

"Yes," I said, thinking of my days in the pond.

"How did it make you feel?"

"I don't know," I said thoughtfully. "Light?"

"Free to fall, free to fail . . . simply free. You did not worry about who would catch you or what you had to do to stay on the surface. That is what being a child is like."

I'd never had that confidence with my parents. I was always worried about the state of chaos in my house, when we would get our next meal. There was nothing about those days in Dyer when I could remember being cradled so safely. I nodded in understanding as he took my hand and led me back to the bedroom. When the door closed and we resumed relaxing in the bed, I braved one more question.

"Did the alligator get away?"

Daniello hesitated only briefly before answering. "They never get away."

CHAPTER 2

Taylor

LATER THAT MORNING, I STOOD AT MY SISTER'S BEDROOM DOOR. Daniello was long gone, and I was sure he'd meant me to hear his parting words as he stood at the door while I lingered between sated and sleep.

"I will return."

It was a new addition to our arrangement. He'd made a sort of promise to me that he would let me know when he wouldn't be returning. I dreaded that day but pushed it to the back of my mind. As I watched my sister sleep, a bottle of prescription pills next to her from a doctor I insisted she see, I wondered if I hadn't aided in her detachment from the new world she was in.

I gave her door a sharp knock. "Amber?"

She stirred slightly and then slowly opened her eyes to catch me fully dressed at her door.

"Shower and dress. We meet with a lawyer today." I searched for the appropriate words to try to make my statement more casual and couldn't come up with anything. I didn't know how to handle the niceties of normal. I knew how to suck a cock and conduct a business meeting that could earn me millions. I didn't know how to be personable, my forte being more . . . formidable.

"Half an hour?" I asked as she sat up in bed in a daze.

Still in her pill-induced haze, she nodded before I closed her door.

Amber came into the kitchen half an hour later, freshly showered and in one of the several outfits I'd given her. Though she was still ghastly thin from her addiction, she wore a simple black dress well. I offered her coffee, and she accepted as she sat on a stool on the opposite side of the counter. Our resemblance, despite her weight, was remarkable. I briefly wondered if she thought the same.

"I'm sorry I haven't been around much," I offered, making myself busy by cleaning my cup.

"I've been tired," she murmured.

"I've been busy," I spouted at the same time. I gave her a small smile.

"Let's go," I said, ushering her into the garage. Amber rounded my Mercedes and got in without a word.

"Starting tomorrow, you will work at Scott Solutions. I'm sending you to Human Resources, so they can assess your skills. Your best bet at getting Joseph back is having a job and a stable place to live, right?"

"Right," she agreed absently as she looked around the cabin.

"I can give you enough money to get you started in a place of your own. Depending on your salary, we will find something," I rambled on nervously.

"How much is this lawyer going to cost?"

"Do you really care, Amber?" I said, rolling my eyes as I took the downtown streets toward Scott Solutions.

"What's that supposed to mean?"

"It means you know I have enough money to pay for your lawyer, and I'm not expecting to be paid back."

"Well, that's up to me, now, isn't it?" she snapped.

Taking a deep breath, I looked over at her as I slowed at a light. "Do you really intend to stay here when you get your son back?"

"Yes," she replied tightly as she looked out the window.

"Look, I just wanted to know you again, to make sure you were okay. You don't have to do things my way. I just—"

"Things are fucking fantastic, sis, thanks for asking." I took a long look at the thin ghost of my past in the passenger seat. She winced under my scrutiny. "Shit, Taylor. I'm sorry."

"No, Amber, I'm sorry. I should have come sooner . . . but why didn't you show up when I came for you?"

She let her eyes drift down my tailored suit. "I was still angry with you for leaving. I was scared Momma would catch me. I was just . . . scared, period."

I nodded, knowing she was telling the truth. The state I had seen our mother in when I had attempted to come back for Amber was downright terrifying. Still, I pressed on.

"And you didn't think to leave? Ever?"

"I'm not like you, Taylor. I just can't leave everyone I care about." I gestured to the parking attendant as we exited the Mercedes, our conversation paused as we entered the elevator.

We rode up in silence, an uncomfortable and expectant air between us until I spoke up. "I did come back . . . for you."

She bit her lip around her words. "I know."

When the elevator opened, we were met by Nina and her brother, Aaron, who took one look at us both and smiled deeply. "Hello," he said directly to Amber.

"Hello," Nina repeated, her smile just as welcoming.

"Nina, Aaron," I introduced, "this is my sister, Amber. Nina is my partner, and Aaron is her brother. He's visiting from Florida."

"Just moved here, actually. Nice to meet you," Aaron said,

sticking out his hand to take Amber's. She hesitated briefly and took his with a small smile.

"Sister," Nina said, widening her eyes at me. I flicked my hand at her as if to say I would explain later while Aaron made small talk and Amber gave polite replies.

"Well," I interrupted, "we have a meeting in five."

"Nice to meet you. I'll be around if you need a tour guide. Taylor knows how to reach me," Aaron offered, giving Amber a lingering glance.

"Would you stop drooling, you moron? She's obviously shy," Nina scorned him in a whisper as they entered the elevator.

"That woman will have my babies, sister," Aaron said smugly.

I saw Amber's eyes light as she caught his comment and turned to look back at him. He winked at her, unashamed, just as the doors closed.

I pressed my lips together to keep my laughter in from his cocky comment and felt a tug of recognition for Daniello as I made my way to my office. Amber took in her surroundings, her steps faltering slightly as we entered my expansive corner of the top floor. As soon as my door was closed, I briefed Amber.

"Your attorney's name is Janet Adler. She specializes in family law and is the best in Charleston. I'm assuming the grandmother isn't well off and can't afford much in the way of representation."

"She's broke," Amber agreed, taking a seat behind my desk.

"And the father?" I stared her down as she twisted in her seat and darted her eyes to me. "Tell me, Amber, what is Joseph's last name?"

I could feel it. The name pained her. "Walker."

"Jesus Christ, Amber!" Despite my suspicion, instantaneous anger boiled through me.

I knew it.

Laz was the father.

"That's the only reason he didn't kill me last week."

"Yes and no. I never thought he wanted to *kill* you," she defended weakly.

I crossed my arms and sat back in my chair. "And you two thought, what? That I wouldn't put this together until after you got your son back? Did you think I would just throw some money at you and not be involved? Are you both that ignorant?"

Her posture stiffened in ready defense. "I planned on telling you. I just didn't know how. I thought Laz might've told you when you spoke to him, and that was maybe why you had avoided me all week."

"We had no chance to discuss paternity, Amber, considering he was kicking the shit out of me!"

How the fuck did this happen?

The intercom interrupted my next question.

"Taylor, your nine o'clock is here."

"I'll be there in a minute, Ross," I snapped and looked back at my sister, who was watching me with guilt-ridden eyes.

"So, what's the plan, Amber?" I crossed my arms. "If you think I'm going to help you regain custody of your child so you can go back to that *monster* and to meth, you can forget it." I paced my office, furious I hadn't seen it more clearly. I looked out my window and down at a few bustling tourists and shook my head, trying to take calming breaths.

"Listen, Taylor—"

"I'm listening," I said, keeping my back to her.

"Laz and I aren't together," she assured carefully. "It was only one night, and it was a mistake. I love him, but not in that way."

"Uh huh, and now this is where you tell me that he's a good father." I turned to her, noting the color coating her cheeks. She didn't like defending herself. It ran in the family.

"No, this is where I tell you that I will do whatever I have to do to get Joseph back. That I will never set foot in Dyer again, and that for the first time since he was born, I feel like I may be able to be a decent mother."

"And you think Laz will just let you have his son?"

She blew out a breath and slunk back in her chair. "No."

Hands on my desk, I leaned forward. "And what do you propose we do when he comes for him?"

"I hadn't thought that far ahead," she said exasperatedly.

"But *he* has. What's the plan, Amber?" I gritted out, knowing this whole setup stunk of preparation. Probably the weeks that led up to her phone call.

The intercom interrupted us again. "Ms. Adler insists she only has twenty minutes."

I reached over and picked up the phone. "Then make her wait another minute and send her in."

I slammed the phone down, trying to get a grip on every emotion I had. I was boiling.

"If money is what you want, Amber, I will give it to you. I was hoping to—" I dug my nails into my palms as I tried to find the right words "—to know you again."

"I want that too," she said softly. "This is my mess. I can clean it up."

"No, you can't, not alone in a city where you know no one and still have addiction running through you. I just want to know right now—"

"Ms. Adler," my receptionist, Ross, interrupted.

For eighteen minutes, I listened to Amber recall the events that led up to her losing her two-year-old son. Apparently, Lucy Hardin had run her mouth to a grocery store clerk about what a shame it was that "Amber Ellison had the most beautiful baby boy. Too bad his mother was a druggie" while Laz's mother stood in the checkout line behind her. Child Protective Services was called, and they located Amber smoking a meth foil in her car with Joseph in the back seat. I sat back and watched the remorse intensify on my sister's face and knew she was telling the truth. Still, a part of me condemned and convicted her for falling victim to meth after all we'd been through at the hands of our addicted parents.

The lawyer instructed her to do exactly as we'd planned: obtain a job and residence. Apparently, there would be several months of counseling, along with random drug tests. And then there was the issue of bringing him out of state. It was a process, but one the lawyer was confident about as long as the rules were followed.

When the door was shut after the lawyer's farewell, Amber turned to me with a heartfelt smile and a thank you.

Unable to hear anything more about Laz with my mind still reeling, I sent Amber down to HR for job placement, unsure if she would qualify for anything. I was already exhausted, and it was only ten thirty. I would get everything from her later. At that moment, I couldn't look at her without feeling resentment, and I didn't want that for our newly kindled relationship.

Laz was a father.

What. The. Fuck.

Sitting at my desk, furiously rushing through my workload, I remembered Ray's words to me the first time he saw my temper.

"Presentation is everything, kitten. You can make your point without having to act out like an animal. If you lash out that way, the reaction will more than likely mirror yours. Nothing gets resolved, and you are left having to explain yourself, and we both know you hate that."

I sat back in my chair, thinking of Ray and the proposition he'd made me exactly one year after I met him.

CHAPTER 3

Taylor

"You are a lot thinner than I remember," Ray remarked, circling me.

"I don't eat much," I offered as I stood in the foyer of his expansive house, as if my eating habits would be reason enough to keep me there. I felt filthy even though I had washed off the bus ride before taking the cab to his address. I spent a few minutes just standing at the entrance to his massive mansion before finally coming up with the courage to knock. I had no idea what was about to happen. I felt like there were eyes on me as I stared at the lion's head doorknocker that seemed to smile as it held the metal ring in its mouth.

"You will eat here," Ray declared with confidence. "And you will eat well. The body is a temple. Did you know that, Taylor?"

"Yes."

"Yes, sir," he scorned as he stopped in front of me. "And you will treat it as such. What makes you think your parents won't come for you?"

"They won't. They will never come looking," I assured him then added, "meth."

Realization dawned on him as he scrutinized me. "And do I need to *worry about your drug use?"*

"Never," I assured adamantly.

"Never, sir," he corrected again with slight agitation. His eyes lasered their way down my body. "You're too young."

I winced. The night we met, Lucy Hardin had painted me up to look a little older. I took in his sharp black suit and perfectly cropped hair while he circled me. His steps were precise, purposeful. I could feel his hesitation.

"I'm an adult."

"You're a baby," he concluded. "Have you ever been fucked, Taylor?" My eyes widened at his sudden change in conversation.

"No . . . no, sir," I answered back, suddenly on the defensive. I crossed my arms over my chest, and he quickly pulled them back down to my sides before resuming his intimidating dance around me.

I saw his eyes light and a small smile grace his full lips before it fell away. He looked entirely comfortable in his skin. It was the first time in my life I had ever envied a man. I assumed he was just home from work considering the hour. He was far better looking than I remembered with deep blue eyes and sharp features. His light brown hair was tamed and perfectly shaped to suit him. He was half a foot taller than me with a strong build, but it was the air about him that was intimidating. I wanted to have that air.

He commanded respect at all times and would not settle for anything less. This I knew from our brief meeting a year ago and even more so as I stood under his scrutiny.

"So, you want to attend Harvard? By my calculations, that's four years at around sixty-five thousand dollars, an apartment around another hundred and twenty. Prep school is going to cost me around another fifty thousand. Then there are your tutors, which will be another thirty or forty grand."

I stood as he listed just how expensive Harvard would be and felt the large lump of defeat fill my throat. I knew it would be impossible. I mentally kicked the imbecile in me that wanted to believe that I had a chance. The endless hours of studying I did in Dyer. All the extra attention and effort I put into my education would be fruitless.

"I understand, sir."

"You understand what?" he asked, discarding his jacket. He rolled his sleeves up while he tilted his head at me in question.

"Harvard, the cost, it's too much."

"So, you are saying you aren't worth half a million dollars, Taylor?"

I was finally free from the hell I'd endured for eighteen years. I was free from Dyer, from my mother, from Laz. I had nothing to fear except where to find my next meal, and I had absolutely nothing to lose either. Digging in, I suddenly had the courage to answer him.

"I guess that's a question you should be answering . . . sir."

"You do understand what I am proposing here?" he asked as he stood in front of me.

"Yes, sir."

With a snide smirk, he looked me dead in the eye. "Well, if I do decide you are worth it, I think that may just make you the highest paid whore in Tennessee."

With confidence I didn't know I had, I gave as good as I got. "A whore that is going to attend Harvard, sir."

CHAPTER 4

Taylor

NINA WALKED IN JUST AFTER MY LUNCH HOUR AND SAT ACROSS FROM me without a word, but expectant just the same.

"I have a sister," I said absently, clicking my emails to avoid her confrontation.

"I saw that one that looks very much like you," she said in a way I knew she was chewing her cheeks off to keep from prying.

"She's staying with me now," I added, giving her more.

"Taylor," she warned.

"When I took time off, I went to get her. She lost her son in a custody battle, and she's here to get him back. She needs my help, and I want to help her."

"Wow, a full confession in less than a minute. I'm impressed," Nina said, standing. "Whatever you need, whatever resources we have."

"I am giving her a temporary to permanent position with us. I cannot vouch for her character."

"And I don't need you to," she said confidently.

"Why thank you, Mrs. McIntyre," I said, getting a playful

dig in.

"Bitch . . . I'm leaving," she huffed and shut the door behind her. I laughed softly as I thought of the hundred and one ways things could go wrong having Amber in Charleston.

I texted Cedric, who was probably ready to strangle me for lack of communication. And the irony was he was my protector and the person I trusted most in the world.

Me: Amber is here.

Cedric: That is good news.

Me: Laz may not be far behind.

Cedric: I'll see you tonight.

Me: Wait. I'll call you.

Cedric: No.

Me: I'll call you.

I wanted to give Amber a chance to explain without assuming the worst, which was hard for me because, as far as I was concerned, everyone had an agenda. The broken little girl I left had turned into a broken woman; a woman whose past had yet to be buried and future lay in limbo.

Why had I expected any differently? There was so much to be said for the hell she'd endured. I could only imagine the thoughts that raced through her head daily. And coming off an addiction, in a new city, living with me—practically a stranger—I was sure she was shell-shocked. I just needed a little time to assess the situation. To see if her loyalty truly resided with Laz or if she genuinely wanted a new life.

I owed it to her. And I would give it to her.

"Taylor, line one," Ross chimed into my silent office.

I picked up the phone to lay into her. "Ross, I'm out of patience. I am not to take another phone call without an announcement of who is calling and what it's regarding. Am I crystal clear?"

"Yes, ma'am."

I waited impatiently, and soon after, she buzzed back in. "He said he's your dance instructor and would like to schedule a lesson." I scrambled to pick up my phone quickly with an embarrassed and curt, "Thank You."

"Taylor Ellison," I announced through gritted teeth.

"I take it you are having a rough day, Taylor Ellison." I cursed the instant smile on my face and the fact he was the one capable of putting it there. Still, I kept my tone impatient.

"Daniello, I have a cell phone."

"And I have that number," he mused. "I think we should discuss last night."

Interest piqued, I took the bait. "Which part?"

"The part where you asked me not to stop."

"Okay."

"Meet me downstairs."

"Daniello, I'm at work."

"I know. And I am becoming impatient outside of your door." He hung up without my reply, and I cursed as I looked at my schedule and saw I didn't have another meeting until later that day. I briefly entertained the consequences of ignoring him altogether and dismissed it. If he wanted a quick, satisfying, afternoon fuck, I would happily rid myself of the tension building in my shoulders.

I made my way toward a different SUV than the one I had become accustomed to and ignored Rocco as I climbed in.

I narrowed my eyes as I saw the small victory in Daniello's. He was gloating at my appearance.

"You are the most arrogant ass I have ever met." Dark locks of hair rested neatly on the top of his head. His suit was an immaculate black. He looked every bit business as I did sitting opposite of him.

"I need an opinion," he replied, ignoring my statement.

"Yes, you could use a new driver," I said loudly, knowing full well Rocco had heard my comment due to the open partition.

"That is one mutt you should not tempt to bite," Daniello reminded as his eyes darted over my dress. It was if he was visually deciding how he would remove it. Heated by his attire, his smell, his demeanor, I did my best to try to hide it.

"How can I be of service, Mr. Di Giovanni? As you know, I have a corporation to run." Our eyes remained locked, both of us filled with renewed desire yet neither of us acting on it.

"Just a few minutes of your time." He winked as we entered a private parking lot. When we exited, I looked around the empty garage at the construction going on then back to Daniello, puzzled.

"It is almost finished," he remarked as Rocco eyed us with distaste from the front seat and we made our way to an elevator. Once inside, I couldn't help but note Daniello's size in the small space. We stood opposite each other in the elevator until I took a step forward and unbuttoned the top of his collar.

"You have no patience today, Taylor?"

Rolling my eyes so he could clearly see it, I examined the cut underneath his bandage.

"It is fine," he protested, grabbing my hands and holding them in his. "Your concern is not necessary."

"Fine . . . What am I doing here?" I asked defensively, taking my hands from his.

"This," Daniello answered as the elevator door opened, "is where we will meet."

"I'm confused," I said as he entered a code on a pad next to a sleek metal door and opened it, ushering me in.

"Your circumstances for entertaining have changed," he whispered into my ear, "and I am very fond of hearing your screams."

My eyes closed at his confession, heat building throughout my abdomen. I noted the place wasn't finished. The cabinets weren't installed, and I doubted the plumbing was either. The space took up the entirety of the top floor of the building. A small spark of hope ran through me.

"Are you buying this place?"

"No," he dismissed, his hands in his pockets.

"Daniello," I blew out as I walked past him to explore the penthouse. It was expansive and modern chic with corner-to-corner views, an exposed open ceiling, and dark hardwood floors.

"It is a loan from a business partner. I helped with the design."

There was no way to conceal my shock. "You design high rises?"

Daniello shrugged. "It is a—" his lips twitched as he searched for the word "—*passion*. In a different life, I would have trained for it."

"It's beautiful." Fully impressed, I walked over to the floor to ceiling wall of windows and took in the bird's eye view of the harbor that led out to open ocean. The sea was turbulent due to a coming storm that was evident by the massive wall of clouds that gathered in the distance. "This seems like a lot of trouble for such a short time. I mean, we could've gotten a hotel." There was little to no activity on the water, and I found it fascinating. I could feel Daniello's proximity by the energy wafting through the air, or maybe it was just wishful thinking that he would close the space between us. Lightning struck in the distance, and I saw the bolt so clearly. I jumped as another struck and then another. Afternoon lightning storms were common in Charleston, and though I had witnessed a few, I had never been so front row.

"Definitely a million-dollar view, there is no denying that."

Another comment without a response had me turning to look back at Daniello, who stood watching me, his posture the same, his hands in his pockets. He was the epitome of tall, dark, and dangerous.

"What?"

"Would you say this view is suited for a king?" he asked, taking slow steps toward me. The room was quickly darkening with the cloud cover, and another series of lightning strikes had me on edge as I saw his face light with each of them.

"I would say that, yes." I gave a nervous laugh. "Is that your big secret? Am I fucking the king of Egypt?"

"No." He grinned wickedly as he reached me and shifted me, so I was again facing the window. "But what is fit for a king is also fit for a phoenix." It took me only a moment to realize his logic and fight his grasp. He stopped my protest. "You may rule the world now, Taylor, but you limit yourself to live in a box fit for a shoe."

"And that is *my* decision," I hissed as he pulled off my suit jacket. Lightning struck close but the thunder never came, or at least I couldn't hear it.

"And that is why you are here," he insisted as he squeezed my ass painfully through my skirt. "You have come so far from your home, Taylor."

"I am aware," I whispered as he placed my hands on the glass above me then unzipped my skirt, letting it fall to the floor. I stepped out, keeping my hands where he put them as he reached around and stroked my neck with one hand while the other unbuttoned my blouse agonizingly slow. Lightning struck again, but I gave it little attention as I leaned back as much as possible against him. My blouse was moved to reveal my peaked chest, cupped by lace. I felt my wet heat coat my panties as Daniello whispered to me while he pulled the lace down just below my needy chest, so it held each breast up for his inspection.

"The next time I fuck you," he lifted my hair and trailed his tongue across my neck to the opposite ear before finishing, "I will think of you like this." He raised his thumb to my mouth, and I sucked it before he brought it to a straining nipple. He stroked across it slowly as I started to pant. Pulse kicking, breathing erratic, he took his time with his seduction. I obeyed without command, my hands still planted against the glass. The storm arrived along with a downpour of rain. Ribbons of water slid past my firmly planted hands as Daniello moved underneath the tails of my blouse, around the edge of my panties, playing with the lacy elastic.

"Please," I begged on edge.

His tongue continued to trace the back of my neck. I remained at his mercy with another plea on my tongue when his hand finally slid down the front of my panties. He sank his teeth into the sweet spot between my neck and shoulder. I moaned out my relief as his thick finger stroked my clit.

"Ah, that is what I needed to hear before I make my way home." He quickened his strokes stifling the throb of my needy clit but leaving the ache inside of me. I moved to touch his rock-hard cock poking me in the back and was rewarded with a harsh, "No."

"I want you," I said breathlessly as he moved his digits faster over my clit, his free hand molding my breast.

"I know you do, and you will have me when I want you to." I braced myself as my orgasm built but not before I asked him again.

"Not this way, please. I want your cock, Daniello. I want all of you."

"And I *will have* all of you," he declared, running his thick bulge over the top of my ass. I split apart at his coaxing, and he turned my head and kissed me deeply while I shuddered. No longer able to hold myself up, I cradled his neck, keeping him there. He continued his tongue exploration for several minutes, even after my body stopped convulsing.

He was so thorough in his quest to sate me, and yet he hadn't given me what I truly wanted. I moaned as I reached a second peak and had to mentally bite my tongue to keep from begging again. This was another game, a way to conquer me, keep me hungry. Fuck if he hadn't won, but I did little to let him know. Yet, he knew. He was strangely intuitive when it came to me, like we'd been lovers for years and he could anticipate my every need without words.

He kept his fingers running over my sex as a fresh orgasm leaked from me. The act alone seemed to please him as his cock pulsed against my back.

"Let me taste you," I requested as he pulled away from our kiss.

"No," he barked before he lifted my bra into place and began buttoning my blouse at the same slow pace. When he'd dressed me in the exact same way he'd disrobed me, he stood behind me for a moment longer, staring into the cloud we were surrounded by, watching the water drip down the large windows.

"It is a pity that you do not feel yourself worthy of a view like this Taylor Ellison."

"I never said I wasn't worthy," I corrected with absolutely no fight in me. "This is too much for just me."

"Ah, but you are so much woman," he teased as he gripped my hair roughly and brought his mouth to mine one last time. "Come, let us go. I have a plane."

"Going home? Italy home?" I asked gathering my wits and taking one last look around. I could see the potential and for a moment entertained the idea of what it would be like to live there. I had grown accustomed to working in a high rise, but living in one had never crossed my mind. I studied Daniello's profile as he closed the door and handed me the key card for the elevator with the house code written in bold on the back.

I studied Daniello as we took the short walk back to the elevator. "Why would you look for a place for me to live?"

"Why do you question everything?"

"Why do you not answer any of them?"

"You know why," he said sternly as the doors closed.

I hid my smile, knowing I was getting under his skin. "We may not have anything in common, Daniello, but our path is the same. We will both be eighty and will have only lived to work."

"I had a wife once," Daniello admitted, surprising me. "I was young. She was beautiful." I stood, waiting for more, and when he remained silent, I pressed on.

"What happened?"

"She belongs to another now."

"Why?"

Daniello stared at the floor between us while he spoke.

"I wanted to make a fortune, and she wanted to make a family. I left her. She found a man to give her a family. She is very happy." Something about his tone and the distance in his stare told me there was more to that story.

"And are you happy with your fortune?" I asked as the elevator stopped. Daniello took a step forward, blocking the door, and they closed again, leaving us face to face.

"I got exactly what I asked for."

"That's not an answer," I said, growing weary of the circles he had me spinning in.

"I am a rich man with no family. I got what I asked for."

"Good for you," I said, motioning with my hand for him to let us exit. He ignored me, his eyes penetrating and inquisitive.

"You do not think I made the right choice?"

"It's not my concern." He smirked and pushed the button, so the doors once again opened.

Rocco was leaning against the SUV, speaking his usual, angry Arabic into his cell phone. I took in his appearance. Rocco was an attractive man, but his demeanor made me incapable of nothing but distaste for him. His dark hair was cropped short, and his build was much smaller than Daniello's, though he was just as sharply dressed. He eyed us both, finished his call, and climbed into the driver's side as Daniello opened the door for us.

"You fault me for not being open to you, but you have not once revealed anything to me."

I shrugged. "You know enough about me."

"I know what I have observed."

"I have never been married." I crossed my arms defensively, and he reached for me across from him and pulled me to sit beside him. I let out a harsh breath I hadn't realized I was holding.

"You do not like to answer questions as I do not."

"Agreed." I didn't know where the sudden contempt for him came from. I had agreed to keep our relationship sexual. Suddenly, the need to know every detail of who he was ate at me, but I couldn't deny, as intrigued as I was, he was right. I didn't want to reveal more details of my life to him or anyone else, for that matter—something else we had in common. I wanted to know if he felt guilty for leaving his young and beautiful wife. If it ate at him the way I had abandoned Amber ate at me. I wanted to know so much, and as the SUV pulled to a stop, I was frustrated that, once again, our time was up, and I had no more room to maneuver any information from him.

Daniello looked down at me as I hesitated briefly before positioning myself for the open door. He stilled my movement, pressed his lips to mine, and opened my mouth with the slow taste of his tongue. I clung to him as his kiss ignited me, his movements slow, deliberate. Daniello brushed my hair away from my cheek with his thumb as he pulled me closer, his hands circling my neck, his gentle fingers caressing me. Dazed and ready to bend to his will, he pulled away and took his hands with him. "That is how you tell a lover goodbye. I will return."

Instead of giving him my usual sarcastic bite, I simply nodded and exited the SUV without looking back. Because if I did, I was afraid he would see what I was terrified to show him. Biting the inside of my cheek, I forced one foot in front of the other, passing reception without a word. I was still holding my breath when I held a hand up to Ross to keep her from interrupting my retreat. Alone inside my office, I stood with my back to the door and buried my head in my hands. I was bred by my mentor to be 'in the know' of *all* situations I walked into, without a chance to be blindsided. With Daniello, I was at risk.

Silver-blue eyes I could never erase from my memory trickled into the forefront of my thoughts. "Ray," I said his name aloud for the first time in years in silent prayer and remembered the night everything between us changed.

CHAPTER 5

Taylor

"Fork etiquette, attire, and you have even sharpened your verbiage. Not bad, Taylor."

"I don't want to look like a foo—I have no intention of looking foolish."

Ray grinned at me as if I was his favorite new toy. I'd been at his house three weeks, and though he'd held up his end of the bargain, enrolling me in prep school the following day, he hadn't laid a hand on me. I was beginning to wonder if I'd imagined his proposition. I rarely saw him aside from dinner; even then, he was quick to dismiss my company for a phone call.

In a way, I felt like a stray dog he had picked up from a pound and was now being taught to adhere to my new master. Oddly, I did not feel free. I felt more captive than ever. My life had changed so dramatically, and I had no time to process. I was up at 5:00 a.m. and given an hour to exercise. Ray, of course, conveniently had a gym room, so the new routine was easy. I'd spent years walking long miles on dirt roads, so I had no issue working up a healthy sweat on the treadmill before conquering the rest of the room's equipment and its benefits. I was fed breakfast by a quiet wait staff at 6:30 a.m. and at 7:00 a.m. I met my first tutor. Because Ray insisted linguistics *was my biggest issue to tackle, he had the tutor work with me for three days before unleashing me on the population of Mason Prep. Dropped at school no less than half an hour early, I was expected to be outside immediately after and transported home for my four o'clock tutor. Grasping the work-load had turned out to be far less challenging than I'd expected. My tutors had repeatedly commented that I was a sponge and would require very little remedial help. I was, of course, far less advanced than my peers due to the Dyer curriculum, but with each day that passed, my confidence began to soar. I didn't need another to conclude I would be able to handle Mason, and I would graduate with honors as part of their elitist group.*

And even if it were the false confidence of an eighteen-year-old girl, I would make it a reality.

"You look tired," Ray quipped, jolting me out of my stupor. He took a long drink of his bourbon.

I had been toying with the same forkful of food for several minutes, and it hadn't gone unnoticed.

"I'm fine," I answered, setting it down with defeat.

"You're tired," he assured me. He sat to my right at the head of the table in his formal dining room. Though I had taken the seat on the far side the first night, assuming he'd preferred it, he kept us at the same end of the ridiculously long table. It was strangely intimate for the curt conversations we'd had, and I couldn't help but squirm under his scrutiny. The air of intimidation choked me with each of our dinners. He asked questions, and I gave him polite answers, but we were nothing short of formal.

"May I be excused?"

"No." Typically, he granted my request, so when I moved to get up, I stopped myself. "How far have you gone?"

"Sorr—pardon?"

"How far have you gone with a man?" he asked again, no shame in his voice, his posture candid.

I felt a small amount of heat grace my cheeks but pushed my shoulders back and replied, "Close."

"Close?" He smirked. "Close to what?"

Searching for an answer to appease him, I used his words. "Close to being fucked."

He sat back in his seat and motioned for me by holding out his hand. Tentatively, I took it, having talked myself into giving him whatever it took to finally be free, and not only that, successful. I knew that no one in Dyer would ever know that I'd made it that far, so I was sure then I was doing it for me.

When I was standing in front of him, he inspected me closely.

"Pull down your panties."

I did as he asked, my skirt covering everything but a small amount of thigh. I wondered if my uniform turned him on. I wondered how bad it was going to hurt. Ray leaned in and pushed my pleated skirt up slowly as his eyes took me in. I stopped wondering altogether when he reached out with gentle hands and began to stroke my thighs.

"Look at me," he ordered. I did as I was told, my nipples beading under my starched white shirt as I saw the desire in his eyes. He softly and slowly ran his fingers through the soft red curls covering my sex.

"You know this is wrong, Taylor," he said in a whisper as he slid the pad of his finger through my slit. Tumultuous dark blue eyes beckoned me to agree, but budding desire told me otherwise. My lips parted at the feel of him, and my body made the decision. And for the first time in my life, I felt empowered by something I held. Something I knew that he wanted. Something I wanted to give him.

I'd been watching him for weeks, studying his face, his eyes, and his lips, curious how they would affect me. I felt nothing for him on a personal side but was just realizing my attraction toward him. As I stood before him, closer to those lips, completely captivated by his eyes, I knew for certain what I felt for him was desire. Something I'd never had the mind to delve into, until recently. I was too preoccupied with survival. Even with Laz, our intimacy had been short lived due to his drug habit. Being high or cooking meth had always mattered more to him.

Ray looked at me as if I was perfect.

"What if I want it to?" The words fell from my lips so easily I had

to wonder where they came from. They were the words of a ready whore, a willing whore.

No longer afraid, I spread my legs a little wider, letting the warm sensation wash over me. His lips quirked up on one side as he watched my reaction to him.

"Put your foot here," he said, palming his seat, spreading his legs on his chair. I inhaled a stifled breath as I saw the outline in his pants. I put my foot between his thighs, and his hands caressed my bare leg. I closed my eyes, loving the feel of his touch. Once his fingers drifted further inside of me, I let out a low moan, my legs trembling.

"It was your desperation on the phone," he murmured as if he was answering his own questions, while his fingers slipped in and out, stretching me. "I felt it. I can still feel it. We have this in common, Taylor." He quickened his fingers as he unzipped his pants, released his cock, and began to stroke himself. Our connected eyes began to convey just how much we both wanted it to happen until Ray shook his head, breaking our heated stare. "I can't take your innocence, Taylor."

I felt the ache, the need to let go as I studied the long, vein-filled muscle in his hands. I pulled away from his fingers and straddled him, hovering above his ready dick. My hands on his shoulders, I looked him right in the eye. "Then I'll do it for you." I pushed his hand away from his hard length and put him at my entrance. His eyes lit fire as he cursed under his breath. I gasped in surprise as I let my hips sink slightly on the width of him. Mouths parted, my pussy gripped him further as I let more of him inside me and welcomed the sting.

Ray froze, biting his bottom lip so hard I thought he would draw blood, his fingers dug into my hips painfully. "If I'm going to hell, then this is worth it." He began to slowly move under me, coating his cock with my wetness as I sank down the rest of the way, feeling the burn and discomfort. Once seated, I wrapped my arms around his neck and leaned in to take his lips. He moved his face away and took a nip at my neck and lips before whispering in my ear, "Kissing is for lovesick fools. You get my fortune and my cock. That has to be enough. My heart is no good."

I nodded as I pushed through the pain and began to move on top of him. Maybe it was his hesitance to uphold this part of our deal. Either way, I knew this move had sealed my fate and made our contract iron-clad. He was risking everything to keep me with him. His reputation was at stake. I knew that.

I winced as he picked up his pace underneath me, feeling all of him. It was uncomfortable and not at all what I thought it would feel like. But as soon as he spread me across the table, driving into me, still in his suit and jacket, his eyes covering me with their lust, it began to feel better, much, much better. He didn't take it slow; his strokes were deep and painful. My virginity was no longer a question as he dug in deep, his frustration rolling off him and into his fucking.

"Jesus," he grunted as I writhed beneath him, taking his thrusts and choking on the full feeling. He circled his hips, and my eyes widened when I felt pleasure began to swell inside my abdomen. Ray grunted and pulled his cock out, coating my thighs with his cum. He looked right at me as he finished himself with his hand. Once he recovered and caught his breath, he pulled a linen napkin off the table and wiped me down before running it through my sex. Shortly after, he hit his knees then placed my legs over his shoulders. His tongue flicked over my middle, and I gasped at the feeling. Before I had a chance to process, he dug in deeper, his fingers inside me while his tongue lit my whole body on fire. The feeling of falling came over me as I gasped out his name and my body shook with my release. Warmth leaked out of me as Ray slowed to a stop and lifted from his knees, his fresh erection bobbing proudly. He took off his jacket and tie then held me still with his hand on my thigh. I looked up at him, eager and willing to do whatever he had in mind. When he was fully naked, I studied his toned body and thick arms, and my desire grew more intense. I noted a huge scar in the middle of his chest, and before I had a chance to ask, I was turned on my stomach, my hands bound behind my back with the tie. Ray gripped my fastened hands, spread my legs and entered me again slowly. As uncomfortable as it was on the table, the rush of him inside me for a second time had me pushing through the pain.

"This will be quick," he assured me as he began to pound away. My heart hammered as I pushed through with gritted teeth, loving the foreign feeling, the distraction. My body was coated with a thin layer of sweat as I began to twist my lower half to move with him, feeling him even deeper. I reveled in the fullness, the heavy bite of each stroke. He pulled out of me with a grunt, and I felt the spray of his release all over my exposed ass. Exhausted and sore, I lay panting on the table as he freed my wrists and collapsed in the chair behind me. I remained still, waiting on him. I maneuvered my face and neck, so I was able to see him and noted the weary look in his eyes.

"Everything that was decent in me is gone," he whispered. Discouraged by his words, I moved to get up, and he helped me, pulling me to my feet. He corrected my skirt, pulling it down from my hips, and then looked up at me. Though I was standing in front of him, I felt he was looking past me.

"You should go to bed," was all he said as I waited for some sort of confirmation, anything to tell me what we had done wasn't wrong. I needed his acceptance. I needed to know that I was enough. I needed to know that I still had his home as a retreat and that Harvard still belonged to me. Whether he sensed my unease or not, his words were bone dry as they came out.

"We will meet with my lawyer tomorrow to discuss your inheritance." His eyes finally focused on me, his voice full of finality. *"You will be my greatest investment, my legacy."* He stood towering over me and then added, *"And my downfall."* I felt the ache in my chest as he walked away. I stood for what seemed like an eternity, staring at the table and reliving what had just happened. I let a few tears trickle down as I thought of Laz, feeling as if I'd betrayed him in some way. He'd been the one I'd always pictured taking this part of me. I'd loved him, but not enough to throw my life away for it. Drying my tears, I let my contempt for Laz overshadow the new scar I'd just helped to create. I pushed my shoulders back, did as I was told, and after a thorough shower, went to bed.

The day after I lost my virginity, I signed a non-disclosure agreement regarding my relationship with Ray and was rewarded as a beneficiary to a trust I would have access to on my nineteenth birthday.

The minute I saw that sum, I became addicted to the source of the power: sex.

I no longer needed validation from Ray.

Sex, money, and power would be my new motivation.

They ruled the free world.

And I would have it all.

CHAPTER 6

Taylor

AMBER STARED AT THE VAST EXPANSE OF THE SEA BEFORE HER. HER mind seemed adrift in its contents. I understood her fascination. I too had very much been just as in awe of the ocean the first time I'd seen it. It was confirmation for her that she was light years away from the hell that she'd called home her whole life. Seagulls drifted above, their cries echoing as she sank her bare feet into the soft sand. The water put on a spectacle as waves crashed into the shore. Though the beach was crowded near the pier, we'd found a quieter place to dwell. I'd told her when I brought her to Charleston that this was the first place that I would take her, but her recovery had taken a bit longer than expected. And with her meeting with the lawyer and starting her new job at Scott's solutions, it had taken the better part of two weeks to get her there.

"I don't belong here," she whispered on the wind. I wasn't sure if she meant for me to hear her or not. I took in her appearance as she stood in awe of the sight before her. She had gained a small amount of weight. Her color was a lot less gray.

Her beautiful auburn hair was slightly windswept as she hugged herself, staring at the water.

"Neither do I," I said as I walked to stand next to her. She turned to look at me, a small smile on her lips.

"You look like you do."

"I'm polished brass, Amber." She nodded as if she understood. "And no one really belongs anywhere. It's up to you to make your place, stake your claim. This world will not apologize to you for what you have been through, *ever*. You take what you want and never use the past as an excuse for *anything*. And you do that by deciding you do belong here and are entitled just as much as anyone else."

"I'm not like you," she said weakly. "I don't have an inklin' to run a corporation. I just want my son back. I just want to raise him and make him strong. He's my life. I don't care about anything else."

"This isn't about turning you into someone you aren't. *This* is about giving yourself a chance to be who you are without the world you lived in dragging you down. Once I got used to having . . . just simply *having* whatever I needed, it was easier to concentrate on what I wanted to do, who I wanted to be."

"Looks like you did good," she whispered as she looked back to the water.

"I did well," I corrected, unable to help myself. She turned to me again with twisted features. "When you came back, you know, to get me, I couldn't believe it was you at first. You were so well dressed, so put together, so damned pretty, and I was so shocked that you came. I was afraid to go to you, afraid that somehow me being around you would ruin this new version of you. I didn't want to screw it up for you."

I tried to understand her selfless reasoning because deep down I knew my selfishness was the reason I stayed away for so long.

If there were ever a time to open up to someone, that was the moment. For years, I'd kept a side of myself hidden from my every business associate, every acquaintance, from every lover, every friend. Aside from the small piece of myself I'd revealed to Daniello, I had maintained my silence regarding *that* part. But Amber was here now, just as broken as I was when I left Tennessee. I moved to stand closer to her as I freed myself for the first time in years to finally tell her all that I felt.

"Some days I am paralyzed with guilt over having left you. I try to wrap myself up in justification for leaving, but it didn't matter how I escaped or how well I did with my freedom after or how successful I became. I couldn't stop the horrible guilt attached to leaving you there. I—" My voice cracked as a flood of emotions took hold of me. "She was a terrible mother, a monster, and they were horrible parents. What she did to you, to us . . ." I paused again as I choked on a sob. I saw twin tears slide down Amber's face as she listened to me finally come clean.

"I did everything I could to protect you and in the end, I just . . ." I let a sob escape me. "I just left you there. To fend for yourself. God, you were so small, so helpless. You needed me, and I ran. I'm so sorry, Amber." She lifted her hands to her face as her whole body began to shake. "I don't feel like I deserve your forgiveness, but I want it. I so selfishly want it."

"There's nothing to forgive."

"That's not true," I said, taken aback.

"I'm a mother, and so I see it a bit more clearly than you." She pulled her hands away from her face, scrubbing her tears before she looked at me. Her red-rimmed eyes kept me still as she spoke. "It's the mother's job to protect her child. You did the right thing by leaving. You would have just been another version of me, or maybe worse. It wasn't your job to protect me. It was our mother's. And she can burn in hell for what she did to *both* of us."

We stayed silent as I stewed on her words, knowing even if that were the truth, I'd never really see it that way. I could have done more. But my selfish reasons for staying away would always haunt me. So, I gave her more truth.

"I still get scared, Amber, afraid that this life I built will all disappear one day and I'll again be that penniless kid surrounded by a world of shit. That's why I work so damned hard, to make sure it doesn't happen, to make sure I never have to go back to that. Even if my thoughts are irrational, even if with every dollar I make and with every mile I keep between me and that fucking place, I still have that fear." I felt the heavy weight of my next words but pressed on, knowing she deserved the truth.

"It will never go away. At least it hasn't for me. I can go for days, and if I'm lucky, months without thinking of her, of the past. But when I do, it can hit hard. That sick feeling creeps in, and I can't do anything about it."

Amber looked over to me. "You put on a brave front."

"It got easier. The more time I spent away, the longer I was able to maintain. I got stronger. That's what I'm hoping for, for you."

"Are you happy?" It was the same question I'd asked Daniello and just as hard to answer. Knowing I had already bared the deepest part of myself, I told the truth.

"I'm busy. That's all I've ever been since I left. Lately, I've been restless, so much so to the point I've been reckless. Content . . . maybe. God knows I've worked hard enough for it."

She nodded as she watched me. We stood quietly for several minutes.

"About Laz," she started.

"Please, Amber, don't try to plead his case. Your history

with him is very different from mine. I *am* curious how you even became involved with him."

She swallowed and took a step toward me. "It was right after you left. A few days after you went missing, he came to the house." I waited, a dead part of me threatening to come to life as she continued. "He was out of his mind high and threatened Momma, telling her it was all her fault. She was scared. I could tell. Daddy wasn't home." Amber bent down and picked up a light orange seashell, brushed the sand off, and then put it in her pocket. "Before he left, he looked over at me and promised he would bring you home."

I fought my budding emotion, pressing in hard to keep it down. Laz was dead to me. He'd almost killed me. I could still feel his hands on my neck, squeezing the breath out of me.

"He would come by every few months when Momma and Daddy weren't home. He would give me a little money, check on me, and make promises he never kept."

"He's good at that," I countered.

"I never expected to see you again, and I knew he didn't either. He disappeared for a few years without a word. I knew he was still around because I heard stories about his run-ins with the law at school. He had made one hell of a reputation and was feared by a lot of people."

I bit my lip, remembering the days and nights I'd run alongside him, causing just as much chaos. Sometimes it was hard to believe it was the same lifetime I was currently in.

"When I turned sixteen, I started working at the gas station. I did whatever the hell I could to make money and get out of that house, but Momma always took my paychecks." She looked at me and rolled her eyes. "That's when I saw Laz again. When he spotted me the first time, it was as if he saw a ghost. I knew he had mistaken me for you until he got a good look at me. After that day, he just kept coming by. He would talk to me a little and be on his way. I didn't think much of it, but . . .'"

I turned to her, patient, silent.

"I kind of developed a crush on him. It was stupid, really. He was so much older, but I found myself looking for him every day."

I shut my eyes tight, trying to keep myself even.

"Do you want me to stop?"

"No," I replied quickly. With certainty, I gave another quick, "No."

"Nothing ever came of it back then. Laz didn't look at me that way. I kept my crush a secret, and he kept coming to see me. We got closer, and I told him momma wasn't any different. He saw the bruises. Even when I defended myself, she still gave them to me. It was always worse when I tried to stop her."

"Jesus," I whispered as my chest ached and my head began to pound. The ever-present guilt I felt deepened slightly with her admission though I knew she wasn't trying to guilt me.

"When I turned eighteen, I had managed to save enough money to get a place with a girl I worked with. Momma refused to let me leave when I told her. I didn't expect that. I thought she'd just accept it and tell me to get. Instead, she tore my room apart and took all of my things, my clothes, even my underwear, and refused to give them back. She stayed home watching my every move, threatening me. When I told Laz what was going on, he made it to where I could leave."

"How did he manage that?" I asked.

"He gave her the only thing she cared about more than keeping me hostage."

"Meth."

Amber absently nodded.

CHAPTER 7

Taylor

"Your invitation will be with the driver, and he will pick you up at six," Ross said as she brought in the black bag that held my dress and hung it on the back of my office door. "I've arranged hair and makeup to be here around four thirty. Are you sure you don't want me to look through your contacts to find you an escort?"

"No, that will be all, Ross. Thank you."

I sat back in my chair, contemplating my next move. I'd thought about inviting Amber to the event but wasn't sure she was ready for something as formal as a corporate party. She had been working her ass off, and we'd been spending all of our free time together—what little we had—to get to know each other again. After her confession that Laz had finally freed her from the hell of that house, she'd told me of her loyalty.

They had been close due to their circumstances. Laz came clean one night when he was coming down off of a high and told her everything about his relationship with me. After years of his protection, Amber had confessed to me that her feelings for him had only grown deeper. She was confident that Laz saw her differently than she'd hoped, but she'd thrown herself at him in a moment of weakness. He'd been drunk and down, and she'd been convenient.

"It only happened once," she said one night as we dined on my back porch. "I thought I was in love with him. It's just . . . no one had ever looked out for me like that, cared for me like that. He regretted it the minute after it happened. It took me a long time to forgive him. And when we found out I was pregnant, something inside of him broke. He knew . . ." She looked at me with careful eyes. "He knew you would never forgive him. I think he assumed you would eventually come back, that one day the two of you would be together again."

"He was delusional," I said with contempt. "The man was morally bankrupt when I left Dyer. I was never going back to him. I was finished with him the minute I left."

"He began to hate you then," she said as an afterthought. "I could never really understand what went through his head, but I knew. I've always known he loved you. But when he spoke about you after I got pregnant, it was like he blamed you for everything. I can't explain it, but it was like he wanted you to pay for everything. When Joseph was born, he became fiercely protective over us both. Our relationship changed. He saw our son as a kind of ownership over me. Things got worse. He started using more and began to really become reckless. Joseph's arrival did absolutely nothing to slow him down."

I cringed at the thought of Joseph trapped in a world so hopeless.

"I began using after Laz decided I needed to 'earn' his protection. I would make runs for him and collect money. I was trying to keep Laz content while trying to take care of Joseph. My first excuse for using was to keep up with Laz's never ending demands and then . . ."

I looked over at her as she wiped a stray tear from her face. "You liked it."

"I loved it," she said as she looked over at me carefully. "It made everything disappear in a way. I wasn't numb, but I could ignore it all."

I nodded, but without a true understanding of the effect of the drug.

"Laz just got worse. He was never hands-on with Joseph, just protective. He found me using one day and went ballistic. I tried to quit so many times. And Laz still forced me to make deliveries. It was too tempting. I'd traded one hell for another, except I had this precious little boy," she whispered tearfully. "If I didn't have him, if he hadn't needed me, I probably would have ended it."

Fear crept through me as I heard the desperation in her voice. "I could never leave him, and then I screwed up, and they took him from me." She looked at me, destroyed. "I can't do it without him, Taylor."

"You won't. We will get him back."

"But Laz," she said with fear in her voice.

"He's a thug and a criminal, and no matter what power he has in Dyer, he's just a street rat anywhere else. I'm not afraid of him."

"Taylor, he's unpredictable and crazy," she warned.

"I saw it."

"What do I do?"

"We will figure it out. Right now, he's waiting on us." I looked at her. "Are you talking to him?"

"Yes," she confessed. "He thinks we're in this together. He wouldn't have let me leave otherwise."

"Are you?"

She paused from gathering the breakfast plates. "No."

"Keep him pacified, Amber. I'll figure out the rest."

"He will not give up his son, and he's hell bent on making you pay."

I looked at my sister with certainty. "He's not in control."

A knock on my office door brought me out of my haze. I opened it and greeted the lady who stood with a large case of makeup and an overly exaggerated smile. "Ms. Ellison, nice to meet you. I'm Gloria Runnel."

"Please come in."

"I see you aren't in your dress. We can work around that. Where should I set up?"

An hour later, I was fully impressed with Gloria and her abilities and tipped her twice her rate before I turned down a photo and closed the door behind her. I had ten minutes to dress and slipped the silky midnight fabric over my head and pulled the floor length hem past my hips. The dress itself was spectacular, but Ross was right in that I had no escort. This Cinderella had no prince waiting, but she didn't need one and never would. No, this Cinderella had run with the rats, fucked a prince or two, and decided that self-worth was superior to being second to a man's ego.

But that wasn't how Daniello made me feel. Not at all.

He had plenty of ego, no doubt about that, but I only played second to his need for me. He fed off our lust first and always.

"You're getting soft, Taylor," I scolded myself in the mirror as I admired the waves in my hair. My dress fit my every curve then flowed from mid-thigh down.

The girl inside me covered in Dyer, Tennessee dirt jumped up and down with glee, and I smiled back at her.

We did okay.

CHAPTER 8

Daniello

Rocco glared at me before testing my patience. "She is a whore."

Barga was supposed to be my sanctuary. At least that was the idea. Aside from my time with Taylor in the States, my home was the only place I truly let my guard down. At that moment, in my villa, where discussions of all business were off the table, I had a two-hundred-pound fly to remind me it was never safe to let my guard down. Rocco was in a rage. So far inside his head, he couldn't see reason.

"Stop your tongue, or I will cut it out of you. She has been through much in her life and deserves your respect."

Rocco scoffed at me, his face covered in his usual scowl.

"Why her? Why this temptation? This is not the way you do things. No entanglements!"

I sipped my coffee before I spoke. "Rocco, are you a robot?"

"What?"

"Are you a robot?"

He scowled before he spoke. "What a senseless question."

"Do you find woman entertaining?"

He shrugged. "I fuck."

"Imagine a woman so beautiful, so entertaining that her pussy was the only one you wanted."

Rocco waved his hand and said in Arabic, "Never for me."

"You will speak in *English*. And, Rocco, that is your choice. If you want to treat women as a resource and not a gift, that is your choice."

He glared at me over the solid oak breakfast table my grandfather hand carved. On the way into my villa, he must have missed the inviting rows of olive trees, the calm of the large statue fountain in the center of my courtyard, and the early morning chatter of the birds, to bid war on me. Rocco's menacing presence washed out the early morning sun perched in the sky. He was a dark cloud.

"Rocco, *she* is my choice. And it will remain that way until I say so. She knows nothing."

"You are risking our dealings. Imbecile."

I glanced up from my paper. "Is this jealousy? Do *you* want to fuck me?"

Rocco moved toward me with more argument. I lunged from where I sat and nailed him to the wall. "Say one fucking word, and you will regret it."

Rocco gritted his teeth as he hissed through them, "I'm not your second in command, Daniello."

I slapped his face playfully. "Oh, Rocco, right now, you *are* my side man. *His orders.*" I snapped my fingers next to his ear. Rocco's eyes bulged as he did his best to hold in his temper. Neither of us had a long fuse. It was ingrained in us as young men.

We'd been forced into the Egyptian Army by my father, who refused to let us have dual citizenship with Italy for the specific purpose of serving as he had. Amon Naifeh, a soldier first, family man second, had even gone so far as to bring us back and forth from Barga to Cairo to ensure we remained on the government's radar even though Italy was our true home. Our fathers had served together, and when Rocco's father was killed, my mother embraced him as her own. When we returned to Italy after our compulsory stint in the service, we were different men. Rocco grew fond of the corruption and kept a thirst for power while I declared war on men like him. And when opportunity knocked for Rocco to follow in the steps of my family, he was the first to open the door. I took my own path, determined to keep my freedom, and Rocco's temper kept him where he started, at the bottom. He'd grown just as rich as he was bitter. I slapped him again just for my amusement. "What is that name of the Indian to that cowboy?" I grinned as he glared at me. "That show we watched as children?"

"Take your hands away from me." More Arabic. I slapped his face again, this time with a heavy hand. "*English*, Rocco. I will not ask you again. Ah," I said as the name came to me. "Tonto. That is your new name. You are dismissed, Tonto." I resumed my seat at the patio table and gripped my paper.

He slammed his fist down in front of me. "He will not approve of this."

"He knows *nothing* of her and never will. He does not care who we fuck."

"You're a fool," he scorned before he pointed to the open air between us. "He is *God*. And what will you do with your whore when he tells you he knows of Taylor Ellison?"

"This is your obsession, not his. This will not be a problem."

He leaned in. "She is too close. She is a weakness. You are *weak* with her."

I lunged for him. My knuckles cracked against his jaw, and I only felt satisfied when I saw blood trickle out of his mouth. I landed another blow, making sure I bruised his face so he would see the evidence of his tantrum. "You are the one that is weak.

You are not your own man. You have no freedom. You wanted to be a part of my family so much, you lost yourself. You are no one without your orders. You act like a jealous wife. I am tired of your temper, Rocco. Tired of you. My sentiments for you as family are long past. When our dealings are done in the States and I am finish with you. I do not answer to him. He is not my fucking God. You can kiss his feet if you wish. Take your moody away from me."

"It's finished and mood, imbecile. Keep your whore but keep her out of my way." He faced me head on. "You are a disgrace to your father, to this family, and to your dead brother."

We glared at each other, and I spoke slowly, so there was no doubt in his mind that my next words were truth. "I *will* kill you if you say another word."

I grabbed my paper and adjusted the antique chair before taking a seat. He stormed away, cursing, with a wish of death . . . a death wish. I smiled to myself.

I will conquer this English.

CHAPTER 9

Taylor

I LEFT THE PARTY EARLY AND WALKED AROUND THE BATTERY IN MY ball gown. There were few people there, and most were decent enough to spare me strange looks. After a few hours of polite conversation and one too many dance invitations from business associates, I felt suffocated. I'd damn near ran over the doorman of the hotel trying to get out of the posh party. I found it ironic that I'd spent so many years in an effort to be a part of that circle. It bored me. Closing deals and tripling my investment on a good idea never got old. It wasn't the pot of gold; it was the rainbow that appealed to me. And I'd chase that rush my whole life.

The breeze from the harbor refreshed my sweat-covered skin as I pounded around the history filled sidewalk while it whispered its secrets to me. I still loved the city, the texture of it. The smells, the glimpses of old world and new combined into a sweet, melodic southern cluster fuck. The swooning trees and ever-burning lamp lights, the secrecy of the never-ending hidden alleys. The sculpted hidden gardens. A late-night walk downtown was a silent symphony which the city richly played. I covered my bare shoulders and leaned over the railing on the cement wall that separated me from the harbor. A silent sailboat drifted by, slicing through the dark water. It was the perfect summer night. My phone buzzed in my pocket, but I ignored it. I'd given enough of my time to everyone who deserved it. I was mentally drained from endless conversations. I had meetings between meetings set up for the next week.

I needed a break. I needed clarity.

Ray always told me there were two realities and that work was the safest.

I didn't understand it then. But at that moment, it was becoming clearer that I had no second reality.

Daniello crossed my mind briefly. I wondered what his second reality was. I wondered if he was afraid to quit being the bad guy because he too had confused his priorities. Most people worked to live. But most people hadn't whored their way to get to Harvard.

Ray's voice whispered over the water. If I closed my eyes, I could see him in his office. His fingers tapped on the rich oak wood of his desk. In the weeks after he took my virginity, I was robbed of his company. He'd spent endless days away from his own home to avoid me. In the few times we locked eyes in passing, he'd been the first to let his drift away. I'd become close to one of his maids, Olivia. She had watched me carefully the first week of his absence and made extra rounds at the dinner table, making small talk. She was the closest thing to a friend I had. I'd been dealing with the bitchy future WASPs at my school and had no desire to befriend any of them. And now that my "Uncle Ray" was missing, I craved the small talk.

Something inside me was hurt by his dismissal, but every day he remained away, a different kind of anger brewed.

When I watched his car pull up a month after he took me on his kitchen table, I raced down his marble staircase and flung open the door. My anger was replaced by shock when I saw a woman on his arm. A woman his age.

Ray barely glanced my way as they descended the steps that led to the foyer. Her perfume hit me as they walked past, indifferent eyes for me from Ray and a smile from the woman on his arm.

I addressed Ray, doing away with rehearsed formality. "I need to talk to you."

"It can wait, Taylor. It's late. Go to bed."

"I'm not a child!"

He paused his steps as the woman looked over her shoulder at me. She was dressed in black silk and high heels I couldn't imagine being able to walk in.

Ray took the coward's way out and called for Olivia.

Olivia came running with wide eyes in my direction. She read the situation and motioned for me.

"Taylor, come on now."

"What the fuck, Ray!?"

Ray's companion spoke first. "Whoa, the mouth on this one. She could use some discipline, Ray."

I held my tongue. I wasn't about to lose it all due to a tantrum. But then she looked down at me with pity.

"I'm not his child. I'm his obligation." I gritted the next words through my teeth. "His niece."

"She's beautiful, Ray."

Ray nodded, and with glossy eyes, looked me over.

"Bed."

I looked between the two of them, and all the fight left me. I was being treated like a child because I was acting like one. If I wanted Ray's company, I was doing a bad job of requesting it. I was at his mercy, whether I liked it or not. Still, I knew he had a soft spot somewhere for me, so I decided to manipulate it. "My apologies for interrupting your evening." I turned to Ray, who saw through my insincere bullshit. "I just wanted to thank you for taking me in, Uncle Ray. I really am grateful."

His eyes sliced through mine as I looked over to the woman who scrutinized me curiously. "I'll leave you to it. Goodnight."

The next morning, Ray was gone. He—like Daniello—was a ghost, and I lived in the shadow of his rejection.

I smoothed my hand down the silky fabric of my dress and looked back at the Battery. I was at a standstill. All dressed up, and I didn't want to be . . . anywhere. But the flutter in my stomach told me that was a lie. I knew where I wanted to be and whom I wanted to be with. I reached into my purse and pulled out the key card. Even if he wasn't there, I could chase his ghost.

Inside the penthouse, I flipped the light switch and gaped at the finished space. It was a different world. It had only been a few weeks since I first set foot inside and it had completely transformed. The furnishings were nothing short of luxurious, and I loved the exposed copper fixtures, the espresso-colored floors, and the metal reflection in the ceiling. It was a palace. A mix of earth and metal. I took long strides over to the king sized bed that sat in front of a diamond shaped, copper fireplace. It wasn't the place for a bed, but I knew it had been my lover who ordered it to be placed in that exact location. He, much like the intrusive furniture, didn't belong in my space. But his presence was entirely alluring. I unzipped my dress and slipped into the bed. It was plush and comfortable, though I was unsure if I was supposed to be there without my lover. I assumed Daniello would demand my presence when he wanted me. But he'd given me access, and somehow I felt his absence a little less in the last space we shared. And though I had no intentions of staying, I fell asleep and drifted off to the memory of his voice.

"Phoenix."

Taylor

Another day, and another, and another. Nothing. No word from my lover, just the looming feeling that I was drifting on a road to nowhere. I was becoming dependent on my surfacing feelings for Daniello, and I hated it. The longer he stayed away, the more the resentment grew for the man who controlled far too much of my time and my imagination from whatever world he escaped to. Whatever walls we'd managed to let down between us in Dyer began stacking up, twice as impenetrable with every day I slept alone in the penthouse. He'd revealed so little and expected so much. Too much. Despite my hesitance to share, he knew details about me, secrets about my life, who I was. And still, he kept me at bay and picked me up on his whim like a toy.

I was no one's fucking toy.

I had to face facts. I wasn't happy with the situation. It was time to take back some control. I needed some say. Our involvement and his disappearance had only amped up the unrest in me over time. I was fighting hard to keep my emotions out of it. And still, my heart ached, my brain was fed up with thoughts of him. I was tired of waiting.

A creature of habit, I slipped on the most revealing dress I had, cut deep in both front and back and left nothing to the imagination. It fit every curve of my body, and I stared at my reflection, satisfied

Without giving it any more thought, and furious with my situation, I fired up my Chevelle and drove downtown on a mission. I mentally dug through every conversation I had with Daniello in a fruitless search for something more than what I felt at that moment: used. I felt discarded, no matter how hard I tried to keep the connection in his endless silence.

But words were bullshit. I'd learned that from Laz. Actions

always spoke louder, and Daniello's consistent absence was screaming at me to wake the hell up.

"I will return," I mimicked snidely, as I tore through midtown and fled to King Street. I pulled up to the piano bar I'd seen Daniello at months ago and tossed my keys to the valet before I moved to the back patio. In the midst of neon blue lights that covered the dark patio, I surveyed the bar for a suitor and saw Damien Baldwin sipping expensive scotch. He drummed his fingers against his glass in time with Kings of Leon as "The End" rang out through the deck. I assessed his relaxed posture and easy smile, as if he hadn't a care in the world. But it was just the opposite. He was on the prowl. Women flocked toward his kind of look and charm. My tastes were now on an entirely different planet than the one Damien dwelled on. But it was exactly why he was the perfect fix.

A cure for the alien who'd stolen my identity.

Harvard graduate, business mogul . . . and doormat? *Fuck that.*

Damien was one of Charleston's most notorious playboys. And on that night, he'd made himself one of the most delectable by pouring himself into a perfectly fitted Brooks Brother's suit. His thick, brown, cropped hair was styled in a mix of class and sex. Within seconds of my arrival at the bar, his light brown eyes flicked my way. His warm smile was genuine in greeting, but his eyes screamed "Wanna fuck?"

"Ms. Ellison—" he tipped his glass my way "—you look stunning tonight."

"White wine, please," I said to the bartender before I acknowledged him. "Mr. Baldwin, thank you."

Several words popped into my mind at that moment and then a name. Handsome, entitled, wealthy *Ray.* Damien kept in his seat as he angled his body toward me, his eyes trained on my face before they slid down my body. "You know, red is my favorite color."

I took my wine and gave him a sly grin. "And how would I know that?"

"I guess you wouldn't," he drawled with a hint of southern tongue. "Why don't you let me buy you that wine so I can tell you more about myself."

"Narcissism is unattractive, Mr. Baldwin."

"Call me Damien." His lips twitched. "And I believe I'm pretty sure I can figure out a way to make the conversation all about you."

I scoured him. He was truly a beautiful man. I took the two strides toward him and stood by his side. He studied my profile and then smirked at his scotch.

"Something on your mind, Damien?"

"I find myself thinking that we may have a little in common, Taylor."

Lust-filled eyes met mine as he inched closer, the smell of his cologne inviting as his breath hit my ear. "Let's discuss it over fucking."

"Wow," I mused, "two sips into my wine."

Damien quirked a brow. "I'd say that dress did the conversing for us. Let's not bullshit each other, Taylor."

He stood and tossed a bill on the bar, winking at the younger girl Daniello had finger-fucked months ago in front of my eyes. My lover later revealed he fucked her that night, which only fueled my anger. It was a game.

He was a predator and I his prey.

I was Daniello's mouse.

With a fresh drink in hand, the bartender bent low in delivering it, giving Damien an eyeful of cleavage, which he had the good sense to ignore. I remembered the heat I felt when I watched Daniello touch her, fuck her with his fingers, and then bring her to orgasm for everyone on that deck to see. The desire that built that night slowly seeped into me as Damien turned his gaze my way.

Full of anger and desire for a man I couldn't grasp, I homed in on the man in front of me—starving. Damien read my mind. "Let's go get comfortable." I followed him to one of the unoccupied couches away from the crowd. Damien crossed an ankle over his knee and patted the couch beside him. Exhaling out the idea that what I was doing was wrong, I took my seat and let him do his bidding. It was easy, too easy, and I found myself deflated at the lack of connection. Still, I forged on, unwilling to admit defeat. Two white wines and a filthy whisper from his lips later, his mouth was on mine in the parking lot. Without a firm answer to him stating where I wanted to go, he nailed me to my Chevelle and tore into me, thrusting his tongue into my mouth as his hands explored beneath my dress. It was quiet in the tree-covered and car-filled yet otherwise deserted parking lot.

Damien took his fill before he pulled his lips away for a quick proposition. "I have a place down the street, four beds, nice kitchen, big bathrooms," he mumbled as his lips traced my neck. "I could fuck you in every one of them."

I gripped his hair as he roamed my skin, and I tried to will myself into the moment, my head and heart at odds as I forced myself open and molded my body to his. Pulling away, I sank into the Chevelle as he dove in, misreading my defeat as an invitation. "Jesus, you are beautiful, so fucking hot, Ellison."

Awareness hit me like a ton of bricks, and I felt a piece of me break when I searched for and found the dark eyes a foot away. My whole body jolted as Damien backed away to study my face before he took a look in both directions, his back to Daniello.

"What's got you spooked?" Damien asked as he slipped a warm hand behind my neck.

Averting my eyes to his, I felt the unspoken threat as I

gripped Damien's jacket, keeping his attention on me and not the certain death that stood behind him. "Nothing."

Daniello's eyes screamed murder as Damien's lips brushed my shoulder. Two men I didn't recognize emerged from a sedan and walked toward Daniello. They were oblivious to us as they spoke rapid Italian. Daniello paused only a second after his name was called before he tore his gaze away and walked with them toward the club.

He was in Charleston, and he hadn't come to me.

He. Was. In. Fucking. Charleston.

My heart sank as I abruptly pushed Damien away. "What the hell, Taylor?"

"Just give me a second, okay?" I fumed as I looked toward the building.

I straightened my dress as Damien smirked down at me. "You don't strike me as the indecisive type."

"I'm not," I snapped as I tried to gather myself. I weighed my options as Damien patiently stood next to me, confusion covering his handsome face. "I'm suddenly thirsty again." I saw irritation flash through his eyes briefly before he extended his elbow. "Tonight is about you, right?"

"Thank you."

He gave me a sideways glance as we walked back toward the bar. "I have a good feeling you're worth the wait."

Seated on the same stool I'd recently occupied, the curious bartender passed out a repeat of drinks while I did a horrible fucking job of not looking in Daniello's direction. He was seated on the couch as he had been a few short months ago, surrounded by the men he'd come with, and didn't once glance my way. My heart pounded as Damien's fingers trailed casually across my skin while I sipped my wine at a snail's pace. I heard Daniello's laugh bellow out in the night air, and the bartender noticed his arrival. A playful "I remember you" smile graced her lips as she sauntered over and took drink orders. Daniello dismissed her without a second glance, and I couldn't help the slight satisfaction that lay in my gut as she stomped away, forgotten.

But then again, I was walking a mile in her shoes.

Damien, too transfixed with seduction and the cock that pulsed in his pants, was completely ignorant to my shift in attention. The man I longed for was feet away, and I was fuming at his indifference toward me.

It was punishment. But why? I obviously meant nothing. And if that were the case, message received.

I inched toward Damien as he turned my way, encasing my legs between his, and leaned in. "Now you're just fucking with me," he whispered before pushing the hair away from my neck. It was at that moment I finally caught the eyes of my lover. "Fuck you," I mouthed as I moved to stand. It was a game. I was a game. Emotional involvement was for fucking fools, and I'd played one long enough. I snapped and gripped Damien by the arm before I leaned in with a promise, my lips ghosting against his skin. "I'll be right back."

I made my way to the ladies' room and paced the floor as I tried to rationalize my anger.

Sex is not love. Sex is not love. Sex is not love. Sex is not love, Taylor! And I was a fool, again.

I checked my appearance and fixed my lipstick before I stormed out of the bathroom. When I returned to the bar, Damien was gone, and so was Daniello.

I raced to the penthouse, my blood boiling as I rode up the elevator. With my keycard in hand, I stalked toward the door when the elevator opened behind me.

Turning on my heel, ready for war, I began to pale when I saw the man who greeted me.

His face was twisted with anger while his eyes scoured me.

Rage.

Jealousy.

And more painfully, disgust.

My galloping heart kept my tongue still. The current in the air pierced my insides with the precision of a sharp knife. Daniello took a single step out of the elevator and froze. Fully lit by the hall light and dressed in a fitted suit and tie, his beauty was only amplified by his anger. I ached to go to him. Touch him. Slap him.

Cold eyes had my flesh crawling with anticipation. The sick idea crept over me that I wanted him this way, in this state. I wanted his anger, if only to solidify my suspicion. He had to have felt something. Because I was practiced at the art of playing immune to emotion, and with Daniello, those emotions now ricocheted between us and felt like daggers as they buried themselves deep.

"I'm not happy with our arrangement."

His hands fisted at his sides repeatedly, as if he was trying to figure out what to do before he punched the button behind him and the door reopened.

"So that's it? You're just going to leave?" I took angry strides toward him.

His voice was venom. "I need to be away from you, Taylor."

I shook my head and scoffed indignantly. "Well, that's nothing new, now, is it, you bastard! How long have you been here? How often do you do this?! Leave me here waiting for you to play with your friends!" Daniello stood his ground as I reached him and pushed his chest. "This is not who I am! I wait for no man!"

Daniello gripped the flesh of my upper arms, picked me up, and carried me as if I was weightless as he growled, "You would let another man touch you, fuck you?!" His voice was evidence of the deceit he felt as his eyes pierced me. Anger rolled off him as he slammed me flat against the door of the penthouse and smashed his palm against it while he cornered me. "You want to be fucked, Taylor, but he would not have satisfied you. I am inside you. You want me. You need my cock. Your thirst is not for him. You fool yourself. You make me a fool." He tore the fabric off my shoulder with a vicious swipe of his hand, exposing a breast. He kept our eyes locked, green to brown. "You let him touch you." He grasped my dress in annoyance.

Rip.

Rip.

My shredded dress hung at my waist as he tore himself from the frame of the door before he pounded his fist to his chest. "You reduce yourself to being some faceless man's whore when you are my fucking sun!"

Unable to contain them, angry tears streaked my cheeks. My eyes widened as he pushed the dress down, so I was reduced to wearing nothing but my thong and heels. I stood bared to him, defying his attempt to weaken my state.

Sex is not love.

I kicked the ruined fabric aside and faced him head on. "You owe me a dress and a fucking explanation!" Exchanged energy pulsed between us as his chest bounced with quick breaths. He gripped my hair and leaned in an inch from my mouth. "In that bed, behind that door, you put your fingers inside your pussy with my name on your lips. I am the man you want. There is no other explanation."

Realization dawned. "You watch me."

There was no apology in his eyes or his tone. "I watch you with my cock in my hand, Phoenix, with my need for you. I know who you are. I know what we are. Do you?" he sneered as I snaked my tongue out to wet my lips. Tumultuous eyes narrowed as his lips turned up. "I can smell him on you." He gripped my hair and tugged it until I was kneeling. Sparks prickled up my spine to my screaming scalp. "You need me, here I am."

His words bit and stung as he challenged me. "Fuck you."

He leaned down. "I am what you crave. Dare to deny it." My eyes watered from the sting. He stood, a picture of pure temptation, while he kept my hair fisted, and slowly unzipped his pants. His bulging length sprang free and my mouth watered.

"Deny it, Taylor. Lie. To. Me."

Sex is not love.

Warmth soaked my panties as I reached out and scratched his thighs before I enveloped his hard as stone cock in my mouth. Scalp screaming from his angry pull, he thrust his hips, and I choked as he made sure it hurt. Stroke after stroke, he satiated his rage as he kept our eyes locked. He punished as I took every inch and moaned, fueling his anger.

He hissed through his teeth while he demanded remorse from my lips I refused to give, opting for delicious punishment. His eyes closed briefly when he saw a solitary tear streak my cheek. His misread it for hurt when it was an elation of sorts. I'd never felt the passion I had for him for any other man. The want, the need, it surprised me, but I knew it was lurking. I'd ignored it before, but my eyes were wide open. He knelt in front of me as he gripped my throat. "Do you need me?"

"No."

He wiped my mouth with the back of his hand before he pulled me to the concrete floor, his back to the door. His eyes searched mine as he gripped my ass and pulled it apart, teetering me on his spread thighs, his cock displayed between us. I eyed it with hunger before he thrust two fingers inside and pushed a third into my ass. I pumped his cock as his fingers teased. With hooded eyes, he spoke. "Impossible fucking woman. You need me." Built up to the point of breaking, he gripped my throat again. "The truth."

Emotion-filled words slid off the edge of my tongue as his eyes implored mine. He wanted to break me. He was blurring the lines. I knew better. But I tipped over anyway. "Daniello, don't."

He let go of my throat and gripped my hips, robbing me of my orgasm. Lust-filled black eyes dove into me as the silky head of his cock nudged my backside. Inch by inch he filled me as I crumbled in his arms, full of emotion and on the brink.

His grip tightened as we connected and then collided.

Fully seated, he waited as I gripped his shoulders to ease the burn. It was a blissful pain. "Do you feel me, Taylor?"

"Yes," I gasped, my heart plummeting as he kept me idle.

"I cannot see that, Taylor. I cannot see that man with his hands on you, his lips on yours." Pressing his thumb to my clit, he resumed pumping his fingers while I scratched his shoulders, drawing blood. He eased his hips up from the cold floor and fucked me, claimed me, owned me, possessed me, and took the rest of my control.

"Taylor." With a hoarse whisper, he demanded his answer. "Tell me."

"I need you," I gasped before his lips claimed mine. With one deep thrust of his tongue in my mouth, I burst, inside and out, my heart heavy between us as we worked into a frenzy, mouths and movement and deep-seated need.

We clung to each other as he tore me apart piece by piece and fed me for his absence. My body repeatedly shuddered as he commanded it. At his mercy, an ocean of feeling swept between us as he silenced my doubts with every soothing touch of his hands. Devoured and defeated, he took my lips again before he filled me with a heavy release. Touching his forehead to mine, he eased me off his cock and pulled me to his chest. "I just want to know who you are."

Gentle lips brushed my temple before he whispered, "You know."

We lay in bed, the penthouse silent hours after the most intimate sex I'd ever had. The early morning light covered the penthouse in an eerie blue hue. Daniello slept next to me as I pulled his dress shirt around my body and looked out at the harbor. I fed on the feelings that surfaced from simply being with him and had done my best to sabotage it. I knew why. He knew why. Emotions were becoming a thick cloud between us, far too hard to ignore. Denial was my only escape, and he was doing his best to stop me. But why? We had no future; we barely had the semblance of a relationship. We were fiery sex and stolen moments.

And still on his terms. I hated myself for it, but I'd lost the battle. I wanted him, that much I knew, but he'd just proved to me I needed him.

His silky, sleep-filled voice drifted through the air. "You think too much."

"I think too little," I said as I turned to look at him. He was a perfect picture of masculinity. Dark, ominous, and fully alluring. No man had ever compared. No man after him ever would. "When it comes to you, Mr. Di Giovanni, I think too little."

"You regret this?"

I nodded slowly. "In a way, yes."

He looked down briefly at the bed before his eyes shot to mine. "I do not want that, Phoenix." I shrugged as I turned back to face the water because looking at him hurt.

"It's too late."

CHAPTER 10

Taylor

CEDRIC LOOKED AT ME THEN TO AMBER, WHO SHRANK IN HER SEAT.

"Laz isn't just going to go away."

I spent the next few minutes filling him in as Amber silently cried on the couch. Every day, even with her progress, she was raw with the loss of her son.

I was sure Cedric's tongue-lashing after I told him about what went down in Tennessee could be heard by every resident in my complex. Once we moved on, I pleaded Amber's case.

"It could take months to get custody. But from what the lawyer said, things are moving faster than she expected." I briefly gripped my sister's hand and felt her return squeeze. We finally had a reason to be thankful to have lived in a town with a minuscule population. There wasn't much on the court docket.

Cedric palmed the top of his freshly shaved head and scrutinized Amber. I trusted him more than anyone in my life, and the worry on his face was doing a number on my mental state. I called him in for reassurance, and he looked like he was about to pass sentence.

Cedric narrowed his eyes when he questioned Amber. "You're clean?"

She looked up at him from the couch with a nod. "Yes."

With worry-riddled features, Cedric warned us, "He's going to come, no matter what. We just have to make sure we're prepared." Cedric paced the condo and stopped with his hands on his hips. "Christ."

Amber bit her lip, her meek posture a sure sign of her guilt. I gave her a reassuring nod. "We're in this together."

She smiled weakly. "Okay."

Cedric turned to both of us. "We can get the local PD on this."

"No cops." I shook my head. "No cops."

Both of them turned to me in surprise. "Slapping him with a restraining order will only get him here faster. We have to do this legally and by way of custody. And then deal with whatever he brings with him when he comes for Joseph."

Cedric blew out a breath. "I agree. Any sort of drama between you two could hold up the case. Laz is behind you having full custody?"

Amber nodded.

"Then security is our only other option."

Cedric and I spent the next hour picking through his list of capable bodyguards. Amber fell asleep on the couch while we sat at my dining room table.

He leaned over and whispered, "It's not going to be enough. If he's as crazed as you say and still getting high, a bullet might not be enough to stop him. He's not just coming after Joseph."

"I know."

"How do you feel about this?"

I looked up to see Cedric's eyes on me. "I'm nervous, of course. You should have seen him, Cedric."

"I mean the baby." Cedric brushed a finger over mine, and

for a moment I saw the boy who taught me how to shoot a gun at his parents' property, the one who tried to warn me away from Laz. The man who told me he loved me and offered to take me away from Dyer. Cedric would have been a good choice.

"I'm concentrating on too much to think about it. I left her there. This is my mess."

"Bullshit, you can't blame yourself."

"But I do. And that won't change. I should have fought to get her out of there sooner. This is on me. She couldn't see past the drugs, and then when Joseph came, she was trapped."

"So were you, and you found a way out."

"She's not like me," I whispered.

"No, she's not." Cedric gripped my hand and held it.

"Help me protect her, Cedric. Please. I won't ask anything else of you."

Cedric moved to the seat next to mine. "You know I will. But I can offer you peace from this. There's a fast solution."

And there it was. An offer to rid Amber and me of our burden. I had no doubt Cedric could get it done and was as capable of Daniello. The skip of my heart told me I could never be the one to make that call, even though it would simplify everything.

Cedric read my hesitance. "You still love him."

"No, no I don't." I pulled my hand away. "He almost killed me. I can't love that monster."

"It's not the monster you love. It's the memory."

CHAPTER 11

Laz

I THUMBED THE GLASS PIPE AND ROLLED IT AS THE RED FLAME produced sweet smoke. I inhaled deep and felt a quick release from the throb in my veins.

Release. Escape.

My phone lit up, and I turned it over before taking another hit. My skin began to crawl with adrenaline as the high built. My high was my home.

Amber: Met with the lawyer again. She thinks it will take another two months. But she says I'm doing everything right. We will get him back.

Trust. That's what it all boiled down to.

My own mother refused to let me take Joseph this morning. She told me she didn't recognize me anymore, that I looked nothing like her son. But she had stolen mine.

My. Fucking. Son.

And he was growing used to being without his mother and me.

Joseph made me nervous. I never told Amber that, but in a

way, I was too afraid I'd fuck him up. I couldn't be hands on with him. He was too pure, too much of a good thing. But leave it to a fucking Ellison woman to ruin the only good thing in my life.

He was all I had left. So, the question was, did I trust Amber?

I rubbed the scar on my leg that I knew was underneath my jeans. I'd spent years tracing its location with my fingertips. It was the evidence of her sister's betrayal. Taylor thought that the years between us would give her a pass for what she did to me.

But everything I did back then was for her, to protect her, to help her and her sister escape that house.

Ungrateful bitch.

She was every inch of the woman I thought she'd grow into. Fierce, strong, and beautiful. And she was fucking some foreign piece of shit, who I knew wasn't legitimate.

How the hell was he any better than me?

I would never forget the satisfaction of seeing her afraid of me that day at our spot. I wanted to kill her, but first I wanted to fuck her so hard it hurt. Hurt to the point she would never forget who her rightful owner was. She was meant to be mine. Always. We had promised each other.

"Laz, stop it!"

"Come on, you know you love it." I smeared the sugar all over her lips as she fought me.

"Damn you, stop it." Taylor pushed against my chest as I leaned in and began to lick up my mess from her face and neck.

We were at our spot, next to the pond. It was one of those days where the trees remained still even with the cool breeze beneath it and time lasted. Taylor brought strawberries and sugar for dipping, and I managed to get a bottle away from my mother's house. It was the first time in months we'd been in the sun together. I'd smoked a foil before we left the hotel and Taylor made me promise it would be my only one for the day. I was hitting the bottle hard to fight the urge as I watched her take a dip in the pond. The itch subsided with each pass of drink through my lips, and every time she looked over at me and smiled, it was a reminder. I didn't need anything but her. I loved her. I'd told her so many times lately, I feared she'd never say it back to me. She wanted me sober. That was her reason for keeping the same words to herself. My chest banged from the rattle of my heart as I feared I might never get those words to pass her lips. I was done denying my addiction, and she knew it too.

But Taylor was my air, the only thing that kept me going, the only thing I looked forward to. The drugs were distracting me, but getting clean meant creating a different plan, and we didn't have time for a plan B. We were getting close to leaving Dyer and everything behind us.

She lay beneath me in the warm sun and fought for air as I smothered her with my kiss. I tasted her sweet tongue and pulled away as she looked up at me with eyes the color of jade stone.

"Laz."

"Yeah, baby?"

I circled her mouth with my tongue, taking the sweetness off her face and then slowly dipped to nibble at her ear.

"Thank you."

I peered down at her in confusion.

"For what?"

"For coming here, for being . . . you. I've missed you."

"I'm always me."

Taylor's eyes filled. "I think you know that's not true anymore." Before that day, I'd only seen Taylor cry once. And the sight of it had damned near killed me the first time. She was the strongest girl I'd ever met. Her tears weren't even for herself when she shared them with me. They were for her sister. Her mother had gotten rough on her with a broom handle and Taylor had taken it so hard she didn't speak for days.

She had so much love for her little sister; it hurt to watch it all happen. My parents weren't much better in the way of provision. I, more often than not, had to fend for myself, but I had it better in the way that I didn't have to defend myself. They never once raised a hand to me.

I looked down at the girl who had stolen my heart and told her the *words again to make myself clear because I had done a shit job of proving it.*

"I love you."

She paused. The words were so clearly returned in her eyes but still fell mute on her lips.

"Laz."

"Tell me. Just tell me. I want to hear it." She smiled and lifted to press her lips to mine. "You're drunk."

I lifted the bottle and brought it to her lips. Lifting to her elbows, she took a guarded drink and then coughed it down. "That's awful, what is that?"

"Whiskey. We do live in the state of Tennessee."

"Not forever."

"No, baby, not forever," I said, capping the bottle and laying it next to her. She had on a blue sundress and her fiery hair cascaded over her shoulder and onto the blanket I brought. Her lips were swollen from my kiss. She was the most beautiful thing I'd ever seen. I wanted so much to take it further. Every touch, every slide of her tongue against mine brought me closer to being inside her. But I knew one day soon she'd ask, and though my dick was raging, my heart refused to press her. It was just a matter of time. And we were getting creative enough to keep me satisfied. Still, I needed reassurance. I needed to know she was mine, though I felt it deep. "But when we leave, no matter where we land, no matter how far we end up away from this shithole, you belong to me."

"Of course," she promised as she snaked her arms around my neck and brought me down to her lips for a slow kiss. When I pulled away, I felt the static start as her breathing picked up.

"Promise me you belong to me, Taylor."

"You know I do," she replied breathlessly.

"I'm your always."

Sincere eyes penetrated mine as she twisted us so she straddled me. "You know you are."

She rubbed her panty-covered middle along my jean-covered cock and lifted a brow.

I grinned up at her. "You feelin' playful?"

"I'm feeling something." She lifted the bottle and took a hearty sip.

"Take it easy," I warned before I gripped the bottle and capped it.

"I can handle it."

Twenty minutes later, I held her hair as she sprayed the lawn with strawberries. When she recovered, we took a dip in the pond and then she slept it off in my arms. Her last mumbled words were "Always, Laz."

But she broke that goddamned promise and me in the process.

Young or not, we'd lived through hell. She knew exactly what she was doing when she stole from me and left me bleeding in that motel room. She might as well have put that fucking bullet in my heart, or mercifully in my fucking head. At least then I would have to think about the life she lived without me.

But she left me. She left me to rot in the goddamn hotel room without a plan, without my air, without her.

And the fucked up part was the life I lived without her had everything to do with her. Taylor was in possession of the only link to my son. Amber was the way.

I tossed my pipe onto my dresser and began bagging product. Amber didn't love me. I wasn't fucking clueless to it, but she owed me. And I couldn't help but think her texts were a way of keeping me at bay. Regardless, I would have my son, and Amber would just have to deal with being a casualty as his caregiver. I'd left her the job of raising him while I kept him safe.

I knew Amber had dreams of leaving Dyer like her sister, but no matter what, the Walker boys would come first. And if she so much as tried to stop it from happening, I would have a pile of red hair in my fist and crush her fucking skull into the other until she believed it.

But Amber wasn't Taylor. She *was* loyal and had never given me any reason not to trust her. While Taylor saw me as a parasite, Amber saw me as her lord and savior. Something Taylor never had the fucking good sense to acknowledge. But I would make sure Taylor prayed to me one way or the other.

Amber would come back to Dyer.

I would have my son back.

And Taylor would pray, on her knees, right before I returned the favor and broke her.

CHAPTER 12

Taylor

I DREAMED OF RAY . . . AGAIN. FOR REASONS I COULDN'T UNDERSTAND, he'd been on my mind. It was half memory, half fiction, and wholly painful. I'd woken in a daze, feeling foolish for entertaining my wishful thinking when it came to Daniello. Too much wine, too much imagination. Still, the ache in my chest wasn't imagined. The ache belonged to Daniello, and my need, my craving for his company, the weight in my stomach came from my memory of Ray and the day he returned home.

I was in my room reading the thirteenth novel on my tutor approved reading list. Ray had waltzed into my room like his absence didn't make us strangers. I sat up on high alert with his aggressive stance in front of my bed.

He was dressed casually—dark jeans and a button down—something I wasn't used to. His blue eyes sliced through me with contempt, and he reeked of alcohol.

"I don't like it that you're here." Pure anger leaked from him as he glared at me with disgust.

I stood slowly and faced him head on. "We have a deal."

"I'll pay you for your absence." I ignored the hurt and demanded an

answer instead.

"What have I done?"

"Pack your things; you need to go. I'll make arrangements for you."

I looked around the large bedroom I'd grown used to isolating myself in and started mentally packing a list of things that belonged to me. And then I realize not a single thing did. It had all come from Ray. Even the clothes on my body. I tore off my shirt and threw it down at his feet.

"What the fuck are you doing?"

"Leaving the way I came. I don't want a damn thing from you." I pushed my shorts down and then my panties. I moved toward the white-washed dresser that held the clothes I came with and was caught by the wrist.

"You can take everything, Taylor."

"Go to hell."

Ray's chest heaved as he looked me over. The awareness of his touch betrayed my body. I had spent a month remembering the look in his eyes, his mouth. I refused to regret what we'd done. I'd been a willing participant, the instigator.

He released me, and I ripped open my dresser, my back to my captor. I didn't want him to see the tear he was causing with his rejection.

"It wasn't right." His words were a whisper.

"No, this isn't right. This, what you're doing to me now, isn't right."

"You're a baby."

I turned to him, vulnerable, bared. "I'm eighteen. I'm an adult, and I'm not sorry. I agreed to all of this. I started it. I knew what I was doing. You were saving me. You are supposed to teach me how to do this, Ray. I still need you. Please don't throw me away. I can't go back. I don't want to go back. You said—"

His eyes trailed down my body. "I changed my mind."

"You want to change your mind, but you haven't. You want me. I can see it in your eyes despite your lying lips. Well, I'm right here. I want this. I want you. I want you to teach me. I want to be your legacy." I took a step forward. "Ray—"

"Don't." He closed his eyes and shook his head at the floor. "Jesus

Christ, don't."

I took another step and then another until we were chest to chest. He opened his eyes when he felt my fingers unclasp the buttons of his pants.

"Stop," he hissed. I ignored him and resumed my workings until I freed his rock-hard cock from his briefs. He opened his eyes and glared down at me. I gripped him hard. "I'm going to give you what you paid for, and you're going to give me what you promised." I did what I thought felt right and pulled at his cock like Laz taught me. Ray gripped the back of my head as I stroked him.

"I want this, Ray."

I moved in and kissed his jaw. His posture was stone, his breathing labored. "Show me how to please you," I whispered between kisses along his neck.

I gripped his hand and brought it to my middle. Ray snapped. A hungry mouth landed on my shoulder as he spread me with angry fingers and plunged two in my wet center.

His touch was deep and seductive. I moaned as his fingers fucked me and pulled a sharp gasp from within. He ripped his lips away from my neck.

"Goddamn you."

He gripped me hard and pulled me up to straddle him before he walked us to the bed. We landed in a heap, tasting, touching, both needy for the other. I wanted to feel the way I had months ago, but I hated his hesitance, his disgust. He twisted my head and spent minutes on my neck before his kiss trailed down my body.

"Ray." It was a breathy whisper. He moved away from me and pulled off his shirt. Completely bared to me, he looked down at the bed, and I spread my legs wide. He cursed again as he rejoined me, his hands snaked underneath my back and moved up to grip my shoulders. The tip of his cock nudged me before he pressed all the way in. We both moaned out at the feel as he hovered above me. I moved and twisted at the slight discomfort, and he stilled me with his mouth on mine. It felt so natural, so right. Ray moved inside of me, hard and punishing as I wrapped my legs around him and gripped his head. We got lost in our hunger, our anger, until he spent himself.

Gasping for air, we lay in a naked pile on my bed. His heavy breath covered my chest as my heart hammered against his.

Maybe it was wrong in the eyes of others. But I saw it differently. He was a lonely man. A sordid king of a cold castle and I was a lost girl who desperately needed the promise of a future and the safety of his kingdom. Everything about my future depended on the whims of the angry king.

"Taylor, line one."

I was just about to fire Ross when she chimed in, "It's the attorney, Ms. Adler."

"Taylor Ellison."

"Hi, Ms. Ellison. I just wanted to let you know that we've managed to secure a date in Dyer with the family court. Things are progressing faster that I'd expected, but this is a good sign."

"When?"

"Six weeks. Chances are, with Amber's established residence, your reputation, and financial situation, not to mention Mr. Walker's record, we should have little issue bringing Joseph across state lines."

"Thank you."

"I'll keep you updated. I've already spoken with Amber."

I sat back in my chair and sighed. I had six weeks to prepare for all hell breaking loose. If I didn't go back with Amber, I risked the safety of both her and Joseph. There was no way we would make it over the Tennessee state line with Joseph. Amber was announced and walked through my door minutes later. She had a healthy glow, and the expression on her face was purely joyful.

"Six weeks! Can you believe it? I've upped my meetings to six a week, and it's paying off."

"That's great, really," I said absently, my head somewhere between hope and dread. Amber paused at my door. "I thought you'd be happy about that."

"I am. Really, Amber."

"It's Laz." She sighed. "You're still angry."

"Not at all." I met her timid gaze across the space. "But I think we should bring Cedric with us and hire more security. Does Laz know there is a court date?"

"I haven't told him. But the minute we get back, he will know."

"Keep it quiet for now. But update him on your other progress and meetings."

"Okay."

Amber lingered in my office doorway. "Thank you, Taylor." She closed the door as I texted Cedric.

We go back in six weeks.

I'll be there.

Somewhere between work and sleep, I zoned out in my office. The sun was setting outside my window, and a velvet haze filled the room with soft light.

I sat back in my chair and sighed. It had been almost three weeks since I'd seen Daniello. I'd slept in the penthouse on several occasions in hopes of being surprised, but it was all in vain. I needed a distraction. Amber was soaring. So was Scott Solutions, thanks to order and excellence.

Amber's words hit me in the chest.

"Are you happy?"

No. That was the truth. I had all the money I would ever need, but I was entirely lacking in my second reality. I was attached to a man who consistently cut our ties, to a man I swore I wouldn't bind myself to in both heart and mind. And flashing images of his perfect smile beneath deadly sexy brown eyes did little to ease the ache.

"I don't need love, Daniello."

"I know."

Was I a liar? All that I felt seemed to be brimming to the surface as I thought of how he'd taken me from a place of denying everything related to my heart and hammered his way in, regardless of the space between us. I was falling.

"Where in the fuck are you?" I hung my head in defeat. Just as I'd decided to suck it up and dig back into my workload, Nina chose that moment to knock on my door. "Taylor?"

"Come in."

She graced me with a soft smile as she sauntered into the room. She looked happy. "What are you doing?"

"I'm looking through Vogel's proposal. Did you see his latest numbers?"

She nodded as she took the chair opposite of my desk. "I did."

I closed the thick file. "I think it's a no-brainer. You should do this deal."

"Agreed. I'll call him in the morning."

Nina sat patiently and studied me.

I met her eyes. "Is there something else?"

"Nope." She moved to leave her chair and then slid back in. "Got any wine?"

"Where's Devin?"

Nina chuckled and shook her head. "While you're making it clear, dear partner, that you're in need of privacy, I'm doing the same by way of your company. Humor me."

I smiled across my desk at her. "I have whiskey."

"My favorite."

"Mine too." I pulled a bottle of Maker's Mark from my desk and grabbed two glasses from a side cart I kept on hand for clients. I poured us two fingers each.

Nina sipped her blend and sat back, the instant effect of the burn putting her more at ease. I too felt the remedy in my long sip and sank a little in my seat.

"We work too much," Nina said with a sigh.

"We're good at it." It was the truth. Scott Solutions had only grown, and we were two of the most watched businesswomen in Charleston. A sudden onslaught of guilt ripped through me as I thought of the repercussions that my personal life might bring, not only with Laz but also with Daniello. I was relieved the moment had presented itself.

"I'm actually glad you're here. I need to tell you something." I bit my lip as she looked me over apprehensively. I took a long pull of the whiskey before I spoke. "My past. It's scandalous. More than that, it's illegal. In the future, if we're spotlighted for our success, some things may come out."

An intrigued Nina sat up at full attention. "Like?"

"I grew up extremely poor. My parents were meth addicts, and my mother was deranged and *very* abusive."

"Really?" Nina's reply was a whisper as her eyes filled with pity.

I lifted my hand, palm out. "Don't, seriously don't do that or this story ends."

She gripped her glass close to her chest and nodded.

"I was involved with a man before I left. We'd been together for years, and when he started selling meth, I helped him. The whole town was addicted."

"Jesus, Taylor."

"You can't be that surprised. I gave you your first gun. Introduced you to Cedric. I told you I lived in the Wild West; I just didn't explain the extent of it."

Nina worried her lip with her fingers as I tossed back more courage.

"We planned on getting out of Dyer and taking Amber with us, but he got addicted himself and became something else, so I escaped by putting a bullet in his leg. And it's a severe understatement that he hasn't forgiven me."

"Oh my God." Nina sipped more of her whiskey.

"It gets a bit more interesting."

"Fuck, I thought my life was complicated." Nina chuckled ironically.

I stood and walked around my desk and took the high back leather chair next to hers.

"Nina, I fled to a man who paid my college tuition and gave me room and board in exchange for sex."

"What?" Her eyes widened as she looked at me like I'd just shot her.

"He was a tycoon, one of the richest men in Tennessee. I was still in high school when we started sleeping together."

"Jesus, Taylor!" Nina stood and paced the room, covered in shock. Her dark locks twisted in a no-nonsense chignon while she marked the carpet in three-inch heels.

I voiced the words aloud for the first time. "I was a paid whore in exchange for my education."

Nina paused and then turned to look at me.

I faced her head on. "And I can't say I'm sorry for it."

Nina tossed the last of her drink back, gripped the bottle off my desk and poured. "Fuck it, Taylor, if the last year of my life has taught me anything, it's that some people will do whatever it takes to survive."

"And that's *all* I've been doing, Nina. This success we're experiencing isn't a surprise to me. It was all carefully planned, calculated, expected. I had no other option."

Nina cringed. "What do you mean?"

"When you grow up with absolutely nothing, it can instill fear in you once you've actually got *something*."

She nodded.

"I was bred to be an addict *and* a tycoon. It's evident which part of me won. And I'm proud of that, but I can't say that I've kicked my real addiction."

Nina brought the whiskey bottle to my glass and poured. "Explain."

"At first I thought it was about kink, rough sex, control, and power, but now I know."

"Stop being so vague. There is no way you are leaving this fucking office without telling me." Nina sipped more whiskey and then looked at me pointedly. I spent the next few minutes divulging as little as possible about Daniello with uttering his name. Nina sat back and listened without judgment.

"I'll sell you back my shares before this thing explodes. And make no mistake, it *will* explode, Nina. But I want you to know, I had no idea any of this was going to happen with Amber when I agreed to partner with you. And the man, well, that's on me. I was going to wait to resign closer to Amber's court date, but I think it's best if I do it now."

"You will do no such thing."

"I'm putting you in danger. Laz is unpredictable, and I have no idea which way he's going to come at me. He's had thirteen years to get creative. You've been through enough."

"We'll up the security," she said with finality. "Everywhere."

"Your loyalty is appreciated, Nina, but it's too much. It could get you killed, bankrupted, or both."

"I don't give a shit who comes out of the woods to bury you. I'll be there to hit them with their own fucking shovel."

I laughed and let a single grateful tear roll down my face. "Thank you."

"No, Taylor, thank you. If it weren't for you stepping up when I needed someone most . . ." She expelled a long breath. "Does Cedric know?"

"He's all over it. I have two guards now. Amber does as well."

Nina winked at me. "You probably don't need any."

"At this point, I'm a little bit less practiced at guns and sharper at paperwork. I need the protection."

Nina shook her head. "I admire you, Taylor, for how far you've come. I'll never utter a word to anyone outside of this room. Your secrets are safe. Now grab your purse and let's go blow off some steam."

CHAPTER 13

Daniello

"I WAS A PAID WHORE FOR MY EDUCATION."

I jerked in my seat as Taylor confessed to her partner.

Rocco faced me with alarm. The private plane touched down in an uneasy bounce so that his question came out in an uneven rush. "What?"

I waved him off as I homed in on Taylor's words. "He's dark enough on his own."

I bit my lips to hide my grin as I pressed the buds in my ears so I wouldn't miss a word. It was wrong. They were her confessions to tell, but I didn't give a fuck. I couldn't afford to. Every day we were together we were on borrowed time, even though I was trying my hardest to change that.

Rocco attempted to interrupt me again, and I glared in his direction, unwilling to stop the recording. I was far too intrigued. I had bugged her office the day I made my proposition. And after that, her condo. I had visual and audio at the penthouse, and she had basically gathered that because I told her I watched her. But I left nothing to chance. A woman with her resources could discover a lot. Still, I was untraceable, and I had to make sure she remained faithful to our arrangement. She hadn't uttered my name to her partner.

She was loyal.

Rocco and I grabbed our bags from the overhead compartment as I heard Taylor unveil more secrets to Nina. She was careful with her words and said little about me. But it was enough to let me know my place with her.

"It is your whore," Rocco concluded as he watched my face with contempt. He ignored the warning in my eyes and made his way to where our SUV was parked. I checked my phone and saw she was at the penthouse, most likely asleep. She'd been there many times in wait for me.

And that meant something. More than it should. More than was allowable, even by my own standards. But I knew back in Tennessee I was far too engaged with her.

At home in Barga, I'd watched her undress in the penthouse and touch herself with my name on her lips. She knew of my eyes on her. She knew I would see her. I heard her every plea as she beckoned me with her touch.

It was need that drove me to her.

Lust.

And I could handle lust in all forms.

Intrigue kept me there.

And now . . .

"Imbecile," I muttered to myself as I slid my key into the door and opened it to find her sleeping. I knew the real danger lay in the way my heart beat in my chest—sharp, painful, needy.

She was right. I could ruin her.

No matter how careful I was, it wouldn't be enough to save her if things went wrong in the States and word got back home. I could leave and forget my foolish plans for stolen moments with her. I could give her any number of reasons to end our time together and be a better man for it.

But I wasn't a better man. I couldn't be. And that decision was made long before I met her.

I removed my shoes as I watched her. Her silky red hair lay against the pillow, and her eyes fluttered within a dream.

She had given her body to a man for money and gave it freely to me without regard to the price she would pay. Like me, she made no apologies for the actions that led her to the woman she had grown into. She was no whore; she was untouchable. A self-made picture of perseverance that drew breath and exhaled fire. A phoenix.

My phoenix.

I tried to wipe the foolish sentiment from my thoughts as I sat next to her on the bed. She slept soundly. I studied the rise and fall of her chest before my gaze drifted to her face. She winced, and then all her features slid back into place. Whatever dream she was in was no doubt a battle. The woman was in a constant state of unrest.

I slept in pitch black.

And that was the part of my soul that refused to apologize for the man I had grown into. No matter what act I committed, guilt eluded me. And I'd spent that decade of my life testing my limits. To others, I seemed ruthless. To my clients, invaluable.

And Taylor appealed to every part of me.

Even the man who would burn down a village to prove a point.

I was that man, and I wanted this woman. But I had years of scattered ashes in my wake. And though she'd risen from hers, I washed daily in mine.

Taylor

"Daniello." Somewhere in my dream, I felt his arms grow tight around me.

"Sleep."

His scent filled the air around me. I inhaled deep and let out a slow breath. My eyes threatened to water, and I knew it then.

It wasn't just his darkness, the intrigue that surrounded him. It was Daniello.

I gripped his arm and pulled it further around me, and he reacted by closing all of the available space between us and kept me tight in his grip.

"Did you think of me?"

I choked down my budding emotion. "Often."

He turned me over to face him as the morning sun streamed through the windows, showcasing his perfection. His dark hair was still neatly manicured and encased his sharply etched jaw. Brown eyes doused with uncertainty glittered over my face. He was gloriously naked, the evidence apparent against the outside of my thigh. He moved to hover above me, his needy cock at my entrance, his lips inches away. "Tell me to leave."

"I can't."

He closed his eyes briefly. "Tell me to go. You know this will only end bad."

"Then let it end badly." His mouth was on mine before I finished the sentence. He invaded my body, hungry and demanding, pulling out only to get my lips to beg and then throwing his hips so I felt every steel inch of him. I screamed out his name as we lost ourselves, completely immersed in satisfying our need.

We feasted and fed until we were both full.

Daniello lay in a sweaty heap as I moved to take a shower when he gripped my wrist. "My cum is still spilling out of you. Be still, Phoenix."

I raised a brow. "You want to cuddle, tough guy? I don't cuddle."

The lines in his face went hard. "Fucking do it!"

"What!?" I ripped my wrist away from him and stood my ground.

"Goddamn woman," he barked as he yanked me down to lay with him. I laughed at his outburst as he nailed me with angry eyes. We lay there quietly as a silent war raged on inside him. He looked up at the industrial ceiling in confusion as I nudged him with my elbow.

"What is *wrong* with you?"

Daniello turned to me as soon as the words came to him. "I have come to vacation with you!"

Another bout of laughter had him growling as he took residence on top of me and peered down at me, aggravated.

I lifted a brow. "Do villains get a vacation?"

He smirked. "Villains take whatever they want."

"And where would you take me?"

"Here," he said as he motioned toward the bed and then nodded toward the newly delivered sofa. "And that couch."

I pushed out a sarcastic laugh. "I'll be spoiled for other men."

He gripped my throat in warning. "No other men on vacation."

"Noted. And as tempting as it sounds and as flattered as I am that you cleared your schedule for me for 'vacation,' I have a business to run."

But I didn't. Nina and I had worked out the details. I was on leave for at least a week to "mentally recoup," as Nina had coined it, and then after I could rework a few proposals from home. Light duty until the mess blew over. And for the moment I was free. And I knew it.

Daniello didn't know of my sudden freedom, but his eyes told me differently. His shoulders fell forward as he pressed me down into the mattress in silent aggravation and then released me.

"Then go, Taylor."

I moved to take a shower and figure out how in the hell I would spend the next six weeks of my life. I paused my feet to look back and saw him watching me. "You have made a different decision?"

"I'm not good at this. I don't know what to do."

Daniello's brows furrowed. "There is nothing to *do*."

"I'm boring. I'm not any fun."

Daniello reared his head back in a laugh before he came toward me and pulled me into his hold. We stood naked with slowly building smiles. "You know, Daniello, this means you thought of *me*."

Daniello looked down at me with soft eyes. "All the day."

I rolled my eyes with a soft laugh as I gripped his hand and led him to the shower while he questioned my back with a clueless "What?"

"Amber." My breathing was erratic, and I did my best to temper my moan as Daniello planted a tongue-filled kiss on my thigh. I pushed his head away as I set my purse on the counter. We'd just gotten back from dinner, and apparently, Daniello felt it was time for dessert. He followed the slit up my black dress and invaded as

I tried to hide the overwhelming feel of him.

"Taylor, what's going on? You weren't at work today, and you didn't come home last night."

"I'm taking lea . . . leave." I fisted Daniello's hair in an attempt to pull him away. He knelt at my feet with explorative lips and eager fingers. "Just until this thing with Laz blows o . . . over!"

"What's wrong with you?"

"I'm probably going to be absent for a few days." Daniello shook his head and bit the soft flesh at the top of my thigh. ". . . a week? A week!"

He seemed satisfied with my timeline and confirmed as much as he pressed his thumb to my clit.

I could hear Amber's accusatory tone. "This wouldn't have anything to do with a sexy, dark haired god with a thick accent, would it?"

Daniello's unmistakable smile confirmed he heard every word. I gawked down at him and attempted to push him away. "I'll call you tomorrow. And call . . . call me if you need me!" I hung up just as Daniello moved my panties to the side and darted his tongue out for a long leisurely lick up my slit. I gripped his ink black hair in frustration.

"That was my sister!"

Daniello ignored my scolding completely as he fed, and my screams followed.

CHAPTER 14

Laz

"She's got that guy with her. They are holed up in some high rise." I white knuckled the wheel to my truck as Lucy whimpered next to me. "It's locked up tight, Laz. There's no way for me to get in."

"Then you fucking find a way, Derek!" Lucy turned to me with wide eyes and let out a shriek as I jumped a curb and made a beeline for her apartment. It had been a long night of running supply, and I felt a crash coming.

"No can do, Laz. I'm telling you, brother, they both have armed guards too."

I gathered my conclusion. "Cedric."

"Yeah. He's got a hawk eye on them both. New security on all fronts. He's not fucking around."

That piece of shit always had a hard-on for Taylor. It wasn't news, and I was sure he would lay his life on the line for her. I would make damn sure he lost it because of her. But tight security meant they were scared. It also meant it would be a fuck of a lot harder to get the job done once the time came.

"I just don't know how were going to get past some of this shit."

"Figure it the fuck out."

"I'm on it, man."

I hung up just as I took a parking spot in Lucy's complex. Lucy opened her door and began to cry in a pathetic attempt to gain my sympathy. I walked the path that led to her apartment with her hot on my heels. She didn't bother to wait until we were safely behind it to start her begging. "Please, Laz, I'm sick. Please, just give me one hit."

I picked up my pipe from her table, lit it, and inhaled before I blew a cloud of smoke in her face. "And what are you going to do for me?"

Her skin was ripe with new scabs, and she was pale and filthy. Her faded red hair was matted on the top of her head.

Her lips trembled as she scratched at her arms. "I feel like I'm dying."

"You look like it too." I smiled down at the almighty Lucy Hardin. The girl voted most likely to succeed. The prom queen and pride of Dyer. She was ruined, and she deserved it. Her mouth was the reason my son was no longer with his mother or me.

"Please, Laz, I'll do anything." She moved toward me in an attempt at seduction. I rolled my eyes as my phone buzzed in my pocket. She ran her hand down my chest. "Tell me what you want." My spine pricked as she lowered her head and dropped to her knees, rubbing my dick through my jeans. "I can be anything you want." She pulled the button free of my jeans and released my cock. She licked the underside of my length and gripped the head as she began to pump, her eyes down. "I can be her."

I ripped my body away as she went down on all fours. I gripped her hair and pulled it back as I looked down at her. "You can be who?"

"Taylor. I can be Taylor." I bent over, level with her face. "You don't even come close." I yanked at her head with a fistful of her disgusting locks and dragged her down the hall as she screamed for me to stop. Inside her bathroom, she shrieked as I kept her in my fist while I turned on the scalding water and discarded her in the shower.

Lucy screamed as the boiling water hit her flesh. "Take a shower, you fucking reek. And don't ever say that goddamned name again. Don't ever compare yourself to her!"

Lucy stood and quickly tempered the water and stripped. Just before I made my way out of the door, she spoke.

"Everybody knows you still love her." I moved toward her with a raised hand. Wide-eyed, she cowered in the corner.

I pulled my hand away as fear raced through her. "Not so high on the hog, now, are you, Lucy?"

"You're a monster, and you will burn in hell, Lazarus Walker. Mark my words!"

"This is hell. *Your* hell." I slammed the door and heard her cries behind it.

"I said I'm sorry! Please, Laz, please just let me go!"

I rolled my eyes as she pleaded for me to stop. I would have to cut her loose sooner or later for my own benefit. Even for an addict, she was high maintenance. I'd held her at gunpoint with a rehearsed script when she called her parents, and it seemed like enough. They were socialites in a town without Joneses to keep up with, and they would eventually require her presence at some bullshit benefit to better the shithole they reigned over. She was becoming more of a liability, and though I'd instilled enough fear in her to keep her quiet and enough meth to make her the slave I needed her to be, it could still backfire. The Hardins had enough money and connections with the Feds to chase me across state lines. But for the moment, I held the cards, and I had to play my hand just right.

I inhaled a stream of smoke again as I checked my phone.

Amber: Can we talk?

I dialed her number, and she picked up on the first ring.

"Laz, we are close to a court date

"When?"

"Soon, less than a few months."

"You getting cozy over there, Amber?"

"I'm clean. I have a job."

"That's not what I fucking asked." Her long pause was enough.

"It's different here, Laz."

"Not fucking homesick, are we?"

"I miss our son."

And there it was, the one fuck I gave about the world wrapped up in a single word.

"Then get him the fuck home."

"Laz, Taylor—"

I ended the call and scrubbed my hand down my face. I had three counties chomping at the bit for my supply. I had no one I trusted enough to care for my business, and I was losing control of Amber.

Goddamn you, Taylor.

She'd manipulated her sister the way she had me. I was completely helpless to it all until my son was legally back in his mother's arms. And even when that happened I'd have a fight on my hands.

And Taylor hadn't, for one second, forgotten how to do that. Lucy blistered my ears from behind the bathroom door while I rubbed at the scar on my leg.

"Laz, you think rich people are happier?"

Taylor was staring out the window of my truck, her body present, her mind somewhere in a daydream as we drove down the back roads toward another sunset.

I looked her way. She had on the same jeans she's worn the past three years and a lightly stained tank top, her ratty clothes did shit to taint her beauty. "I don't think money solves everything, Red."

"I think it does." She looked over at me with glossy eyes.

I shook my head. "Look at George Hardin. Big house, beautiful wife, he owns half the county and fucks his secretary on the sly. That ain't happy."

"I'll never get married."

"The hell you won't," I said with a wink her way. "You're going to marry me."

Taylor rolled her eyes and looked out the window again as we passed the Rucker farm. It had been the latest in a string of family farms to go bankrupt.

"We can buy that place, make it our own."

Taylor's head snapped to me before her eyes narrowed. "We aren't staying in Dyer."

I shrugged. "What's so wrong with home? It's where we met. Nothing wrong with staying close. Hell, if it will make you happy, we can move two counties over. I've got friends out there."

Mouth parted with accusing eyes, she scoured me. "Are you serious?"

"Why the hell not? This place is as good as anyplace else."

That was the moment I lost her.

It took me years to figure it out. But I saw it that day, in her eyes. Her decision. A month later, she put a hole in my leg.

"She became Ray Tyco's whore when she left here, you know."

"What?" I turned to see Lucy wiping her hair with a towel while a satisfied smirk played at her lips. She had my attention, and she knew it. "He was my father's business associate. Ray Tyco, he—"

"I know who the fuck he is."

Her smile went full Cheshire. I would knock every tooth from her lying mouth. "Give me a hit, and I'll tell you the rest."

I pulled the gun from the back of my jeans, and she shook her head. "Do whatever you want, Laz, but I'm not telling you shit until you let me hit that pipe."

With a plan to make her pay, I motioned toward the pipe, and she snatched it up without a second thought and inhaled deeply. Once she was flying, she began to sing like a canary. It was the first time Lucy Hardin's big fucking mouth had ever been useful.

CHAPTER 15

Taylor

"Where are we going?"

Daniello drove my Chevelle with ease as he navigated his way through the crowded peninsula.

"It is a surprise."

"I'm not a fan of those." Armed with only my purse and my clothes from the previous night and a slight headache from the whiskey, I was forced to play along. Daniello's mood was light and playful, and I was curious to see how our day would pan out. He glanced my way as I winced at the sun invading the car.

"I may need a little hair of the dog."

Daniello pressed his lips into a line, his eyes full of question.

"A shot of whiskey," I explained. I spotted a liquor store. "Can you stop here?"

Daniello parked. Armed with a small bottle, I rejoined him in the car, uncapped it, and took a hearty sip.

He scrutinized the bottle, looking for answers. "Hair of the dog?"

"The same of what you drank the night before to get rid of

the headache."

Daniello's lips twitched. "And do you feel better?"

"I will." I took another pull of the whiskey and the corner of his mouth lifted while he raised his brows. "I suspect it is time for more south woman."

I capped the bottle and threw it in the back seat. "Not a chance. Take me home, please. I want to change."

"You can change when we get to where we are going." There was no sense in arguing, so I let him drive. "Daniello, we can't go far. Amber may need me."

"Rocco is watching Amber."

"Is that supposed to make me feel better?"

Daniello turned to me. "He will not let harm come to her."

Cedric was also watching her along with a team of body-guards. It was more protection than I could offer. I sank back in my seat.

"Tell me more about Barga."

Daniello paused in thought before he spoke. "My villa is on the outside of the city. I live there alone now when I do not travel. My mother died a few years ago."

"How did she die?"

"She slept into her death."

I saw no emotion or change in his posture. "You weren't close?"

"She lived her life. I do not have emotions for death."

"So, you don't get sad at funerals?" I had only been to one.

"I do not attend funerals."

Daniello turned onto the interstate, pulled up a small black box, and placed it on the dash.

"What's that?" I moved to grab it, and he swatted my hand.

"It is not a toy."

"Fine," I said, massaging my reddened hand. "Barga."

We drove for hours past the Georgia and Florida state lines

as Daniello spoke in cliff notes about his life. He spoke of his favorite bakery. Of the olive trees that surrounded his property. About his sister, Tula, and nine children and how she ruled her home with an iron fist. I had to admit I was curious.

"She is stronger than any man I have ever met and has hard will close to yours."

"Iron will," I corrected carefully.

He nodded. "Iron will. She and I are very much the same. We are very protective of each other." His eyes were transfixed into a distant memory he didn't share.

"When did you meet your wife?"

"Before I left for the army."

"You were in the army?"

"For a short time, yes."

I pressed for more. "And then you became a bad guy?"

Daniello paused and then turned to me. "We spoke of this before."

"But you *know* my secrets."

"Do not ask me again," he threatened, his voice full of finality.

Mafia.

He had to be connected. Of that I was sure. The intimidation he brought with just a look spoke volumes and only confirmed the fact that he was a shot caller.

The more I swore I wouldn't press, the more curious I got. And the less he revealed to me, the more I was convinced that no matter what, when I was ready to resume my position at Scott Solutions, Daniello would have to be far removed from my life. I felt the clock begin to tick on our involvement at that moment and dread coursed through my veins.

"Whatever it is, Daniello, you can trust me."

"It is not about trust," he gritted out. "But you have made it difficult."

I felt the jab, knowing he was referring to the night I let Damien kiss me.

More doubts seeped through, and I could only think of darker scenarios.

"Have you ever killed a lover?"

"Goddamnit, Taylor!" Daniello cut off every car in the lanes to the right of us as he pulled onto the shoulder and glared in my direction. "You are still reckless with your tongue, with your life. Even with my warning. You demand patience, but you expect too much!"

"I just want to know who you are!"

"And I am giving you all that I can!"

Out of nowhere, a truck pulled up a few hundred yards ahead of us on the shoulder and began backing up in our direction. It came to a halt just inches from my bumper. The angry driver—no doubt a result of Daniello's erratic parking—got out of the truck and came barreling toward us as I gripped Daniello's arm. He had Daniello's weight by at least a hundred pounds and was covered in tattoos. Daniello didn't so much as glance in his direction, his eyes fixed on me. "You want to know?"

I glanced at the man as he stalked toward us. "Daniello, don't. Oh God, don't. Daniello, *please* don't."

"Get the fuck out of the car, asshole!" Hundreds of cars whizzed past us while he beat on Daniello's window with an intent fist.

Daniello moved in close, his lips a whisper from mine. "Don't close your eyes, Phoenix." In a flash, he was out of the car. The man had one threatening word out of his mouth before Daniello made his move. In seconds, the man was screaming in pain, mutilated and bloody, as his eyes searched fruitlessly for help and met mine through the windshield. Before I could open my door, the screaming stopped, and the man went completely limp. Daniello dragged his body to his truck, placed him in the driver's seat, slammed the door, and made quick work of getting us back onto the interstate.

All of it lasted fifteen seconds.

It took fifteen seconds for Daniello to show me who he was.

We pulled to a stop at a hotel on Amelia Island, a sleepy beach town off the Florida coast. A valet opened my door, and Daniello tipped him as I moved in a zombie-like stupor into the hotel. I waited by the elevator as Daniello checked us in and then followed him into the small space as he pressed the number to reach our floor. He gripped my arm by the elbow and guided me into our room. I sat at the edge of the bed in the massive suite with my eyes to the floor.

"I am hungry." Daniello loosened his tie and opened the mini bar fridge. He plucked a Jack Daniels mini from it and tossed it on the bed next to me. I eyed the bottle and then looked to him.

Daniello's expression was completely void of remorse.

Death was his business.

I uncapped the bottle, swallowed all the whiskey, and motioned to him for another. He brought this bottle to me and tilted my head with a fistful of my hair and brought it to my lips.

I swallowed the bottle as he stood with me in his grip until my throat was coated with whiskey. His eyes danced over my face with a touch of apprehension before he freed me.

"I will not force you to stay."

I bit my lip and nodded.

"I will leave you to your decision." He picked up his jacket and walked out of the room.

CHAPTER 16

Daniello

"YOU ALONE?" A WOMAN TOOK THE SEAT NEXT TO ME AT THE hotel bar. She smelled of too much perfume. I glanced her way as she smiled at me. "I could use some company, handsome."

She brushed her leg against mine, and I expelled a harsh breath as she forced my reply. She was a woman in her late forties and wore too much makeup to disguise it. "I am in no mood for company."

"Oh, I love your accent! Come on now, don't be shy." She had a southern accent that made my chest tighten. She slid a careful finger down my arm. "We're in this beautiful place; we should have some fun."

The bartender greeted the spirited woman with a smile. "What'll it be?"

She wrinkled her nose as she sniffed my drink. "Strawberry margarita."

I pulled some money from my pocket and threw it on the bar in front of her. "I wish you well."

"Bummer," she said to the bartender as I took my drink

and walked poolside and took a chair to stare at the sea. I had no business here. I had taken too many liberties with Taylor. Her tantrum with that man at the bar still cut me deep. She wanted truth, pushed me for it, and now she had it. She would never look at me the same, and it was for the best. I had to instill fear into her. I had to make her believe. It was the only way we could continue. *The only way.* I had just taken a man's life, but I would do anything to keep her.

Anything.

Death was easy. Too easy.

It had been my life, my way, my reason for existing on this fucked up Earth, until I saw her at that club in Savannah. Years of living like a savage had forced me to a place where very little light existed, but Taylor's light forced her way under my skin and into my veins.

I had seen all sides of her and accepted them. But even with all her strength, she had human limits I'd grown immune to over time. For years I'd watched unimaginable and vicious slaughter due to man's greed and became indifferent to the effect of death, to the act of taking life. I had just shown her the darkest part of me. And it was just a glimpse of my capabilities. I was a trained killer. Emotion played no part in it. It did not affect me to take a life, not the type of life that I felt I had to extinguish. And I did not spare her from the truth.

My only regret was that I had burdened her with it.

I sat for endless minutes, watching the sun disappear below the sea. If she had left, fled from me, I knew my place with her. I would accept it.

"It was my fault."

I released a breath and closed my eyes. When I opened them, I saw the guilt in hers as she stood above me.

"You did not kill him."

"I pushed do you to do it."

"You have no such effect over me." I watched her as she regarded me carefully like the dangerous man I was. It was exactly what I needed her to do. I needed her to believe. It kept her safe. I was quickly discouraged as she knelt down by the side of my chair, her knees on the concrete, with forgiving and desperate eyes. Her life, the struggles she'd faced, had led her to understand me. It made me feel more human. Capable of more than the pain I've inflicted. That was her effect. In her eyes, I didn't exist as a shadow but as a worthy man. She reminded me of a past life, where I was capable of being flesh, bone, and a beating heart.

Watching her reaction to me, I'd never seen a woman so beautiful, and in the depths of her carefully guarded but soulful eyes, I saw the sadness that went with that understanding. My chest seized when I realized I was a part of that sadness.

She leaned in and whispered over my lips, "You promised me you would be as truthful as you could."

"That is the truth. I took his life for my own protection, for yours. If I left him to live, there would have been a struggle. The police maybe would have been involved. I have made every trip in and out of this country undetected."

Taylor sighed. "I'm sorry. I don't know why I did that."

I heard it on her recording with her partner, Nina. She was attracted to the darkness; and I was the abyss.

I pulled my drink to my lips, and she took it and placed it on the ground beneath us.

"Do you want to return home?"

"No." Taylor gripped my fingers, kissing them one by one before she brought them beneath her dress to the lace of her underwear. She was wet for me.

So. Fucking. Wet.

I gripped her throat, and in a quick invasion, plunged my fingers into her as I whispered in her ear, "Who do you want to fuck you tonight?" Her breath hitched as she looked between us at my working hand and then rode my fingers with abandon. Without regard to anyone who lurked around us, she faced me head on.

My phoenix.

"Give me everything, Daniello. I want *all* of you."

Relief and hunger flooded my veins as she melted into my touch.

I pressed harder against her delicate neck as she came on my fingers and whispered her request. "Fuck me."

Taylor

Daniello stood at the foot of our destroyed hotel bed the next morning with a small bag. I winced at the discomfort between my legs and looked up to see the smug satisfaction in his eyes.

"What's in the bag?"

"Your work suit for the next days."

He tossed the bag in my direction, and I pulled out a solid green string bikini. It looked ridiculously expensive, and the price tag confirmed as much.

"My uniform, huh?"

Daniello nodded. "Yes, uniform."

And what will you wear?

He was sporting the same suit we arrived in, and it looked worse for wear. He lifted his hand. "I bought a bag of my own." He pulled out a pair of the loudest yellow swim trunks I'd ever seen, and I laughed as he deadpanned, "It was either this wetsuit or birds." He shrugged.

"You've got something against birds?"

We shared a laugh as he bent down to take my lips. I pulled

away swiftly as my body reminded me of the damage inflicted the night before. "No, no, no."

Daniello pulled back, gripped my hand, and pulled me from the mattress.

"I will maybe give you a break."

"Gee, thanks," I said with a sigh.

"Gee, thanks," he mocked poorly and then slapped my ass. "Put on your uniform. We have much to do."

"Oh yeah, like what?"

"This is your idea of vacation?"

We lay on the beach, side by side, on plush, hotel-supplied beach towels as I slathered on sunblock. The golden man beside me watched the beachgoers.

"This is American vacation tradition, no?"

"We could have done this in Charleston."

Daniello raised a brow as he watched a toddler prance past us with a new sand shovel. "No one knows who we are here. You are known well in Charleston."

"True." But I doubted any of my associates would stoop to a Charleston beach day. They spent their time in places far more exotic.

Daniello turned to me. His dark eyes followed the path of my hands as I massaged the lotion in.

"In Florida, we are Mr. and Mrs. Di Giovanni."

"No thanks," I said with as much sarcasm as I could muster. Lightning fast, he pulled me on top of him so we were chest to chest. His skin was on fire as he smiled up at me.

"Why not live like the rest of them? These people are stupid in bliss."

He gripped the sides of my face with imploring eyes.

"Blissfully ignorant." I gave him a wicked smile. "And we'll do it our way because we aren't like the rest of them."

He leaned in close. "I agree."

I placed my head on his shoulder while he wrapped his sculpted arms around me.

"This is a cuddle." His shoulders moved, and I heard the rumble of his laugh as the sun beat down on my back. I ignored his remark and let myself relax into him.

What he'd done the day before had shaken me, but I couldn't for one second deny that I knew the truth before he'd revealed it to me. He'd killed three men in Tennessee without regard for who they were and only because they were a threat to me.

For the first time in my life, I felt the protection of a man. As perverse as it was, as immoral and corrupt as Daniello seemed to be, he fed my sick need. My sinner thrived on his chaos. And for just a few more stolen moments of my life, I would indulge her.

"I'm not afraid of you."

Daniello paused the easy exploration of his soothing hands. "So foolish."

"I'm not afraid to die."

"Ah, but you would fight to your death, Taylor."

"Goddamned right I would."

Daniello's chest shook as he gripped me impossibly closer. "I find you *very* fun."

For six days, we lived like a king and queen, feasted on the fruits of the ocean and then each other's bodies. Daniello took an occasional angry phone call from Rocco. The hatred spewed was unmistakable as he quickly exited the room to spare me from his wrath.

Aside from that and an all clear from Amber, we were free to just . . . be.

Without a real agenda, we were slightly lost and stumbled through Amelia Island like any other tourists. But the hotel provided so much sanctuary, we rarely left. Daniello spoke freely of his life, his family, his sister. And every so often I would see a looming sadness in his eyes when he talked about home. There was a missing piece.

I knew he was just as out of his element as I was, but we sank into a new rhythm together. We were making memories far more unforgettable than the ones we shared in the beginning.

I was toweling off another day in the sun when I caught Daniello staring at me. He was gloriously naked with his hand clasped behind his head on the king bed I was sure they would have to replace when we checked out. Squeezing the water out of my hair, I gave him a small smile.

"What?"

"Are you happy with this vacation?"

I sat bare next to him, the towel in my lap forgotten. My breath hitched, and it had everything to do with the intensity in his eyes. But it was more emotion than heat.

"I think you know that answer."

My belly fluttered as his eyes implored mine. "If I have made you feel . . . alone . . ." He faltered as he swallowed hard. It was an apology.

He grabbed the hand on my thigh and held it. I looked down at him with confusion. "What?"

"Lay here. With me." It was a question and, of course, an order. Without waiting for a reply, he pulled me into his arms and buried his nose in my hair. I felt the need between us and some of the pain from missing him slip away as we drifted together into the darkness and both dreamed of light.

The morning of our last day, Daniello decided we would both be "fat as pigs" if we didn't get in some rigorous exercise.

After breakfast, armed in matching island T-shirts, Daniello proceeded to strip me bare.

He pushed his well-used banana swim trunks down, his thick cock on proud display.

"I think we've covered *this* exercise."

"Get on your knees, hands to the floor." His eyes were fire as he commanded my attention with a simple change in tone.

On the floor, I waited with bated breath. Daniello moved behind me and pushed my thighs apart. I felt his breath tickle my sensitive flesh as he leaned in and darted his tongue out.

"Ah."

I gripped the carpet as he slid the pad of his finger up my thigh while the ache began to build. He traced my entrance achingly slow before I felt his tongue flutter over my clit.

"Fuck."

Silence behind me.

I hated that I couldn't read his reaction to me. My legs began to shake as he licked me from bottom to top in one slow sweep. My knees buckled, and I was brought back up with commanding hands. A thick finger dipped in, penetrating me for mere seconds before the flick of his tongue replaced it.

"Jesus." I ripped at the carpet as I fought my tongue to keep from begging.

Another slow lick had me reeling. I moaned out his name and felt the tickle of his hair as he nestled his head between my feet and brought me down to sit on his face.

"Oh GOD!" I rode his hungry mouth and felt his chest

vibrate with satisfaction. Just as I was about to peak, he pulled away. "I love the taste of you." He slapped my clit with his fingers, and I damned near hit the ceiling.

"Please."

Daniello pulled me from the floor and flipped me to hover above him. I gripped his cock and centered myself. Just as the full feeling hit, my instinct to ride it out was cut short with a clipped order.

"Do not move."

Daniello drew his knees up behind me, crossed his arms over his chest and pulled up so his breath hit my hardened nipples. My body jerked on top of him with every subtle thrust of his, hips in need of more friction. I was dripping while his cock pulsed with every movement. He was the picture of control as I fought my every instinct to move. He pulled up repeatedly, his stomach tensing, chest rippling, and robbed me of his feel, only to impale me when his back hit the floor. His dark eyes were fire as he worked his torso, his abs glistening, his eyes liquid pools of ink.

"Fuck." I tilted my head back as he lifted up and captured my nipple between his teeth and bit down before he resumed his torture.

His thick cock slid slowly against my clit as I panted in wait. Unable to handle another second, I clawed at his chest as his hands gripped my ass and spread it.

Eyes locked, I pumped my body faster and harder than I ever thought possible. Daniello hissed as he gripped me in his hands and I rode him like a woman possessed.

His praise hit me right in the chest. "So. Fucking. Beautiful."

"Daniello." I whimpered as my hips buckled and my orgasm breached.

"Cover my cock," he growled before he thrust up and jerked my hips back and forth with bruising fingers. My orgasm spiked to an explosion, and I screamed out his name in defeat as my body pulsed and shuddered.

Daniello pulled air through his teeth, pushed me onto my back, and dipped his head between my thighs, sucking my clit as I quaked beneath him, gasping. He fed and fed until I was drawn tight and went over. Once satisfied, he lifted my lower half off the floor and buried himself as I choked on the fullness.

His eyes closed as a powerful current passed between us, and my heart tightened when he opened them.

"Phoenix."

"Don't stop."

"Jesus Christ," he grunted out while he pumped furiously until we were both in a frenzy, breathless and full of emotion. Hot tears streamed down my face, stemming from pleasure, our connection, and belonging. Because it had never been clearer.

I belonged to Daniello.

I came, clenching him as he submerged himself. One powerful thrust after another, praise and lust in his eyes. His cock jerked as he brought himself down to the carpet to hover above me. He moved us both while he gripped my hair and slammed his lips against mine, invading my mouth with a hungry tongue. Answering that hunger with my own, I gripped his shoulders as I pulsed under him before detonating. With one last thrust, I felt him fill me before he ripped himself away and spilled over, his fist pumping the very last of him onto my chest.

He collapsed next to me as we lay recovering on the carpet, both moved and speechless.

Minutes later, I gripped Daniello's hand and turned to him with a smile. "I'm willing to bet the blissfully ignorant don't vacation like this."

Daniello's dead expression wiped the smile right off my face.

CHAPTER 17

Taylor

"WHAT'S WRONG?"

Daniello's golden eyes swept my body as he stood and gripped my hand. "We must go."

"Why must we go?"

I felt my heart sink as he distanced himself from me and began to dress. "Rocco is not a happy man."

"That's not news." I slipped on one of the three sundresses I'd purchased at a local shop and played immune to his sudden indifference, though it tore me to shreds. Whatever was happening between us wasn't supposed to be happening. This much we knew. Still, as I checked the room for any of my newly purchased possessions, I felt the weight of his stare.

"What, Daniello? Just say it." I braved a glance his way as he cast his eyes away.

"Let us go."

On the way back to Charleston, Daniello kept his eyes on the highway as I masked my sulking in my seat. Indifference. I knew indifference. I'd been its whore.

"Your GPA is down."

I gave Ray big eyes. "I've been up late a lot lately." My smug smile was ignored as he tore into me. Blue eyes scorned me from across the table. "Don't waste my money."

"I'm not wasting your money. It's a half point. I can handle a half point."

He forked a bite of his steak. "Long days and late nights are the way to success."

I sipped my white wine, exasperated. "Maybe if I cut out the exercise. Lord knows I'm getting enough with my gentlemen caller."

Ray's jaw flexed, his lips tight. "This isn't fucking funny."

"Jesus, stop playing the part of father." I rolled my eyes and jumped when he knocked my plate from underneath me.

Incredulous, I lashed out. "I was hungry!"

"Stay that way!" He moved to get up with his plate in hand. "I'll dine in my bedroom."

Hot on his heels and stomach rumbling, I refused to let it go. "Maybe if you weren't fucking me every night, I could get more sleep!"

He paused before he turned to me with menace. "Not another word."

Exasperated, aware no defense would work, I knew it was pointless, but I dug in anyway. "I'm exhausted! And it's a half a point!"

Ray's brows drew together. "It's the difference between the school you want and the school you settle for."

I shrugged. "So what! Princeton, Brown. I'll take any of them."

Ray walked toward me and pinned me to the table. Setting his plate down he looked behind him to Olivia. "Shut the door."

"Yes, sir."

Once we were alone, I felt my skin start to thrum with anticipation. Ray had other plans. "So now we're backtracking? Any of them? Any. Of. Them? That's not how you win. You set your sights on one fucking thing, and when you attain that, you move onto the next. You don't settle."

I shrugged with a bite in my voice. "Fine, I'll work harder."

"Smarter," he corrected as he gripped my face. "Smarter. Order and

excellence, Taylor."

"Yes, sir," I snapped as I pulled my face away. My disobedience seemed to eat at him as I refused to indulge. I was exhausted. I had months left and a lot to prove before I flew his coop with my inheritance. Not that being with Ray was so horrible. He showered me with gifts and gave me the attention he was capable of. There were no more women, at least, not at the house. It seemed he'd finally accepted our situation. And I loved the things he did to my body. It always came with the price of his immediate absence. We never slept in the same bed. And he never, not once, let me forget my place.

He peered down at me with intent eyes. "You . . ." His breath came out harsh. "You can do this, Taylor."

"I will," I swore as he tipped my chin up with his finger. "I will, Ray. I promise."

"You never take second, ever."

"I got it." Ray's forehead began to bead with sweat, and he was paling rapidly.

I wiped the moisture off his brow with my palm, and he jerked from my grasp. "What's wrong?"

"Flu or something. Go to bed. I'll see you in the morning."

"What are you thinking of?"

Daniello's voice was distant but snapped me out of my haze. "A friend."

"You do not have any friends." His voice was cool, much like that of the man who had been haunting me. I couldn't help but think Ray's manifestation in my thoughts was a warning of sorts. A way of telling me I was throwing it all away.

"You don't know everything," I said with pure contempt. I didn't know what his issue was, but he had just ruined a good amount of blissful days with his temperament. "Fine, I was thinking about a man I used to fuck."

Daniello's jaw ticked as he glared at the Chevy in front of us. "I do not wish to know this."

An hour later, he pulled into the garage, and as soon as he

was parked, I jumped out of the car and rounded the bumper to take the wheel. "Thanks for the vacation."

Daniello stood with the door open, the key ring on his finger. "It is not over."

"I've got news for you, buddy—"

Daniello frowned. "What news?"

I let out a sarcastic laugh as he gripped my shoulders. "I was deep in my thoughts, Taylor Ellison."

"Fine. Can I go?"

"No." Daniello slammed the door behind him as I held out my hand for my keys. He put them in his pocket and began to walk toward the elevator.

"I'm leaving!"

"You are staying." It was a warning. One I didn't give a shit about.

"You can't force me to stay," I snapped as he made his way into the elevator. He turned on me and gripped me to him as the doors closed. "We have vacation to do."

"Daniello—" His mouth crushed mine as I pushed at his chest. His tongue prodded in possession until I had no choice but to open for him. His kiss filled me, unlocked something inside me, and his tongue claimed the rest. When he pulled away, he left an inch between us. "I will stay for more vacation."

"What?" I stared up at him, dazed, his dark eyes trying to convey more than his lips.

"You. Are. Staying." It was an infuriating order.

I pushed at his chest in vain. "If you want a fight, you're about to get one."

His slow smile told me everything before his lips moved. "Then let us fight."

"No, Taylor."

"Just try it."

Daniello lay in bed, gloriously naked and draped in a sheet with fresh nail marks covering his chest, his nose upturned at my offered cracker.

"It looks like a child's vomit."

"It's pimento. Olive-flavored cheese."

He pushed at my intrusive hand. "I do not want it."

With his protest and open mouth, I took the opportunity and shoved the cracker in. His eyes widened as I wiped at the spilled cheese over his lips with my fingers. He glared at me with a mouth full as he chewed. Within seconds, his eyes glittered over the tub in my hand.

"Delicious, right?"

Around his bite, he answered enthusiastically, "It is *very* good."

"It's the caviar of the South." I laughed as he pulled the tub from my hand and devoured it.

Through heavy mouthfuls, he questioned me, a man in love. "How much is this caviar?"

"About six dollars. A little less if you buy the cheap shit."

Daniello looked at me with wide eyes. "Six dollars? For caviar?" He harrumphed as I kept my laugh inside. After shoving the last cracker in his mouth, he patted his loaded stomach and stretched out with a smile. "Maybe that will be one point for America."

I rolled my eyes. "I'll let the others know."

With full bellies, we lay in bed "vacationing" and watching the sailboats in the harbor. Charleston was our version of reality TV. We'd spent the last few days playing penthouse. I'd taken a few business calls, and Daniello had disappeared for a few hours to meet Rocco, but other than that, we were inseparable.

The previous night we'd drank a couple bottles of wine while he made me his favorite Italian cookie, Bruttiboni. He said there was only one bakery in Barga that made them "to his liking." I watched his every move, slowly seduced as he spoke. He was at ease and totally animated while he destroyed the kitchen. Flour clung to his eyelashes, streaked his nose, and covered his T-shirt. I couldn't help my smile as I realized the most lethal man in Charleston was baking cookies for me.

It was only minutes after the last batch was cooling on the rack that he'd tied me up and slapped my pussy until I begged him for his cock.

The man was anything *but* boring.

"What are you thinking of now, Phoenix?"

Daniello traced my nipple with his finger before he closed his mouth over it. I sighed out the truth as I gripped his thick hair. "You."

His lashes fluttered as I opened for him and he nestled between my thighs. He ran his hands through the length of my hair as he looked down at me. "No thoughts of friends?"

"No."

He placed an unusually soft kiss on my lips and pulled back. It was there. All of it.

He scrutinized me as his phone rang somewhere in the mess of sheets. He retrieved it with a pained look on his face and then answered it to angry Arabic. He shot out of bed and was dressed and out the door within a minute with a rushed, "I will return."

I spoke to the ceiling as the door closed behind him. "I guess vacation is over."

CHAPTER 18

Daniello

"You fucking fool," Rocco spit out as I jumped into the passenger side of the truck.

"I will change this. I will make this right."

Rocco whipped the SUV around the sharp curves of the garage as I glanced in his direction. His tone was full of contempt as he tore into me. "You cost us the contract playing with your whore!"

"I did no such thing." I pulled my phone from my pocket.

"Too late!" Rocco sat at the exit and glared at me. "I already spoke to him."

It took everything I had not to rip him apart where he sat. "Tell me what he said."

"He asked what kept you."

My whole body tensed as I looked to my cousin. "You told him."

Rocco nodded as he sped out of the garage.

Taylor

"One week!" Amber pranced around my condo, full of excitement. "God, that lawyer is a miracle worker!"

One week meant it had been a month since I'd heard from Daniello. With every day that passed, I grew more frantic. I slept at the penthouse for a solid week then gave up. Our vacation was most definitely over. But were we? And my worry for him in the state he left only worsened the dread in my chest. Was he alive?

I shook away the thought as the heavy feeling threatened to overtake me. We weren't supposed to have lasted this long. It wasn't supposed to be this hard. But it took very little to stir the feelings I had for him, even in his absence. I felt our connection no matter how far the space between us. I bathed in his soap and was clouded in our memories. I needed answers, but mostly I needed to know he was still out there.

"Earth to Taylor."

"I'm sorry, what?"

"I was thinking we could go shopping for a toddler bed to put next to mine."

"Amber," I said carefully, "if you don't get custody—"

"I will. I just know it." She shook away my doubts. "I've called every night sober. His mother knows I'm clean."

"If she's attached to Joseph, we have to be prepared for a fight." I shrugged after seeing Amber's light dim. "But let's just think positive, right?"

"Right." Her phone pinged with a text, and she looked over at me.

"Laz?"

"No. It's a work friend." She sent a text and set her phone face down. "You will love Joseph, Taylor. He's so smart. He's such a happy little boy."

"I will," I agreed, though I had little to no experience with children other than Amber.

Her smile disappeared as she studied me. "If Laz tries anything—"

"We'll be ready. He has no idea we're coming, right?"

"Either that or he's playing ignorant. His mother won't speak to him. Won't let him over. There is a good chance we could get in and out."

"Then that's the plan."

"And if he catches us?"

"Cedric will step in."

"Right." She nodded as she looked at screen shot she took of FaceTime with Joseph. "Right."

The flight to Memphis and the short car ride after to Dyer felt like the longest trip I'd ever taken in my life. Cedric had eyes on Laz, and from what he was told hourly, Laz hadn't emerged from Lucy's apartment since he went in late the night before. Our court time was at 8:00 a.m. There was a good chance we could pull it off. I drove the rental with white knuckles as we passed the desert I swore I'd never return to for the second time. When we got to the courthouse, Amber could barely control herself when her son came into view in the arms of his mother.

"Taylor?" Stacy Walker looked between the two of us as Joseph squirmed in her arms. The minute Joseph saw his mother, his excited screams turned into a pleading wail. I studied Joseph for the first time. He was a duplicate of his father.

"Wow, Taylor, you look so fancy." Forcing my eyes away from the baby, I turned to greet his mother.

"Hi, Stacy."

"You look . . ." She bit her lip as Joseph reached for Amber. "You look *so* nice."

"Thank you." Amber's eyes implored hers, and Stacy handed over the baby, not taking her eyes from me. "I always wondered what happened to you."

"I went to college." *I left your son shot in a motel room to whore my way through business school.*   ,

"Amber never told me she was staying with you."

Surprised, I looked over to Amber, who shrugged. "I didn't know if you wanted anyone to know."

"Yes, she's been with me the entire time. Things are good. She's sober." Stacy's shock was unmistakable as she looked over to Amber. "I can see."

"Janice Adler." Amber's attorney intervened with the presentation of her hand in Stacy's face and shook it before she addressed the three of us. "We really shouldn't communicate too much before the hearing."

Stacy was still fixated on me, and I saw an opportunity. Ray's voice a whisper in my ear. *"You can do this, kitten."*

"Actually, Stacy, do you mind if we talk privately for a moment?"

Laz's eyes stared back at me. She looked older than her years, and I was positive she had on the same blue dress she wore the day I met her. It was far worse for wear and stained from years of heavy use. "I guess that would be okay."

CHAPTER 19

Taylor

AFTER A STERN WARNING FROM THE JUDGE, AMBER HELD JOSEPH tightly to her chest with relief-covered features as we walked out of the courthouse. Our lawyer reminded us we still had work to do upon our return to Charleston with a curt, "I will be in touch."

Fearful of an impending backlash, I darted my eyes around as Cedric opened the car door for the three of us, an unmistakable smile on his face. He knew how much the day meant to me personally. We were a family. For the first time in our lives, we were *truly* a family. Amber buckled Joseph into the new car seat she bought only an hour before. She sat in back with the baby as Cedric and I kept our eyes peeled. I let out an audible breath once we crossed the county line and made it onto the interstate, headed toward the airport.

"I don't understand. Are you sure we aren't being followed?" I glanced in the rearview and saw nothing but pavement and blue sky.

"I'm just as fucking surprised—

"Hey, language," Amber protested.

"Sorry," Cedric apologized as he darted his eyes my way. "He's still at Lucy Hardin's apartment. My guess is he crashed."

"This was just too easy." I glanced back at my sister, who shrugged. "He goes down hard after a week sometimes."

New hope filled me as I realized we were going to be safe at home within a matter of hours.

Cedric gripped my hand. "Let's go catch a plane."

Amber smiled down at her son. "Ready to go on your first airplane, buddy?"

"Truck," Joseph replied as he pointed to his T-shirt.

Amber's tearful laugh was music to my ears.

It seemed, for fucking once, life had cut the Ellison sisters a break.

Laz

I woke up with the worst headache of my life. I'd been going hard for a week straight and finally managed to pass out. I gripped my head and yelled for Lucy.

"What?" It was obvious she'd found my personal stash; her pupils were blown.

"Get me some water. Bring me my pipe. If you smoked more than I gave you, you're fucked."

"Whatever." My phone buzzed on her bedside table, and I reached for it as she walked in with the water and my fix.

"How long was I out?"

"Night before last."

"Fuck."

I opened my phone to see the damage. I was responsible for too much supply. I knew it would take a couple of days to catch up.

I sorted through the endless mess of texts when I saw Derek's.

11:00 p.m.

Heads up, they're on the move, and Cedric is with them.

11:15 p.m.

Where the fuck are you?

11:30 p.m.

Answer my goddamn call. I think they are on their way to Dyer. They just hit the interstate.

12:00 a.m.

What the fuck, Laz?

1:00 a.m.

Stay or go, man?

2:00 a.m.

I'm three hours behind, now answer the phone!

Fuck it, I'm coming.

I shot out of bed as a fist landed on the front door.

"Jesus, what now?" Lucy said as she reached the door and eyed the peephole. I knocked her out of the way and ripped it open to see Derek with his fist up, ready to hammer again.

"Finally, man, what the fuck!" He was strung out and smelled like garbage. I had no doubt he'd smoked everything I sent with him, and his main reason for coming back was for more.

Everyone's favorite drug was more.

He palmed his greasy blond hair off of his forehead. "Gotta foil?"

I clenched my fists. "Where are they?"

Derek barreled through the door and barked at Lucy. "Get me something to drink."

He turned to me with his hands up and spoke to me like a parent talking to his child. "They were here. I talked to my sister who knows a girl who works at the courthouse. They had a hearing today. Judge handed him over to Taylor. She's got temporary custody." I could fucking hear the *I told you so* in his tone.

Rage boiled through my veins as I gripped him by the collar. "Where's my fucking son?"

"I didn't make it back in time, Laz. They're gone."

Derek sat in the cab of my truck and spouted off his excuses. "I tried, man, but there was nothing I could do. I was waiting on orders. I didn't know if I should stay or go. I'm so fucking sorry, Laz." Glaring at Derek, I threw the truck into gear as we backed out of the motel. I didn't trust Lucy enough around a fresh stash, so I kept it there. The cops I kept on my payroll sat in the parking lot to watch over it. No one fucked with me in my own town. *No one.* And that goddamned bitch had managed to sneak in like a thief and take my son. And I knew the judge who handed him over so easily was the same bastard who had sentenced me to months in juvie. He would pay too.

"Fuck. It's good to be home." Derek inhaled a foil and tried to pass it my way. I waved it off as he rolled down the window and lit a cigarette.

"Want one?"

"Yeah." I took the butt from his fingers and smoked as he rattled on.

"It's a nice place. And Amber is clean. Like really clean. She looks good and has a job working for Taylor. Someplace downtown called Scott Solutions."

My pocket buzzed.

Amber: Court date in two weeks!

She was trying to buy time. Amber was no longer loyal.

Swallowing down the urge to react, I drove out to the back-woods while Derek smoked the rest of the foil. "Seems to me, Laz, Joseph is in good hands out there. It's a beautiful city. You could work this out with Amber. You could get a spot out there. Open a market out there too. I wouldn't mind a little beachside place."

Loyalty.

It didn't fucking exist.

"Yeah," I said as my face flushed and my body boiled. "Tell me about the building."

"Taylor's boyfriend's place? He's fucking hard to keep a thumb on, man. One minute he's in the building, the next he just fucking disappears. I don't think he's a guy you want to fuck with."

I cut my eyes his way.

"No offense, man, but he seems like the fucking type that would excel in body disposal. He's Armenian or some shit. He's not around a lot. Except for last week. He and Taylor disap-peared while I was watching Amber."

I gripped my wheel as Derek lit another cigarette.

"How long?"

Derek exhaled and scratched his head. "It was about a week, I think. They came back and holed up in that building. Amber stays at work late and then goes to NA meetings. You should be proud of her."

"Where is the building?"

"Uh, I think it's Bay Street."

I pulled to a stop and grabbed his foil, taking the last of it. "You sure it's Bay?" I expelled the smoke out of my window.

Derek nodded with certainty. "Yeah, man, you can't miss it. It's massive. I'll go back with you. I can show you everything."

"Nah. I can handle it," I said as I reached under my seat.

"You sure—"

I landed the first blow with the butt of my pistol and cracked his nose. I reached over and opened his door then pushed him out as he screamed. Getting out, I rounded my truck and stared down as he bled at my feet.

"Jesus, Laz. I said I'm fucking sorry!" he pleaded on the ground with hands up, his eyes wide. "I called you, man. You fell asleep. Fuck, dude, put the gun away. We've been friends for ten years, man! I'm sorry!"

"Sorry?" Cocking the gun, I broke some teeth as I shoved the barrel into his mouth and gripped his hair. "Say it." I kicked dirt on him as he cried. "Say 'Sorry, Laz, I lost your son.'"

"Please." He managed around the gun with blood pouring from his nose and mouth. "Please don't shoot me."

"I'm not going to shoot you." Derek's shoulders slumped as I pulled the gun from his mouth. It was only when he looked at me with relief that I shattered what was left of his face with my fists, even after he took his last breath.

Satisfied with my fingers covered in Derek's dried blood, I set out to multi-task and dialed Lucy. She answered on the first ring. "Yeah?"

"Get some of my clothes to the motel and get Perry there." Perry was the motherfucker I should have sent to get the job done. He would never have let my son slip through his fingers. We worked together on a few jobs over the years when I was short on money, and he had a controllable habit and could keep his fucking mouth shut.

"What are you going to do for me, Laz?"

"Lucy, you are taking too many liberties with that fucking mouth. You should be more careful. But don't worry, I'm going to remedy that. Tell him to meet me there in twenty minutes."

"Fine."

"Twenty minutes."

Perry's eyes closed as he gripped Lucy's hair while she bobbed on his cock.

"Fuck yes, prom queen, suck it." She began to choke as he fucked her mouth.

"Goddamn, Laz, get some of this."

I tossed weighed bags aside and scraped the remaining powder onto a foil. I took a hit and watched Lucy squirm on her knees while she clawed at his thighs. "She's baggage, man, all yours."

Perry leaned down and winked at her as she tried her best to keep up with his hips. "Hear that, baby? You're all mine."

Perry would do. He had a similar build and enough ink, and with Lucy by his side and the right clothes, he could pass. I had no doubts Cedric had eyes on us, and I needed them both on board without too many fucking questions. I couldn't let word get out that I was leaving. It was too risky with the amount of vultures after my supply. And with Perry, I could be at two places at once. He could also keep Lucy occupied.

"Fuck yes, bitch." Lucy gagged as Perry wasted himself in her mouth and then pushed her to the floor while she gasped for air. "I've got a lot more where that came from. Hope you like the taste." Lucy glared at him as he buttoned his jeans. With a lit cigarette dangling from his lips, he joined me at the table. "So, what's all this about?"

"You know how you've been asking to get dealt in?"

"Yeah, man. I've been ready."

"I'm about to give you a fucking hand of aces."

"Laz, don't move."

"I'm not moving, Red."

"I can't do this. Please don't make me."

"The fuck you can't."

"I don't want to hurt you!"

"Then don't, baby. You've got this."

The guys stood around me, laughing as she aimed the pistol.

Taylor's eyes shot to them, and she shook her head. Her voice quivering, she said, "Laz, I can't."

"Look at me. Fuck them, okay? School them, baby, show them what's up."

Taylor aimed and shot the beer can out of my hand.

The guys quieted as she took aim again and hit it on the ground where it landed.

The reaction was instant.

"Goddamn, man, watch your balls."

"Fuck, man, better keep one eye open at night."

I held out my hand. "Pay up, motherfuckers."

Taylor smiled as I came toward her with a fistful of cash. I scooped her up in my arms and kissed her deep. When I pulled away, she looked up at me. I grinned down at her, my chest filled with pride. "Told you."

"I can't believe I let you talk me into that. You weren't worried?"

"Not for a single second."

"That was so stupid."

I inhaled her smell. "You like living on the edge."

"No," she whispered. "No, I don't."

But I knew better. The guys huddled around our circle of trucks in the middle of the hayfield, giving us shit for our PDA. I shot the bird over my shoulder as someone turned some music on and fresh beers were popped.

"I bet you're wet."

Taylor smiled as I leaned in.

"And I bet it's not just 'cause I kissed you."

She lifted a brow. "Bet you won't ever find out."

I ran with her in my arms as she threw her head back, laughed, and tightened her legs around me.

"Where are you taking me, Laz? There's a mile of field around. They can see us."

I tossed her in my truck and sped out of out of the circle as empty beer cans were tossed our way, hitting the side of my truck.

"Laz, I don't have to be home yet."

"I'm not taking you home, home, baby."

Taylor slid next to me as I raced down the gravel road to the Mason farm a few miles away. "What's going on?"

"I need to make you mine."

"I am yours," she said with a glance my way.

I slid to a stop in front of the barn. Taylor glanced around, uneasy.

"Laz, they'll catch us."

"He's at a horse show. He asked me to keep an eye on the place." Out of the truck, I gripped her hand and slid open the door. It reeked of damp hay, but it didn't matter. I saw her smile as I sat her down on the pile of quilts I'd laid down.

"You planned this?"

"I just thought . . ." My chest ached with a feeling I couldn't control when I was around her. "I know you hate that motel."

She nodded as she looked over to me.

"You're high."

"Please don't. Just don't, okay?" I kissed her and felt it the moment she gave into me. My eyes stung from the ache that burned in my chest, while my heart hammered for her. I kissed her deep before I slowly pulled off her jeans. She panted beneath me, her eyes a little fearful.

"I want you so much, Taylor. It's all I can think about."

"Laz."

"You're all mine." I pulled her panties down as she tentatively watched me and parted her thighs.

"You won't remember this," she objected. *"Not the way you're supposed to."*

I pressed her hand to my chest. *"This is all you. All of it."*

Her breaths came fast as I closed my eyes, moved in, and tasted her.

"Oh my God."

She tugged at my hair as she squirmed. I slid my tongue over my coated lips. *"Stay still, baby. I promise you this is going to feel so good."*

"Okay."

Trust.

That was what I saw in her eyes as I dipped my head again and darted my tongue out. I added a finger and her back arched as she wrapped her legs around my head and moaned.

"Laz." Her voice was hoarse as I licked and sucked until her body shuddered.

Bracing myself over her, I leaned in and kissed her while she opened for me. Completely wrapped in each other, she pulled off my shirt before she unzipped my jeans. It was permission, and I took it. I leaned in on a whisper. *"I love you."*

I centered myself at her middle and dipped my fingers in to stretch her, determined to take what had always belonged to me.

Breaks squeaked outside the barn just as I began to push inside her. *"Laz, you in here?"*

Taylor was up in a split second, struggling to get back in her jeans just as old man Mason opened the barn door.

And when she snuck back through her window that night, her mother was waiting. She wore fresh bruises the next day when I pulled up to her walking home from school.

"Don't Laz, drive away. She's got Amber in the closet until I get home. You have to get. My mother is watching."

"Fuck that bitch. I'll take care of this. Get in the truck."

Taylor stopped and threw her hands up. *"Amber is in a closet! You can't take care of anything!"* She narrowed her eyes at me. *"You're high right now. You don't understand this. You don't have to live there. My baby sister is in a closet! I have to get home!"*

I pulled the truck to a stop and nailed her to it. The side of her face was swollen and purple. She cried as I tried to console her but pushed at my chest. *"I have to get out of here! I have to get the fuck out of here!"*

"Baby, I'm sorry. I'm working on it."

"Lies, more lies. She's suffering because of me. It's my fault."

"It's not your fault."

"I have to go, Laz." She fought me as I tried to wrap myself around her. *"It's going to be okay."*

"Go smoke another foil, you fucking liar!"

I jerked back as she ripped a hole straight through me with her tongue. *"All you do is lie. You don't love me. You won't help me. You're just like my mother! Look at you!"*

"That's bullshit," I defended weakly.

"Yeah?" she challenged. *"Then let's leave now. Let's just go. Screw the money. We can just grab Amber and leave. You promised me, and I'm holding you to it, right now. I don't care what happens, Laz, get us out of here!"*

"Now, today?"

"Now, today. If you love me, let's go. Right now."

I looked at the ground between us. *"We can't do it today."*

"She could kill me, Laz. Kill us both."

"Red, I know it's hard. Just give it some more time."

Even disguised in anger, I saw disgust. I looked at the road between us.

"I'm taking back all my hopes I had for you, Lazarus Walker."

I snapped my head up and took a step forward as my chest exploded. *"You don't mean that."*

"Leave me alone," she barked as she stalked toward her house.

"Take that shit back, Taylor!" She was just out of reach before she began to sprint.

"I won't. Stay away from me!"

"Red!"

She ran on as I jumped into my truck and beat on the wheel until she disappeared. I reached into my glove box then grabbed and lit a foil. I swore I would make her eat her words. I would pull her through. I swore it.

But instead, I smoked her away.

I wiped my face of the memory as I sped down I-40.

She forgave me a week later, and the week after that.

And still, I smoked her away.

And she took away my hopes for her when she left.

Then the smoke stopped working.

She tossed my love aside like trash, whored herself out to some man she hardly knew just to get away from me. He would get his too. I waited too long. But I knew one day she would come back for Amber.

But she came back with another man beside her.

He is probably fucking her right now.

I saw red as I pressed the pedal to the floor and tore through the Blue Ridge mountains. I might one day be able to forgive her. And it was time she came home, one way or another, permanently. The boy she left in the motel was a pussy in love. I was a new man now. And that man would erase everything that stood in the way of her homecoming.

Perry's piece of shit truck blew smoke midway between Dyer and Charleston. I was forced off the road for a full fucking day while I waited on repairs.

I'd spent my first day staking out Taylor's condo. Hate brewed as I watched my son come and go in the arms of his lying whore of a mother with a few of Cedric's fucking minions on her heels. I only caught sight of Taylor as she drove past to reach her garage. Her condo was locked up tight. There were eyes on them both. It would be a hard breach but not impossible. Apparently, when it came to opportunity, Derek was always looking at doors and never thought about the windows.

Taylor and I were good at windows.

Just when it seemed I couldn't catch a break, the minute I pulled onto Bay Street I spotted the building Derek described. And with the silky stroke of lady luck, I managed to catch Taylor's boyfriend pull into the garage in his SUV. Slipping in behind him, I drove past the elevated security bar.

When the SUV pulled to a stop, I tucked my pistol in my waistband and followed him into the elevator. Awareness struck as I crossed the threshold. He turned on me lightning fast, but I already had the barrel aimed as the doors closed.

"'Sup, motherfucker."

CHAPTER 20

Taylor

"Mommy, have some?" Joseph squeaked in offering to his doting mother.

"No, baby, that's your ice cream."

He sat in a high chair, managing to get his chocolate scoop everywhere but in his mouth as Amber watched on in pure adoration. It had been the perfect two days. According to Cedric, Laz was still in Tennessee, so we took our freedom and spent the last few days with Joseph at the beach and took turns with him on our hips playing in waves of salt water as they rolled through us. Joseph loved the water and even more so running through the crowds of seagulls who fled as he screamed his way past them. We built sun castles, ate peanut butter and jelly sandwiches, and fell asleep under our umbrella. With Laz safely in Dyer, we dismissed our sweaty security to embrace our new dynamic. Amber and I exchanged happy smiles as we, for the first time in our lives, lived like two sisters, like family, without fear.

She texted Laz regularly to keep him in "the loop," and his replies raised no red flags. The night we brought Joseph home, we'd sipped champagne late into the night and talked candidly in an attempt to close the remaining space between us. It was one of the best nights of my life. My sister was warm, caring, had an incredible sense of humor, and was extremely quick-witted and intuitive despite her lack of healthy education. She was a capable woman despite the life she'd been forced to endure, and I was proud. Proud of her strength and resilience.

Not only had she bounced back from addiction, Amber looked radiant and the happiest I'd ever seen her. Her healthy smile was a mix of her getting her bearings and her little boy back, a boy who owned her heart and had managed to steal a piece of mine in less than a few days. He reminded me of another man who had consumed me, especially when he misspoke my name.

"Let's grill," I declared as she wiped Joseph's face. "Sound good?"

She glanced at the small gas grill on the porch as I slid open the glass door adjacent to the dining room and glanced at the marsh. It had been another perfect day.

"You ever used that thing?" Amber laughed as I spent a few minutes trying to figure out how to light it.

"Nope," I replied as I found the safety switch and got it going.

"Nope," Joseph mimicked. "Nope, Aylor."

Every time he said my name, my heart sang in a way I never imagined possible.

"So, I guess you two should look forward to burned chicken."

"Nuggets," Joseph declared with an open mouth and excited eyes for his mother.

"Black nuggets," Amber piped sarcastically in reply before she turned to me with a grin.

I shrugged. "One of us has to be the man of the family."

"He's right here," Amber said as she readjusted the bib

around Joseph's neck. It was no use. The ice cream was on every imaginable surface and crevice of his little body.

He stuck his fingers in his mouth managing to coat his chin. "Let's give it a year or two before we put him on grill duty."

"Maybe until he's out of diapers." Amber chuckled. "Better fill up on this, buddy, or you'll starve."

I deadpanned, "Keep it up, you will too."

She didn't let up. "Have you ever cooked in your life?"

"Does macaroni and cheese count?"

She shook her head with an incredulous laugh. "No."

"Well then, no."

"Spoiled ass, better let me handle this," she said as she moved to help me.

"No, let me have this. Really. And cooking for one never appealed to me." I looked down at Joseph just as he managed to get the chocolate in his hair. "Is it weird I'm excited about it?" Looking up at me with a sincere smile, she shook her head. I felt the same burn in my throat I'd had for the last few days. It wasn't painful; it was freeing and close to what felt like healing. Understanding passed between us. Something as ordinary as grilling for my family had me emotional. To other people, we might seem like lunatics, but for us every second was monumental. Every new experience was a finish line. Ignoring the fear that always accompanied me when I allowed myself to feel, I moved to the fridge to grab a beer and begin dinner when a text pinged on my phone. I spent a few minutes gathering ingredients before I glanced at it.

Cedric: Get the fuck out of there!!

My heart seized as fear sent a shock wave through my body. I heard the glass door from the patio slide open. A wave of cigarette smoke hit my nostrils, and a chill went straight up my spine when I heard his voice.

"Well, isn't this just a fucking Hallmark moment."

318 | KATE STEWART

"Da!"

I leaped for my cabinet where I knew my special sat.

"Don't bother, momma bear, I took that one off your hands." I pulled at the cabinet anyway and felt my heart sink when I found it empty. He'd climbed up the goddamned balcony. I turned to see Amber paling rapidly as she snatched Joseph from the highchair and hugged him to her chest.

Laz glared at her with disgust, his voice filled with the promise of punishment. "I fucking knew it, you lying bitch."

Amber started rambling nervously as Joseph looked at his father, clearly sensing the tension. "Da!"

Amber began rambling quickly. "Laz, I just got him. I just wanted to get him used to me again."

"So, you had to lie about it?" Laz dipped down to be eye level with Joseph, who gave him a sideways smile before burying his head in his mother's chest. Laz ignored his son's dismissal and lifted accusing eyes at Amber. "You think I didn't know the minute my son crossed state lines? Fucking stupid." It was if the devil himself had walked into my house. Dressed in blue jeans, a T-shirt, and boots, he towered over my sister in silent threat. His menacing presence pushed my fear into the back seat as I braced myself for his wrath.

"It was my fault. I told her to lie to you." Laz turned his volatile eyes in my direction. He looked sick. His skin was gray, and his hair was a slick mess. He was beauty hidden behind his disgusting drug. The best years of his life had been wasted, as was he.

"Of course you did. We'll get to you soon enough. That's a promise, Red." Laz moved toward Amber and gripped her chin. "Get your fucking shit and get in the car."

Amber's first tears appeared. "No, Laz, please, we're happy here. Please, we can work this out!"

"This isn't his home, Amber. And if you think for one

fucking second I'm about to let this happen, you're wrong."

"Please," she pleaded. "I have a job here, and Joseph loves the water."

"Get. Your. Fucking. Shit. Amber."

Amber glanced my way with fear-covered features as the light in her eyes dimmed.

"They aren't going anywhere." Laz's head snapped to me as I made a move to my kitchen drawer, grasping at straws for anything I could find. I managed to find a meat mallet before I felt his fingers grip my neck.

"Laz, don't!" Amber shrieked, and a startled Joseph jumped in her arms and began to cry.

Laz spun me to face him, the ominous twist in his lips a preview of what he had planned for me. All the scenarios that Cedric and I had prepared for slipped through my open fingers like sand because I'd let my guard down for a moment to live in it. I didn't know why I hadn't learned my lesson.

I was never supposed to be happy.

I was never supposed to have a family.

I would never have a second reality. My mother's words hit me like bricks as dread filled me. I looked over to Amber whose face was twisted in horror. She loved me, despite my failure to save her from a living hell. She still loved me. And her little boy had the possibility of a future without a trace of Dyer in it. Maybe I was never meant to have family or a second reality. But I would make sure Amber did. Even if it cost me my last breath.

Laz's grip tightened on my neck as he eyed the metal in my hand with a devilish smirk. "What are your plans for that, sweetheart?"

"Bury it in your skull, asshole." His fingers tightened as Amber screamed out another plea. Joseph wailed as I looked over at a helpless Amber, who clutched her son.

"Go, Amber." She shook her head, our argument pointless.

"Go, get your stuff."

"Yeah, Amber," Laz said, his focus solely on me, his nicotine-tinged breath hitting my face, "go get your stuff."

I faced Laz, who had me tight in his grip, my back folded over the counter top. "Your move, Red."

Fury raced through me as I did my best to push him back to swing the mallet. Laz laughed, and my stomach rolled as he kept me pinned tightly.

"How will this end, Taylor?" Laz leaned in close, our eyes locked in battle. I pushed my fear down, my need to protect Amber and Joseph outweighing any thought of self-preservation.

"You're going to have to kill me to get them out of this house."

His fingers cut the rest of my breath as he spoke. "And you think I won't?"

I flailed beneath him and brought my knee up between his parted legs. He managed to move before I could land a blow. He gripped my forearm and slammed it against the counter top until I dropped the mallet. "Just so you know, baby, I took the liberty and ended your relationship for you. He's resting peacefully in your favorite elevator. Bay Street, right?"

No.

Tears sprang up instantly as I looked at him in question. "I can see your tastes have changed. Italian, huh?" He pressed his fingers in as I fought for air. "Oh, sorry, your turn to speak." He loosened his grip as I gasped and inhaled all my lungs could hold.

"Fuck you. Goddamn you, Lazarus Walker!" I pushed away the agony that threatened to seep in.

"Such a pretty face on such a deceiving bitch. Did you ever even think about the mess you left me in?"

"You made your own mess. You're still an addict. I made the right decision leaving you."

His blue eyes lit up with pure fury. "I'm talking about the

day you put a fucking bullet in me." Spittle dripped from his mouth as he leaned in closer and dug his nails into my neck. "You. Just. Fucking. Left!" Laz raged as I tried to think of any way to shift my weight to my advantage. I had only one choice, and I took it. I jerked back and then forward with all my might and nailed him in the nose with my skull. I heard bone crack and was instantly freed. Still gasping, I gripped the mallet on the floor and came back at him with a hard swing. Laz was fast and caught my arm before he landed a hard backhand to the side of my face. I screamed out in rage, the pain a bystander to the anger that fueled me.

"You bastard!"

"I'm calling the police!" I heard Amber scream from behind the door.

"You do that, you join your sister tonight!" Laz shouted right before I reached him. I swung my fists in a futile attempt as he batted them away. His nose was shedding blood as he laughed at my anger and determination to bruise him further.

I cleared my counter, throwing everything I could get my hands on as he easily avoided the debris with hell in his eyes. He was playing with me, and I was fighting for my life. He had me in weight and size, and I was defenseless without my guns. High and out of his mind, it was only when I managed to sting him well with a heavy coffee mug that he came for me. He gripped my T-shirt and nailed me flat on my back to the island. His blood dripped down my neck as he wedged himself between my legs.

"I've been waiting thirteen years for this. It's probably better that you're alive when I do it."

Realization dawned as he pulled at my shorts. I fought hard as he ripped at them with steady hands, despite my angry blows to the side of his face.

Annoyed, and only when I hit his tender nose, he slapped me hard enough to daze me while managing to get my shorts down.

I fought with every fiber of my being to no avail. His fury won.

"Laz." I lay exhausted on the counter, breathing heavy, full of fight and not an ounce of energy to execute it. I needed to buy time. "Are you really going to do this to me with your son in the next room?"

Laz worked himself tighter between my thighs.

He ignored my attempt to appeal to anything decent inside him. "You turned into a whore, right? For that guy in Memphis. Ray? Way different story than that scholarship you lied about. A little birdie named Lucy told me. Said you were holed up fucking Ray before you left for Harvard. And I believe there is some unfinished business between us about some money you stole from me. What's your hourly rate? I'm pretty sure I'm covered."

"You're disgusting."

"You made it that way!" I felt the anger radiate from every part of him. "You think you're so much fucking better than me, Taylor? You're a white trash whore faking a high-class life."

"And you're a drug addict. That's *all* you are."

Another slap had my face exploding with pain. I felt the copper build in my mouth and spit it out directly in his face.

Laz raged on, his face close—too close. I had no choice but to see my death in his eyes.

"Finally afraid, Taylor? That's a relief. It makes you seem almost human. It's deceiving, though. We both know you don't have a goddamn frail bone in your body. Your sister is your only weakness. And I'm going to take her from you."

"Fuck you!" I cried as he snapped my panties away from my body.

"I'll take a piece of you, and then I'll take the rest."

I clawed his arms bloody as he hovered above me. My efforts seemed to satisfy him. It was only when I lay limp again that he stopped the workings of his belt.

He stared at me as my jaw trembled, satisfied with my defeat.

"Laz, please, you want this. Fine, I'll give it to you, okay? Just please don't let them see." I wrapped my legs around his waist and pulled him closer. "You want this? Take it."

"Fuck you." Another slap to the side of my face had me seeing stars.

"Laz." He paused as he looked down at me. I gathered it was something in my voice that made him do it. He studied me like he saw a ghost.

Stopping his hands on his pants, he screamed in rage. "You were promised to me! I did it all for you! Every goddamn thing!"

"I'm self-made, goddamn you! I did it myself! What the hell did you ever do for me!?"

"I killed your fucking mother!"

I lay there in shock as he raged on.

"I made it safe for you to come back, made it safe for Amber. I saved you and your ungrateful sister! I loved you my whole goddamn life, Taylor Ellison, and you left me in that fucking hotel room to rot!"

And then his weight on top of me was gone. It took me seconds to recover, and when Laz came into focus, I saw he wasn't alone. Laz grunted out in pain as Daniello landed blow after blow to his face, alternating his fists and then holding him up by his throat when Laz went too limp for him to continue his brutal beating.

The baby was screaming as I watched Daniello's wrath unfold.

I found my voice and managed to croak. "Stop, Daniello."

Daniello did as I expected and continued to punish Laz with bone crushing blows.

"STOP!" I gripped him by the arm. "Please, you can't."

In a sudden move, he gripped Laz in a headlock with a Glock to his temple.

"NO! No! The baby!" It was all I could bring myself to say.

Daniello scoured my body, his features filled with a rage I'd never seen.

His voice deadly, he leaned in to whisper in Laz's ear, "She begs for your life, you piece of shit."

"Daniello, don't." I stared on at Laz, who I believed with everything in inside, loathed me as much as he loved me.

"Oh, he's going to," Laz said with ironic humor, his face completely broken as he spat the blood pouring from his lips.

"Wise words from a stupid fucking man," Daniello bit out, his face twisted with restraint.

"You'll waste her," Laz grunted out, agony in his fractured face. Two of his teeth were cracked, and his face freely bled as he looked at me with sorrowful eyes.

"And you will never have her," Daniello hissed.

"I did though," he coughed out. "Didn't I?" Twin tears streamed down his cheeks as he looked at me with a mix of need and regret. "Always, right?" He stared at me in the present and the past. I knew exactly what he was referring to—our picnic with the strawberries. It was one of the best days we spent together. Recognition of our past life razored circles over my chest and threatened to cut deeper. Cedric was right. No matter how much I denied it, I loved Laz in memory.

I gripped my chest as Daniello held his life in his hands.

Laz's eyes implored mine as he looked at me, lost. "Red," he whispered, "did you ever love me?"

I stared back at the man who was my nemesis and the boy who was at one point, my hero and my first love. "Yes." Laz's eyes closed in what looked like relief a second before Daniello cracked his neck. Laz went completely limp as I slid to the floor in unison.

The next few minutes were a blur as Daniello barked orders at Amber's closed door. I looked into Laz's cold, lifeless eyes with strangled breaths and glassy eyes. Relief, devastation, and confusion all came into play as Daniello hoisted me up from the floor and slid my shorts back on before he pulled Laz into the dining room, past Joseph's ice cream-soaked highchair. I blinked again and again, completely torn and unwilling to snap out of it. Daniello was in front of me, washing my face, twisting my neck to survey the damage.

"Phoenix, Jesus Christ, look at me. Look at me."

"I'm okay." The words were metal and lead on my tongue. "He told me you were dead." I couldn't control the emotions that surfaced, the confusion, the anger as I let my tears flow.

"It was one of my men." Careful brown eyes scoured me. "Taylor, you saved him from a worse fate. I could not let him live. Tell me you understand."

Still in a haze, I muttered my reply. "I understand." Behind him, movement caught my eyes, and my chest seized when Daniello lifted his gun, his eyes still fixed on me, and aimed directly at Cedric's head.

"No." I shook my head at Daniello. "He's a friend."

"You better make goddamn sure you don't miss," Cedric said as he inched toward us and Daniello turned to fix his focus on Cedric. I saw the fire light between them. I clutched Daniello's arm. "Please don't."

"Nice gun," Cedric complimented, cold as ice. The look in his eyes was deadly. Daniello was stiff in front of me, and I could see his intent as I tried to wedge myself between the two men.

"You do a horrible fucking job of bodyguard." Daniello's voice was full of condemnation as he pushed me away from him and faced Cedric head on. "You tried your best, but you failed."

"Don't!" I begged. "God, please don't."

Cedric didn't flinch. "I trusted the wrong people, and I think a few of us in this room are guilty of that. And you didn't do much better," Cedric noted as he lifted his chin in my direction.

"Stop it, please. I'm begging you both." I turned to Daniello. "He would have killed him, like you."

"Like me?" Daniello's smile was sinister. "I assure you this man is nothing like me."

"Looks like we have a problem then," Cedric said as he took a step forward.

Daniello turned to me. "Take her to the penthouse."

I stood my ground as the air thickly filled between them. "No."

Cedric spoke next. "Take her, Taylor."

I swallowed the scream in my throat as I again pleaded with Daniello. "Please. Don't do this. He doesn't know who you are. He doesn't know your name. He doesn't know *anything*."

"Taylor." It was a warning from Cedric. "I really don't like your new boyfriend. But you need to listen to him. You need to go."

"Phoenix." Daniello jerked me into reality as my eyes finally fixed on his.

"Take her to the penthouse. Go."

"Amber," I breathed out, barely audible to my own ears. I walked over to the door and knocked. "Amber, we're leaving."

Amber slowly opened the door and looked past me. Daniello stood behind me, his gun still pointed at Cedric, blocking her view of the dining room.

"Joseph's bag is still in the car, meet me there."

"Okay." Amber clutched a sniffling Joseph to her and made a beeline for the garage door. I turned back to Daniello who spoke to me without looking my way.

"Go. I will be behind you."

Tears multiplied as I stared at Cedric. His eyes softened on me briefly before he barked his order.

"Goddamned it, Taylor! Get Joseph out of here, go!"

"He's dead, isn't he?"

I nodded as Amber looked at me with tear-filled eyes and then back at her sleeping son. Laz's sleeping son.

An avalanche of guilt covered me because of Laz while growing fear budded for Cedric.

Amber looked over to me with salt-filled eyes. "He would never have left us alone, right?"

"No. Even with the police involved we would have never been free of him."

"Does it hurt?" She lifted soft fingers to the side of my face, and the ache wasn't nearly enough to break through my torment.

"No."

"Jesus, Taylor. Who is that guy?"

She was referring to Daniello, but my thoughts were still on Laz, his eyes, his words, his devastation. I felt it. I felt all of it, and I would probably carry it with me for the rest of my life. In the sickest of ways, he'd remained loyal to his love for me long after I left him. I had no compartment for that, no place to shove it away. He loved me with his last breath, though I gave him no reason to, and I was sure as I stared at his lifeless body that I didn't want him dead. I wanted him gone, I wanted to keep my sister and her son safe, but I never wanted to see him that way. And Daniello would never have let him live.

By the way he handled him, I could tell he would have done so much worse if I hadn't begged him to stop. And if Cedric were lying on my kitchen floor lifeless, I would never get past it.

Laz's words echoed through my head. "Laz killed Momma?"

328 | KATE STEWART

Amber stiffened in her seat and looked at me with wide eyes. "Yes. That's the one secret I kept from you." Amber sniffed. "I screwed up. It's the one thing that could have kept him away from us. But I wanted so much to believe he would do better. God, Taylor, I'm so sorry. He almost killed you. He would have taken us. God, I'm so damned stupid. Please tell me you'll forgive me. Please, Taylor. I wanted Joseph to have a father, but never at this price. And not the way he was. He'd just done so much for me."

But it wasn't for her. That's what he made sure I knew. None of it was for her. The pregnancy might have been accidental, but the rest was part of some sick wish that I would return. He was lost in a world we'd created all those years ago and never got out of it. A world I prayed he'd take me away from. And his life was taken in *my* world, by a man who was even more dangerous.

It had to stop somewhere.

The chain had to be broken.

I couldn't afford any more of the same in my life.

"I understand, Amber. I wanted the same. But we can't change their nature."

Amber wept silently in her seat as I let the words I just spoke pass over me like a sentence. My sister and her son were my priority. I couldn't take any chances with their lives.

If Daniello had ended Cedric, his death would be more than I could bear.

And that meant letting go of another man that I loved.

CHAPTER 21

Taylor

AT 4:00 A.M., I STOPPED TEXTING CEDRIC. I HAD TO PROTECT Amber, and that meant making sure none of Laz's crew were waiting in the wings. When I was certain we weren't being followed, I got us safely to the penthouse and began begging for any word. Amber cried silently with Joseph snuggled next to her on the bed while I sat on the sofa with my anger and grief.

Mountains of tears multiplied as a chest full of despair I could never have imagined threatened to ruin the rest of me.

Minutes or hours later, when the door to the penthouse opened, and I saw Daniello was alone, I bent over in defeat and let my emotions run rampant. I sobbed into my hands, my gun discarded on the couch next to me before I snatched it up and aimed it at Daniello. There was no surprise in his eyes as I walked toward him.

"Where is he?"

Daniello's eyes were filled with emotion as he spoke softly. "Did he get inside you?"

I jabbed the gun in his direction with every word. "Where.

Is. He?"

"Tell me, Phoenix, because if he was inside you, I want that bullet."

I scrubbed my tears with my free hand, my resolve slightly faltering. "Don't pretend to care about me!"

"I assure you I am not."

"What did you do to Cedric?!"

My phone beeped, and I looked at Daniello in shock. With the gun still pointed at him, I gripped it tighter and glanced down to read an incoming text.

Cedric: I'm fine. I'll call you in a bit.

I let out a hard breath as I dialed him.

He answered on the first ring. "I can't talk right now. I'm being patched up by a hot nurse."

Nervous laughter spilled from my lips as I glared at Daniello. "Patched up?" I surveyed Daniello and saw he had a purple bruise on his jaw. "You two got into it?"

"It was a discussion of sorts about future security."

"But you're fine. You're okay?"

"You have the absolute worst taste in men. I seriously couldn't pick worse."

I sobbed again in relief. Daniello's concern for me hadn't swayed as he watched me carefully.

"It's over." Those words came from Cedric. I felt the finality as I studied Daniello, who nodded slowly, obviously able to hear our conversation.

I'd been so damned selfish, so blind, and it almost cost me Cedric.

Daniello had told me the truth all along. There was no future, no fix. We could never flip and fit into each other's world.

"I . . . Cedric, I—"

"I love you too. Get some sleep. I'm going to follow Laz's trail. I promise you no one will come looking for either of you.

I'll call you later."

Cedric ended the call as I let the anger consume me.

"You son of a bitch!"

Amber spoke up. "I'm just going to take him home." I looked over at my sister and her terrified son with apologetic eyes, cursing my stupidity. "I'm sorry."

"It's okay." She turned to Daniello as I handed her my keys. "Is it safe to go there?" Daniello gave her a solemn nod as he brushed Joseph's cheek with his finger. "You are safe. Your guard is waiting at the elevator."

Amber disappeared behind the door with her son in tow as I glared at Daniello. My insides deteriorated as I let the phone and my gun slip out of my hand and made my way forward in a cloud of rage.

Daniello braced himself as I delivered one punishing slap after another. He took exactly two, then gripped my arms, bringing his face an inch away from mine, demanding answers. "Tell me right now, Phoenix, did he hurt you? Was he inside you?" I continued to fight as he growled and shook me in his arms. "Tell me!"

"NO!"

I felt the air leave him as he gripped me to his chest like a lifeline.

I pushed at him as he kept me locked within his arms. "Get the fuck away from me! You don't get to have that kind of power in my life. You don't get to decide who lives or dies! You aren't GOD!"

Daniello jerked me back to him. "I am your God! If there is a fucking man out there who wants to hurt you, *I* am the fucking man they answer to! Do you understand me, Taylor?"

"He was my friend. I told you that!"

"That was for me to decide," Daniello snapped as he gripped my arms and challenged me. "*I* am your lover. *I* am your protector. I am all of these things!"

"How could you do that to me?!" My voice was gravel.

"Do you think that is the worst I could do, Taylor? Ridding your life of a man like that?"

"No." I swallowed. "Just leave."

Daniello's anger and apparent hurt bled between us as I broke apart. "I can't do this anymore. I can't have you around them. It's too dangerous. They are my life now."

A loud knock at the door interrupted our argument, and in seconds Rocco was in the kitchen speaking rapid Arabic. Daniello stood stunned and turned to study the silent television in the kitchen. On screen, twenty or more agents were unloading cargo from one of the shipping containers at the Port of Charleston.

The details began to scatter on screen. *Biggest Firearms Seize In South Carolina History* ran across the CNN banner. Daniello turned back to me.

I looked at him incredulously. "You're an arms dealer?"

Rocco barked out a laugh and turned to me with pure hatred. "Stupida cagna!" *Stupid bitch!*

"Phoenix." Daniello drew my attention back to him, and his words disintegrated me. "I will not return."

Rocco spoke rapidly, as Daniello and I remained motionless, studying one another. I nodded slowly, as I shattered piece by piece. Rocco moved toward the door and called Daniello's name. He remained still, memorizing me. So much unsaid, so much that would never be said. Our situation was impossible, our lives even more so. Seconds ticked by as Rocco's voice turned more frantic.

As if a flip switched, Daniello's eyes hardened, and he turned and walked out the door.

I fought every urge to go after him. I gripped my hair as tears escaped and I sobbed out his name.

I loved him, and I would never see him again. I loved him

though I shouldn't. I loved him against all reason. Against everything I was taught, everything I taught myself.

He was a threat to all I had built. A fatal blow to the reputation I had carefully crafted. He would tear my castle apart and ruin my kingdom if I let him.

Because I loved him.

Someone had to love the fucking villain.

Two weeks later

Taylor

"Okay, yes. I think so too. K, bye."

I raised a brow at my sister's sheepish smile.

"That was Nina's brother, Aaron."

I hid my smile. "I know his name."

"Uh, right. Well, he says he has a golf buddy with a little boy Joseph's age. He wants to come pick us up this Friday." She smiled sheepishly and then looked over at Joseph, who was playing on the carpet in the living room. "Can I make a confession?"

I nodded, knowing that she would tell me they had been seeing each other for over a month. Nina had spilled after their first date. I wanted Amber to come to me with the information freely.

"I've been on a few dates with him. I'm crazy about him."

"Really?"

"He's so different. He's so nice to me, so good to Joseph. Taylor, I've never had a man kiss me like he does."

Every part of me that could feel happiness felt it for her. Despite what happened, she was still a picture of health, and Joseph had adjusted smoothly. I knew she was still mourning Laz in some form, the sporadic appearance of red eyes a sure sign of her grief. We would be forced to keep his death to ourselves indefinitely. I knew the guilt would eat her alive if she let it. But she was a fighter, and somewhere inside her, she knew the outcome would have been worse had Laz taken her from Charleston.

My sister had created her own skeletons, and they'd mingled with mine. And with Cedric's quick cleanup, we both helped to bury them. Cedric had made certain Laz was found in Tennessee in the motel he'd spend half his life in. Laz's mother had called to give us the news. It was open-and-shut shitty Dyer police work that saved us in the end, and Cedric assured me from the buzz in Dyer the pointed finger was nowhere in our direction. They'd found the body of Laz's right-hand man a few counties away. Cedric had only stopped by once since that night and spent only a few minutes with me, prepping me for the phone call from his mother. When I mentioned Daniello, he cut the conversation short.

"What happened?"

"We had more in common than we thought."

"That's all?" I demanded.

"That's all you need to know." My refusal to drop it led to a closed door with Cedric behind it. He knew his slight hurt me, but refused to tell me anything further. Even so, I texted him an hour later with a curt "Thank you." Amber and I owed him our life, and I couldn't let my involvement with Daniello affect our friendship or the fact that he had cleared the way for us to finally be a family.

Laz's voice haunted me at night. His shrieks and bloodied face, his love, his hate. It was etched inside, and I could only pray it faded with time. My days at the office were the only things that kept me going. Nina could see the distance in me but refused to grill me about it. I threw myself into cultivating new deals and succeeded. It's what I did. Order and excellence had been restored.

And in my idle time, aside from the battle with my conscience, I had to beg my heart to keep beating.

"You sure you want us to take this place?" Amber said as she looked around the condo with appreciative eyes.

"Yes. There's a room for you both."

"You bought that penthouse?"

I nodded as she whistled. "Good for you. You deserve it."

I felt the sting of her words as she looked over to Joseph and then back to me. Her guilt took a back seat at that moment to her hopes of a new future.

"Thank you, Taylor." I shook my head as a lone tear slipped down my face. "I know you don't want me to thank you. I know you don't want to talk about it, but I don't think there was a soul in that situation that didn't love you."

My head snapped up.

She gave me a sardonic grin. "You, sister, make the men in your life insane with love."

I chuckled ironically. "I've never had love, Amber."

"Oh, yes you have. It might not have been the kind that goes on to the grave—well, maybe that was a poor choice of words." Her shoulders slumped.

I put up my hands. "Just stop right there. There is no way to glorify this situation."

Amber smirked and moved from the counter to pick up Joseph. "Are you saying good things can't come from bad? Because me and this little man disagree, don't we, buddy?"

Joseph gripped his mother's hair and then looked at me with Laz's eyes. I choked on my tears as they moved toward me. I shied away, too afraid of scaring the baby with my emotions. Unable to resist, I took him in my arms and studied his profile. He was a replica of his father, which kept the burn brewing in my throat. Amber looked at us as I gripped him tightly to me and cradled Laz's son. "Everything you loved about him is in this little man. The rest, the world did away with."

"Hey!" Joseph shrieked as he waved a chubby arm at me. "Hey!"

I chuckled as tears slid down my face. "Hey!"

"Another man in love with you," Amber said with a sigh. "I'm kind of relieved I have a date."

"Hey!" Blue eyes I'd dreamed of for years stared back at me with complete trust. I had failed Amber, but Joseph was my chance to make things right. And I would take it.

Amber lay in my bed while Joseph napped. I pulled an overnight bag from my closet. "You are just taking clothes?"

"Yes," I said, looking around the room. There was nothing sentimental about leaving the condo. "New place, new stuff."

"That's the fun part, shopping." She offered as she texted on her phone.

"Hardly," I disagreed. "I hate shopping. The movers will be here tomorrow to pick up my wardrobe."

Amber snorted. "Wardrobe. Jeez. Is this real life?"

I smiled at her despite my ache. "You aren't doing so bad as a temp. You may have your own soon."

"I'll earn it," Amber piped.

"I'll make sure you do," I said sternly. Amber rolled her eyes as she glanced at her phone and blushed.

"He's a dirty talker."

I grabbed a pair of jeans from a drawer. "You don't say."

"Too much?"

I let out a breath and looked her way. "Probably. I don't know. Do sisters talk about sex?"

She shrugged. "We could." She pushed herself to kneel

on my bed, her phone resting on her legs, eyes wide. "Tell me something."

I pulled a shirt off a hanger and made my way into the bathroom.

"Aww, come on, Taylor. That gorgeous man had to be good at it."

I poked my head out of the door. "He was." I shut the door and locked it with a chuckle.

"Really? Way to let a girl down!" she said through the door.

"Sorry."

In the shower, I washed the lazy Saturday off me, intent on moving into the penthouse and making Sunday a workday. I picked up the last of Daniello's soap and lathered my hands. Maybe there was some sentiment after all. The smell brought me to instant tears. The shower had been my retreat. The only place I let my emotions go. I was anxious to take up residence in the penthouse so I could mourn without watchful eyes around me. I cupped my hand over my mouth as I sat on the tiled bench seat and brought my legs up. No matter how hard I cried, the ache wouldn't leave. He was still there, still inside, and so deep there was no way to exorcise him. His permanent absence left the deepest hurt imaginable. He'd saved me and imprisoned me. Bone-deep sadness was my new companion and threatened permanent residence. I couldn't shake it.

A loud thud interrupted my thoughts, and I called out to Amber.

"What was that?" I stood, washing the soap off my body, waiting for a reply.

Silence.

"Amber, what *was* that?"

More silence.

My heart raced as I gripped a towel and stumbled out of the shower. Sliding over the tile, I unlocked and opened the door, relieved to see Amber sitting straight up in my bed.

"Amber? Damn, you could have answered me. I'm soaking wet," I said as I wrapped the towel around my body and tucked it closed.

Amber turned to me slowly, and it was then that I saw the blood begin to drain from her stomach. Her eyes were wide with terror and blood laced her teeth as she screamed out a raw, "Nooooooo!"

Dread coursed through me as I jumped into action the second she went down against the mattress. I picked up the cell from her lap and dialed 911 as she stared up at me, gasping and wide-eyed. "Jos-Joseph! Taylor, get J-J-Joseph!" It was an agonized cry from her lips as I frantically spoke to the operator. Amber fought me frantically in fear for her son. I ripped the towel from my body and pressed it to her bullet wound and noticed a second bullet hole in the wall behind her. "Hold it there. Press hard!" With an ambulance on the way, defenseless and naked, I let the adrenaline do its job and made a beeline for Joseph's room. I burst through the door and felt my whole chest explode when I saw dark hair surface at the top of the crib.

"Oh God," I exhaled as I moved toward him and scooped him up. I raced back into my bedroom and covered the baby's eyes so I could drape Amber with my comforter.

"Keep holding it, Amber!"

I rushed to my closet, threw on some clothes, and then lifted the comforter to see too much blood had leaked from her. She twisted in agony as the pain tore through her. "Oh, no, no, no," she sobbed as Joseph began to sense something was wrong. His lips began to tremble as Amber's eyes searched mine.

"It's okay, buddy. It's okay. Mommy is playing." I turned to my sister, frantic.

"Who . . . who was it, Amber? Who did this? Did you see?"

Amber shook her head as she looked over at Joseph while a

solid stream of blood slid down her chin. I wiped it away as tears streamed down her face.

"Hang in there; you can do this. Nod your head, you can do this."

She nodded as Joseph bounced on the bed beside her. "Was it Dyer? One of Laz's crew?"

She shook her head as the last of my hope was washed away.

I heard the sirens approach and was forced to leave her to open the door.

"Amber!" She began to spit up blood as she looked over at Joseph.

"Oh God, please hold on," I begged as I pressed the towel to her stomach to keep more blood from spilling out.

"What's her name?" the paramedic asked as he reached her.

"Amber," I said as she went deathly still.

"Oh God," I sobbed as Joseph began to whimper at the commotion around us.

"She's in shock." They frantically worked on her until they got her to the doors of the ambulance and then left us there, standing in their wake. I looked down at Joseph who turned to me with a quivering voice. "Mommy?"

I was forced to stay behind with Joseph as the police questioned me, all of my answers useless. No forced entry. My alarm had been disarmed. I was defenseless against this enemy. And I knew without a doubt that that enemy had come to finalize the end of my relationship.

And if that were the case, we would never be safe.

CHAPTER 22

Daniello

Kiev, Ukraine

I MADE MY WAY ACROSS THE STREET AND INTO THE ALLEYWAY WHERE my target stood with his back to the wall. He studied the cigarette in his hand as if it had answers. I wondered if he thought it would be the cause of his death.

I had that answer.

I took careful steps his way and gripped the gun inside my jacket just as he took one final puff of his cigarette.

The irony was not lost on me.

When I was five feet away from him, he finally looked up just as I aimed the gun at his head and pulled the trigger. I never gave my targets time to speak, to plead for their lives. It was an act of mercy on my part. I could do far worse if commissioned to do so. But I knew their sins before I accepted every contract.

It was an easy job, one of many I had taken since I returned to Italy. I had no time for thoughts that weighed me down. There was never any shortage of work. Never any lack of men who were too much of a coward to dispose of their own enemy. My vengeance for my brother's undignified death had led me down this path. Matteo was murdered before my eyes by an evil man full of greed, much like the man I'd just left a corpse in the street. And he too had been tracked down and suffered the same fate as my brother.

I touched the untouchable.

The piece of shit that lay bleeding behind me had fled and believed himself safe. That morning he woke up with a clear conscience and deemed himself free of the consequences of his actions. But shadows always lurked in the most secretive places. And I was good at searching the earth for those places.

My reputation preceded me, though no one had ever seen my face unless I escorted them to their death. And the dead could keep a secret.

I was fine with the progression. I was always hungry, waiting to conquer the next untouchable.

Until I saw her, touched her, felt the warmth of her light, the deliverance of her eyes in the way she looked at me.

In the States, I had attempted to live a life with a woman who moved me toward something better, something more than the life of a man without a conscience. More than the shadow of the man he once was, who became what he despised most.

But she extinguished that light.

And now I dwelled in darkness.

CHAPTER 23

Taylor

"TAYLOR." CEDRIC STRODE THROUGH MY CONDO WITH AUTHORITY past the officers who were leaving. "What the fuck happened?"

I nodded toward Joseph, who slept on my chest, and walked into Amber's bedroom and laid him in his crib.

When I closed the door behind me, I walked Cedric out to the patio. "They shot Amber."

"What!?"

"They shot Amber. I need you to take the baby. I have to end this."

I moved toward my bedroom, leaving Cedric temporarily stunned on the porch, and paused at my bedroom door when I saw my sister's blood. Cedric was behind me an instant later.

"Taylor—" he gripped my wrist gently "—talk to me, start from the beginning."

My thoughts raced as I looked back at him. "They must have thought it was me."

"They who?"

"That's what I'm going to find out." I unpacked the bag I

was working on before I got into the shower and began cramming in street clothes. "Do you know the temperature in Barga in August?"

"Barga?" Cedric looked at me incredulously. "Fucking Italy? You think he did this?"

I shoved another T-shirt in my bag. "I have to get away from them." I pointed in the direction of Amber's room. "I have to. Move her out of here, Cedric, until you know she's safe." My heart cracked. "If she survives, keep her with you. Okay? Just get the baby and go."

"Wait a fucking minute." Cedric gripped my arm and spun me to face him. "You aren't going after him."

"That bullet was meant for me."

His eyes penetrated mine. "Fine, so it was meant for you. We'll up security."

"No." I shook my head. "No locked boxes. I didn't come this fucking far to look over my shoulder. And you met him, Cedric. Do you really think that would work?"

Cedric took a step back and crossed his arms. "So, what? You're going on a suicide mission?"

"If I'm there, they aren't looking for me here. I'll make some noise. It will keep her safe."

"Do you hear what you are saying? No fucking way." Cedric pushed my bag off the bed.

I picked it up and faced him head on. "I did this. I brought him into our lives. *I did this,* and I don't give a fuck what happens to me."

"That's your broken heart talking."

I deadpanned, "Fuck you."

"No, Taylor. Fuck you if you think I'm going to let you walk out of this house, abandon your sister and that baby when he needs you the most."

"That's *your* broken heart talking," I snapped as his jaw

344 | KATE STEWART

twitched. "I know you love me. But I also know you see my logic. You just don't want to deal with the consequences."

"Yeah, Taylor, goddamnit, I love you, always have, and there's no way I'm letting you go without me."

He towered over me, forcing my eyes to his. "I can't let you go."

"You don't have a choice. I need you to stay here and take care of them. Jesus, Cedric, they are a step ahead at every turn. Amber is my benefactor. I changed it weeks ago." I looked up at him. "You're next in line. You'll have my money, my resources to do right by me. Take care of them."

Cedric shook his head. "Sorry, ain't happening."

"The last man who cornered me got a hole shot through his leg."

His lips twitched as he stared down at me. "You threatening to shoot me, Taylor?"

"If I have to."

"He didn't do this."

"You don't even know his fucking name. What does that tell you?" I studied him. "Maybe you like him a little more than you let on."

"Hardly. We moved a body together. That hardly constitutes 'bros before hoes' bonding. He's a fucking trained killer, Taylor."

"Start talking."

I moved around my room, packing everything I could find that didn't pair with heels.

"He ex-army special ops turned rogue. My guess is he's a contract killer. Mercenary."

I shrugged. "Your guess? You know shit."

"I know he wouldn't fucking shoot you." Cedric ripped up the bed sheets I hadn't realized I was staring at and threw them into a ball to cover the dark stain that lay underneath.

"Well then, maybe he can tell me who would." The thought

of Daniello being the one to pull the trigger was too much to process.

"Ah, but you would fight to your death, Taylor."

"Goddamned right I would."

"The alarm was disarmed. It was him or one of his."

"Fuck this. I'm not doing this shit for you. I can't sign off on this. You'll have to find someone else. I can't let you do this, Taylor."

"Then I'll find someone else." I gripped my bag in an attempt to move past him but grabbed my arm. I could feel his desperation. He peered down at me, his eyes begging mine. "Give me time to assemble some men."

I huffed out a laugh. "This isn't Dyer."

"So then you know you won't survive it!"

"Amber is lying in the goddamned hospital, and it's my fault!"

Cedric crossed his arms. "Then you should be with her."

"You're done protecting me, Cedric. I've asked too much. Just take care of them. Joseph is in my custody. If she survives, she could lose him all over again. I fucked everything up. Just let me try to figure out a way to keep them safe."

"By dying?"

"Maybe. Maybe my momma was right. Maybe I'll go out in a spray of bullets. It's so fucking ironic."

"Goddamn it." Cedric sat at the edge of my bare bed and looked up to me with unshed tears in his eyes. "I'm fucking begging you. Don't do this."

"She's got a chance to live the life I always wanted her to have."

Cedric stood and moved toward me with a set jaw. He didn't stop until I was wrapped in the strength of him. His lips covered mine before he invaded my mouth and kissed me thoroughly. Feeling his need, I pushed out a surprised breath as he tasted and teased until I was breathless.

When he pulled away, he peered down at me with angry eyes. "If you make it back, I'll never forgive you for this shit."

Still enveloped in his steely arms, I wrapped my own around him. "I can live with that."

He whispered into my temple, "I'll send you a care package. You aren't going in without a few old friends."

I smiled with my head on his chest. "I'm counting on it."

"Find him *first*."

I let out a breath. "I'm pretty sure he'll find me."

CHAPTER 24

Taylor

"Excuse me, let us through." I jerked out of my stupor as they wheeled Amber back into her hospital room. I must have fallen asleep because the room was filled with fresh daylight.

"How is she?"

One of the nurses at her side glanced my way. "I'll have the doctor come and update you." They had to rush her into a second surgery when I arrived at the hospital. I couldn't find it in me to skip town without saying goodbye, without knowing.

And knowing was so much fucking worse.

Her body had begun dumping acid, and her lungs had collapsed. A gut shot brought on the worst imaginable pain. Someone had intended for me to suffer. Amber lay lifeless, attached to several machines, her porcelain face swollen from her struggle. I gripped her cold hand as she fought for her life, the way she had since she was a child. Remembering the little girl I had comforted after long, exhausting nights of cleaning. The sweet child who curled up next to me in bed, who smelled of bleach, and cried silently after a day of relentless torture at the hands of her mother. And the day I left her to fend for herself in a world she was defenseless against.

"Here, Aylor." Amber handed me a macaroni plate she'd made at school, and I studied it. The macaroni was dyed green and glued to a hand drawn brown tree trunk. Amber's leaves were sloppily placed, but I knew she had tried her hardest. There was a note attached that read: To my mommy. Thank you for helping me grow.

I handed the plate back to her. "Amber, this is for Momma."

Amber looked behind us to make sure our conversation wasn't heard before she whispered, "You are my momma."

I cupped my mouth as I sobbed out my apology. "I'm sorry. I'm so fucking sorry, Amber. Please don't leave me."

Amber lay limp, machines doing her breathing for her as I begged her forgiveness. "Fight, baby, fight so hard. I know you can do this. You've come so far. I love you," I sobbed, unable to control it as the pain seared through my chest. "Please don't go."

"Ms. Ellison."

Wiping my face with the back of my hand, I met the eyes of her doctor. "Yes?"

He glanced at Amber and then to me, no doubt comparing our similarities.

"Your sister is still critical. Abdominal trauma is tricky, and post-op is dangerous due to the high risk of infection and other complications. We will have to wait it out. For now, we have her under for pain and to keep her as stable as possible. I'll keep you updated."

"Thank you."

I walked back over and gripped my sister's hand. "You can do this, Amber. Fight. Just one more time, fight *hard.*" I kissed her temple as I took one last look at her. When I moved to leave, I noticed Aaron standing at the door with Nina behind him.

I was sure Cedric had updated them both. Aaron looked destroyed as he walked into the room.

I spoke to him as he passed me. "Tell them she's your fiancée, that's the only way they'll let you stay in here." Aaron nodded, his cloudy eyes on my sister. He looked over to me, brimming with tears. "Is she going to live?"

I bit my lips together in an attempt to tamp down my emotion as Nina moved to my side. "They don't know. She's critical. The doctor said it's a waiting game."

Aaron questioned me with an anger-etched face, "Who did *this*? Who in the hell would do this to her? Don't they know what's she been through?! Don't they fucking know what she lived through!?"

He didn't bother waiting for an answer as he sat in the chair next to her and gripped the hand I had just let go of.

Amber had told him everything. She'd only been dating him for a month, and she'd opened up about her life in Dyer and her addiction to a man she barely knew. At that moment, my sister was the bravest woman I'd ever known. I'd been such a coward, afraid of anyone finding out my truths. But it didn't matter. Those who loved you didn't care about your past or your skeletons. They embraced them.

As Daniello had embraced mine.

How could he let this happen?

"Was it him?" I'd almost forgotten Nina, who stood at my side watching her brother shatter.

"I honestly don't know. I can't live with it if it was." And that was the truth, but nothing had kept him from ending me in that penthouse the night he left. It would have been the perfect opportunity. "I think it was one of his associates. I have to find him. I have to know either way."

"What are you going to do?"

I looked at my sister on the hospital bed, with the man

who could have been her future falling apart next to her. I turned to Nina as the anger began to seep in. "Bring a little Tennessee dirt to his doorstep and end things badly."

"Taylor—"

I continued to retreat down the hall with purposeful steps. "We talked about this, Nina. I can't come back to Solutions. I'm so sorry."

"We'll be here." Her voice shook as I turned on her. Her eyes were murky as she studied me carefully.

"Twelve years I spent trying to be something better, to live better. And I'm not even sure who it was for anymore."

She shook her head. "That's not true, Taylor. You're confused. You're scared."

I shrugged in front of the elevator. "Am I? Or did I know exactly what would happen?"

Nina gripped my hand. "Does Cedric know?"

I nodded. "Everything. He has Joseph."

She held my hand tightly as her chest stuttered with heavy breaths. She feared for me.

"Taylor, just come back, okay?"

I let go of her hand and pulled her to me. We held each other tightly as I let a lone tear slip down my cheek. I whispered to her, "At least I know now *exactly* who I'm doing it for."

"Taylor—"

"Marry Devin. No one will ever love you more than that man."

She laughed. "You used to hate him."

"People can change."

"True," she agreed. "Case in point, you're hugging me. I want you to know, you saved me." She pulled away, her tears still falling.

I shook off her statement. "I know I have no right to ask, but—"

"You don't have to."

"If Amber doesn't make it—"

"She will. She has to, my brother is in love with her."

The elevator opened, and I stepped in. Nina gripped the top of her arms as her face fell.

"Bye, Nina."

CHAPTER 25

Taylor

"You look beautiful," Ray said as he slipped the corsage onto my wrist.

"This is ridiculous," I said as I fidgeted on the three-inch heels I'd been forced to walk in for the last month. "I don't want to go."

"It's your one and only prom, kitten. You deserve a break. Live like a teenager for once."

"I think we both know I'm way past that."

A hint of a smirk traced his full lips. "Still, you need a little more personality." I studied the claw marks I'd left on his arm the night before, hence my nickname. "I think we both know that's coming along nicely."

Ray gave me his first real smile in weeks. He'd been more absent than present, but we more than made up for it when the time came. He'd fulfilled every promise he'd made to me. I was expertly trained on corporate etiquette, not to mention I'd surpassed his expectations, landing first in class at school.

"You really do look beautiful."

I rolled my eyes as the driver knocked on the door.

"This will be humiliating. How many times do I have to tell you I can't stand my classmates?"

Ray's jaw tensed. "You will walk into that room and own the fucking thing. Make eye contact with every person who looks your way. Within five minutes of being there, someone will ask you to dance. Accept the invitation."

"Why?" He pulled and unboxed a solitaire diamond necklace from his pocket then slipped it around my neck.

"Practice."

"So this is another drill? And should I spread my legs to some pompous jock prick to keep the illusion alive?"

Ray didn't flinch. "Up to you."

I studied his beautifully chiseled face as he looked me over. "Why don't you care about me?"

Ray looked down at me with haunted eyes. "Told you. My heart is no good."

"I don't believe you."

"Nine months in this house and you still think there is hope for us, Taylor? Don't be ignorant."

"Ray." I held his arm as he fastened the clasp. Then he pulled away from me. His eyes briefly flicked to mine before they ran down my body. "Worth every penny."

My blood instantly boiled. "Fuck you."

Another smile, this one far less kind. He was insanely handsome and grew more so by the day. I gripped the back of his head with my nails and pulled him closer.

"Let me skip this." His eyes dropped to my lips. "I'll make it worth your while."

He palmed my hands with his own and pulled them away.

"Have a good time, kitten."

I moved to the door and looked back to him. "What if I loved you?"

He flinched as he stood at the bottom of the stairs, his hand on the railing, his eyes on the ascending marble steps above. "Well, that would be utterly stupid."

I bit my tongue and slammed the door behind me.

I did exactly what I was told. I owned that fucking room. I'd even *danced with a couple of guys who eye-fucked me daily in some of my classes. But it didn't last long. Inside the limo on the way back to the castle mere hours after I arrived at my senior prom, I let a few tears fall. Ray was decidedly cold. I knew enough to realize it was against his nature. He didn't want our relationship at first, but he was as equally involved.*

It was impossible he felt nothing for me.

Impossible.

Even with the distance he put between us, something was there. He never strayed far from home for more than a few days. There were no other women. And he fed on me like an addiction.

Pissed off and anxious to finish our conversation, I hit the top of the stairs, prepared for war. I entered his bedroom, and when I saw he wasn't there, I moved to find him in his office when I heard his cough.

"Nice and easy," Olivia's voice sounded from his bathroom. I moved toward his en suite, my heels silent on the carpet, and saw Ray sitting on his toilet seat with an oxygen mask on his face. Olivia spoke in a soothing tone as she pressed the end of a stethoscope to his chest.

"What happened?!"

Ray looked up, and his eyes narrowed. "Get out." It was weak.

I ignored his order and rushed forward just as he jutted his foot out and kicked the door closed.

"Lock it," I heard him tell Olivia.

"Please, just tell me what's going on!"

"Fuck off, kitten."

Angry tears burned my cheeks as I sat on the other side of the door. "I hate you!"

The plane touched down in Florence and jolted me awake. I discarded the onset of fear of what lay ahead and made my way to the rental counter to secure a car. I'd gotten the loudest car imaginable: a canary yellow hatchback with a navigation system. I wasn't there to hide.

It was around 2:00 a.m local time when I sped into Barga a few hours later. The sleepy town was the perfect place to hide the bad guys. I was clueless to where I was going, and it seemed the whole town was shut down. I needed daylight to begin my search. Daniello's descriptions of his home were my only guide. I dialed Cedric as I began to circle a shopping area.

"Where are you?" I could hear the grudge in his voice.

"I just got to Barga. I don't think I'm going to find a place to sleep tonight."

"Find a shopping center and park there and get some shut eye until morning."

"I'm already working on it. I just got a crash course in European driving. I'm a fucking fan."

"Speed demon." Cedric chuckled. "Feeling a little out of place?"

"That's an understatement."

I spotted a row of specialty shops and parked directly in front of a bakery—Pasticceria Celeste *Heavenly Pastry*—and got out of the car. I looked over the glass and gold-framed menu with satisfaction and returned to my lemon-yellow hatchback.

"I think I've found something. He grew up here, so it's only a matter of finding someone who knows him or his family."

"It's not too late to turn around."

"Drop it."

Cedric sighed. "You'll have mail at Ville Le Pergola in about eight hours. I've booked you a room with my card."

"I'm not hiding, Cedric, but thank you." We sat in silence for a few moments. "How is she?"

"She's still asleep." I heard the hesitance in his voice, and dread coursed through me.

"Tell me."

"She's had another surgery."

"And?"

"She won't survive another setback." I swallowed the threatening emotion in an attempt to let the anger resonate.

"Taylor?"

"I'm here," I said hoarsely. "Joseph?"

"He's fine. He's actually with Nina and her brother tonight. I had a job."

"That's okay, that's good." I stomped down the guilt at abandoning him. But he was safer without me.

Cedric kept me in the present. "You want to tell me what your plans are?"

"Nope."

"Taylor, I can be on a plane in a few hours. Don't do this alone."

In a blatant attempt to change the subject, I gave Cedric some truth. "I regret not leaving Dyer with you."

He paused, and it made the distance seem more endless between us. "But you wouldn't have loved me. You would have resented me eventually."

I gripped my phone and sank into the stiff seat. "You're probably right."

"You're an impossible woman, Taylor. But I think that's what I love about you. You can't be tamed."

"I can't lose you too, Cedric. I can't."

"You won't."

"If the past has taught us anything at this point, we know there are no guarantees. You can't make me that promise."

More silence.

I sighed. "How the fuck did it get to this point?" Cedric stayed mute as I rambled through my thoughts. "Why would he go through all the trouble with Laz if he was just going to let me die?"

"I hate the motherfucker, but I don't think he had anything to do with it."

"Even so, he's been watching me since we started. If he didn't do it, he knew it was going to happen, and he *let it* happen." I didn't bother filling him in on the fact that he'd warned me if I got in the way he'd do it himself. It only made me more of a monumental fool.

"Ask him, and don't be polite about it."

"I don't intend to. I'm such an idiot. I've destroyed everything I worked for. And for what?"

"Would you give yourself a break? You had started this before Amber came back, before you knew about Joseph. And before you knew the extent of who he was."

"I still don't know who he is, but I should have ended it."

"And he wouldn't have made it in time to get you away from Laz."

"Laz wasn't going to kill me."

"Are you sure?"

I let out an ironic chuckle. "Do you see the pattern here?"

"This isn't funny."

I grinned. "It is a little."

"Not at all. Come home. Marry me. I can live with your resentment." It was said in jest, but I felt the sadness in his tone. The longing. I hated myself at that moment for becoming his headache, his heartache. For dragging him into my mess, for making him a target.

"I'm sorry, Cedric. Please just know that."

"We'll get through this."

I pulled the lever on the side of my seat as I looked at the dimly lit line of shops in front of me. At night, Barga was peaceful. There wasn't a car or soul around. I rolled down my window slightly and let in some of the air. It was a cool summer night, and the mountain breeze drifted through the car and put me at ease. Though my circumstances were anything but, I felt strangely relaxed.

"Taylor?"

"I'm okay. I think I might even manage some sleep."

"Tell me his name, Taylor."

"No. Cedric, just let me handle it."

"I fucking hate this!"

"So you've repeated." I smiled.

"I want a check in every hour you're awake."

"I'll do my best."

A tap on my driver's side window woke me, and I shot up in my seat, my body aching from where I solidly slept. I was doing a shit job of keeping my guard up.

"Scuzie, non volevo spaventarti." *Sorry, I did not mean to frighten you.* An older man, who looked to be in his late sixties, smiled at me through the window. I turned the key and let it down fully. He had kind brown eyes and faded olive skin. His hair was solid white and combed back neatly. Underneath an apron, he wore a T-shirt and black slacks.

"Pardon?"

He smiled with recognition. "You are American. I was asking if you were okay. I see you alone here."

I wiped my hand down my face to free it of sleep debris. "Oh, yes. I'm fine."

I glanced at the old beat up pickup truck parked next to me. The tailgate was down, and there were several canvas bags piled on top of it.

"I got in a few hours ago, and I got a little lost, so I decided to wait here until morning."

"Good morning."

I glanced at the clock on the dash. I'd only been asleep for a few hours.

I looked back to him in question.

He shrugged, his palms open. "Well, it is morning for me. You are here to vacation in Barga?"

My stomach knotted at the word and the way he spoke it. "Something like that."

"Oh, well, I feed you breakfast as a welcome. I am Donato." He placed his hand on his chest in proud declaration. The man was slightly frail in frame due to his age. And there was nothing threatening in his posture. My stomach had been empty for days, and I had ignored the rumble that reminded me as much.

"I'm Taylor." I bit my lip as he stared down at me. "I don't want to impose, but would it be possible for me to use your restroom?"

"Of course." His thick accent was charming and upbeat. "Come." He moved to the truck and gripped two heavy bags of flour before he headed toward the door of the bakery.

My excitement spiked. "This is your bakery?"

"Yes. I opened it fifty years ago."

"Wow," I said as I grabbed two of the bags from the truck bed and followed him.

He set the bags down at the door and pulled a large chain of keys from his pocket. "I have not missed a single day," he boasted proudly. The sun was just beginning to light the city and my mouth unhinged slightly as I took my first look around. Barga was nestled in the mountains, and the architecture alone took my breath away.

"This place is beautiful."

"It's old. There is far better countryside further south." Donato turned to see my full hands. "You did not have to help."

I shrugged. "I really don't mind."

"You are kind, Bella." The man had just called me beautiful, and I felt anything but. I was a mess from head to foot. My hair was an unkempt rat's nest. A far cry from the polished professional I was mere days ago.

The bakery had an intimate feel. Once through the doors, we walked past several small tables situated closely together so that anyone who dined there never really ate alone. Brightly colored paintings covered every inch of the walls. The residual smell of baked goods invaded my nose and had my mouth watering. We walked past a service counter and glass case to a large kitchen with a huge wooden countertop. We set the bags down, then we walked back to the truck to grab the rest. Once unloaded, Donato pointed toward the restroom. After I took care of business and thoroughly washed my face, I entered the kitchen to thank him.

"Thank you so much."

"Come sit . . ."

He'd already forgotten my name. "Taylor."

"Taylor. I had a red-haired wife once. She was very full of life."

"I'm pretty boring."

"So you say." He gave me a wink. "Come sit. I make you breakfast."

I was at ground zero. The circumstances couldn't be better. I had no doubt a man who lived in Barga for fifty years knew of Daniello. Even if I wasn't at the right bakery, I was in the right place. If I played it right, I had a small chance at the element of surprise.

"As long as I'm not intruding. I would love breakfast."

Once Donato had situated his supplies to suit his workspace, he washed his hands and threw an apron in my direction.

"You help."

"Oh. Sure." I slipped the apron on, tied a bow at my back,

and secured my hair in a knot.

"Wash hands."

"Yes, sir."

I washed my hands and joined him as he flicked flour all over the counter.

"Let us make a mess."

"I'm good at making messes."

Donato kept at his task as he planted his hands in the bed of flour and shook off the excess. "Everyone is good at something."

"I warn you now, I have never baked."

"Ah, but today you will, Taylor."

My heart seized at the subtle similarities in speech of my new friend and my lost lover.

Donato studied me.

"It has been a long time since I had a beautiful woman to help me in the kitchen."

"Thank you."

"I see no ring. You are not married?"

"No."

"No children?"

I shook my head. "No. I'm more of a business woman than a family woman."

"Ah, but family is everything."

"I'm beginning to understand that. I have a sister with a son. They moved to be with me."

Kind eyes offered me more solace with kind words. "So, then you have a family."

I nodded as I thought of my sister in that hospital bed.

"She is very sick." I was so much better at confessing to strangers.

Donato paused his fingers. "I am sorry for you."

"Thank you."

He drew a handful of flour out of a canvas sack and piled

it onto the table. He grabbed a bottle of olive oil and plugged the top of it with his finger as he sprinkled it all over the waiting flour.

"So you vacation alone?"

"Yes."

He pulled out a smaller bag filled with yeast, cupped his hand in careful measure, then tossed it in a bowl before adding some piping hot water.

"What are we making?"

"New friends bake bread."

Once he had assembled the ingredients, adding everything with a pinch here and there with his hands, he threw the ready dough in my direction.

"Press with this," he said as he tapped the fat bottom of his hand above his wrist. "And separate into four." He placed four glass bowls next to me.

He cleared his side of the table with the swipe of a towel as I began to start a different dough.

I let out an incredulous laugh at my circumstance.

"What is so amusing?" Donato asked as he eyed me with a pinch of salt between his fingers.

"If you only knew how strange this is after the last few days of my life. Being here with you, in this kitchen. It's kind of unbelievable."

"Did you get on a plane to vacation to Barga?"

"Sort of."

"And you slept outside my bakery alone?"

"Well . . . yes."

He tossed the salt into a bowl and began to mix. "Then maybe it is not so unbelievable."

Donato moved lighting fast as he lit every oven at his disposal and began to fill baking pan after baking pan with hand measured concoctions.

"You do all of this alone. Every day?"

He braided three loaves of bread before I had my sentence out.

"Every day. I am a bit of—What is your expression . . .? Control freak."

"I'm kind of the same way." He gave me a wink. "You think?"

I laughed. "I *know*."

"Well, then we both make progress in my kitchen this morning."

I watched him, a master in his element, as the room filled with mouthwatering scents of baking bread and sweet pastry. I followed his every order to the letter as he placed my hands in flour and shook them off when the dough began to stick to them. I forgot myself and became immersed as we "made a mess." Two espressos later, we began to fill the glass cases.

"You have helped so much," Donato complimented as he inspected the fruits of our labor.

"It was my pleasure," I said around a mouthful of rustic bread and basil/honey-flavored butter. "This is truly delicious." I set the bread down as he moved to get up from the table and pulled his keys from his pocket.

"Donato, I am looking for someone."

"Oh?"

"A friend. Daniello Di Giovanni. Do you know him?"

"Of course. He lives not far from here."

My heart spiked as Donato searched through his keys.

"Can I possibly get his address from you?"

"Yes, but he is not home. He is away much. He comes to the bakery for Bruttiboni when he is home. He was fat from them as a child."

I laughed despite my hopes being dashed. Of course, it wasn't going to be that easy.

Donato spoke up, sensing my obvious disappointment. "I'm sure he will return soon. His sister ordered a cake for his niece's birthday party this weekend."

"Thank you."

Donato wrote down the address and handed it to me. "How do you know Daniello?"

"He came to the States. Told me of your Bruttiboni. I had to try it for myself."

Donato twisted the key in the door and opened his bakery for business.

"This is a long way to travel for Bruttiboni."

"I wanted to see Barga." *Before I die.*

"Well, you have much to see. I'll make you a basket. You go enjoy the day."

"I don't want to trouble you."

"It is no trouble, Taylor."

Just as he unlocked the door, an older man came in and shuffled his feet to take the table closest to the counter. "Come va, Barta?"

"Va bene." The older man said as he looked over to me. "Chi è questo?" I knew enough to know he wanted to know my name.

"Taylor." I extended my hand his way as he waved me off.

Donato snapped, which was unexpected. "Do not be rude, you old goat. She has traveled far to see our Barga."

"Espresso," the old man ordered as if he couldn't care less.

Donato shook his head in apology. "He knows he can't have you, Bella. He is grumpy for that."

I shrugged with a wink as Donato moved to grab his espresso. Once he set it in front of him, along with a paper, he motioned for me to join him in the kitchen.

"It is probably not a good idea for you to ask for Daniello to other people. He is a very private man."

Ain't that the truth.

"I am staying in town at Ville Le Pergola. Would you phone me if he returns?"

Donato grabbed a fresh loaf of the bread we'd made and several containers from the fridge. "Take for a lunch."

I moved to grab my purse, and he waved me away. "Bella, do not insult me."

"Thank you."

I picked up the basket as Donato walked me to the door. "Bella, this sadness you keep with you. Is this what brings you to Italy?"

Honest with strangers.

"Yes."

"And does Daniello know of this sadness?"

"I don't know."

Donato waited, his brown eyes searing through my green. A silent understanding passed between us.

"You come to see me again."

It was a polite order. "Okay."

His lips twitched in amusement. "Maybe not so early for you."

He placed the basket in my hand and gripped my face before kissing me on both cheeks.

"Go, enjoy Barga."

I got in my car and placed the bounty Donato gave me in the seat. I checked into Ville Le Pergola, a postcard boutique hotel with small rooms, frumpy beds, outdated linens, and old box TVs. But the iron balcony offered breathtaking views of the city and the surrounding mountains.

It was truly magnificent.

An excellent place to die.

I laughed at the irony. Only in my wildest dreams could I have imagined a place like this in my childhood bedroom in Dyer.

I spent hours on the balcony and broke out the basket, munching on bread and staring into space. I decided to drive past Daniello's at sundown. A knock on my door let me know Cedric had come through as promised.

I opened the door to the front desk clerk, who wore a warm smile. "Buonasera." *Good evening.*

"Grazie." I handed him twenty euros and grabbed the massive box from him to avoid conversation. He took the hint and his leave. On the squeaky brass bed, I shredded the brown paper to reveal a Tennessee Vols care package.

"Funny asshole."

I rolled my eyes at Cedric's sense of humor while I ripped it apart. Inside, I had everything I needed. A loud, orange T-shirt, matching socks, and twin Glocks buried in an oversized *Smokey* mascot doll with enough ammo to take out every pedestrian in Barga. He'd managed to stick a nine millimeter in an orange foam football.

I knew it was pointless, as did Cedric, still I texted him to ease his mind.

Me: Love the shirt. Thanks for the friends.

Cedric: I said every hour.

Me: Not going to happen. He's not here.

Cedric: You work fast.

Me: I have his address.

Cedric: Wait for him to come to you.

"Don't I always," I said to no one. I loaded both guns and tucked them under my pillows. I sat on the balcony in the lone chair provided and watched the sun drift from one edge of the sky to the other. Restless and curious, I slipped into my hatchback and typed in Daniello's address. Five minutes outside of Barga, I turned onto a dirt road. I spotted the villa in the distance and his plane on a hill next to it. There was one way in and one way out. Anyone who occupied the house could see who was coming half a mile away.

Despite the fact that the villa was lifeless, it made it no less beautiful. Stone walls and iron gates surrounded the large home. I could only see the bones of the house from a distance; up close it seemed impenetrable. I stopped outside the walls and got out of the car. I saw a security camera in the corner of the fence and turned to look directly at it. I choked any emotion I had down and let my anger through.

"That's not how you say goodbye to a lover."

I got back into the hatchback and kicked up dust. I raced down the road and couldn't help but to take in the countryside.

Such a different world.

He lived a different life in Italy. His second reality. I wondered how many secrets he kept from me.

I felt a sick gnaw start as I thought how uninvolved we really were.

CHAPTER 26

Daniello

"SONO QUI." *I AM HERE,* I SAID AS I SHIFTED MY CAR AND GRIPPED my phone. "Stop bitching at me, Tula."

"Your English is getting better." My sister's smile could be heard over the phone. "Tell me, brother, at your age, why this sudden interest in speaking English? God knows you were too stubborn to use it before."

"I have been to the States."

"And you have met a woman?" I could hear the smile in her voice.

"Stop talking nonsense."

"Hmmm. She would not have forgiven her uncle for missing her party."

"She will not need to forgive me. Domani." *Tomorrow.*

I hung up just as my phone pinged with another security alert reminder as I pulled up to my Villa. The gate was still intact. Sometimes animals set it off. I pulled forward and saw everything was as it should be. Rocco pulled up behind me seconds after I grabbed my bag from the trunk.

"Where have you been?" he barked in Arabic. I walked past him without a glance his way. His presence alone set my blood boiling.

"Fine, in English. Where did you go?"

Inside, I threw my bag down on my couch, grabbed a beer from my kitchen, and took a swallow. "I do not answer to you. Get the fuck out of my house before I kill you like I should have a month ago."

Rocco stepped toward me like the fool he was. "He wants to meet with you."

"And you are being a good little dog. Tell him I got the message."

"You are working alone?" Rocco pulled out his gun and set it on the table before he removed his jacket.

"I have always worked alone. The States were a mistake. Do not make yourself comfortable. You are not welcome here."

Rocco threw his head back in a laugh. "All because of you and that whore. We are no longer in the States. We have no issues."

I shook my head. "If you call her a whore again, I will pull every tooth from your head."

Rocco lifted his palms. "Fine."

"Get out. I have much to do."

"I will stay for dinner."

I reeled on him, and he smiled. "Ah, ah, ah, cousin, you cannot touch me now." Rocco's eyes narrowed in challenge.

"Get. The. Fuck. Out. You are no more than a trained dog."

He shook his head and tapped his temple. "I have accomplished much."

"You have an owner. And I will always be free."

"You will always be a slave to your vengeance."

I swallowed the last of my beer and set the bottle on the counter.

I shoved my hands in my pockets in an attempt not to break the bones in his face. I took a step toward him and met his black eyes. "When we were boys, and we moved from Egypt, I was forced by my father to be friends with you and play games with you. I did not like you then, and I do not like you now. I no longer wish to know you. Get the fuck out of my house."

Rocco's face reddened with each word I spoke. He shrugged on his jacket and grabbed his gun, tucking it back in the holster. "You have no loyalty."

"I have found it does not pay off."

"There are still games to be played, cousin." Rocco chuckled as he slammed the door behind him. I finished my beer and took a look around. Weeks on the job had done nothing to ease my ache for her. I sat at my desk and opened my laptop. During my missions, I had succeeded in avoiding her. I'd resisted every urge to watch her. As I sat at my desk with the possibility of seeing her a click away, I lost the battle. I pulled up the footage of the penthouse and rewound it to the last time I saw her. Nothing. She had not been back to the penthouse. A dull ache ripped through my chest where she had resumed her place. No matter how hard I tried to rid myself of thoughts of her, they pushed through the recesses to the forefront of my mind and tortured me in waking dreams.

Rocco had been right. Taylor was a weakness. And my father had seen me as a disgrace up until the day he died for not being one to follow his footsteps. His disappointment in me was the result of my hatred for him. He had pre-destined his sons to become his disciples, soldiers and the predecessors to the family business. He, like Rocco, fed on power and corruption. He was the evil I despised. He had lost one son to his iron will and another to his depravity. Rocco was his only heir.

My security alarm pinged again as I pulled up the footage. I moved my mouse to pinpoint the time of the alert and saw a yellow hatchback pull up to my gate. *Probably just some lost traveler.*

I froze when I saw a glimpse of red hair when she exited the vehicle. She walked up to my gate and peered through the iron to survey my property. All the breath left me when she turned and looked right into the camera. My heart thundered as she spoke directly to me.

"That's not how you say goodbye to a lover." My chest recoiled as I gripped my keys in my hand and I paused at the door of my villa. Dread filled every part of me as I recalled my cousin's parting words.

"There are still games to be played, cousin."

Taylor

I'd spent the time in Barga, unsure of my next move, walking the streets, taking long drives through the Lucca countryside, and living like a tourist. Metal-gray Dyer seemed light years away from the countryside filled with trees, lush green fields, pastel flowers, and a mountain backdrop. I felt like I was driving through a picture I'd seen in an art gallery when I lived in New York. With the sun nestled into soft white clouds, the hills in spun gold, I turned a drive into a dream. As angry and lost as I was at the hot mess my life had become, as tortured as I felt about everything I left behind, including a suffering Amber, I found a sort of peace as I drove.

At night, I lay wondering about the lover who left me so abruptly, who had tortured me with his hello and goodbye. I hated that I loved him. I hated that I couldn't find it in me to resent him for any part of what happened when I was with him. I hated that I played with fire and burned my sister, the person I loved most in the world. I hated that in order to protect her, I had to stay away from her.

I was never meant to have a family or love. I had resigned myself to that fact long ago. And those thoughts had been stripped away once again with Daniello's absence and the nightmare after. I'd been conditioned to believe emotions were for the weak. I should have trusted my mentor and not my heart.

"You ever heard the saying 'Don't ever tell your problems to anyone. Twenty percent don't care, and the other eighty percent are glad you have them'?"

Ray ignored my teary eyes. "Handle it."

"What if it's positive?"

Ray's eyes scoured me briefly, his face void of any emotion. "Handle it."

"Ray, you can't be serious."

He shot up from his chair. "You're going to finish first in your class. We should be hearing from Harvard any day. You want to give that up for a mistake?"

Bile threatened as my stomach churned. "You are a cruel bastard."

"I'm a sensible man. And you've let your emotions run rampant, which is exactly what I taught you not to do. You need to figure it the fuck out."

"Jesus, what is wrong with you! I came from a family incapable of love, and even I know this isn't right! You . . . you are all wrong."

Ray straightened his tie and sat down again, his breaths coming fast. "I don't want a child. I don't need obligations, and neither do you."

"Ray, we don't hate each other. We get along—"

"Us again, Taylor? There. Is. No. Us. There's an arrangement, a contract. And until I decide to fuck you again, I don't want to see your face. Understood?"

All I felt for him threatened to die away at that moment.

"You are going to hell."

He flipped a page and picked up a pen. "I'm packing my bags, kitten."

I stalked toward his study door as my stomach churned then looked back at him one last time in a plea. "Ray?"

His face was pale, and his eyes weren't focused. "I can't do it. I can't. Please just get the fuck out."

A few days after I had arrived, I'd rejoined Donato at his bakery before sunrise to help him open. He'd seemed pleased at my reappearance. In need of answers, I decided to ask questions as he rolled out a table full of dough, but he beat me to the punch.

"You have questions, Bella?" He peeked over at me expectantly with a freshly made batch of dough.

I nodded. "How do you know Daniello?"

"I am family. His father married my brother's daughter."

"You are his great uncle?"

Donato nodded. "His mother, God rest her soul, was not happy in Egypt. She wanted to return home, and so his father brought them here."

"Them?"

"Daniello and Matteo."

"Matteo?"

Donato punched the dough with his fist. "His brother."

Daniello had never mentioned a brother. All of his stories in Italy had consisted of him and Rocco.

Donato's kind eyes scrutinized me. "You did not know of him?"

I shrugged. "Like you said, he is a private man. I don't know *anything*."

In an attempt to hide my sulk, I kept busy with the dough.

"Matteo is a very painful subject for him. Daniello was only eleven months old when his brother was born. They were very, very close."

"What happened?"

"Amon, his father, made them join the Egyptian Army, and Matteo was killed. He was slaughtered by a commanding officer in front of Daniello, and he left the army a changed man."

My body tensed in recognition as I thought of Daniello and the hard edge he carried with him. The guard he rarely dropped. The anger that radiated from him, the grudge his eyes held. When Daniello spoke of his childhood, even his memories with Rocco, the stories were laced with happiness. I'd pictured a world of beauty and adventure like he had described, so very far from the childhood I'd lived.

Donato paused. "I have said too much."

"Not at all," I said while I began to braid some dough. "What about Rocco?"

Donato raised a brow. "What about Rocco?"

"He's an angry man."

"He is a foolish and jealous man. His father was killed in the army as well, but he does not concern himself with sentiments for the dead. He is also a *selfish* man."

I deadpanned, "He's an asshole."

Donato chuckled as he threw several loaves into the oven. "Rocco was the soldier his father wanted Daniello to be. Right before Amon died, he burdened Daniello with that truth. But it was no secret. Daniello remained a stranger to Italy for many years before his father passed."

"Rocco is jealous?"

"Rocco has always been second best; a man determined to prove his worth."

"And Daniello?"

"He is very much the soldier his father wanted him to be, but he serves no army."

Daniello's words in my office months before rang home.

"Who are you?"

"I am the man who will disappear from your bed one night without

any explanation."

You see, there are bad men out there who will not hesitate to pull the trigger . . . rape, steal, and climb with hungry claws to get to where they want to be."

"And you are one of them?"

"No. I am the man who stomps on those men with my heel."

Donato had paused his hands and was staring at me intently. "What are you thinking of?"

What if he isn't a villain?

Donato wiped the counter with the towel as he spoke. "I have said too much. This is not my story to tell. Please do not mention this to Daniello."

"You have my word."

CHAPTER 27

Taylor

I was living in limbo. The only news that kept me going was that my sister was still breathing. Nina had taken it upon herself to keep Joseph. I had no objections. I had no clue what the right move was, aside from taking the danger away from them. I couldn't find my strength. I had no order. Love had ripped away the hard lines in my heart, weakened my walls.

Love in any form made me weak. That was the truth of why I'd avoided it for so fucking long. Whether it be the love for Laz, Ray, my sister, or for the man I met just a few short months ago, it was a weakness. All I'd worked for I'd lost due to my weakness.

And still, when it came to regrets, I felt like I hadn't fully lived until I admitted loving every one of them. Tracing my steps back, Laz had turned into an abusive liar and became impossible to trust. Ray had always thrown away my attempts at mending the bridge between us, and Daniello, well, he'd blown my life to hell with his sudden appearance, his secrets, and he had exclusive claim to the heart I had left.

And he took it with him.

I had no future. Just a path to right the wrongs I had buried with a new life that no longer belonged to me. I pulled at the bottle of whiskey and tossed it up in the air, shattering it with three bullets before it hit the ground. I stared at the peaceful hillside I'd taken residence on as I thought of Ray and his hopes for me.

Ray came to me a week after our blowout, hungry and eager as he spread me with his hands and licked my center. Enraged at my body's response to his touch I clawed at his skin before he entered me slowly while he hovered above. "Fuck, you feel good."

I lay back, lifeless, my jaw clamped, refusing to meet his eyes.

"Still angry with me, kitten?"

He pumped slowly, purposefully forcing me to face him as tears streamed down my cheeks. It was the first and last time he would ever see me cry. He paused above me and pulled out as he sat on the bed, his face to the carpet. "Don't mistake sex for love and love for loyalty. The minute they stop paying attention to you is the minute it's over. Stay loyal to your end game."

He and I had been mute ghosts drifting through the hallways of a cold mansion. His silence was deafening. He never asked the question that I knew weighed heavily on his mind. "I wasn't pregnant."

Ray inhaled deeply, his brow covered in sweat. He said nothing.

"What's your end game, Ray?"

"I thought I made that clear." He slipped on his boxers and turned to me before he walked out the door. "You."

Ray had shown me the thin line between love and hate, and I had walked it with him until the end of our time together. It felt like a different line with Daniello.

But was I confusing sex and love again?

I watched the sun descend behind a line of Cypress Evergreens and made my decision. I was done waiting. It was time to make some noise.

I'd spent the next day in the heart of Barga at the various shops, making small talk with the owner's using the small amount of conversational Italian I knew, while I made random purchases and my presence known. I walked down the street, scantily clad in barely-there shorts and a tank top paired with three-inch heels. I was a walking neon sign and for no other reason than I was tired of the charade. I counted on small town talk, the way I did back in Dyer, to get word to my enemy, and I would bet my fortune it was Rocco.

I was restless, determined to protect my family, and itching for a fight.

That night at L'Osteria Di Riccardo Negri—a local bar—I made friends with Gian and Omero, two men passing through on business. They were bored with the sleepy town and a perfect excuse for me to behave badly. I stood at the blue, red, and gold neon-lit bar with Gian's arm wrapped around me while Omero chatted me up about his time in America. Gian's fingers drifted down my low-cut dress and massaged my back as Omero fucked me with his eyes. The two men were in no competition for my attention as I gave them both false impressions in equal measure. I had no expectations. I only hoped I was being watched. It wasn't hard to slip back into sexual indifference with a stone heart. I'd been doing it a long time.

"You like Italian?" It was a shitty attempt at flirting from Gian as he slipped his fingers between the low part of my dress and my skin. I didn't object as I leaned over, a whisper from his lips. "I've gotten a taste for it." Gian grew hard in his seat, an apparent outline in his pants, and squeezed my flesh as Omero ordered us another round. "Excuse me, I need to use the restroom." Gian's hand tightened briefly as he stared straight at my peaking nipples. And it had nothing to do with him. The room was freezing, and I was wearing a whore's scrap of a dress. I grabbed my purse, which barely fit my Glocks and a second round of ammo, then made my way toward the back. While pulling up my dress, awareness hit me like a ton of bricks. Underneath the narrow stall and to the right I saw wingtips. Unlocking the door, I made my way to the sink. I placed my purse next to it and ran some water before I pumped soap into my hand then met his eyes in the mirror.

"Rocco, what a surprise."

His eyes narrowed as he stood, his arms crossed. "You are already dead, whore."

"Nice to see you too." I gave him a wink as I turned and wiped my hands on the waiting linen. "Can I buy you a drink?"

He pulled his phone from his pocket and sent a text before he lasered his focus on me. I gripped my bag as casually as I could right before he snatched me by the hair.

"It disgusts me he was going to go legitimate for you."

Shock filled me, and I winced as he pressed me against the wall with a hate-filled face.

"You have done nothing but bring ruin to our family."

"Your family?" I spit out with pure contempt. "Not what I heard. I heard you were an orphan."

He slammed my head into the tile wall as I pressed the Glock I'd already gripped to his crotch.

Ignoring the throb at the back of my head, I dug into him. "You started this fight motherfucker and I'm about to end it."

Rocco laughed despite the gun firmly pressed to his dick.

"You have no idea how wrong you are."

"I'm pretty sure I have the upper hand at the moment. Turn around and open the door."

"I don't think so." Rocco smiled and leaned in. "How *is* your sister?"

In a split second, the butt of my gun connected with his chin before I pressed it to his temple. Rocco leaned in with zero restraint or fear of my itchy trigger finger. "I could have her dead by morning."

"Fuck you!"

His laughter echoed throughout the bathroom. "You think killing me will fix your problems, *cagna*? They have only just begun."

"What the fuck did I ever do to you?"

"You exist. We had him close, and then he dreams of a life making puppies with you."

"Close to what?" Rocco grabbed the barrel of my gun, and it took everything in me not to pull the trigger.

Rocco feigned a sigh, "It doesn't matter. Daniello will *do* what he must."

Against my better judgment, I pleaded with him. "My sister is innocent, Rocco. She knows nothing. Jesus Christ, I know nothing!" I gripped his hand and placed my gun inside of it. "Take me somewhere. Let's end this."

Rocco barked out another laugh before he took a step back and spit a mouth full of blood on the floor between us. "I could shoot you now and have the busboy clean the blood from my shoes. Like I said, whore, you are already dead. And I will not have to lift a finger." He watched my face twist as he took another jab. "You are now the price he has to pay. And make no mistake, he *will* pay it."

He let the gun drop from his hand. "You keep your toy. You need it more than I do."

He pulled the door open and walked out without a backward glance. Even with me in Barga, my sister wasn't safe. I pulled out my cell phone.

Cedric answered on the first ring.

"Taylor."

"Is she safe?"

"Yes. I'm with her now."

"Cedric, don't let her out of your sight."

"What the fuck is going on?"

I paced the bathroom and shoved my Glock back into my purse. My voice was hoarse as I admitted my worst fear. "She's not safe, no matter what I do. You are being watched."

"I won't leave her side, Taylor. What the fuck happened!?"

"I don't know."

"Taylor, talk to me."

"I'm fine. Nothing happened. Cedric, just keep her safe. It's time for a Hail Mary. I need you to promise me."

"Goddamnit, Taylor. I won't. That's a promise."

"No matter what?"

"Taylor, please tell me his name."

I shook my head, unwilling to bring him into the crosshairs. He already knew too much. "We both knew I wasn't going to live through this. Take care of my family. I love you."

I hung up as I sank against the wall.

"Taylor?" Gian was at the door.

"I'll be right there."

Mustering up all my strength to keep it together, I pulled my dress back into place and ran my hands through my hair. I reapplied my lipstick and met Gian at the bar. "Where is Omero?"

"His wife called. He had to return home." He gave me a sly grin as he handed me a whiskey. Apparently, there had been a conversation between the two men and Gian wanted to claim his prize. I gulped down the drink and ordered another.

"Are you okay?" Gian resumed his grip around my waist, and I nodded. I was anything but okay. I was terrified to walk out the door, unable to think about anything but an impending fight I had no chance of winning. I tossed the whiskey back and let it burn.

If I ended up buried in Barga that night, there was no guarantee that my sister wouldn't suffer the same fate. That fear kept me planted as I tried to think of a way out of it.

But there wasn't a way out. I still had no idea what I was dealing with. And if Rocco hadn't bothered with the opportunity to take me out, there was only one other person that would do it.

The rest of my hope sank inside of me like a heavy stone drifting into the dark depths of Mediterranean. I was no closer to saving my family even as I sat as a sacrificial lamb for slaughter.

I needed to relocate. I needed to grab the rest of my ammo. I had to figure it out. I pushed away my drink and turned to Gian, who watched me carefully.

"Gian, take me to my hotel?"

Gian threw some bills on the bar and leaned in close, his tone low. "Show me the way."

Outside the bar, a step from the door, he made a sudden move to press me to the brick wall in an attempt to kiss me, and I refused him. He was a smoke screen, and I'd got the attention I sought out, but looking at Gian's eager face, it was an easy decision. I'd been selfish with people's lives long enough.

"Actually, Gian, I'm not feeling well. I'll see myself to the hotel. Goodnight."

"Oh, woman, you cannot do this to me now." He was all smiles, eager and ready for the chase as I opened the driver door and sat in my seat. He blocked my attempt to close it as he leaned in to save what would never happen. Daniello had made me a monogamous woman.

Bastard.

Determined to get the poor man out of harm's way, I opened my mouth to speak and felt a whoosh of air.

Before I knew what was happening, Daniello had him pinned to the hood, his hands wrapped around his neck, his face twisted in rage. "Leave now, and I will spare your life."

Gian screeched in terror as I pulled my Glock from my purse and pointed my Glock at Daniello's temple.

"Let him go."

"Do not test me, Taylor." I watched Daniello, his eyes trained on Gian—the same eyes that I saw that day in Florida.

Guns meant shit to these men.

Gian's eyes flitted between us as he choked under a death grip. I lowered my gun.

"Okay, just let him go, please." Daniello gripped the hand Gian had on his shirt and I heard the crack of bones before he screamed.

"Stop!"

He released him abruptly, and Gian gave no fight as he bounced off the car and made a beeline for the safety of the bar. Daniello turned to me, a picture of darkness.

"Get in the fucking car."

Sirens sounded in the distance as I weighed my options. Daniello came toward me, a flash of lightning. Thirty seconds later, we were speeding away from the bar.

Daniello was excruciatingly silent as we rode out of town toward his villa. I made peace with fate as I tried to appeal to the man who once cared for me.

"Please don't let them hurt Amber. Please, Daniello. Call them off! She doesn't know anything. They don't even know your name!"

Daniello sped up and into his driveway then slid to a stop, forcing us both forward.

"I'm begging you. If I mean anything to you at all, don't let them hurt her. You *know* I know nothing!"

He slammed his hand on the dash and killed the running car as he turned toward me with dark eyes.

"Do you have any idea what you've done by coming here?!" I moved to get out of the hatchback, but he gripped my wrist. I slapped him hard as he took all the air out of the space between us with his roar. "Do you know what you've done, Taylor?!"

"What I've done?! How could you let him hurt her! How could you let him come after me!"

I escaped the car before he could reach for me. He got out on the opposite side, peering at me in shock. It separated us enough that I was able to let my anger fly.

"You horrible bastard! How could you let him hurt me this way! After everything . . ." I let my tears fall as my anger consumed me. "You were too much of a coward to do it yourself, and your fucking dog shot my sister!"

Daniello studied me with confusion as I crumbled in front of him. "So finish this, but do it yourself, you bastard, because I can't live with this." I gripped my hands to my chest. "But you tell them to leave my Amber out of it!"

Daniello stood deathly still as he spoke. "Taylor—"

"God, I should have known I wouldn't matter. Why am I so damn stupid when it comes to you? I'll make it easy for you." I leaned in the car, pulled the purse from the seat, and aimed my gun at my temple. "Tell me you will spare her life, and I will pull the trigger right now."

Daniello flinched in front of the headlights. "Taylor! Stop!"

"No." I shook my head as he moved toward me and pressed the ready gun into my skin. My body racked with sobs. I was hysterical as he inched toward me, and I took a step away. "If you wanted to destroy me, you've done it. I'm a woman with no control. I've lost *everything*. And I would do *anything* for her. Anything! Promise me!"

His words came out in a low rush. "I cannot make that promise."

I crumbled as I tapped the gun against my head in frustration.

"Then I won't give you a goddamned easy way out," I said before I threw the gun at his feet. "Do it yourself."

In three angry strides, he was in front of me. His hands gripped my face. "You think I would kill you, Taylor? You think I would do this to you? To Amber?"

I sobbed as he gripped me tightly. "I could never hurt you."

"Liar!"

"Phoenix, believe me."

Overwhelmed and exhausted, I gripped his shoulders as I sank into the darkness.

Daniello

I gripped my phone as I watched her sleep. "I want a meeting. *Now.*"

"Ah, cousin, are you happy to have returned to your present? I would have delivered it myself, but she was busy whoring at the bar. I thought it was far better you saw her true colors."

"You will die for this, Rocco."

"You cannot touch me, cousin. You forget you have your mother's name for protection. That name is the only reason she is still breathing. *His* orders."

"Meeting. Now," I seethed.

"Perhaps tomorrow after the party. That would work best. I have ordered a special doll."

"You have gone too far."

"But you will bend now, won't you, cousin?" I threw the phone against the wall and Taylor shot up from the bed. Her face paled as she took in her surroundings and her eyes found mine.

I was the first to speak. "I did not know. I did *not* know."

"I don't care anymore." She lay back down and turned to face away from me. "We probably should have died in that house in Dyer anyway."

I moved my mother's old sewing chair next to my bed. Taylor kept her eyes on the floor. "I would not hurt you this way, Phoenix."

Taylor's eyes closed as she sank into the bed. "I'm tired of the fight. I'm just tired. Surviving shouldn't be this hard." Her face twisted as she touched the back of her head.

"You are hurt." I moved to inspect her as she spit her venom. "Don't you dare fucking touch me." My chest ripped open as she glared in my direction. "My mother beat me over half of my life. I can handle a bump on my head."

Her words struck me hard as I gripped the chair next to me. "Broom handles, anything that was close. She damned near killed me with a can of Lysol. But Amber—" she closed her eyes as she confessed her deepest hurt "—she tore her apart. She doesn't deserve the life she was born into. She was so little," she choked out as she kept her cries inside.

I scrubbed my face as she gripped the pillow beneath her. The fiery woman I met was breaking in front of me. "Don't look away from me, Amon," she snapped. "I'm showing you who *I* am. Not so fucking pretty, now, am I? Not so alluring. Did you know I was a whore?"

"Stop."

She met my eyes. "I was a whore for a wealthy man to ensure I had a place to sleep while my sister was beaten."

"No more," I growled before I stood to look out the window next to her.

"He used me and threw me away like trash. Because make no mistake, *lover*, that's what I am. Rocco was right."

"Stop! Right now, stop!" I clenched my fists beside her.

"I really should start believing people when they tell me who they are. But I think it's because I have been a liar for so long. I'm not powerful. I'm not strong. I'm a chicken shit. But I guess it doesn't matter." Her phone buzzed in her purse on the bedside table. She didn't even glance that way as she looked at me, her eyes void of soul. "This body is a lie. It's a shell."

"Phoenix."

"I wanted you so much, I buried myself." She laughed without humor. "That's my addiction: beautiful men without souls." Despair of the worst kind filled my body as she gave up on me. "How could I convince you to love me when I have no fucking idea who I am?"

"Phoenix—"

"You don't have to love me. But I'm asking you to save me. For the first time in my life, I'm asking a man to *save* me. I'm begging you, Daniello, finish this. Finish me."

I knelt by her side, my eyes intent on hers. "I would never harm you, Taylor."

"It doesn't matter anymore."

Her phone buzzed again, and I searched her purse then answered the call.

"Taylor?" The voice on the end of the line was that of a man destroyed.

"Cedric. She is safe. She is with me."

"Goddamn you, man. I swear to God if you hurt her—"

Taylor looked up at me with no sign of hope as I spoke. "She will be home soon."

"Put her on the phone."

"She cannot talk."

"Then I guess I'll see you in a few hours."

My patience ran out. "Do not threaten me, bald man. You should not have let her come."

"Really? Have you met the woman? How the fuck was I supposed to stop her? Call your goddamned dogs off. I just stuffed my trunk with two."

"I will work on that."

"I'm not letting this go until I hear her voice. You aren't the only motherfucker with friends overseas."

I did the only thing I could do to try to convince them both. "My name is Amon Daniello Stamatio Di Giovanni. I will not let any harm come to her or Amber. I will keep them safe. I promise on my life."

Taylor's eyes held mine as she sat up on the bed and grabbed the phone before she spoke softly. "It's almost over." She glanced at me warily and without trust. "It's almost over, Cedric."

She ended the call and handed it to me. "Your move, lover."

She turned over as her body shook silently in my bed before her breath went shallow and her shoulders stopped moving.

CHAPTER 28

Taylor

"TAYLOR."

I opened my eyes to see Daniello towering over me, his face etched with hours of lost sleep. "I need you to dress."

He pulled out my suitcase he must have retrieved from my hotel. I glanced down at it and turned over in his bed, staring out his iron-covered bay window at the statue in the center of his large patio. It was filled with dancing angels, and the water trickled down their joyful faces.

"Why am I still alive?"

"I never would have harmed you."

"Lie."

He sat down on the edge of the bed. "I threatened you to keep you safe and from asking questions."

"I don't care."

He gripped my shoulder and turned me to face him. "It is truth. I had to convince Rocco I had no feelings for you. I failed." He pulled at my hand until I stood in front of him and snapped the spaghetti straps of my dress before he pulled it off of me. Still sitting on the bed, his eyes roamed my body as he pulled me toward him and buried his head in my stomach. My hands lay lax at my sides.

"Forgive me, Phoenix."

Naked and raw, I looked down as he gripped me tightly to him. "I have ruined us both."

"Just do it, Daniello."

"No," he snapped as he looked up at me. "No." He placed a soft kiss against my stomach.

"Rocco told me you would be the one to kill me. What the fuck are you waiting for!?" I pushed at his shoulders as he gripped me tighter.

"Don't lie to me anymore. Don't be such a goddamned coward. Don't drag this out!"

He stood and lifted me, carrying us into the bathroom as I fumed. He started the shower and brought us both in.

"You think fucking me is going to make this go away?! I hate you!"

Daniello pulled off his T-shirt and jeans as I glared at him from under the running water.

He remained mute as he washed his hair and then mine. I pulled away from him and soaped my own body as he watched.

The smell of the soap hit me, and I bit my trembling lip. Daniello saw my reaction and closed the space between us. "This pain that you feel right now, this missing of me, I have felt this every minute since the penthouse. I had no knowledge of Rocco's plans. I stopped watching you. I was trying to break myself from you. I wanted to keep you safe. It was the only way to convince him. I did not know he would go this far."

I pushed past him and grabbed a towel. "I don't care."

"You do fucking care!" Daniello turned off the water. "You are not lost, Taylor, you are angry. I understand this." He looked down at me and gripped my face. "I am your mirror, Taylor

Ellison. Look at me, I am your mirror!"

With a burning throat, I swallowed. "What the hell are you talking about?" He pressed his forehead against mine and took several breaths.

"We are the same. Get dressed."

He walked out of the bathroom and closed the door.

Dressed and numb, I found Daniello at a large oak table on his patio. He was dressed casually in a chalky white button down shirt and slacks. The sheer beauty of him was only enhanced by the backdrop. As many times as I pictured him in Italy, it was a bleary contrast to the sight before me. His golden eyes found my green as he gestured for me to sit. I took the seat next to him.

"Are you hungry?"

I shook my head as he poured a cup of coffee for both of us, then pushed my cup toward me. I accepted it as we sat in silence.

Several times he looked my way, but I refused to meet his eyes.

"My mother was a mafia princess, and my father made sure she chose him."

I sipped my coffee and looked past him at the rolling hills surrounding his villa.

"She took her last breath believing they met by coincidence. I think that is the word?"

I nodded.

"But it was his plan. He was a career soldier. He married her and kept her in Cairo, away from her family, with the help of the military until a few years after my brother, Matteo, and I were born. My mother was unhappy in Cairo, and by order of my grandfather, we were made to move back to Italy. My father brought us back to avoid a small war. His intentions were to use her as a way of earning a place in the Di Giovanni family. By holding her there, it was a way of sending a message."

I furrowed my brow. "By holding his daughter hostage?"

"These were the ways of the old world. Bold moves meant much then. And my father wanted to prove himself a powerful man. Powerful enough to stand against the entire family. My mother was my grandfather's world. His only child. And my father was not of Italian blood."

Daniello's eyes glittered over me. I could feel his need for forgiveness. I could feel the ache between us. Daniello felt my hesitance and closed his eyes.

"When we arrived in Italy, my father was beaten terribly in front of the whole family and almost lost his life. My mother saved him from certain death. Still, he was not accepted as a son or into the family, but he had his children. Matteo and I were accepted, and at my grandfather's insistence, we took his last name for the protection it brought. Rocco was left with his father's last name but was never given the same treatment.

"My father saw it as a good sign, but he grew bitter. He focused his life energy on the three of us. He brought us to Cairo often and told us when we were of age we would start our duty as soldiers. He programmed us early to believe it was the only way to truly become a man."

Daniello sat back in his chair. "Rocco was meant to believe his father died in the army."

"He didn't?"

"My father killed him. I overheard him talking to one of his army brothers. My father *was* Rocco's father. That is why his biological mother did not protest when he took him away from Egypt. She did not want the truth discovered. She would have been shamed, and she feared my mother's family."

"Rocco is your brother?"

Daniello gave me a sharp nod. "I have never told him, neither did my father. And he would never reveal that to the family. It would have ruined his plans."

"Jesus."

"Still, my grandfather was no fool. Upon his death, he made certain that Rocco could not have a place in the family. He was a bastard son with no Italian blood."

"And Rocco has no idea?"

"I will never tell him. I loathe him. Inside of him is the evil that was my father."

"And your mother?"

"She played blind, but I did not fault her. She cared for us all the same but never interfered with my father's plans. So, when it was time, my father took us back to Cairo. Matteo and I enlisted with our Egyptian last name, Naifeh. He had three soldiers. It was his biggest accomplishment."

Daniello's eyes glossed over as he turned to me. "Matteo knew right away that we were in a very different army than what father had described. He warned us both. Rocco embraced it, and I stood beside my brother and witnessed the true evil of men."

"What happened?"

"We took part in the corruption in order to survive, but Matteo was not the type of man who could be silenced. One day, Matteo refused orders. The captain slit his throat in front of me."

I twisted my hands in my lap as Daniello's body tensed. "When we had served our time, and my grandfather became ill, I was ordered home to take my place in the family. I had other plans."

He looked over to me with a grief-infused face. "I freed my wife and left Italy."

Daniello clenched his fists. "I had to change myself. It took several years to execute the man responsible for Matteo's death and those who watched it happen. I was not ever a suspect. And even when I had finished my mission, I did not stop."

My whole chest ached as Daniello turned to me. "I *am* the evil man I despise, Taylor."

My mirror.

A world away from my life lived a man who fought his family for his own freedom and became someone else for the love of a sibling.

"Since I have returned to Italy, I have been pressed to join the family. And I have refused each time. I have always worked alone. I have no interest in it."

"Why were you in the States with Rocco?"

Daniello stood. "The first time, I had a contract for someone who used to own The Rabbit Hole. And then I needed a reason to return."

"A reason to ret—"

Daniello's intense stare cut me off.

"Me?"

He leaned down and placed his hands on the side of the table, caging me in. "You. Most of my clients are not in the States. And I was growing tired of the . . . job. So I thought of a way to bring peace to my family and return to you."

I scrubbed my hands down my face. "And?"

"I had connections with the US through my time as a soldier. I was met by a contractor who sold guns to the military. I took guns from those I killed and washed them through customs and sold them back to US soldiers."

Everything began to click into place. "You shipped them to Charleston."

Daniello nodded. "As long as I was giving the boss a part of the profit, I was becoming an earner, and it gave me an excuse to come to the States, to be with you. But I know now who made it impossible."

"Rocco."

Daniello paced. "Rocco remained home while I was away and had befriended the new boss. He has tried in every way to get into the family, but he saw this as his chance and accompanied me. I had to honor his wish because of their friendship. It was my biggest mistake."

"He sabotaged you."

He gave me a sharp nod. "And he told of my involvement with you."

"I could have shot him last night," I pointed out dryly. "I should have."

Daniello shook his head. "He is a made man, a captain now."

"The boss let him into the family?"

Daniello nodded. "It is still my place to take."

Realization struck as I looked over at him. "No."

"I do not have a choice. I have struggled with this, but they have found my weakness, a way to force my allegiance."

"Me."

Daniello's lips twitched. "You, pig head."

I ignored his attempt at a joke and remembered his words to me the night before. He asked me if I knew what'd I done by coming to Italy, and at that moment, I knew. We were each other's downfall.

My whole body filled with dread. "You'll be trapped in a living hell."

Daniello leaned in, now eye level with me. "You are worth it. Every minute, every second with you has been worth it."

Emotion bubbled up, threatening to spill over. "There's got to be another way."

"There is no other way." He pulled me from the chair. "I am a killer, Taylor. This life is not so far from the one I have been living. I fool myself that I am a better man. But that is not the truth."

I gripped him to me and searched his eyes. "You are a better man." He leaned in close. "I won't let you do this."

"You do not have a say."

I ripped my arms away. "Tell me this isn't real! Who is the boss? Can we not reason with him?"

"Good morning." Donato stood to the side of the table in a manicured suit with a massive cake in his hands, his eyes drifting between us. "I apologize, Bella. Have I interrupted you?"

Daniello tensed as I turned to look up at him. Contempt, anger, and resentment twisted his beautiful features. I drew my brows together as I looked at the older man. Donato chuckled at Daniello's visible response to his intrusion then set down the cake and winked at me. "She is one beautiful woman, Daniello."

Daniello's jaw ticked as he glared at his great uncle, and a shock wave hit me. I stood, mouth gaping, as I followed his eyes to Donato. "You?"

"I have already agreed to pledge myself to this family!" Daniello said as he pushed me behind him protectively.

"I am aware." He studied me with amusement. "You, Bella, have become my greatest ally. I am in your debt."

"No," Daniello snapped before he looked over his shoulder at me with solemn eyes. "This is not your mistake."

"Good morning." Rocco walked up and looked between the three of us before he pulled some icing off of the cake with his finger, making a loud sucking noise as he cleaned it off. Delighted with my misery, he eyed me over Daniello's shoulder. "You are pale, Taylor. Should I put you down for a nap?"

"Donato," Daniello snapped, "if she is threatened again by this animal, I will withdraw my offer."

Donato nodded and turned on Rocco. "This is a party, Rocco, careful of your manners. I have grown fond of Taylor Ellison."

Rocco gave Daniello a wicked grin. "Happy to, boss. I would say this is more of a celebration, wouldn't you, Uncle?" He turned back to Daniello and me. "I hope you brought a party dress, Taylor."

"Do not look at her. Do not speak to her," Daniello seethed. "She will be gone by nightfall."

I moved from behind him and glared at them both. "I'll be staying. Let's break out the champagne."

Donato laughed as Rocco stared on. "You will be gone or dead by nightfall, whore." In a sudden move, Daniello was in front of Rocco, his hands on his throat, and then they were both on the ground. Rocco's eyes bulged as Donato stepped over them and shrugged. "Boys will be boys."

Rocco gasped and gripped Daniello's hands as Donato moved toward me, oblivious to the struggle on the ground. "I meant it, Bella. I owe you. Sometimes it takes the love of a good woman to change a man. He has been gone for far too long, and you have brought him home." Rocco twisted his body in an attempt to get away from Daniello. Donato glanced back at Daniello, who clearly had the upper hand. "He will be the greatest asset to the family. We will go far."

I watched the men fight behind him as I spoke. "He doesn't want this. Doesn't that matter to you?"

Clicking his tongue, he scolded me. "Oh, Bella, did we not just agree days ago that family is everything?" He pulled a gun from his jacket and pointed it at my face. "Enough, Daniello."

Daniello looked our way and released Rocco as he gasped on the ground, his white suit soiled.

Daniello rushed toward us in a blur. "Goddamn you, Donato! Take the gun from her face."

"Ah, so this woman really is your weakness, Amon." Donato's brows furrowed as he morphed into the most dangerous of men. "Watch your mouth; I will not tolerate disrespect."

"Daniello!" A woman's voice broke the tension as Donato sheathed his gun and his face twisted into a smile, the same warm smile I knew to be an illusion, as he greeted the woman with Daniello's eyes who held a baby on her hip. She looked down at a recovering Rocco, who was still gasping. "Rocco, did you get burned by Daniello again?" She laughed as she looked over to her brother, whose face was deadly. "I see you are in the same mood you've been in for years, dear brother."

Tula.

Her eyes found me next. "Ah, this must be the mystery American." She moved toward me with kind eyes and extended her hand. "Tula. I'm this giant ass's sister."

I extended a shaky hand her way. She took it and scowled at the men around her. "Why is she upset? Who is responsible?" She shook her head and bounced the baby, who was so perfect she looked like a living doll. "Just ignore them." Her accent was thick, but her English was perfect. She seemed to read my thoughts as well as her brother could. "*I* was born in Italy. And I hate to say it, but I think Italians have a better temperament than Egyptian men. I've lived through it to tell the story."

Her eyes reassured me in a way her casual conversation couldn't. I knew she was trying to tame the fire. I felt consolation in her soft eyes before she surveyed the giant icing covered masterpiece on the table. "Donato, what a beautiful cake. Thank you."

Donato took a step toward Tula and eyed the baby on her hip. "My pleasure. Let me have her."

He took the baby and sat with her in one of the chairs next to the table as Rocco stood and brushed his pants off before he shot a glare in my direction. Just like Laz, he was highly delusional and seemed to blame his issues on me. I was over it.

I took a step toward him. "This isn't over."

"Yes, it is." He turned to Tula with a smile. "Let me get

changed and I will be back for the party." He nodded in Donato's direction before he made his way down a path past the olive trees. Daniello watched his retreat before he turned to me. His eyes said it all. This was his life. This was his fate. This was everything he didn't want, and it was because of our relationship he would continue to live in his personal hell. He had risked just as much as I had to be with me. We were mirrored, but he had ended my nightmare with his sacrifice. I heard the tires of several cars arriving in the distance, and minutes later, several men in white aprons began to drop off food. Daniello and I desperately scanned each other as Tula chatted with Donato.

"Where is your Capo, Tula?

"He will be along with the rest of the children shortly."

"Ah," Donato said. "You left him with eight children?"

"He is the one who made it this way." Donato chuckled as if he hadn't a single care in the world.

Daniello moved to stand next to him. "A word, Uncle."

"After the party," he dismissed as he continued to bounce the baby in his lap. His eyes found mine. "I am sure there is something more suitable for you to wear, Taylor."

"Not at my daughter's party, Donato, do you hear me?!" Tula spouted off before she turned to her brother. "Daniello, take Taylor to change," she demanded as she nodded toward the door. The Italian began to spill between the two of them before we were a step away. It was an argument, of that I had no doubt. Tula towered over Donato as she rapidly berated him while he smiled on at the child on his lap. Something she said struck a nerve with Donato, and I could see the opposition in him begin just before Daniello pulled me into the house.

Inside, I sat on the edge of his bed, my mind racing. I gathered my clothes and picked out a sundress and grabbed the makeup I'd purchased from the shops on my day in the town. I hadn't a single lifeline left, and I was unsure of what was about to happen. But I gathered myself into the dress and applied make-up, simply going through the motions.

Rocco had assured me I would not leave Italy alive. And even if I managed to escape the country without a scratch, it would still be the truth.

"You are so very beautiful."

My heart sank as Daniello watched me from the door of the bathroom. I leaned over the vanity mirror as I camouflaged my face to keep up the lie.

Inside, I was dying.

"So are you."

I lined my lips as he watched me closely. He moved toward me, but I cut him off with my words. "Please, I'm hanging on by a thread. If you touch me right now, I won't survive it, Daniello. I won't." I let a single tear fall and saw his eyes close before he walked out of the door.

Surrounded by Daniello's family, I sipped the proffered wine and finally gave into my hunger. Tula sat next to me, her beautiful eyes lit with sincerity as she complimented me. "You are beautiful, Taylor. I can see why my brother is so captured by you." Her husband, Capo, sat next to her with one of their children in his lap. I'd recognized his face the minute he sat down at the table. He was one of the men Daniello had with him the night at the club. The other man must have been the one to take Laz's bullet in the elevator. As if Capo sensed my stare, he looked my way with a short nod of acknowledgment.

He was the silent brooding type, much like Daniello.

"Thank you, I've heard good things about you as well, Tula." I braved a glance at the end of the table, where Donato sat with Tula's little girl planted in his lap. She opened another doll and held it up proudly for the table to see. I'd been greeted endlessly by the family with hugs and dual kisses. I was dizzied by the affection and at the same time mystified by the undercurrent of danger that went with the false atmosphere that seemed so genuine.

Italian mafia.

And that wasn't even the extent of it.

I had no clue of the amount of threats Daniello had earned after the reign of revenge he had brought down on his enemies or the families of those whose lives he took.

Contract killer.

Daniello watched me closely as Tula poured more wine. "You will get used to the pressure. And eventually it will become your life. We are a very close family."

I moved my gaze away from Daniello to face her. "I don't think I'm staying."

Tula frowned and glanced toward her brother. "He is in love with you."

My lips parted as he ignored the chaos and chatter around him to watch me.

I mouthed his way. "Stop staring."

He ignored me and kept guarded eyes in my direction.

"He was away so long from Italy, and not just here, but from himself. I had hoped one day he would return. I think you are responsible for bringing him back."

"I'm responsible," I whispered too low for her to hear. *For his demise.*

We'd ruined each other's lives with our love for each other.

Still, the paths we were on were destructive in their own way. The lives we'd formed separately were leading to a different kind of death. One where our humanity was stripped away, and we survived as lost souls. No second reality, no love, no life. Machines.

I felt the weight of it all as I gripped my glass and met his eyes.

"Where in America are you from, Taylor?" one of his aunts asked as she stood with a bottle of wine and began to fill every empty glass.

"Tennessee."

She was a robust woman with a booming voice dressed to the nines. "I don't know of Tennessee. Daniello, have you gone?"

"I have," he answered as one of Tula's boys came up to him. He looked to be around three years old. "Uncle Nello, take us on the plane."

Daniello could only give him a small smile. "Not today."

The boy stomped his foot as his mother scolded him. "Daniello, this is Mia's party. Let him be!"

The boy's—who had my lover's name—lips began to quiver. "You are never home, Uncle you promise me too many times!"

Daniello offered Mia to the woman next to him and pulled the boy to his hip while whispering in his ear as he kept his eyes fixed on me. The boy smiled and looked in my direction and nodded. "Okay!" He jumped from Daniello's lap and made a beeline for me before he stopped and gripped my face, placing tiny hands on my cheeks before kissing me on the mouth. He pulled away with a whisper. "Ti amo, Taylor." *I love you.* My chest exploded as I met Daniello's gaze while his nephew looked back and squeaked. "Okay, Uncle?"

Daniello nodded, his eyes filled with emotion as I bottomed out. My breath hitched in my throat as I stifled a sob, and Tula gripped my hand under the table. She spoke to those sitting near her, keeping our moment in a cocoon as life moved on around us, as if we weren't being torn apart. Unable to handle another second, I ripped myself away from the table with a curt, "Scuzie."

I walked away slowly, as not to draw attention to myself, and then ran deep into a row of olive trees as I let my tears fall. I placed my hand on my chest, unable to breathe through the pain. Daniello appeared a few seconds later.

Raw and exposed, we crashed together before he took my mouth in a hungry kiss. Our tongues mingled as he tasted me for endless minutes, his touch turning carnal as he pulled up my dress. "I have to have you right now." He snatched my panties from my body and pulled out his cock. He lifted me onto him, and we both cried out as soon as we connected. "I love you," I whispered as he buried himself deep and reclaimed my lips. I wrapped my arms around his neck and ground into him as we kept our eyes locked, our bodies immersed. Lips parted, we lost ourselves in an alternate reality where we were possible, our souls and heart in sync. He whispered kisses along my jaw as he took me to the safest place I'd ever been. "Taylor," he rasped out as he thrust himself deep. "Mio amore, mia sola vita." *My love, my only life*, he murmured as he again took my mouth and absorbed everything between us.

"I'll stay. I'll stay with you. I'll be with you, Daniello. I want to stay," I pleaded as he kept us connected. The voice of a shrieking child brought us back to reality, and he reluctantly let go of me to pull up his slacks. His eyes never left mine.

"I cannot be both men."

"You can, you *have.*"

"No, Taylor."

I faced him head on, fighting for a different life. "It's my decision."

"I will make sure it is not. You will be a happy woman. You will live a long life. You do not deserve this one. I will not let my life taint yours again."

I took a step forward and wrapped myself around him. "Please, don't do this. We can leave."

"You do not understand. He will not stop until I am his slave."

"Then I'll stay." I looked up at him as he cupped my face. "I'll stay. I won't leave your side. I'll make you happy."

"You have made me very happy. You have brought me back from a dead man."

"Please, Daniello."

"You will leave tonight." He whispered a kiss on my lips and grabbed my hand to lead us back to our end.

Taylor

As the party wound down and guests began to say their good-byes, Donato took his leave with Rocco, who only showed at the end of the party. The man I'd met a week before, who had disguised himself as a friend only to become my worst enemy, walked my way, kissed both of my cheeks, and before I could utter a word, turned his back to me. Rocco sneered my way before he nodded at Daniello, a warning in his callous eyes. Daniello remained silent as the guests trickled out of his villa. The wait staff cleaned up the table, and in less than twenty minutes, there wasn't a trace of a celebration. Packing up her daughter's toys, Tula and Daniello argued briefly as her Capo gathered their children. They spoke far too rapidly for me to catch any of it. Once alone, Daniello and I stood staring at the sun that threatened to set on the both of us.

"Daniello," I whispered as I walked over and entwined my fingers with his. He stared at our clasped hands and then turned pain-filled eyes to me. I walked him into his bedroom and slipped out of my dress as he watched, his eyes murky. I undressed him slowly and stood bared to him. His chest heaved with rare emotion as I sank to my knees and wrapped my lips around his cock. He gripped my hair as I enveloped him in my ready mouth in worship.

"I need you," I prayed as he looked down. "Fuck me." He closed his eyes. and I could feel the rip as he broke and began to fuck my mouth. His hands gripped me as he pulled himself from my lips and brought me to stand. He pushed me gently onto the bed as he followed, our mouths colliding in need. With the first thrust, my body coiled tight as he branded me with his bite, and I screamed out a welcome. He wore through me, the ache radiating through his strokes and between both of us. He bruised us both and buried himself so his mark would never fade. "You will belong to me, Taylor."

"I do."

"Goddamnit." He thrust harder, and we both fell apart, our body's convulsing together. Our breathing erratic, he lifted me to a sitting position, my legs wrapped around him as our hearts pounded.

"Again," I begged. "Take me away. This hurts too much. Please." Daniello buried his head in my shoulder as he grew hard beneath me, and I began to move to keep us tangled in our fantasy. It was all we had.

Sometime later, fully exhausted, we lay tangled in his sheets, our fingers lazily exploring the other.

Daniello's sudden chuckle broke the underlying tension.

"What?" I asked as I turned to study his face. A small smile played on his lips as he palmed my stomach.

"What would you do here?"

Hope rose in my chest, and he shook his head, stifling it. I ignored his dismissal in an attempt to convince him, to convince myself.

"I would figure it out."

He harrumphed as he looked down at me skeptically. His dark lashes hit his cheeks as he looked down to where his hand rested before deep brown inquisitive eyes met mine. "You would let me pregnant you?"

"Impregnate me?" I shrugged. "Why not?"

He chuckled as he kissed my shoulder. "Do you have any idea how mean those children would be?"

I grinned up at him. "Pig heads?"

"*And* chicken heads." We both laughed as Daniello looked down at me. "I would give you no choice. I would fill you with my sons and daughters."

"Mutts."

Daniello smiled. "Yes, red head, south mutts."

I gripped his face with wide eyes. "Whiskey filled baby bottles?"

Daniello grinned. "Of course. And you would marry me."

I felt my heart began to pound. "I *would* marry you. Make mutts. Ask me."

Daniello sighed as he pulled me tightly to him. "You do not want this life."

I cupped his jaw. "I want you."

Daniello sat up in alarm as his phone pinged. "Get dressed. We are not alone."

Less than a minute later, we were dressed and waiting on the patio as Donato emerged from the trees with Rocco behind him.

"Your meeting." Donato nodded in Daniello's direction.

Daniello stepped forward without hesitation. "If you want me to be your new dog, I want him dead."

I gasped as Rocco stood back with smug features. "You

seemed to have forgotten your *place,* cousin."

Donato stared at Daniello with interest as he spoke, never once looking at Rocco. "He has caused much trouble. He is the reason we were discovered in the States. He is the reason your pocket is short."

Donato turned to Rocco. "Is this true?"

Rocco shrugged. "I did what you asked me to. She was a distraction and he had plans to stay in the States. I told you this." Rocco glanced my way. "As long as she lives, he will never truly be family."

"And so you attempted to take her life?" Donato's presence was different from the kind man I'd baked with. I could feel the malice within him. I suddenly understood what Daniello meant by not being able to be both men. He had struggled with his demon long enough. One or the other had to take over in order for him to be what he needed to be. And he had to let the demon win to save me.

"I did what I had to do to make sure he returned to Italy."

"You are a fake man, *Akhom,*" Daniello hissed. "You are not even of Italian blood. You are my father's bastard. You have no place in this family."

Rocco stood, mouth gaping, as Daniello took a step forward. I could feel the hate emanating from him as he lifted his chin and commanded Donato's attention.

"This is not the truth," Rocco said weakly as he frantically flicked his eyes back and forth. "These are lies." Rocco looked at Daniello, his olive skin paling as he pleaded to Donato. "I have been loyal to this family."

"You are my father's bastard. But you will never be my brother," Daniello declared as Rocco turned back to stare at him incredulously.

With an exasperated sigh, Donato retrieved a gun from his jacket and pointed it at me.

"I have pledged my allegiance!" Daniello reminded him as he stepped in front of the gun. "If you kill her you must save a bullet for me. I will not do your bidding. I will not so much as lift a finger for Di Giovanni." Heart pounding, I eyed my bag on the bed that held my gun before I glanced back at Rocco, who smirked at me just before his face exploded. He went down with a thud on the concrete as his remains bled out onto the colored tile.

Daniello didn't flinch as he shielded me from Donato, who took a menacing step forward with anger clouding his face.

"No more fucking games, Daniello. As of this moment, you belong to the family. You will follow orders. You and your affair with this woman have just cost me a loyal captain. This ends here." Donato glared in my direction. "No harm will come to you or your family. You leave now and never return."

"No." I moved from Daniello's back and faced Donato head on. "No! Donato, please don't do this. Please." He took a look at Rocco and returned his resentful gaze to me. "It's done, Bella. Go home."

"No," I whispered to Daniello as I saw the light in his eyes grow dim with defeat.

"Daniello, come," he ordered as he made his way into the trees.

"Wait, no, NO!" I shrieked. "Please."

Daniello paused his back to me, his frame stiffened with my plea as if I had just shot him. He remained there only a moment before following behind Donato.

Every piece of my heart ripped apart in those seconds I watched him disappear. I knew without a shadow of a doubt it was final.

Minutes later, with absolutely nothing left but an empty soul, I was escorted by one of Donato's men to a black SUV for what I was supposed was transport to the airport, or to my certain death. I had no will to fight, no will to keep breathing, but I owed it to the man who had just chained himself for my protection. I ripped my arm away from my escort as I slid into the back of the SUV. I looked back at the villa, praying for just a glimpse of him, just one more kiss, a touch, a moment, and was splintered when we pulled away.

I gasped out a throaty cry, my heart making its final descent as the driver watched me curiously. Unashamed, and for the first time in my life, I cried openly for a man. The irony was not lost on me. My walls were down, and there was absolutely no reward behind that. What existed there now belonged to a man I could no longer have and would never see again. I hiccupped as my chest heaved with my endless tears. No relief came as I tried in vain to flush out the pain radiating through me. My life was spared, my sister was safe, and there was not a single fucking scenario in life that waited for me that I wanted to return to. Before him, I was an empty woman, void of love. Without him, I'd lost my soul. Uncontrollable sobs racked my body as I wept for the man who had continually tried to save me since the minute we met—from myself, from the dangers of my own life, and his. He'd walked into the fire to save me.

And I'd asked him to.

The SUV came to a sudden stop and my door opened. Daniello pulled me from the back seat and sandwiched me between him and the door. The same pain I felt twisted his features as he watched me fall apart.

Raw and out of my element, I confessed the truth. "These tears are for you. They will always be for you." He cupped my face and kissed a trailing tear down my cheek before he whispered. "Phoenix."

"What kind of monster does that make me? I'm so sorry, Daniello. I can't bear what I've done to you. You fought your whole life against this."

"I did the same as you. I am your mirror. Never forget that. You did nothing but protect who you love. And I will stay and do the same. I love you, Taylor Ellison, with my whole soul. I will not regret this. We did nothing wrong. Our love is *not* wrong. Do not take this on yourself."

"I can't do this. I can't leave you like this."

Daniello's eyes surveyed the villa before he pressed a gentle kiss to my lips. My breathing slowed as I fought for control. "Listen to me. You are stronger than this, you will see. You can come back from this. There is no other way. I would do anything to change this. I wanted you to be mine. I wanted to dine on your body every day and live inside you. That is where I feel I belong. You honor me with what your eyes say, and I cannot deny it anymore. Each breath I take when I am with you goes easy, and I fear I will never breathe again when this door is closed. But I made my choice, and there is nothing I can do, no solution but to obey. And my soul hates me for it."

I crumpled in his arms, gripping him tightly to me. "Daniello, you are the only thing that I have ever wanted in my life that I didn't have to earn. And you are the only thing I want to keep."

"Look at me," he pleaded. I looked up into his eyes as he confessed to me, "Taylor Ellison, you have won me in every way. My love for you fills my every cell brain."

A loud and inappropriate laugh escaped despite the horrific crack in my chest as he looked on at me, amused.

"Daniello," I pleaded.

"Yes," he asked, his eyes searching mine.

"Shoot your tutor."

He leaned in before his next confession. "I did not speak fluent English the first time I saw you."

"What?"

"I wanted to approach you, I wanted to know your name,

but I spoke so little English, the conversation would not have gone far."

Shocked by his confession, I stood, mouth gaping.

"I wasted no time when you returned to the club. I had to know you, speak with you, so I forced Rocco to teach me, and then I listened to a tutor on the plane. Thirteen hours a day every day for months I listened, just to meet you."

More tears slid down my cheeks as he looked down at me, just as ripped open as I felt.

"You are the strongest, most beautiful woman I have ever known. You have forever changed me as a man. I will miss this, I will think of you, and I will not want another."

"You won't be alone," I whispered before he claimed my lips slowly. We clung to each other tightly, desperately kissing and losing ourselves in each other one last time. When he pulled away, fresh tears emerged as I felt my heart being ripped away from me a second time. His eyes shimmered with unshed pain. "Go, Taylor."

"I'll wait for you," I promised.

"I will not come." A sob escaped as I tried in vain to pull myself together.

"Taylor, go." He gripped my neck as his mouth descended one last time, and all too soon retreated. "Please, go." I heard the watery edge to his voice and saw the break in him. I climbed into the truck and braced myself as another wave of searing finality hit me. I studied Daniello and realized out of all the men in my life, he was the only one who taught me the truth about love.

He had come into my life as a threat to all my principles and fully wrecked my line of thinking. Order and excellence had their place, but so did passion, spontaneity, and love.

"I love you," I whispered to him as he lingered at the door, his hands on either side of the frame. "Thank you for showing me it was still possible." He closed his eyes tightly as if to keep what I said burned into his memory.

The driver shouted in warning and darted his eyes at Daniello in the rearview.

"Goodbye, Phoenix," he murmured before he shut the door and the SUV sped away.

CHAPTER 29

Taylor

I DIDN'T RETURN TO CHARLESTON, DESPITE DANIELLO'S SACRIFICE to keep me safe. I had to be absolutely sure. And once again, that meant I had to keep my distance from those I loved.

And nothing about the life I left appealed to me without him in it.

The doctors had declared Amber out of the woods when she woke up. She would soon start therapy. When my sister opened her eyes, she was met with a new future. A man by her side who truly cared about her and a son to raise. She would never again be in the kind of danger that she'd been exposed to. She wouldn't be a target for anyone or anything, except the bastard called life. And I knew without a doubt she could manage her way through the bad. She was well armed for that. She'd endured so much, her day-to-day problems would seem totally trivial. She would thrive, and so would her son.

"Where are you?" Cedric asked as I gripped my phone in another rented car.

"I'm home." I looked up at the mansion I hadn't visited in

years as Cedric questioned me.

"You aren't home."

"I'm where I need to be for now."

"If I ever see you again, I won't know whether to kiss you or kill you."

I heard the longing in his voice. "I'm sorry for what I've put you through."

"Do you want me to come?"

"No. I need to just be alone for a while."

"Back into old habits, huh?" It was a dig, and I knew he meant it that way. He was still angry with me.

"One day you'll forgive me."

"I gotta go."

"Cedric—"

The phone went dead. I would let him have his space. I knew his love for me surpassed friendship a long time ago. I knew what unrequited loved felt like. I'd experienced a good bout of it on my own by the man who owned the mansion I stared at.

There was a chill in the air, alerting me to the arrival of fall in Memphis. I let down my window, and a few leaves drifted across the hood. Automatic lights flicked on around the property, giving it a regal, white glow as I stared at the lifeless house and remembered the last time I saw Ray.

"I've arranged for you to have a brownstone in Boston. It will be easier if you don't have to come home for break."

"What?" I paused my packing and turned to him. He shrugged, indifferent.

He wore his usual suit and tie, as he looked over my luggage and then back to me. "No sense in coming back here, kitten. This isn't your home anymore."

"I can come back for Thanksgiving in a few months and Christmas. What about summer, Ray?"

Ray moved in front of my suitcase and resumed packing for me. "I assume you'll be fucking some college Joe by then." I moved to stand in front of him and ripped the T-shirt from his hands. "You know that won't happen. You are the only one I want."

He looked down at the floor between us. "How many times do I have to tell you this? You aren't for me."

I stood my ground. I could hear the lie in his voice and feel it in my heart. "I am for you. You're twenty-nine fucking years old! Ten years is not that big of a fucking age gap, Ray. We have nothing to be ashamed of!"

He gripped my arm. "So then pay me back. When you've made enough money to pay me back, maybe I'll take you seriously. Until then, stay gone."

I bit my lip to keep it from trembling. "That's what it's about? That you paid me?"

Ray faltered, his whole frame dropping as he looked me in the eye.

"You want love from me? That's what you want?"

"I want you to admit it's already there!"

"I have to respect you, kitten." I faced him head on. We were in negotiations, something he'd made sure I'd mastered.

"You do respect me."

"No, I don't. I think you're brave. I think you're exceptionally smart. I think you've got a goddamned mouth on you that would make the devil weep, but respect has to be earned. You want mine? Go kick some ass, make your fortune, and come back to me then and ask for love." He crossed his arms, and I took an aggressive step forward.

"You love me."

He shook his head, his blue eyes resolute. "I don't. You want me to, but I don't. This is it for us. Contract is over. Let's say goodbye like adults, kitten."

I tamped down my tears as I looked him over. "I'll hate you for this."

"You might, or you might thank me."

I maintained my composure as he tried his best to rattle me. I held my head high as the seconds ticked by.

A slow smiled traced my lips as I pushed my anger aside and gave him a wink.

"Have it your way, Ray." I could feel the pride on his side as I fought the battle with my anger and my pride and won. He confirmed my suspicion when he reached me. We fought breathlessly to get our clothes off, and once he was buried deep, his emotion-filled eyes cloaked me in what I needed to feel. No gentle words, no soft whispers, just deep blue eyes. When we'd both come, Ray leaned in and kissed me for the first time. It lasted endless minutes, and it was filled with every unspoken kindness he'd deprived me of. I moaned into his lips, and he took and took and took some more. Our tongues tangled and slowly broke apart as he sealed it before gracing me with one last lingering look.

"Offer stands, kitten. Come back when you make your fortune."

"Ray?" My heart sank as he leveled me with his goodbye.

He looked at me without an inch of fight. "I'll be waiting."

Outside, on the front steps of his castle, I shivered as tears streamed down my cheeks then rushed to the front door and unlocked it. "Ray." I needed him now more than ever. I leapt up the stairs as I had three months into my first semester at Harvard.

"Ray!" I yelled, excited after the all-night drive from Boston to Memphis for winter break. I knew it would aggravate him to no end that I was yelling throughout the house. Still, I couldn't stifle my excitement. I had just been granted enough in student loans to carry me the first semester and maxed out six credit cards to pay for the rest.

I moved toward his bedroom as memories rushed toward me from all sides. Deep blue eyes, his rare smile, his hungry lips on my skin, his reluctant friendship.

"Ray?!" I barreled down the hall to his bedroom at six in the morning to see it made. Thinking he might have been early to rise, I rushed into his office and stopped short when he wasn't there.

"Taylor? Is that you?" Olivia rounded the corner from the foyer with a warm smile on her face.

"Olivia, hi!" I moved toward her, filled with excitement, and gave her a brief hug.

"Where is Ray?"

Olivia's smile faltered. Instant tears surfaced as I shook off the impossible. "Is he out of town?"

Powerless against the memory of my last trip to the house, I hung my head as I reached the door to his bedroom. I stared at his empty bed then walked in and closed the door behind me.

"Taylor, he's gone."

"Gone."

She nodded as she took my bag off my shoulder, gripped my hand, and led me to the couch.

I swallowed as I stared at the high heels I'd worn to show him what a grown up I was. It seemed so childish to me then. "His heart?" I braved a glance her way.

She nodded and took a seat on the ottoman across from me.

I let the tears slip down my cheek. "I mean, I knew. I knew something was wrong. I just didn't know how. . . bad. . . Oh my God, Ray!" I let myself free fall into devastation as she did her best to calm me.

"Why . . . why?" Confusion and anger overpowered me as I lashed out at her. "Why didn't you call me?! Goddamn you, Olivia, you knew I loved him!"

"So did he, Taylor. He knew. He wanted it this way. He didn't want you to suffer."

"Well, I'm suffering anyway! He was only twenty-nine! He was rich! Why the hell didn't he save himself?"

"Money doesn't solve everything, Taylor." I cringed at her words because they belonged to Laz. "It was his second rejected heart. He said a third would be too selfish."

"Selfish?" I scoffed. "That bastard was worried about being selfish? He's the most selfish man that ever lived!"

"Taylor, he knew you wouldn't go to school. He knew."

I let my body dissolve as she spoke softly.

"He never really said much, but I know you were his world, Taylor."

I cut my eyes at her. "I was his whore."

"That's not true and you know it."

"I know nothing." I stood, wiped my tears away, grabbed my bag, and barricaded myself in his room. On top of his bed was an envelope for me. I stared at it for three days before I slipped it in his bedside drawer and returned to Boston.

I pulled one of the shirts from his closet and slipped it on. Nothing smelled of him anymore, and in my anger, I hadn't taken the time to do anything that a women in love would do with her grief. I'd kept it all inside at school and used my pain as my anchor. Even with my hurt, I'd set out to do everything we talked about. I'd made my fortune. I'd conquered. I ruled my share of the corporate world, and I'd done it all for a dead man's acceptance. For myself, but mostly for Ray. He was the voice in my head, my mentor, the whisper in my ear for the better half of ten years . . . until I met Daniello. I knew grief had its limitations, but I found myself in a heap on his bed minutes after I'd arrived, swallowing chalk with desperate sobs. I released years of pent up sadness, grieving my losses, my failures, and the three loves of my life.

Ray had left everything to me. His home, his fortune from the quick sale of his Fortune 500 company, even the Studebaker he refused to let me drive. I was a millionaire my first semester in college, but I refused to cash in. I was self-made, and somehow, even from the grave, I knew I had his respect. But I later realized it was just an excuse. He'd bred me to be a winner, and I'd become one, in a sense. But his cruelty had stunted me in a way that refused to let me embrace my feminine heart. I was a working robot, and only Daniello had been able to break through the façade. Ray was wrong to hijack my emotions. He'd ripped away life from the living.

Still, somehow, I needed him to come back, to remind me of who I was, of my capabilities. I was frozen and drifting, and I needed the kind of slap only he was capable of giving. I needed to shed the emotions and get back to the heart of what I was. But who the fuck was I?

I wiped my face as the sun peeked inside his massive bedroom and gripped the envelope I had placed in his drawer ten years ago. I held it to my chest and swallowed hard, mustering the courage to open it. Slipping the letter out of the envelope, I paused when I saw the length of it.

Kitten,

In another life, I would have loved you.

Ray

I gripped the paper tightly as I read it over and over before I tucked it back in the envelope and felt another folded letter inside of it. I gripped it like a lifeline, hoping for more from a man who had never given it, and gaped when I saw what it was. I took a seat in the chair next to his bedroom window and stared at the crumbled paper.

Dear Committee,

I was born into a nuclear family. I've had a swell life. I attend church with my loving and supportive parents every Sunday. My hobbies include feeding the homeless, daily bike rides with my high school sweetheart, and visiting old folk's homes to ensure they are entertained and rarely lonely.

I've read three thousand books in my high school career. I was valedictorian of my class, and my SAT scores are well above average. With a degree from Harvard, I intend to make a difference in the world. With an MBA in business, I intend to become a leader my parents will be proud of. I intend to cultivate fresh ideas, benefit from them, and return the profits to the business community. I see a bright future riddled with prosperity. These are my plans.

But that is complete bullshit.

My name is Taylor Ellison. I come from a tiny town in Tennessee that the world has forgotten about. My parents were addicts, and I didn't own a pair of shoes until I was two years old. My hobbies included escaping my house and the wrath of my mother to read one of a thousand books I couldn't understand. On weekends, I would help my toddler sister scrub the walls of our house to keep my unhappy mother at bay. I spent a majority of my days at the local library, which housed exactly three thousand books. I read every one of them until I memorized them. It took me eighteen years. I managed to escape the clutches of my parents my senior year through sheer ingenuity and graduated valedictorian of one of the hardest prep schools in the country. My scores speak for themselves, but this is where you want to hear about who you will be letting into your school and the carefully laid plans for my future.

I'm a child of abuse and neglect and an adult who doesn't use it as an excuse. I want to rule a boardroom, found a company that will support a life without financial worry, and maybe use the money to mentor someone like myself. I'm thirsty for whatever knowledge puts me in this position. And I know that I can gain that knowledge at your school. I've brought myself to your door. Please open it.

Sincerely,

Taylor Ellison

Tears streamed down my cheeks as I choked out a laugh. I had no idea Ray had seen that letter. It was one of a thousand I had written. It was more of a joke for myself, the bitter ramblings of an eighteen-year-old girl whose background couldn't compare to a majority of those applying. But it was my heart, the truth of who I was, and he wanted to let me know it. Ray had loved me as the penniless girl he took in as well as the woman full of confidence he sent back into the world.

The only thing bad about his heart was that it wouldn't let him love me.

"Oh, you bastard." I turned my head and sniffed the shoulder of his shirt and caught a subtle, if not imaginary, whiff of his cologne.

My heart wrenched as I thought of my mirror, a man who had taken the woman Laz and Ray left broken and smashed the pieces of her back together in their wake.

And he loved me anyway.

It was time to mourn.

I'd never given myself a chance. I wrapped myself up in the three men who had, in some form, shaped and ruined me. But I guess that's what love did. It built you up to believe and broke you if you didn't get to keep it. And I was comfortably broken as I stared out of Ray's bedroom window at the falling leaves.

"You're right, Ray. This isn't home, but mind if I stay a little while?"

Taylor

Eight months later

"Oh my GOD!" The speaker of my phone pierced my ears as my sister screamed in excitement.

"Amber, seriously, stop yelling."

"I'm getting married! MARRIED!"

"I'm on my way."

"You staying longer this time?" I closed the door to Ray's house and locked it with a bag in hand. "I don't know."

"Okay, but as soon as you get here, I have plans."

I cradled my phone in the console and turned on the Bluetooth.

"Shopping?" Dread coursed through my veins. "We'll discuss it."

But—"

My phone beeped and I smiled.

"Amber, I have to go."

"But—"

I clicked over. "How's it going, partner?"

Nina all but growled her reply. "Sometimes I really hate you for leaving me with this mess."

"I'm doing my part."

"I know, but it would be easier if we weren't conferencing every ten damn minutes."

"I'll be back soon. I'm on the road now."

"Thank Christ."

"Get off the phone," Devin ordered in the background. "You were the one bitching about date night."

"I have a company to run, deadbeat," she murmured.

"That's going to hurt you," he quipped as she shrieked in pain. Devin's silky voice summoned me over the phone, "Hello, Taylor, you ready to come out of the woods yet so I can spend a day with my fiancée?"

"I'm not marrying you," Nina barked as she snatched her phone back.

"You are marrying him," I argued.

"I know," she said, and I heard a door close behind her. "I'm thinking a solid year of groveling."

"It's been a year, Nina."

"Okay, two."

I laughed as she dug in. "How are you?"

"You saw me three months ago."

"And you were too thin."

"I'm fine."

"Have you heard from him?"

"No, and I won't." I killed any emotion the idea brought. "Did you deal with the Organic Orange disaster?"

"Taylor Ellison, back to all business," Nina mused.

"Always." If there was one thing I discovered about myself on my hiatus, it was that I loved my job.

"I'll take it as a good sign. Yes, it's dealt with, thanks to you. I could really use you back. I mean, I know you are working your ass off, but it's not the same."

"I know." I wanted to offer her more, but I couldn't. I was consulting for her but, I couldn't bring myself to dive fully back in. I was getting there.

"Hurry up, okay?"

"Okay."

"Nina!" Devin barked in the background.

"I'm coming!" she yelled. "God, he's such an ass."

"So, go kick it."

"I will, bye."

An hour and a half outside of Memphis, I drove past the dilapidated town square and felt my chest tighten. I let out a heavy breath as I drove the rural route past a haunted house where my nightmares played out and down the road that divided my heart. I stepped out of the car and stared at the pond and the faint outline of a little girl with clown hair and a dark headed boy splashing in the water. The new spring breeze whispered through limbs full of leaves above me and an eerie calm settled over me.

"I'm your first kiss, Red. Nothing will ever change that and you can't do a thing about it."

I let myself break for the boy I fell in love with. The boy

who tried to protect me from the monsters lurking down the hall from my bedroom. The boy who gave me as much of a childhood as he could. The boy who loved me. I thought of our last day at the pond when I'd made a promise I would always keep to *that* boy, and I kept my memory there and didn't let it drift to a single day after. And then I thought of the son he left behind with the same beautiful blue eyes.

"I'll teach him how to ride a bike. I'll show him how to float. He'll have it all, I promise you. I love you. Always." I wiped my tears as I took one last look at our forgotten pond. "Goodbye, Laz."

I drove out of Dyer for the very last time.

"Okay, just let me show you this last thing." Amber scrolled through her phone and began sorting through the fabric samples in front of her while Joseph looked up at me with big eyes. "I bored." I laughed as Amber frowned between us, then sighed.

"Okay, maybe this is a bit much. You look tired. We can do this another day."

"Tank weezus," Joseph said as I burst out in hysterical laughter.

Amber cut her eyes at her son. "Okay, monkey, you get dressed for bed."

"Wead me a book?"

"I'll be right there," Amber promised.

Joseph shook his head. "No, Aylor." He turned to me with a smile.

"Okay, buddy," I agreed.

"Tank weezuz."

Amber straightened in her chair. "Aaron?!"

Aaron poked his head out of the kitchen. "Yeah, babe?"

"My son seems to think thanking Jesus is a necessary period to end each sentence. You wouldn't happen to know where he got that from, would you?"

Aaron winced with guilt. "Sorry, babe. We'll get it right with the next kid."

Amber shook her head. "So cocky," she said with a smile as he gave her a wink. She turned to me. "I worry, though," she said as she looked toward Joseph's bedroom. "He's having problems with his speech. He's just not getting it."

I looked over to my sister, who had transformed in the time I was away. Her recovery from the gunshot had been a slow nightmare, but Aaron had been there every step of the way. I'd visited often enough, but it was clear to me after a few trips she had someone new to look after her. In fact, I'd been visiting Charleston as an out of towner, not a resident.

"You had speech problems too."

She looked at me in shock. "I did?"

"You did, and a lisp. Don't worry. He'll get it."

"I don't remember that."

"It was adorable," I pointed out as she gave me wide eyes. Joseph called from bed. "AAAAYLOR. I WEADY!" We both chuckled as I moved to get up. "*That* kind of adorable."

Amber looked me over with a small smile. "You've changed a little."

I raised my brow. "How?"

"Just a little softer around the edges," she noted as she glanced back at Aaron, who was busy in the kitchen. "Nothing wrong with that."

Honesty. "I've been trying to figure some things out, let sleeping dogs lie, you know?"

Amber's faint dimple appeared. "Sleeping dogs can't lie.

They're asleep." We shared a smile at one of our old corny but shared childhood jokes.

Amber stood and gave me a hug. "We miss you. Really. I know it's hectic when you come, but Joseph asks for you all the time. I don't mean to twist your arm, and I know you've been through a lot but—"

"So have you," I pointed out.

Amber shook her head. "I don't want to get emotional."

"Good," I deadpanned, and we both laughed. Her eyes watered anyway. "What you did for us—"

I cut her off, unwilling to take the credit. "You brought yourself here. Don't forget that."

Amber took a step forward and wrapped her arms around me. My reaction was instant. We hugged for a silent minute as Joseph peered out his bedroom, a replica of Lazarus Walker, with an open hand waving for me to come to him. "I think it's time I came home too."

"Good, because I'm pregnant."

CHAPTER 30

Taylor

THAT NIGHT, I CHECKED INTO A MOTEL AS I HAD IN MY PREVIOUS trips to Charleston, never staying more than a day or two before retreating to Ray's mansion—*my* mansion. I hadn't been back to the penthouse. It was the last step of my self-imposed mission to try to move on with my life. In the late hours, I tossed and turned in that hotel room, desperate for some much-needed sleep, my body exhausted from hours in the car, my mind racing with thoughts of a new future. Against all odds, my position was still safe with Scott Solutions, and my partner had made it so. Still, even with my brief visits, I always worried there might be someone lurking in the shadows, some circumstance that would prevent me from resuming my life, from making another transition into the rest of it. I'd had to fight that fear every day for years, and it was time to put it to bed.

I walked down Bay Street in the French Quarter with the key to the penthouse in hand. The garage was brimming with cars, a far cry from the deserted parking space of a year ago. Daniello and I had alone occupied the building. Even the elevator had a different feel. Opening the door to the penthouse, that feeling dispersed. The bed still sat near the fireplace, the sheets tangled. The stale smell of an unoccupied space drifted over me.

Empty.

I laughed at the irony. Through all the trials I'd been through in the last year, I was still inevitably alone.

"But you aren't alone." I smiled as I thought of the baby boy that fell asleep on my chest, of my sister's plea for me to come back *home*. I had family. I had friends. I had a career waiting for me.

I walked over to the bed and stared at the sheets, the only sign that he truly existed. He'd left me nothing but his memory. I tried to shake my emotion away as rain began to pour down the large panes of glass in front of me. I gripped my arms as I stood at the window and spoke to a ghost.

"I won't say goodbye to you. I won't. I can't. *Not you*."

Taking a deep breath, I lay in our bed and stared at the ceiling as visions of my love danced around me, the way I knew they would if I returned to the only place that belonged to us, and finally drifted to sleep.

"Taylor Ellison speaking." I moved through the penthouse as the movers set Ray's desk in the corner. My door sounded again as I looked at one of the men who'd just finished hanging a painting on the wall. "Do you mind getting the door?"

"Sure, Ms. Ellison."

My penthouse was a madhouse of workers. I dove into the task of creating some sort of semblance of a home once I decided to stay in Charleston. I needed order, and that would never change.

"Hey, partner, you getting set up?" Nina asked with syrupy sweetness on the other end of the phone. "I'm attempting to," I said as I motioned to the men carrying the desk.

The man I asked to answer the door called out behind me, "Ms. Ellison, it's a grocery delivery."

I let out a sigh as I addressed Nina. "I may lose my shit today."

"I just heard that southern twang," Nina chuckled as she refused to let me off the phone.

"Get used to it." I called out over my shoulder, "Money's on the counter. Please have them unpack them."

"Yes, ma'am."

"So, I'll see you tomorrow?" Nina pleaded.

"I'll be there. Look for a six a.m. email."

"Wait—"

I smiled as I hung up.

Careful what you ask for, Nina.

The truth was, I couldn't wait to dive back in. I sat down behind Ray's desk and spread my hands over the surface before I glanced at the two men exhausted from the haul. "Perfect. Thank you."

One of the men pulled a towel from his back pocket and wiped his brow. "No problem. Need anything else?"

"I'm all set."

Within a few minutes, I was alone. My penthouse was full of décor I had handpicked, a new personal hurdle I'd cleared. There was nothing staged about my new house or my new life. And for the first time in a very long time, I was excited.

I still gave fuck all about shopping. And I'd actually purchased a floor of the garage for my cars and added a Studebaker to the mix. My stomach rumbled as I started to set up my office equipment, and I moved to make a quick trip to the fridge to temper it. I glanced around the nearly finished space with pride.

Opening the refrigerator door, my smile vanished when I saw my grocery order had been royally screwed up. Rows and rows of pimento cheese sat on every shelf—in the butter box, in the door, in the vegetable bins. It was everywhere. In every available space.

"What. In. The. Hell!?"

"The South caviar."

I froze as my heart leaped to my throat and instant tears sprang to my eyes.

"Do not turn around."

I struggled to find my voice as I sobbed out my reply. "Please let me see you."

"I fear I am not the man you remember."

I pushed out an "I don't care," and inhaled hard as his scent hit me. "Oh, God, please let me see you."

His breath hit my ear. "Have you thought of me?" His words were hoarse as he gripped my hair and his lips ghosted over my neck.

Still reeling, I gripped the door as my legs threatened to give out. "You said you wouldn't come back." My heart leaped to a runner's pace as I felt his chest at my back. "Please let me see you."

"I am a changed man, Taylor Ellison."

"I don't fucking care." I moved to turn, and he stilled me. Kissing my neck, he pushed my shorts down and slipped his fingers between my folds before he pressed on my clit.

"You are wet for me."

"Please, let me see you."

He rubbed his thick length across my lower back as my whole body convulsed in need.

"I am thinking you have missed me."

I shuddered at the feel of his fingers and tilted my head back.

Pushing my T-shirt up over my breasts, his warm hand

cupped one of them just before he pinched my nipple through my lace bra. The cool air from the open fridge that swept over my body did nothing to stifle the heat between us. We were both match and gasoline, and the inferno grew hotter as he whispered to me.

"You are always mine."

Warm tears ran down my cheeks as I embraced the moment. Even if it was stolen, even if it was all we had, I was his, and I let him know it.

"I love you."

In a quick move, he captured my chin and then my mouth with a fiery kiss. I exhaled the months we spent apart and reveled in the feeling of our mingling tongues. He devoured me as I shook in his arms.

When we pulled apart, I caught his lust-filled eyes as he peered down at me.

"Phoenix." He withdrew his hold as I twisted in his arms and gripped him to me. We collided.

Angry.

Hungry.

Desperate.

And in love.

Every part of me was molded to every inch of him. Shedding his clothes, we moved to the bed, where he pinned me down and hovered above me. Full lips twisted as his emotion-filled eyes told me nothing had changed, his heart had remained faithful. There wasn't a trace of indifference, only love.

He leaned in carefully and took my lips again as he thrust inside me. Wrists pinned, I screamed out as he poured himself into me with every deep stroke. Buried fully, he fucked me as he watched my reaction to him, capturing my gasps with dark eyes and the rest of me with his greedy body. He gave and took as he claimed me until my cries satisfied him. I shuddered beneath him, each orgasm only spurring him on. Our breaths mingled as he lifted my wrists and re-pinned them above my head, only giving me access to his mouth. I tugged at his lips, begging for them as he swiveled his hips and went deeper. My whole body arched as he pressed in with one last thrust and freed my hands. I clutched him to me, my heart pounding as he collapsed.

"I just want to go to my death fucking you. Is that so much to ask?"

I chuckled as I gripped his hair and he smiled up at me. "Hi."

Trying not to ruin the moment, but terrified of not knowing, I had to ask.

"How are you here?"

His smile deepened. "I got on a plane."

"Please don't." I pleaded. "Please don't joke. Not now."

Daniello lay back into the bed and pulled me to his side. "The boss freed me."

I reared back so I could see his face. "Donato?"

"Tula."

I lifted to sit as I peered down at him, not wanting to miss a word. "Tula?"

"She is the rightful heir of the family. Has always been. My father and Donato were set on the old ways, and many of the family would refuse to take orders from a woman." Daniello surveyed the penthouse with pride. "I believe you and I know that a woman is *very* capable." He chuckled. "Well, maybe not a moody south woman."

I slapped his chest with unbelieving eyes. "She just freed you?"

He grimaced. "It is a little more complicated than that."

Blood pulsed in my face. "I swear to God if you don't start talking—"

Daniello clamped my lips together. "Tula has always wanted

to be boss. She embraced the life very young." I recalled how Tula played nonchalant at the chaos before the party. Remembered the command in her voice when she spoke around the table. Her menacing tone with Donato. She was more than capable.

"How did she do it?"

Daniello traced my nipple with his finger, and I grabbed it as he sighed in frustration. "Capo is a captain. He was next in line."

"And?"

"*And* she made it happen."

"Donato?"

Daniello nodded slowly. "He was never supposed to rule the family. And after me, Capo was the only other choice. He has the title, but he will not rule. And she will do it better than anyone before her." Daniello winked. "I feel bad for Capo. Tula will be boss and bitchy wife." Daniello chuckled as he ran his fingers down my side.

"Did you know this when you said goodbye to me in the SUV?"

Daniello frowned. "Yes and no. It was Donato's driver who took you, so I had to make sure he was convinced I was taking my position. And there was also a chance it would not work. Donato had gained much loyalty with his reign. But he underestimated Tula. And I have a persuasive way of making things work." Donato was dead. I was sure of it. He pulled my hair away from my neck and placed a tongue-filled kissed next to my ear. "I have missed you, Phoenix. My world grew so dark without my sun. I watched for you every night. Why did you not return for so long?"

I clutched him like a lifeline. "I had to let go of my past. It was eating me alive."

He nodded in understanding. Still, I cursed the minutes and months of despair I'd dwelled in.

"What took you so long?"

His eyes softened as he peered up at me. "I had to make sure the family respected the new order of things. Accepted Capo and would not make a move for his place in the family. I had to make sure Tula was safe." He lifted my hand and pressed a kiss to my palm.

"So now?" I refused to let myself hope.

Daniello gripped my chin. "I told you, I am a changed man. I have become *very* boring."

I furrowed my brow as I thought of Amber and Joseph, of the risk of having him in my life. "No more contracts, no ties, *nothing*?"

Daniello held my gaze and made sure I heard his every word. "My sister told me I had sacrificed enough for the family with vengeance for Matteo. Make no mistake, she is serious about her position, but she knows that is not the life I want. She likes you very much."

Gratitude swept through me for the fierce woman who had just given me my life back. I owed Tula my happiness and had no idea how I would repay her. It was the love of his sister that saved us. I knew how powerful that love was.

I cursed my trembling lips, still needing to hear it. "So, you can stay?"

Daniello scrunched his nose. "A green card? *Boring.*"

I straddled his hips, elated tears running down my cheeks. "And boring vacations?"

Daniello cupped my neck and pulled me down to his lips. "The only thing I want now is to be boring with you, Taylor Ellison."

I grinned through the inch between our ready mouths, unable to resist. "Bored."

Daniello narrowed his eyes and fisted my hair. "And now you will suck my cock with no reward."

EPILOGUE

Taylor

Eight months later

BORING. THE MAN THOUGHT WE WOULD BE BORED. I SMILED AT MY fiancé as he ordered Joseph to bed with a gentle tongue. His mother was in labor at the hospital with another son. Cedric was there as well, but I had a feeling it was more for the nurse he'd taken up residence with in the last year. He seemed happy but kept his distance when Daniello came back into my life. I knew I'd hurt him, but it was never intentional, and he seemed to become more accepting as the months passed and found a love of his own.

Daniello lay in Joseph's twin bed, his feet hanging off the edge as he gathered him into his arms.

"Seuss," Joseph squeaked.

"I do not like the Seuss books," Daniello deadpanned to Joseph and waved a palm in the air.

I cleared my throat in the doorway. My beautiful man stared back at me with menace. "I *don't* like the Seuss books, Joseph."

I chuckled as he rolled his eyes. He still had so far to go. As Daniello slaughtered *One Fish, Two Fish, Red Fish, Blue Fish*, Joseph giggled, dwarfed in his massive arms. For a brief moment, I saw a flash of Laz as he looked up at his future uncle curiously. I twisted my heavy new ring on my finger and admired it before I closed the door with a swollen chest and called to check on my sister. Aaron's elevated voice told me enough as he briefly updated me and hung up. Amber had gone through a risky pregnancy with the damage from the bullet she took. Her newest son was a miracle baby. But I believed in miracles.

I had no choice.

My life had made me a believer against all odds.

Behind his bedroom door, Joseph laughed hysterically, and I heard the deep rumble of Daniello's echoed chuckle as I made my way out onto my sister's patio. The crash of the waves pulled a day's worth of Joseph's demands from my shoulders. I felt at peace for the first time in my life. And it had everything to do with the two men who lay on the other side of that door.

Daniello and I had nothing but each other to look forward to. My dark knight had gone legitimate. It turned out his plans for a "different life" had shifted into the one he was living. He'd set up shop on the second floor of the building we lived in, hired the best architects in Charleston to mentor him in plans to start a design firm, and then sank a majority of his fortune into local real estate, mostly undeveloped land. I could see his excitement and feel it roll off him when his drafting table was delivered. His idea of boring was building an empire of his own. Mutts were in our future, of that I had no doubt, but I was still far too satisfied with my corporate life and with a man who was anything *but* boring.

Daniello often visited his family in Italy while I stayed stateside. It was the one sacrifice of our union. I wouldn't for any reason put my family in harm's way. Besides Tula, Italy and the rest of the Di Giovanni family knew nothing of his life in the States or the second family Daniello had, and never would. It was what we agreed was best. The locals of Barga most likely assumed he was the same wanderer he had always been.

But I knew better.

The hard-edged man I fell in love with was still demanding and infuriating, but his unleashed love opened me in more ways than I ever thought possible.

I still fought daily against my life's conditioning, but I was winning the war. I still believed in order and excellence. I still drove fast cars and dodged days of shopping with my sister to have kinky sex with the dark-eyed man who maxed out my body.

I still believed that the world was a scary place.

And I no longer wanted any more guarantees in life. It was meant to be lived, not feared.

And I had a life, one that I could never have imagined for myself, one that didn't keep me in the shackles of fear or harden me to the point of being void of emotion. I was a woman of flesh and blood. Freeing myself, I'd become capable, just as capable as Daniello of loving and being loved, of being hurt, of being *human*.

It wasn't fear that got me to where I was anymore, and it was love that kept me bulletproof.

THE END

LISTEN to the predator and prey playlist on Spotify

ABOUT THE AUTHOR

USA Today bestselling author and Texas native, Kate Stewart, lives in North Carolina with her husband, Nick. Nestled within the Blue Ridge Mountains, Kate pens messy, sexy, angst-filled contemporary romance, as well as romantic comedy and erotic suspense.

Kate's title, *Drive*, was named one of the best romances of 2017 by The New York Daily News and Huffington Post. *Drive* was also a finalist in the Goodreads Choice awards for best contemporary romance of 2017. The Ravenhood Trilogy, consisting of *Flock, Exodus*, and *The Finish Line*, has become an international bestseller and reader favorite. Her holiday release, *The Plight Before Christmas*, ranked #6 on Amazon's Top 100. Kate's works have been featured in *USA TODAY, BuzzFeed, The New York Daily News, Huffington Post* and translated into a dozen languages.

Kate is a lover of all things '80s and '90s, especially John Hughes films and rap. She dabbles a little in photography, can knit a simple stitch scarf for necessity, and on occasion, does very well at whiskey.

OTHER TITLES AVAILABLE NOW BY KATE

Romantic Suspense

The Ravenhood Series
Flock
Exodus
The Finish Line

Lust & Lies Series
Sexual Awakenings
Excess
Predator and Prey
The Lust & Lies Box set: Sexual Awakenings, Excess, Predator and Prey

Contemporary Romance

In Reading Order

Room 212
Never Me (Companion to Room 212 and The Reluctant Romantic Series)
The Reluctant Romantics Series
The Fall
The Mind
The Heart
The Reluctant Romantics Box Set: The Fall, The Heart, The Mind
Loving the White Liar

The Bittersweet Symphony
Drive
Reverse
The Real
Someone Else's Ocean
Heartbreak Warfare
Method

Romantic Dramedy

Balls in Play Series
Anything but Minor
Major Love
Sweeping the Series Novella
Balls in play Box Set: Anything but Minor, Major Love, Sweeping the Series, The Golden Sombrero

The Underdogs Series
The Guy on the Right
The Guy on the Left
The Guy in the Middle
The Underdogs Box Set: The Guy on The Right, The Guy on the Left, The Guy in the Middle

The Plight Before Christmas

ACKNOWLEDGEMENTS

PART ONE

To my Betas: Sharon Dunn, Stacy Hahn, Patty Tennyson, Julie Kerchkof, Cindy Gordanier, Sophie Brighton, Susan Decker, Lina Linalove, Malene Dich, there is no book world for me without you ladies. Seriously, I can't do it without you. Thank you for pushing me, picking me up, and bitch slapping me when needed.

To my Asskickers—thanks for sticking with me through all my writing pens. I adore all of you, and I'm proud to call you friends.

Christin Stanley—I adore you and your blunt ways. Thank you so much for everything you do.

Jessica Berthlelot—Thank you for all your hard work on all of my books and dealing with my insane schedule. I love you to pieces.

Bloggers, how I love thee. Thank you for giving my books a chance, for your endless support, and for performing an often thankless job because it's what you love to do.

PART TWO

Thank you first to my PA, Bex Kettner, for running my shit show with grace and a sense of humor. I adore you, lady. Thank You!

A huge thank you to my beta's Sharon, Heather, Stacy, Anne, Patty, Kelli, Suzanne, Kim, Malene, Christy, Paige, Cindy, and Donna.

A big shout out to all the bloggers who promoted, read, and reviewed this series and took a chance on my erotic suspense. I appreciate you more than you will ever know.

A huge thank you to my amazing group, Kate's Asskickers. You ladies are the greatest. I'm so lucky to have you.

A huge to my cover designer Amy Queau of Q Design. You are brilliant.

Thank you to my amazing formatter, Stacey, at Champagne Formats. I can't wait to share a bottle with you one day. XO

Made in the USA
Columbia, SC
13 July 2025

60516881R00246